# RARE

# TRAITS

## David George Clarke

Cover design by Derek Murphy of CreativIndie

*For Gail, with love*

# Part I

# Chapter 1

## May 2009

John Andrews sprinted through the pelting rain to his ageing Volvo, pulled open the driver's door and threw himself in. He was drenched but he didn't care – he'd sold five large paintings in one afternoon and he couldn't wait to get home to tell Lola. He put the pasta and wine he'd just bought onto the front passenger seat, dug the car key from his pocket and started the engine.

As he reversed out of the parking spot, he was still thinking about his day's profit when he suddenly remembered his seat belt. He stopped to fasten it. He was about to pull away when there was a loud crunch from behind and the car lurched forward, a packet of pasta and one of the bottles of wine jumping from the seat. He instinctively hit the brakes and watched helplessly as the second bottle flew into the air, only to land on the first and shatter.

"Jesus!" he yelled, his buoyant mood instantly evaporating. He got out of the car and saw that the back end of a Range Rover was attached to his car's rear bumper. Looking up from the damage, he saw a heavily built man in a crumpled business suit stumbling awkwardly from the Range Rover, his bloated face twisted with rage.

"What's yer game, Jack?" spat the man, his strong Liverpudlian accent cutting through the rain as he wobbled unsteadily towards John. "Can't yer bloody wait yer turn? Yer must've seen me reversing out. Look at that dent; that's gonna cost yer."

"What the hell are you talking about!" snapped John, tensing with anger, "I was stationary. You reversed into me."

"Yeah, and me dad's the Pope," spat the man, poking a meaty index finger into John's chest. "That's me brand new car you've crunched and you're gonna have to pay for the damage."

John wrinkled his nose in distaste as the man's boozy breath wafted over his face. He knocked the man's jabbing finger out of the way.

"You shouldn't be driving at all; you've obviously had way too much to drink."

"Yer what, yer pillock!" slurred the man, swinging his right fist. John saw it coming and moved his head to one side, raising his own arms and fists in a defensive stance. The man grunted, hunched his shoulders and threw two more punches. John sidestepped the first but he was out of practice and the second glanced his ear, a large signet ring cutting into the skin. He half-turned and gave the now off-balance man a shove that sent him stumbling forward to fall headlong into a puddle. John looked down in shock at the sodden and dishevelled man. He realised he had acted instinctively, recalling automatically the skills taught to him so many years ago. It had been more than a hundred years since he'd had to use those skills. Images of a rock-strewn landscape on the South China coast and his search for Lei-li flashed across his mind.

Red-faced and snarling angrily, the man staggered to his feet and turned round, his chin bleeding. He took a step towards John but stopped in his tracks as a police car turned into the car park, the lights on its roof flashing. It stopped near the two men and a police officer got out. Taking his time, he cast a long-suffering glance at the rain as he pulled on his cap.

"What's going on, gentlemen?"

"It's like this, Jack," shouted the Range Rover driver, wiping the blood from his chin with his sleeve. "This stroppy prat reverses into me, smashes me brand new car, and then the git says it was my fault and starts swinging at me."

The police officer glanced at John, who had blood dribbling from his ear, and then at the other man, whose gashed chin was bleeding freely onto his shirt.

"Certainly looks like you two were having a good go at each other."

His sense of fair play severely threatened, John gave in to his rising anger. He walked threateningly towards the police officer, waving a finger at him.

2

"That's complete rubbish. This drunk is way out of order."

"See, Jack, stroppy bastard, like I said," slurred the Range Rover driver as he wiped his chin on his sleeve.

The police officer fixed his eyes on John, the steely threat behind them stopping him in his tracks.

"Right," he said, "let's get this straight. I'm giving each of you a breath test and I'm arresting you for fighting in a public place."

John took a step forward and opened his mouth to speak, but the police officer's eyes bored into his again. "And if you don't stop, sir, I might well throw in a charge of attempting to assault a police officer."

A frustrated John paced the floor in an interview room at Ambleside police station. His processing had so far taken two hours. Finally, the door opened and the police officer came in carrying a plastic box.

John frowned at him. "What now?"

"Since you've been arrested for a recordable offence, sir, I am going to take a buccal swab sample."

"A what-able offence?"

"A recordable offence. It's one for which, in theory, you could go to prison."

He paused to let John absorb this piece of information while he took a stoppered plastic tube from the box.

"But my breath test was negative," objected John.

"Nothing to do with it, sir, you're still under arrest. Now, it's totally painless. I just need to take this swab and wipe it round the inside of your cheek." He pulled the stopper from the plastic tube and held up the swab. "The sample will be tested and the results put on the National DNA Database."

John felt a twinge of panic. He was sure that there must be something different about his DNA; what else could explain his age? The last thing he wanted was for it to be tested and scrutinised. "Look, officer, surely you're not serious about these charges."

"Just open your mouth, sir; this won't take a moment."

Thirty minutes later, John was still pacing the room when the police officer returned, a nonchalant smile on his face.

"Looks like it's your lucky evening, sir," he said. "There are two people outside, a man and a woman, who say they saw what happened in the car park, and it appears your story holds up. They say they saw you both reversing out at the same time, although it seems you were actually stationary when the collision occurred and therefore, technically, the other driver drove into you."

"There's no technically about it!" snapped John. "He did drive into me."

"The important point as far as you're concerned, sir," sighed the police officer, "is that they both agree they saw the driver of the Range Rover get out and pick a fight with you. Since you just acted defensively and didn't actually hit him, we won't be pressing any charges against you."

"And what about him?"

"Well, he'll certainly be charged with driving under the influence of alcohol, and I've no doubt he'll be found guilty and lose his licence for a year, but as for any other charges, that's really going to be up to you."

"Why me?"

"Do you want to press charges of assault against him, sir? It's a lot of paperwork ..." The police officer had clearly lost interest in the whole matter.

"I'd like to press his face right into the ground," muttered John. Then, as he saw the police officer raise his eyebrows, he added hastily, "No, I won't be pressing any charges, I just want to get home. But what about that sample? Surely it will be thrown away now?"

"'Fraid not, sir. You see, it was taken while you were under arrest. As I explained before, your DNA will go on the database."

"Ridiculous!" snarled John as he marched out of the room.

Back at the Green Man car park, John surveyed the damage. It wasn't as bad as he'd originally thought: his sturdy Volvo had definitely come off lighter.

He started the car, put it into first gear and gingerly pulled away. To his surprise, his car freed itself easily from the Range Rover. Of more immediate concern to him now as he drove off was the fact that his DNA was going to be on record. How much of a problem might that prove? He didn't know.

"Although I think it's a total infringement of your rights, I don't think you have anything to worry about, darling. You weren't a serial killer before I knew you, were you? At least not in recent times?"

John's wife, Lola, was standing with him in the large kitchen of their cottage on the banks of Thirlmere. She had checked his ear, declared it was only a scratch, and was now dishing up penne al ragù for their delayed dinner – their young daughters, Sophie and Phoebe, had long since had theirs and gone to bed. Meanwhile, John was opening the bottle of Merlot that had survived.

"Here's to penne al Merlot," he said. "There's a nice cold pile of it in the car."

"Yuk," grimaced Lola.

They had been talking about DNA profiles, their knowledge, like most people's, limited to the bite-sized chunks of science served up in TV documentaries and CSI.

"I wonder if mine will be different," mused John.

"Of course it will, sweetheart," smiled Lola. "We all have unique DNA, unless we have a twin, so yours being different shouldn't mean much. Apparently they can't tell anything about you from the results they get. So your serial killing will remain a secret."

John smiled, amused as ever by her flippancy.

"I wonder how long it lasts," he said reflectively. "I mean, does it go off if it's been lying around for ages?"

"I think they've been able to get it from the remains of mammoths stuck in ice," replied Lola, "but that's probably because it's frozen. And I did read something about looking at old master paintings and comparing one with another by measuring the DNA that is assumed to be from fingerprints of the artist. The trouble is that Leonardo da Vinci's DNA isn't on the database. Nor your friend Piero della Francesca's for that matter."

No it isn't, thought John, but I'd bet he would have been impressed with the technology.

He stared into his wine as the weight of his five hundred and eighty-two years suddenly pressed heavily on him.

# Chapter 2

## 1467-1492

Luca di Stefano stood back from his easel, linked his hands over his head, and stretched. It was five on a hot July afternoon and he had been bent over his work in meticulous concentration for the past three hours. He wiped a thin film of sweat from his forehead with his sleeve and returned his attention to his work. The board, or tavola, in front of him was well-seasoned poplar wood and on it he was producing a portrait in a tempera and oil mixture. His subject was Elisabetta Costanza Alberti, the supercilious wife of Rodolfo Giovanni Tommasini, a minor nobleman and local councillor. Tommasini had ordered the portrait to be in the traditional style, with no attention to be paid to perspective or realism. He had declared that he wanted none of the modern nonsense that was being produced in increasing amounts by various local artists caught up in what would later be called The Renaissance.

Luca poured himself a mug of water from an earthenware pitcher standing on a corner table, water he collected from a spring on his wife's family's farm three miles outside the walls of Borgo San Sepolcro in Tuscany where he lived and worked. He was convinced that fresh spring water was a source of health. Certainly he couldn't complain. He led what his wife, Maria, called a charmed existence as far as illness was concerned, never once in his life having fallen prey to even the mildest cold.

He cast an expert eye over his work and decided he'd had enough of looking at that face for one day. He was covering the painting loosely with a cloth when his fifteen-year-old son, Niccolò, ran into the studio clutching a small parchment scroll sealed with wax.

"Babbo, I met a messenger on my way home who gave me this," he said eagerly. "It has your name on it and I think I recognise the hand."

Luca glanced at the handwriting and smiled. "Maybe he's paying us a visit, Nicchi," he said, opening the scroll. As he read it, his eyes lit up with delight.

"He is indeed coming, Nicchi," he said, tossing the scroll to his son. "It looks as if he might be with us tomorrow. You have obviously studied his documents well if you recognised his hand. It's been four years since we've seen him."

The documents he was referring to were a number of early drafts on the subject of perspective that had been left with him by the man who, in his opinion, was one of the most talented artists of his time, a man who had become a close friend and who always sought him out on the rare occasions he returned to his native Borgo San Sepolcro: Piero della Francesca.

They had last seen Piero when he had returned from the conservative Tuscan town of Arezzo where he had been continuing work on what would turn out to be one of his most famous frescos: The Legend of the True Cross. Adorning the walls of the choir in the basilica of San Francesco in the centre of the town, the ambitious series of paintings depicted the mythical tale of how the wood from the cross on which Christ was crucified had originated from an acorn deposited in the mouth of the dying Adam. Piero had taken over from the painter Bicci di Lorenzo in 1452 when Bicci had become too ill to continue, and he was in the process of producing a controversial but brilliant work. However, he was a notoriously slow worker and, distracted by many other commissions, he had still not completed it by 1467.

A little before noon the next day, Luca heard a horse's hoofs enter the courtyard. As he rushed outside, he almost bumped into Piero who was running towards the studio door calling out Luca's name. They embraced in delight. A big man with a big personality, Piero held Luca out at arm's length. "My God, my friend, the years are being good to you, I don't think you've changed one jot since we last met."

He screwed up his eyes in concentration and laughed. "You must be dyeing your hair, Luca, there's not a speck of grey in it. Look at mine, greying and tired like the old man who's growing it. You must teach me your tricks. Now, how's my beautiful Maria?"

Ignoring the remarks about his hair, Luca returned Piero's firm grip. "She is in the best of possible health, my dear Piero, and longing to see you. As for Niccolò, he was beside himself in anticipation of your arrival when he left for Lepri's this morning. He would have stayed home if I'd given him the chance."

"You're too hard on the boy, Luca!" They were both laughing and slapping each other on the shoulders.

"Zio! Zio Piero!" Niccolò charged through the doors to the courtyard and nearly knocked Piero off his feet as he greeted him. Piero held him out and looked him up and down. "Niccolò, my boy! No, my young man, my God how you've grown! Look at you! When I last saw you, you were a mere lad. Heavens! You'll soon be taller than I am!"

"What are you doing back here so early, young artigiano?" said Luca to Niccolò, with a mock serious frown.

Niccolò turned, slightly unsure of his father's tone until he saw his face. "I told Signor Lepri that Zio Piero was arriving and he sent me home early for my lunch, Babbo. He said I needn't come back today, but I'll probably go later. There is some glueing I must attend to."

Both men laughed at Niccolò's enthusiasm for his work. "Spoken like a true craftsman, young Niccolò." Piero hugged him again. "Now go and fetch your beautiful mother for me. I can't wait to see her."

Niccolò raced off to find Maria, who was at her dressmaker's inspecting a new delivery of cloth from Florence.

Luca turned to Piero, "What news of your work in Arezzo, the famous Legend? Is it completed yet?"

"Almost, my friend, almost. I have possibly two or three more weeks of work ahead of me before the last of the scenes is completed. It's been a long task. I was summoned to see the Franciscan friars immediately I returned to the city two months ago and I was told in no uncertain terms that they were impatient to see it completed. I can't really blame them – it's been fifteen years since I took over the work. They have even withheld a substantial part of my fee until the last brushstroke is in place. But I had to have a break from it. To appease them, my best assistant, Giovanni, is still there, devoted student that he is. Truth be told, he's been responsible for more of the work than I'd care to admit to my masters."

"Good to see you're as independent as ever," laughed Luca. "What do you have planned here in the Borgo?"

"Apart from a number of long-overdue matters with the council, I have a small commission in Monterchi, a village close to my heart, as you well know."

"Yes, your dear mother, Romana, God rest her soul, was born there."

"Exactly. It's an interesting commission; I'll show you the sketches. The work is well into the planning — I've already drafted most of the cartoons. It's to be in the old church of Santa Maria di Momentana. Fortunately, although it's a sizeable work, there is only one large central figure with two accompanying angels."

"Why fortunately?"

"Simply, my friend, because I don't have very much time."

He paused, a mischievous glint in his eyes.

"The subject is again rather controversial, for a painting at least. It's Our Lady heavy with child."

Luca smiled to himself, not surprised that Piero had yet again moved into potentially difficult waters. Then, puzzled, he said, "But Monterchi is about one-third of the way back to Arezzo. Surely you are not thinking of travelling to and from the Borgo to undertake this work?"

"Not at all. I intend to stop at Monterchi on my journey back to Arezzo in two months' time and complete it then. I have assistants visiting in advance to carry out all the preparatory work."

He paused, spread his arms out wide and shrugged. "I am too busy, Luca, thanks be to God, while you, my friend, one of the most talented artists I have ever met, have chosen a life of peace and serenity with your family."

"It's true, Piero, that I prefer to stay here in the Borgo, even though I'm not normally the first choice when it comes to official commissions with the confraternities and the clergy. I keep my opinions of them to myself, but the fact that I don't play much of a part in their lives I suppose speaks for itself."

"Your views are safe with me, Luca. However, I do regret that your talent is not more widely available."

Luca looked at him quizzically. "You have a twinkle in your eye, Piero. What are you plotting?"

"Ah, my friend, you know me too well. I have another commission while I am here. There is a certain nobleman with a fine villa not far from Anghiari who wishes to have a large fresco adorn his family's chapel. He wants it to have a contemporary setting but a biblical theme."

"He must have offered you a fine purse, Piero, for you to undertake what will essentially be a private work."

Piero smiled conspiratorially. "A fine purse indeed, and one I want to share with you, my friend! I propose that we undertake this work together. But we shall have to work fast – as I have explained, time is short. Tell me you'll work with me!"

"Piero, it would be an honour. What's the theme?"

"The theme is to be Christ explaining himself and heaven to some of the disciples, opening their eyes from the sleep of normal life to the Glory of God. It's a particular obsession of this nobleman and he has quite fixed ideas about how it should look, which, fortunately for him, I am prepared to accommodate. It's to be called 'The Awakening'. I've already made a number of sketches, but I can only undertake it with your help. As you know, I can be somewhat slow in the execution of my work and I don't think that I can do it alone in the time I have available."

"Will the nobleman agree to your having help?"

"From you, yes, since he is familiar with your work. Indeed, I believe you are in the process of completing a portrait of his wife."

Luca shook his head in surprise. "Tommasini? I'm amazed; he's such a conservative man. He'd be the last person I should expect to commission a work that isn't in the tedious style he has demanded for his wife's portrait. I take it that he hasn't insisted on your returning to the dark ages."

Piero laughed at his reaction. "Not at all. He knows that if he employs me he will gain all the benefit of my ideas on perspective and realism. I should not consider working otherwise. It would seem he has a public face and a private face."

They had moved into Luca's studio and were sitting on a couple of stools while Piero was casually looking through a set of Luca's sketches. On hearing a shout from the yard, they looked up to see Maria rushing in. Piero leapt to his feet, his arms outspread. "Maria, how wonderful! You are a joy to behold!" He picked her up, swirled her round and held her at arm's length, smiling broadly at her.

"My dear, you are as beautiful as the day I first saw you, and as radiant as you were on the day of your marriage to your scoundrel of a husband. Oh, Maria! If you knew how many times you have appeared in my work. Your face looks down from on high in many noble and holy locations."

He held his head to one side as he studied her features carefully. "You know, your radiant beauty will be perfect for a work I'm soon to be undertaking in Monterchi."

Maria blushed. "Really, Piero, it's about time you chose a younger model, not an ageing mother like me."

"You may have aged in years, my dear Maria, but you remain as youthful as ever. What is it with both of you? In your presence, l feel far more than my fifty-five years."

He looked from Maria to Luca and back, realising with an inward gasp of surprise that while Luca, at forty years of age, had the youthful looks of a man ten years younger, Maria, at thirty-four, had fine lines starting to etch her eyes.

Two weeks later, Luca and Piero were taking a break in the private Tommasini chapel, having already completed over one-third of the commission.

Luca was delighted to have the opportunity to work with Piero again. He had become a part-time apprentice to him at the age of ten when Piero, who was still working under the guidance of his own mentor, Antonio d'Anghiari, had first seen a remarkable set of Luca's drawings. Realising that the boy possessed a rare talent, Piero had persuaded Luca's recently-widowed mother that he could help develop that talent. From then on, Luca spent all his free time with Piero, listening and watching in wonder as Piero introduced him to his skills and techniques.

In 1439, Piero had left San Sepolcro to study the masters in Florence, but when he returned a year later, he insisted that Luca accompany him as his apprentice on his next trip there. That experience had a profound effect on them both, but at heart the young Luca missed his home. He felt a strong responsibility towards his mother, especially since she had no other relatives in the Borgo.

Although Piero was disappointed that Luca would not develop at the rate he had hoped, he was sympathetic to the boy and decided to set up a workshop in San Sepolcro for a small group of talented youths, Luca included. To run this during his own long absences, he engaged Alighiero Ferrobraccia, a skilled if somewhat unimaginative artist who had also been an apprentice of Antonio d'Anghiari.

Luca had been the star that shone among them and as he reached his late teens, he had again accompanied Piero on his commissions in other towns, helping him on a number of major works. But his concerns over his mother were ever-present. When on a trip back to the Borgo, Luca met and fell in love with Maria, he knew where his future lay.

Piero stood back to review their progress.

"Luca, you work with an impressive speed that I cannot begin to emulate – if you carry on at this rate, this work will be one quarter mine and three quarters yours."

He paused and stared closely at the part Luca had just completed.

"Tell me, my friend, is your brushwork always this close to mine or are you deliberately copying my style?"

Luca laughed. "My style is naturally very similar to yours, Piero. How could it be anything else? However, I confess, I am trying to adjust it to be even closer to yours than I would normally paint. After all, this work is ostensibly by you."

Piero shook his head in admiration. "I should be hard-pressed to tell which of us painted what. Your technique, Luca, has matured from the mere excellent to brilliant."

Luca laughed self-deprecatingly. "You are too kind with your compliments, Piero. Everything I know, I learned from you. Without a detailed understanding of your technique, I could not have begun to paint in this way. I regard myself as immensely privileged that I am one of the very few people who can number themselves among your apprentices."

"Pah! Apprentice! When I look at this work of yours, I regard myself as an apprentice. You could teach me much, Luca. It is a terrible waste that you are not in Rome or Florence gaining a name for yourself."

"Rome, Florence, the other important capitals; they are all appealing, Piero, but as I've explained to you before, I've never been prepared to become an itinerant artist, even if that limits my potential for success. Being with my family is the most important thing for me and I am content with my life in the Borgo. And Niccolò is such an excellent artigiano; he will go far as a carpenter. It gives me such pleasure watching him grow and mature."

"I salute you, Luca, I really do. Perhaps one day I will settle back here."

Piero picked up the sketches that were scattered across a large workbench. "Now, this afternoon, let's have some fun. I've added my own face to a number of my works in the past as you know. It's like a signature. But for a change, I can be the model while you will be the artist who paints me. Who shall I be?"

He studied the figures in the sketches as Luca walked over to his side.

"I think St. Paul's pose would suit me. You may make St. Paul's face mine."

Turning to Luca, he said, "I shall, of course, put your face on another figure once you have completed mine. It will be good to have you present for a change when I include you in a painting."

Luca looked up from the sketches. "What do you mean?"

"Well, as you are aware, I like to paint from life, or at least use the faces and figures of people I know. When they are not around, I paint them from memory. Take your wonderful wife. Her divine face has been the focus of several of my paintings. You too, Luca. Your face is in several groups that the Duke of Urbino sees daily when he reviews his collection of art. And if you were to look closely at the Legend cycle in Arezzo..." He grinned mischievously. "I think in all your face appears in at least two dozen of my works. But for every one of them, I have had to rely on my memory. To have you here in front of me as a model will be very special. Now, who will you be? St. John? St. Matthew?"

Luca shook his head in amazement at Piero. It amused him to think that his likeness would be present in so many works. He wondered if anyone would recognise him from them. He too, like all artists, had used people he knew as models for various figures appearing in the background in many of his works. He had even used Piero's features on more than one occasion, but he didn't want to spoil Piero's fun by telling him that now.

"I don't think it would be right for me to aspire to being a saint, Piero." Luca scanned the main sketch with his eyes. "Yes, that's it. This figure."

Piero looked over his shoulder. "The shepherd?"

"Yes, Piero, I'll be the shepherd."

"I agree, my friend, it's a good figure. But you realise that being a shepherd is a stressful occupation. I insist that even if in real life you manage to maintain your youthful looks, in this likeness I'll give your hair a distinguished grey tone that more befits your years."

Piero laughed, but as Luca looked into his eyes, he saw his great friend was perplexed. He had seen what Luca himself had seen and worried about increasingly over the last few years. He had seen what Maria had seen and had questioned: he was simply not looking any older.

Rodolfo Tommasini was delighted with Luca's portrait of his wife and overjoyed with 'The Awakening'. He proudly recommended Luca to his friends and in the years that followed, Luca reluctantly found himself away from home more than he preferred. Maria was pleased he was getting the recognition she knew he deserved, but now each time he returned home from a commission, she worried about his youthful appearance.

"When you were here all the time, Luca, I didn't really notice it or think about it, but now when you return after three months away, I realise how blessed I am to have such a young-looking husband. It's most disconcerting, you know. In contrast to your wife, whose appearance displeases her more each time she sees it reflected in the glass, not only do you not have a single grey hair on your head, but your handsome features are not disturbed in any way by lines or wrinkles."

"You are as beautiful as the day I first met you, Maria," he said, taking her in his arms. "As for me, people think I dye my hair out of vanity."

"I think you underestimate the problem, Luca. I'm concerned

because one or two of my friends have been making unkind remarks about you. Antonia del Sarto has been particularly cruel, saying you must have made a pact with the saints, or worse, some evil spirits. She claims that in times past, witches would sacrifice various animals as part of a spell to ward off ageing."

"Pagan nonsense!" harrumphed Luca. "That woman should learn to hold her tongue. The confraternities do not take kindly to rumour-mongers."

"It's not the confraternities that concern me," replied Maria, "it's the clergy. Many of them are old gossips themselves and it doesn't take much for them to start thinking about witchcraft. They'd take even less kindly to thoughts like that. Do you think that perhaps we should try to make you look a little older to prevent them from gossiping?"

"What do you have in mind? Should I go grey, or better, white overnight? Start painting lines on my face?"

"Be serious, Luca! Changing your hair colour too quickly would only invite comment. However, I've been thinking, you could wear a beard and colour it grey from the day you start to grow it. I've noticed that men's beards are often greyer than their head hair. What do you think?"

"I could, but I'd have to apply colour to it almost every day to maintain the effect."

She nodded. "You would, but of course I'll help you. It would be a small price to pay for stopping any gossip."


With them both now being away on commissions, Piero and Luca crossed paths infrequently, and it was not until 1479 that they met again in the Borgo. Thanks to Maria, Luca now had a full but neatly trimmed white beard and a greying head of hair.

Their meeting coincided with a celebration of the second birthday of Niccolò's young son, Gianni. Niccolò, who was now well-established as a master carpenter, had married Antonella Maria Donnetti, the daughter of a local merchant, in 1475. Gianni had arrived two years later.

Piero greeted his friend with his usual bluster and enthusiasm, hugging him with the pure joy of seeing him again.

"My dear friend, I'm delighted that you have at last received some of the recognition you deserve, at least in these local towns, even if the steep price I have had to pay is seeing far less of you."

"My recognition, as you call it, Piero, is all thanks to you."

He turned to look at Piero and saw that his friend was studying him carefully. He felt slightly embarrassed when for several seconds Piero uncharacteristically said nothing. Finally, Piero sighed.

"As you know, Luca, I am fascinated by the human form. And your face, well, it doesn't deceive me for one moment. You still haven't aged, have you? This grey and white in your beard and hair, it's false, isn't it?"

Luca looked down, avoiding Piero's penetrating look. He pursed his lips in resignation. "Is it that obvious?"

"No, my friend, not at all. You've done a remarkable job. It's very convincing. But my critical eye can see through it. Even though you've covered half your face with hair, I can see that your skin tone is still remarkable, and those incredible pale grey eyes of yours are as clear as ever."

Luca slumped into a chair. "I simply don't understand it, Piero. I'm fifty-two years old, and yet if I were to remove all this powder mixture I've formulated and cut off this ridiculous beard that I hate, I'd look exactly the same as I did twenty years ago. I'm also – it's strange – I have the vitality that I had twenty years ago; I've retained my fitness; my musculature seems not to have deteriorated and my stomach hasn't rounded and softened like a normal man of fifty. And I'm never, ever, ill – I've never in all my life had even a cold. In harsh winters when Maria tends to get worrying coughs that put her to bed for a week and make me fear she has lung fever, I can tend to her, be around her, and nothing will ever touch me. I have even been exposed to the plague on occasions. It's known, is it not, that people with the plague and afflictions like it have bad air around them that should not be breathed. I must have breathed it, but never once have I shown the slightest tendency to any of these ills."

Piero raised his eyebrows in incredulity. "You are truly blessed, Luca."

"Or cursed."

"Cursed not to catch the plague? A strange curse and one many people would be pleased to have put upon them. How are your eyes?"

"My vision is as good as it was when I was a boy. My hearing too."

Piero sighed. "I can offer you no explanation, my friend. But I can offer you some advice. The Church doesn't like unexplained phenomena and your condition could be misinterpreted. You would do well to carry on with this little pretence of altering your appearance. It certainly seems to be working."

"For now yes, but it requires so much attention. Although this powder mixture is effective, I have to apply it every day. That's why I have taken to wearing a hat so much – it hides most of my hair while emphasising the white beard that is easier to maintain. Maria is most diligent, ensuring that I never go out without looking totally convincing." He smiled wryly at Piero. "Except to you, that is."

"You are very fortunate to have such a wife."

"She has taken to coming with me. For the past year, whenever I've taken on a commission outside the borgo, she has insisted. It's regarded as very unusual, but as well as helping me maintain my disguise, it helps spread the notion that I am ageing and in need of assistance. She's always there to support me, Piero. I think without her my secret would be quickly uncovered. But it worries me; she is not the strongest of women. The loss of our two daughters at birth after Nicchi was born took its toll. She nearly died the second time. I worry that she might fall victim to some illness in one of these fine villas or palazzos. So many of them are cold and dank places."

Piero nodded. He had worked in many such buildings himself.

Luca's fears became a reality in November 1485, when the now fifty-one-year-old Maria caught an early winter chill in a damp and drafty villa where Luca was painting a large fresco. The chill developed into a more serious bronchial condition, confining her to bed with a fever, and her weakened lungs quickly succumbed to the illness. She died with a grief-stricken Luca at her bedside.

The fresco was never finished. It remained on the damp and poorly finished villa walls for another fifty years until, like the surfaces around it, it crumbled and flaked as the building fell into disrepair, lost like so many similar works to the ravages of time and the lack of understanding of, or interest in, maintaining it.

Luca returned to San Sepolcro in a daze. He had lost the love of his life, his Maria. He could see no further point in carrying on and could summon no enthusiasm for painting. He had no more interest in his house in the Borgo where he and Maria had lived with Niccolò and Gianni – Niccolò's wife had died in childbirth along with their second child four years earlier. Every corner, every angle, every surface carried memories of times that had gone forever and it pained Luca to be reminded of them. When Maria's brother, Antonio, who ran her family's farm a short distance from the town, suggested the three of them move into a cottage that was one of the outbuildings, Luca jumped at the chance, and both Niccolò and Gianni readily agreed. They wanted nothing more than for Luca to recover from his grief.

While the move briefly lifted Luca's spirits, he soon returned to his introspection. On the rare occasions he went out he shuffled along like an old man, a scarf pulled round his face and a hat covering his hair.

A change for the better occurred in the late spring of 1486 when Niccolò realised that Gianni, now nine years old, was beginning to show some of his grandfather's artistic skills. He showed Luca some of the boy's sketches and a couple of paintings.

"He is afraid to show you, Babbo; he thinks you would consider them too poor."

Luca sifted carefully through the pile. "He's a silly boy. These are excellent for a child of his age. He has real potential. Perhaps I can help him a little."

Niccolò was delighted. "Would you really, Babbo? He would be thrilled."

"I shall make it my mission, my son. I may have lost interest in painting for myself, but it would be terribly selfish of me if I shied away from the opportunity of bringing on a young talent. Whatever would his grandmother have said? As for Piero, he'd disown me!"

The last time Luca and Piero met was a week before Piero's death in October 1492. Piero had been living back in the Borgo for some years, devoting himself to his treatises on perspective and algebra. The old friends called on each other from time to time, their meetings always resulting in the raising of Luca's spirits since Piero's zest for life and good humour had not diminished as he advanced into old age. They seldom discussed Luca's 'condition', as Piero had taken to calling it, although none of the meetings passed without Piero closely studying Luca's features.

At this final meeting, Piero had taken to his bed following a fever. His face had a sickly, grey pallor that made him look even older than his eighty years. His eyes, however, were alert and fixed on Luca, puzzled as ever by the dilemma he knew he would never solve.

"You behave like an old man, Luca," Piero's now thin voice piped, "but do you feel old? Have you really slowed down in the way you'd have us believe? When I look into your eyes, I can still see that vitality, that young man who's never gone away. And your skin. My God, Luca, your skin is as youthful as ever! If I were to cut your hair and beard, and remove that ridiculous powder, I don't think you'd look any different from when you were a young man."

"Nonsense, I'm feeling my years like everyone else," lied Luca.

"Listen, my friend," whispered Piero quietly, "I'm tired and I have a feeling that this fever might be winning its fight against my body. I need to rest. When I'm gone, I want you to promise me that you will continue to take the utmost care. There are people in this town, particularly among our learned priests, who would not look favourably on your condition, people who would wish to develop all kinds of frightening hypotheses, most of them centred on evil forces. Take very great care my friend." He looked towards the bedroom door, paused for breath and called out, "Nicchi!"

A sad Niccolò entered the room. He had accompanied Luca to see Piero, but realising the seriousness of Piero's condition, had chosen to remain in an outer room so the old friends could talk.

"Nicchi," wheezed Piero, "say goodbye to your old zio."

Forgetting himself, Niccolò buried his head in Piero's chest. Piero gasped and then laughed. "Careful Nicchi, you don't want to hurry my end along too much; I still have a few things to tidy up."

The tearful Niccolò grasped both of Piero's hands, kissed them and looked lovingly at the old man. "I'll never forget you, Zio Piero."

"Nor I you, Nicchi, I'll be watching you from wherever I'm going. But you must promise me that you'll take good care of this other old man." He raised a worn hand towards Luca.

"I promise." Niccolò chewed on his lip.

"And that boy of yours. Your babbo showed me some of his work the last time he was here. He has great potential. Make sure that his illustrious tutor continues his lessons."

As they slowly made their way from Piero's house towards the walls of the town, they passed a street stall selling peaches. Luca stopped in surprise — it was unusual to see them in early autumn.

"Piero has always adored peaches, Nicchi; I think I'll buy some. We'll eat them at home and toast him with a mug of wine."

He took out his purse and was about to remove some coins when he was knocked sideways and the purse snatched from him. A boy of about fifteen who had been lurking quietly in the shadows had decided to take his chance against this old man.

"Hey!" yelled Niccolò, quickly gathering his wits and sprinting up the street after the boy. But the boy was fast and Niccolò, who wasn't in the best of condition, slowed and stopped to lean against a wall to gather his breath. He glanced up as someone else ran past him at full tilt, his jaw dropping open as he realised it was his father. On regaining his balance, Luca had shrugged off his cloak and hat and without a second thought, charged off up the street after Niccolò and the boy.

It had been years since Luca had broken into anything more than a fast walk, but his legs felt good as they pounded after the youth. "Stop!" he yelled as a couple of women and a priest stepped quickly aside. He caught the youth at the corner of the next building as he was about to disappear into a dark alleyway. Grabbing the boy by the scruff of the neck, he turned him round. The boy was filthy, an urchin living on the street, and terrified by this elderly man who had outrun him.

"Give it to me!" demanded Luca, holding out his hand for his purse.

The boy passed it over. Still grasping him firmly by the neck, Luca looked him up and down. "How long have you been living on the street, boy?"

"Five years, signore, since my mother died," he stammered.

"Well, if you want money, ask for it. Don't steal it!" Luca let go of the boy. He was about to open the purse to give him some coins when, in a flash, the boy was gone.

As Luca stood there shaking his head, Niccolò rushed up to him, carrying his cloak and hat.

"Babbo!" he hissed. "Babbo! Half the street is staring at you. They know who you are. Put this on quickly and cover your head."

Luca put on the hat and the cloak and looked around. A small crowd had formed and there was a quiet muttering as they stared at him.

"Babbo, for the love of God. Lean on me, look tired, stagger a little," whispered Niccolò.

Luca took a step towards his son and faltered, reaching out for him. "Help me, Nicchi," he groaned loudly, "I think I've overdone it. Whatever was I thinking of, a man of my age?"

Continuing with the playacting, Niccolò helped his father walk slowly along the street, shaking his head at various members of the crowd to gain their sympathy. Luca sat down heavily on a barrel and asked feebly for a glass of wine.

"You should be careful, di Stefano," called out a shopkeeper. "You're too old to be chasing after urchins."

Luca nodded weakly in reply.

The priest, Padre Bognini, who had been forced to jump out of Luca's way as he raced along the street, stood back in the shadows watching the whole performance with interest. He waited until Luca and Niccolò had disappeared, then slipped away down a side alley.

The relationship between the Church and the lay authorities in San Sepolcro had been complex for more than two hundred years. The town was unusual in that its independently-minded men had a strong control over its clerical life, deliberately limiting the Church's power and influence within the town walls, much to the frustration of the clergy. As a result, the despised bishop of nearby Città di Castello, who claimed clerical authority over the town, had maintained control of only two of its numerous churches for decades. Anything that might swing the balance towards the Church was welcomed by the bishop, who had a number of sympathetic eyes and ears in place in the town to help him gather evidence that the lay authorities were failing in their duty of overseeing the spiritual life of the townspeople.

The following night, Padre Bognini met with Angelo d'Angeli, archpriest of the Santa Maria della Pieve church, one of the two in the Borgo under the bishop's control. An austere and ambitious man, d'Angeli was artfully in the process of increasing his sway with the major confraternities that ran San Sepolcro. As Bognini related his rambling account, the archpriest narrowed his eyes in interest, knowing he could use this information to his advantage. And from what the obsequious priest had to tell, it sounded as if action was more than justified.

"The man is in league with the Devil, Father Angelo, there can be no other explanation for his unholy demeanour. I tell you I saw it with my own eyes – a man well into his sixties running down the street like a youth. And despite his pretence at exhaustion afterwards, there was not a bead of sweat upon his face, while his heavy breathing was clearly a sham. If anything, there was a superior look of joy. He was gloating at his prowess. I am a similar age to di Stefano and I lead a pious life of frugality, yet I think my heart would fail me if I attempted such a feat."

The archpriest cast a glance at Bognini's well-fed torso and doubted his frugality extended to his diet. "A foolhardy endeavour for anyone of advanced years, Father Bognini. Yet I have heard di Stefano looks his age."

"A disguise, Father Angelo, a disguise. After the incident in the street in the Borgo, I took it upon myself to visit him, something I haven't done for many years since he dissuaded his son from taking vows in the Holy Church. What kind of father would do such a thing?" He shook his head in disbelief, and then continued. "Last evening, after Mass, I went to his late wife's family farm where di Stefano lives in a cottage."

"And what did you find?"

"A most fascinating discovery, Father Angelo," replied the priest, rubbing his pudgy hands.

"I was about to knock on the cottage door, when it opened and, to my surprise, Luca di Stefano himself emerged carrying a lantern. He had it held up and I could see his face clearly. He addressed me sternly, showing little respect, demanding I tell him my business. I told him I was concerned that I hadn't seen him for confession for some time, and that given his advancing years, I didn't want him to be surprised by death's often untimely call without being purged of his sins."

"What was his reaction?"

"He laughed in a manner I can only describe as scornful. He then told me he was in good health and did not expect an imminent visit from any representatives of the next world to take him away from this one. The presumption of the man, and said with such arrogance!"

He paused, warming to his theme.

"But Father Angelo, I haven't told you all. As I said, the light was held up against his face. I could see his features clearly. He has, you know, the most unholy and penetrating pale grey eyes. I could see those eyes and the face around them. Unlike all other men of his age, Father, this Luca di Stefano has not a single line around those eyes, and as far as I could tell, not a single line on his face, although much of it is covered by an extensive beard. That beard too is very strange. I only had a brief opportunity to study it before he lowered the lantern and his face was plunged into darkness, but I swear it was far blacker than when I saw him in the town."

He paused again to let this sink in, his mouth salivating freely, his lips moist with excitement.

"I am convinced he colours his beard grey to disguise the youthful looks that have been his reward for being the Devil's agent."

The archpriest rubbed his chin thoughtfully. "You have done well, Father Bognini. Without a doubt, this man needs investigating. If, as you say, he has maintained his youth despite his advancing years, then the only explanation can be that he has made some sort of pact with the dark forces, perhaps with the Antichrist himself."

He paused to cross himself before continuing. "Such behaviour cannot be tolerated. I shall report it to the bishop immediately and to the confraternal council at their meeting tomorrow evening. I shall insist that action is taken."

Archpriest Angelo d'Angeli pounded his fist onto the long wooden table in the meeting hall of the confraternity, his eyes glowing with fervour as he looked around the room. Spittle flew from his lips. "My brethren, it is our holy duty to take action against this man. From the report I have just given you, it must be clear to you that we have the Devil's work being carried out in this town."

The meeting of the confraternity's eight members had been in session for an hour. Archpriest d'Angeli, as a guest of the meeting, had bided his time while its members discussed routine matters, some of which he knew would raise their ire against one member of the town or another for some real or imagined slight against the Church.

When asked to address the meeting, he had started slowly, speaking in a matter-of-fact manner, detailing the report that the malicious priest had given him. He let his voice rise with every new point, adding what he hoped would be fuel to the fire in which he fervently wanted Luca di Stefano to burn.

"This unbeliever must be brought here, stripped, and his body examined. His beard must be removed so that we can see the full extent of his sinful pursuits. I have no doubt we shall see the reward he has accepted from the Antichrist for whatever practices he has been performing is that his body has retained its youth. A most obscene concept."

The group was convinced. It was agreed that a squad of the town guard would be dispatched to arrive at the di Stefano cottage at first light, a time when it was assumed the occupants would still be sound asleep and any danger posed by whatever foul practices they had been performing under the cowardly cover of darkness would have diminished.

Only one member of the group hung back slightly in his fervour at what he had no doubt would result in a public execution. Not that he wasn't convinced: Domenico della Francesca was as devout as any of the men around the table. He was, however, concerned that the justice meted out was often based on what he considered flimsy evidence. Domenico was the son of Antonio della Francesca, Piero's brother, and had taken over his ageing father's seat on the confraternity's administration. He looked on thoughtfully as the other members of the group discussed the plan for the following morning and arranged a time to meet for the interrogation of Luca, Niccolò and Gianni, and he wondered what his dying Uncle Piero would make of it.

# Chapter 3

## June 2009

Claudia Reid stared at her computer screen in total disbelief. Sighing in exasperation, she grabbed the receiver of her phone and angrily punched an internal number.

"Derek? Could you come to my office? Now!"

Thirty seconds later, Claudia's office door opened and Derek Abbott walked in clutching a pile of computer printouts, his body language radiating caution, his eyes wary.

Claudia looked up, her eyes falling on the paperwork.

"What the hell are these results?" she said, her voice rising unintentionally as she waved a flustered hand at the computer monitor. "They can't possibly be correct. It's your first week as a unit head, leading the profiling, and you come up with this. I..." She raised her arms in exasperation.

"I know, Claudia. I've been tearing my hair out since the first result appeared. I've been checking and rechecking everything. That's why I didn't come to see you earlier. I know they can't be right but all the controls are correct; all the other results in the batch are normal. I can't find any explanation."

"Derek, I know with DNA profiling we occasionally see rare alleles. That's what makes it exciting. But now the database is getting larger, we're pretty sure we've seen most of the variants. OK, new ones are still going to pop up and it's great when they do. But there are ten pairs of results here, twenty alleles, and eighteen of them aren't on the list, eighteen alleles that have never been seen before! That's impossible, Derek!"

She breathed out heavily, angry with herself for trusting such a junior biochemist. He'd seemed so good, so competent. She'd given him responsibility and he'd failed her within days. Her eyes fixed on his with a scowl. "Have you repeated the profiling?"

"It's on now, Claudia," stammered Derek. "I've used different controls, a whole pile of them. Look, I'm sorry, I just can't imagine what's gone wrong."

"Let me have the new results as soon as you have them. And leave those printouts for me to look through." She dismissed him with her eyes and he turned to leave.

"And Derek," she called after him, "don't discuss this with anyone. It's too embarrassing."

Claudia spent the rest of the morning analysing the printouts, a sinking feeling in her gut. How could this happen? High technology aside, the raison d'être of her laboratory was very straightforward: it profiled the DNA on the ever-increasing numbers of buccal swabs taken by the police under the Criminal Justice Act from anyone arrested, cautioned, charged or convicted for a 'recordable' offence: CJ samples. The profiles were sent to the National DNA Database where they were run against the outstanding crime database. If there was no hit, the profiles were still added data to the DNA Database – a potential time-bomb ticking against anyone on the database who committed a crime in the future.

It was crucial that all the results were correct; that there were no mistakes, no misinterpretations, no mix ups. As a section head, Claudia was part of a team whose job it was to ensure the system was watertight.

And now this.

Three hours later there was a hesitant knock on Claudia's door.

"Come in," she called abruptly.

Derek shuffled in, the same injured look on his face.

"I don't need to ask, do I?" said Claudia curtly, her hopes evaporating.

He handed her the latest printouts.

"Look, Claudia," he mumbled defensively, "I supervised every step of the repeat profiling myself. I used a whole gamut of controls. There is no reason to believe that these results aren't correct."

"I can see that," said Claudia, frowning at the charts in front of her.

After ten minutes of close scrutiny, she sighed and pushed the charts away from her, touching them gingerly as if they were about to burst into flames.

"OK, supposing they are for real. What would it mean? As far as we know, variation in STRs affects nothing we can measure or observe in an individual. This person isn't going to have two heads. He..." She paused to glance at one of the results that showed the gender. "Yes, he. He could be that very rare beast we assume we'll never see. The one in a squillion that can exist in theory but who is really no more than a statistician's dream."

Derek was eager to agree – anything that would deflect his boss's thoughts away from considering him incompetent. "Yes, he could be the one person in the history of the universe to have such a set of sequences. But perhaps the database simply isn't big enough yet. After all, it still has far less than ten per cent of the population on it. Given another five years, we'll probably regard these results as just another example of relatively rare profiles, but otherwise nothing special."

Claudia looked up at him. She didn't buy it. People had children. Genes were passed on. Why hadn't they seen any of these alleles before? The results couldn't be a one-off. But she was happy that Derek seemed to regard the profile as no more than a statistic. She wanted to keep these results to herself for the time being.

She drummed her fingers on the file. "Right, I have to agree that the analysis appears to be correct, as odd as it might seem. What we've got to do now is find out if this man has any more new alleles by using a different kit. The results will also crosscheck these. You'll need to use the second swab from the donor, by the sound of it."

She tried to get back to her routine work after the conversation with Derek Abbott, but she couldn't get the unbelievable results off her mind. She kept picking up the file and staring at the data. Everything was correct; all the results tallied: the DNA profile in that file was staggeringly different from anything that had ever been seen before. For Claudia it was a gift from the gods, the breakthrough she had been dreaming of for her research.

Claudia's research went against the grain. DNA profiling targets areas on chromosomes thought by most geneticists to have no significance other than being structural links. They even call them 'junk DNA'. Each targeted area is a specific place, or 'locus', where the sequences of DNA building blocks repeat a few times – a Short Tandem Repeat or STR. The number of repeats at an STR locus can vary from one person to another, which is what gives profiling its power. Each different variant is called an allele. Claudia disagreed that the variants were junk DNA and she was collecting data to support her theory. She had to follow this sample up to find out if the donor was different from other people in any way. She had to locate the man and find out more about him.

But there was a problem: the personal data of each person on the database was totally confidential. There was no way a donor's details could be known to an analyst at her level. That was totally against the rules.

Claudia was fully aware of the risks she'd be taking if she tried to find out the identity of the subject and approach him. If discovered, she would be severely reprimanded and probably lose her job. She might even be prosecuted. She had mulled this over while she waited for the latest results, but when they confirmed the findings beyond doubt, she decided that she couldn't let it rest. She would make some discreet enquiries.

When she checked the sample submission ledger, Claudia realised that she might have had a lucky break. The sample came from Cumbria, a county with large swathes of countryside and low population, and the normal delivery routine of samples being channelled through the county town of Carlisle had not happened. On this occasion, a police officer from Cumbria's Kendal Division in the Lake District had brought in the sample along with twenty others. She looked at the name of the delivering officer – PC Jeff Roberts – and wondered.

"Sal? It's Claw. How're you doing?"

Sal was Sally Moreton, Claudia's ex-flatmate from her university days in Manchester and, like Claudia, a forensic biochemist. She worked for Forefront Forensics, one of the rapidly-growing private forensic science laboratories in the UK that police forces were using increasingly. Sally worked on serious crime casework in the new, purpose-built Knutsford laboratory south of Manchester. Claudia had called her to talk over the profile that was starting to become an obsession with her. She desperately needed some sensible, down-to-earth advice from someone she knew she could trust. She knew whatever she discussed with Sally would go no further.

"Hi Claw, great to hear from you. It's as frantic as ever up here. The casework keeps piling up. My bosses might be an enlightened bunch, but sometimes their sales skills outpace what we can achieve on the ground. You should see my pending tray."

"Tell me about it," laughed Claudia. "Crime seems to be one area completely unaffected by global credit crunches and economic gloom and doom. Even with a 24/7 shift system we're finding it increasingly hard to stick to our targets."

"And I'll bet," said Sally, "that the police officers you deal with are as impatient for results as the ones constantly knocking on our doors. I think they all watch too many of these TV series where a one-man-band laboratory staffed with a forensic superhero skilled in everything from handwriting analysis to cranial reconstruction can deliver results almost instantly. They never seem to get it that this work takes time."

"Sal, have you got a few minutes? There's something that I'd really like to run by you. It's work-related, so I don't feel too guilty calling you in office hours."

"You mean this isn't a social call from a friend concerned that I'm going loony and buckling under the enormous pressure of work that's placed upon my slender shoulders?"

In her mind's eye, the diminutive five foot one and seven stone Claudia could see her almost six foot tall athletic friend – her ash blond hair cropped stylishly short for that extra bit of streamlined efficiency in her triathlon-filled weekends. They had been known on campus as 'Little and Large'.

"That as well, Sal, my sweet."

"Oh, it's my sweet is it? It must be pretty important."

"Sal, I want to keep this between ourselves, OK?"

"Goes without saying, Claw. Have any of our heart-to-hearts over the years ended up in the Sundays yet?"

Claudia dropped her voice to little more than a whisper.

"Sal, I've got this incredible DNA result. It's full of really rare alleles. The analyst who profiled it reckons it's a statistical thing, but I'm not so sure. It could be very significant to my research and I'd really like to track down the subject."

"To do what exactly, Claw?" replied Sally, the shock sounding in her voice. "Are you intending to go and knock on this guy's door and say, 'Hi, I'm a high-powered geneticist and I've profiled your DNA, you naughty little arrested person you, and Wow! Your DNA's really weird. Can I have some more sample?' If this guy lives in some inner-city slum, he's really going to respond favourably."

"I know that's the likely outcome, Sal, but if I can get a bit further – and it's a big 'if' I know – and the subject turns out to be someone who seems amenable, I might be able to get somewhere. If it turns out he's a lout, I'll stop immediately."

"Claw, you know you can't do this; it's against the rules. It contravenes the privacy laws; you'll lose your job!"

"Sal," Claudia hissed, "you're talking rather loudly. There's no one who can hear you, is there?"

"Actually, Claw, you've caught me in a meeting with the directors and the local Chief Constable. They're looking rather shocked at the conversation so far and want me to turn the phone on to speaker. Is that OK?"

"What!"

"Claw, don't be a dummy! I'm in my office; the door's closed and no one can hear. Relax and tell me why you want to throw away your career."

"That's the last thing I want to do, Sal, but don't you see how important this is? This person could be very special."

"You know, Claw, it's really only you who's likely to think that. Most people don't agree with your theories about there being a hidden, unknown function of junk DNA. Most people think it is junk. Me, I'm open-minded because I'm your friend and I know you're bonkers. But you've got to admit, with the distributions we now have for DNA profiles, everybody's special."

Claudia was frustrated. "I know we're all different when we go far enough with the profiling, but Sal, most of the alleles in this sample have never been seen before, and they're all here together in one person. I'm not talking rare here; it's unprecedented. I'm talking outrageously unique!"

There was a silence at the other end of the line. Finally Sally said, "So, this really is the big time huh? Why don't you go to Mike and explain? He seemed a reasonable guy when I met him. Maybe the bigwigs could arrange some sort of formal approach."

"First," replied Claudia, "Mike and reasonable have never met. He's an arsehole and he thinks my research is a waste of time. And you know the rules for a CJ sample. The subject is never contacted. Full stop. Period. End of story. Anyway, even if Mike thought he could get beyond that problem because he thought it was special, he'd immediately try to take it off my hands and run with it, and then if anything came of it, claim all the glory."

"I thought he was trying to screw you."

"Well, he's realised that isn't going to happen, possibly something to do with my pointing out that he has a wife, who I happen to like, and kids; so he's now just keen on screwing my career."

"Sounds like you could be handing him that opportunity on a plate, Claw, to screw your career, I mean."

She paused for a moment. "And you say the analyst who brought you the result isn't interested?"

"Yes and no. I think Derek simply sees it as rare. He seemed more concerned that I was going to blame him for getting a wrong result. He's not really interested in the function or otherwise of these alleles. Like everyone else here, he thinks I'm wasting my time researching them – reckons they're structural and nothing else. That's why I'm so keen to follow it up – it could be a big break in my research and I could prove them all wrong."

"And lose your job! What about the review meetings, won't you have to bring it up?"

"Yes, of course I will. But we've only recently had one, so I can sit on the results for now without alarm bells ringing. Even when it comes up, they probably won't be interested. The only things that really concern them are that the results are all correct, beyond challenge, and that we're meeting their gruelling targets."

She paused and took a deep breath.

"Look Sal," she continued, "I know I should probably go about this differently, but I have a strange feeling about this profile and I really want to follow it up if I can. I promise I won't do anything daft; and I certainly don't want you sticking your neck out. What I'm really hoping to do is track down the submitting police officer."

There was a silence at the other end.

"Sal? Are you still there?"

She heard a long sigh. "I can't believe what you just said, Claw. You want to contact the police officer to ask him if he'll tell you the name of someone who gave a CJ sample?" She sounded incredulous. "They'll have you on toast!"

"Put like that, I know it doesn't sound very bright," replied Claudia meekly, "but this sample comes from Cumbria, and if it happens to come from the back of beyond, the police officer might be a bit more inclined …"

"I don't think you should underestimate these guys. They might spend their time cautioning day-trippers for parking their bicycles on a double yellow line, but they're still cops, you know. Many of them are like me – they love running around the countryside all day – but others have a real chip about being stuck in the wilds and are out to prove they're super cops. They certainly wouldn't think twice about busting you."

"God, Sal, I suppose you're right." Claudia sounded utterly deflated. "I know I shouldn't take this further. But when I saw the name 'PC Roberts' in the ledger, I imagined him as a really nice guy who'd be fascinated by my work and happy to turn a blind eye to the rules."

"You're bloody kidding, Claw, right?"

"Yes, I know, naïve, huh?"

"No, Claw, I mean kidding about the name. PC Roberts. What was his first name?"

"Jeff. PC Jeff Roberts."

"Christ, Claw! You realise that you haven't simply phoned your old friend and partner in crime, Sally Moreton. You've phoned your fairy bloody godmother!"

Claudia was confused. "I don't understand."

"Claw. Jeff Roberts and I have a history. We had, you know, a bit of a fling."

"What? When?"

"Well, as you know, before I worked for Forefront, I spent a couple of years in the Forensic Science Service's Chorley lab at Preston. Jeff was among a group of police officers on a training course there trying to absorb what went on in the lab. Most of his grey cells are below waist level, so I think it was all a bit much for him, but he's a bit of a looker and when he asked me to join him for a drink in the pub after work, I wasn't going to say no."

"So what happened?" asked Claudia.

"We sat and discussed roadblock design."

"What?"

"Don't be a plonker, Claw, what do you think happened?"

"Oh."

"Yes, well, it was OK for a while but I then found out our PC Roberts had a Mrs Roberts and a Jeff junior–"

"He's got a son called Jeff junior?"

"God, Claw, I don't know what his bloody son's called and I don't care. The point is, if I ask him for a favour, he'll be shit scared that if he doesn't deliver, Mrs Roberts and I might have a little chat."

"You wouldn't?"

"Of course I wouldn't, but he doesn't know that."

"Sal, I absolutely don't want you asking this guy for any favours. It's my neck and I can't get you involved."

"Claw, have you thought beyond this connection?"

Claudia couldn't always keep up with Sally's rapid thought processes. "What do you mean?"

"Claw, now this might be a leap of logic, so I want you to follow me carefully," she added, with more than a hint of mock sarcasm in her voice. "Our PC Roberts is in the Kendal Division, but he's stationed at the Ambleside nick. Given that he brought in your sample, I'd say there was more than an outside chance that your man lives in the Lake District. Call me inspirational, call me–"

"You're a genius, Sal!"

"Yes, well, don't forget that so far, no rules have been broken. It's not against the rules to check in the ledger and it's not against the rules to put two and two together. But it is against the rules to approach PC Jeff Doe-Eyes Roberts and try to find out who the sample was taken from. However, if you happen to mention that you're my best friend, and that we have no secrets from each other –"

"And I explain that he'd possibly be helping with a huge scientific breakthrough–"

"No, that wouldn't touch him; remember where his brain cells are. But if perhaps you explained that there might be a link between criminality and certain profiles, if he doesn't like the bloke, he might buy it."

"But that's rubbish, Sal, I can't say that."

"Look Claw, he's a police officer, he doesn't understand science. If he ever put you on the spot and quoted it back at you, you could explain in a very scientific way to him that he'd got his backside confused with his brain. Now do you want his mobile number or not?"

"You've got his mobile number?"

"How do you think we communicated, Claw? Smoke signals?"

"Sal, this is amazing," beamed Claudia, excitedly writing down the number.

"Maybe, Claw, but I'm seriously not very happy with it. If you approach this guy, you've really got to do it very, very carefully. If he's obviously not biting, walk away."

"Sal, I'll be careful, I promise. And don't worry; we didn't have this conversation. I found his name and recognised it. I made the association from the chats we'd had."

"Well, I do worry, Claw. It's a rough old world out there."

"I love you, Sal. You're a genius."

"When I come and visit you in prison, I'll be the one wearing a false moustache and glasses," said Sally as she rang off.

Claudia put down the phone and looked at the number Sally had given her. She couldn't believe her luck. She picked up the phone to dial, thought about it, and put the receiver back down. What was she going to say? She'd need to think it through carefully. There was a lot at stake.

# Chapter 4

## 1492

The six guards walked their horses slowly along the pitted, uneven lane to Luca di Stefano's cottage, lighting their way in the predawn darkness with burning torches. Archpriest d'Angeli's stern instructions were still ringing in their ears.

"Seize all three of them, tie their hands and bring them back here for interrogation. They are in league with the Devil!"

The cottage was in darkness. They dismounted and their sergeant indicated to one of them to bang on the door.

"Wake them up, Simone. They have a rude shock coming to them."

The guard walked cautiously to the door, nervous at the possibility of being in the presence of the Antichrist. His blow on the door was hesitant.

"I said wake them," growled the sergeant. "That tickle wouldn't disturb the mice."

Simone hit the door again with much more force, making it rattle on its hinges. Not a sound came from the house.

"Again!" yelled the sergeant.

When there was still no response, the sergeant strode up and pushed the hovering guard aside. He stared darkly at the door.

"May I, signore?" Another of the guards reached past the sergeant and took hold of the door handle. He turned it and found the door wasn't locked.

"I was going to do that, Giovanni," muttered the sergeant, raising his lantern and walking into the cottage.

"You two!" he called back to them. "Search the place!"

After two minutes, they had confirmed that the cottage was empty. Another guard drew the sergeant's attention to a piece of parchment held down by a water pitcher on the kitchen table. It had writing on it.

Snatching it from the table, the sergeant glanced at it and thrust it at the guard who had found it. "Read it to me!" he ordered. The guard looked flustered and offered it back to the sergeant. "Signore, I can't ..." he faltered and looked embarrassed.

The guard called Giovanni took the parchment. "Here, let me," he said.

"Signore, it's addressed to Francesco Marino. He's the farmer who owns this estate – di Stefano's brother-in-law."

"I'm well aware who Francesco Marino is. Just tell me what it says!" snapped the sergeant.

Giovanni looked down the letter. "It's signed by Luca di Stefano, signore, and it says that he apologises for having to leave a note rather than speak directly to Signor Marino, that under normal circumstances he wouldn't have dreamed of being so impertinent as to-"

"Get to the point, Giovanni, there's no need to go through all the flowery politenesses."

Giovanni's eyes darted over the letter. "He's gone to Verona, signore. With his son, Niccolò, and grandson, Gianni."

"Verona! Why? When?"

"It must have been during the night, signore, because I personally saw Niccolò here yesterday in the late afternoon. I was passing to take some bread from the market to my mother-in-law and–"

"For God's sake, man, stick to the point!"

Giovanni jumped to attention and peered again at the letter. "Yes, signore. Er, let me see. It says that he received news from a messenger that his aunt in Verona - that's his late father's sister, I think, signore. I remember my father told me ..." He caught the sergeant's eye and quickly got back to the letter. "It seems she's very ill, signore – the aunt – and there was no time to lose if he wanted to see her while she still has breath in her body." He paused and crossed himself. "It says the three of them had no choice but to leave immediately, riding back with the messenger."

The sergeant considered this news for a moment and then

suddenly banged on the table with his fist. "Well, they can't have been gone long and they wouldn't make good time in the dark. You!" He pointed at Giovanni. "Take the letter to Archpriest d'Angeli. Tell him that I, Sergeant Gallo, have taken the initiative to follow them and that he can expect me to return with all three of them by nightfall. The rest of you, it's light enough now. On your horses! We'll take the main track through the mountains; it's the way they will have taken. We'll check at each village to see if four men riding north in a hurry have been spotted."

With that, the sergeant ran out of the house, mounted his horse and galloped away, followed by four of the guards. The remaining one, Giovanni, was left holding the parchment and wondering if perhaps the sergeant was being rather hasty. But he knew better than to question his orders.

Shortly after eleven o'clock the previous night, Luca had been woken from his sleep by a light but insistent tapping on the cottage door. He made his way from the cot in his studio to the kitchen, stopping at the fireplace to light a candle. He was placing it inside a lantern when the tapping on the door sounded again. It was louder now, more urgent. As he moved towards the door, Niccolò appeared from his room. "Babbo, who can it be at this time of night?"

Luca opened the door a crack and raised the lantern, throwing light onto the head of a hooded figure. He opened the door a little further, enough for the lantern's light to penetrate the darkness a few feet and for him to see that the caller appeared to be alone.

"Signor di Stefano, please let me in. There is no time to lose," urged the caller in a hissing whisper. "And please lower the light, I do not wish to be seen."

Luca knew the voice but couldn't immediately place it. He stood aside and let the caller in, shutting the door after him. The man pulled the hood from his head.

"Domenico!" cried Niccolò in surprise. "What brings you here at–?"

"Sshh, more quietly, my friend," interrupted the caller.

Luca looked at him, his face taut. "Is it Piero, your uncle? Is it … bad news?"

Domenico turned to him. "No, signore, no. He is unchanged.

Weaker perhaps, but still in this world."

"Then what is it? What would bring Domenico della Francesca, councillor and senior member of the most prestigious confraternity of the Borgo, to my humble house in the depth of night?"

Domenico held out a hand. "May I take the lantern, signore?"

Luca frowned, puzzled by the request. "Here," he said.

Domenico held the lantern close to Luca's face and studied it, his eyes taking in the beard, the skin and the hair, before finally settling on Luca's pale grey eyes that in the flickering light appeared liquid, their translucency enhanced.

Niccolò looked anxiously from one man to the other, fear rising within him.

"Domenico," he whispered, "whatever is it?"

Domenico finally sighed and shook his head. "They are right to wonder, signore, and I fear that if they saw you at such close quarters, their minds would be made up."

"Who?" Niccolò was beside himself. "Who do you mean? What are you talking about?"

It was Luca who answered. "The confraternity, Niccolò. The wise men of the town have made a decision about me. I'm right, Domenico, aren't I?"

"I regret to say they have, signore. There was a meeting of the confraternity last night at which Archpriest d'Angeli made an impassioned case for your arrest and examination. I fear if that were to happen, the outcome would be dire. After what happened in the town two days ago, I could have said nothing that would have altered their opinion – the archpriest is a very persuasive man."

Luca sat down on a stool by the table and sighed. "I feared as much. I noticed that priest, Bognini, at the edge of the crowd. He's never liked me."

He put his elbows on the table and rested his head on his clenched hands. Then he glanced up at Domenico. "You have risked a lot coming here. Is your opinion different from that of the council?"

"The confraternity is a charitable organisation, signore. Its members undertake many good works and serve this town well. I believe in the principles of their cause, but some of the more influential members have become extreme in their views. I am not like that, signore, but I remain amongst them in the hope that I can moderate some of their more zealous decisions. Of course, the ways of the Devil are devious and so it is always difficult to make a judgement. But I know that my uncle has always been your very close friend and if he, as a pious man, tells me you are not involved with the Devil's trickery, then I am inclined to believe him. After all, he has known you for very many years and has far more knowledge of you than the confraternity can ever have. This is why I have come here, signore."

Luca sighed and smiled to himself. "Dear Piero, looking after me to the last."

He stood. "I thank you, my friend, from the bottom of my heart. You have given us an opportunity that we could not have expected. If, despite your warning, the guards that I am sure the confraternity is sending do catch up with us, you can be assured that your name will never cross our lips."

Domenico bowed his head to Luca in thanks. "You are right. The guards are ordered to come, but not until first light. So at least you have a few hours to try to make good your escape."

Luca nodded, his head full of rapidly forming plans. He grasped Domenico by the shoulders with both hands. "We are in your debt, Domenico. Good luck and God's protection be with you. I think you should go now, in case the guards decide to come early. You should not be party to any plans we make, so that you can say, before God, that you knew nothing of them." He hugged him and kissed him on both cheeks.

As Niccolò embraced Domenico, Luca added, "I regret that I shall not be able to say my final farewell to my old and dear friend when he leaves this life, as I fear he will very soon. However, I'm sure he will understand."

"I have no doubt he will be with you in spirit, encouraging you on your way," replied Domenico, as Niccolò opened the door. "No light, Niccolò, I shall make my way to my horse under cover of darkness. It is better that way. May God be with you all and protect you on your journey, wherever it may take you."

Niccolò closed the door behind him and turned to his father. "What are we to do, Babbo?"

"I'm afraid, Nicchi, that we must flee this place without delay and leave almost everything behind. We have little time and I regret that there will be no goodbyes to anyone. Whatever work you have in your workshop will have to remain unfinished. Later, once we feel a little safer, we can make our plans."

"I fully understand, Babbo, and I think a new start will be good for us all. These past few years have not been easy."

"I know, Nicchi, and it is my fault. I am truly sorry that it has come to this, but we have no choice. Now, go and wake Gianni and get together what you need to take with you. I shall do the same."

"Where shall we head, Babbo?"

"I think south would be the best option. And I have an idea to send the guards in the wrong direction, for a few hours at least. Please fetch me some parchment, I intend to write a letter to dear Francesco."

An hour later, they were on their way. For Luca, the news had been no real surprise. He had thought for some time that the mood of the confraternity was hardening against him and he had often imagined what he might take with him if he had to leave. It didn't amount to much: a few clothes, a leather jewellery pouch containing a few precious items of Maria's, a selection of his finest brushes and some parchment for sketches. His purses, with what money he had distributed among them, were normally kept about his person.

He had discussed their leaving with Niccolò on a number of occasions. Niccolò had initially been more resistant – his reputation as a carpenter had taken some years to develop and he was reluctant to leave it behind. Recently, however, he had accepted it was inevitable Luca should go and he had no intention of letting him go alone. He too had his list and he very quickly gathered what belongings he needed.

Gianni, by contrast, had never really thought that they would have to leave. The Borgo was all he knew, and while he had thought of travelling to new places, he hadn't imagined it would be as a fugitive. Niccolò had woken him from a deep sleep and in his groggy state Gianni found it difficult to understand the situation.

"You mean we have to leave now, Babbo?" he yawned, even though this was precisely what Niccolò had explained to him. "Can't it wait until morning?"

"If we wait until morning, we'll find ourselves in the Borgo dungeons. We need to move fast, Gianni. Throw some water onto your face to wake yourself up. I'll help you get your things."

While Niccolò was rousing Gianni, Luca walked quickly to the stables, saddled up three of the strongest horses and walked them as quietly as he could to the front of the cottage. They were agitated, not being used to being disturbed in the middle of the night, but after Luca had rubbed their muzzles for a few moments and whispered gently to them, they calmed.

Niccolò emerged from the cottage carrying their packs, followed by Gianni. Seeing the boy was still wide-eyed with shock at this sudden change in their circumstances, Luca took him by the arms as Niccolò arranged the saddlebags.

"Gianni, I'm sorry this has all happened so quickly. I'm afraid we have no choice but to leave immediately."

"Where shall we go, Nonno?"

"We'll decide that once we are well clear of this place. But south, a long way south, far from the clutches of the Borgo. For now I want to head into the forests, remaining in Tuscany until we can find a quiet place to cross over into Umbria. I want to avoid any customs posts. We'll head first for Monterchi and then head through the woods on the mule paths towards Lippiano on the other side of the border. From there I want to follow the path of the Tiber, but remaining in the woods until we are clear."

"Won't the guards come after us?"

"They will, without doubt, but I'm hoping that a little diversion I have left them will send them in the wrong direction for long enough to stay well ahead of them."

Quietly, the three of them walked the horses away from the farm, taking a path on the far side of the property from the Borgo. Once well out of earshot of the farm and its neighbouring buildings, they mounted the horses and rode off into the night towards Monterchi.

Fortune was with them and the lightening skies of the dawn saw them in the hills beyond Lippiano. Deep in the forest, they stopped by a stream to refresh themselves.

As the light improved, Luca removed a razor from his bag and stripped to the waist. "It is time, my boys," he said, waving the razor theatrically, "that I said goodbye to these grey locks and this hateful beard. Losing them will be the best disguise I can adopt."

Returning from the stream ten minutes later with both his head and face completely shaven, he walked over to where Niccolò and Gianni were eating some bread and cheese.

"Good day, gentlemen. Let me introduce myself." He bowed, laughing loudly at their reaction.

"Babbo!" exclaimed Niccolò. "I cannot believe it. You look so young, hardly older than me."

"You are wrong!" a wide-eyed Gianni said to Niccolò. "You, Babbo, have some grey hair, real grey hair, unlike the dyed hair that Nonno had. Nonno doesn't look almost as young as you; he looks considerably younger!"

Luca laughed even louder. "We'll see about that when my hair has grown a little, young Gianni, but for now the easiest way to get rid of all the grey was to shave it all off."

Niccolò was still staring at his father. He shook his head in amazement. "Babbo, you could pass for a man of thirty, maybe even younger. How can this be possible when you are more than sixty-five?"

"As you know, Nicchi, I have no answer to that question. I wish I did."

Looking more seriously at them, he took out a sheaf of papers from his saddlebag. "When I said, 'Let me introduce myself', I was serious. I need to change my name, as do both of you. I have our documents here from the Borgo, written on their finest official parchment. I am an artist, so producing acceptable copies of these should not be difficult. I need to leave Luca di Stefano behind in these woods and emerge as someone else."

"You are right, Babbo," said Niccolò. "Looking the way you do, you can no longer introduce yourself as my father and Gianni's grandfather. That would be absurd. Would it not be better if we became brothers?" He paused and raised his eyebrows in resignation. "And given how youthful you look, I suggest you become my younger brother."

Luca nodded. "You are right, Nicchi. Which will make me Gianni's uncle." He smiled at Gianni. "You'll have to get used to calling me 'Zio', Gianni."

Gianni shook his head. "Zio," he muttered. "But 'Zio' what? I can't call you Zio Luca, that wouldn't seem right."

"I agree," replied Luca. "As I said, I need to change my name, but it needs to be something that we all can remember easily. I was thinking, our family name is also a given name – I could become Stefano. You would call me 'Zio Stefano'. How about that?"

"That should be easy enough to remember, Nonno," nodded Gianni.

"Zio," corrected Luca. "Zio Stefano."

"Yes, of course. Zio Stefano."

"Babbo?" said Niccolò.

Luca turned to him, opening his eyes wide in mock rebuke and tilting his head. "Stefano?" he suggested.

"Babbo. Stefano. No, Babbo, in private I shall still call you 'Babbo'. I might be able to get used to calling you by another name, but I don't think I can with Gianni. Surely we could keep our names?"

"Yes, I agree, I don't really see why you shouldn't. But we need a new family name. Again it should be something that easily comes to mind. My mother's family name was Crispi. Perhaps we could use that?"

Both Niccolò and Gianni repeated their names several times and agreed they could get used to them. Stefano Crispi, as Luca was about to become, removed a small board from his saddle bag, one he used as a support when he was sketching, and set about preparing some official-looking documents. After an hour, he sat back and studied them. Satisfied, he passed them to Niccolò and Gianni for inspection. "What do you think?" he asked.

"They are excellent, Nonn…er, Zio," said Gianni. "Very realistic, but they look a bit too new."

"That's the next step," replied Stefano. He took the documents, sprinkled a little dry earth onto them and put them together in his document pouch. Holding one side of the leather pouch in each hand, he began to work it up and down and side to side. He then rolled up the pouch into a cylinder, compressed it and beat it lightly on a nearby tree stump. Removing the papers, he then worked on each one individually until he was satisfied they looked as old and travel-worn as the originals. He handed them back to Gianni.

"Perfect," admired Gianni. "Look Babbo, your new papers."

Before they mounted up and rode on, Stefano Crispi completed the final stage of his transition from Luca di Stefano. He took his original documents together with his son's and grandson's, tore them into small pieces and burned them on the small fire they had set, waiting until they were nothing but ash. He then ground the ash with his boot until it was nothing but fine powder.

As he watched the powder dispersing in the light breeze, he thought of Maria.

"Farewell, Luca di Stefano," he said quietly.

As an extra precaution, for the first few days of their journey they separated during the day, with Gianni and Niccolò riding about an hour ahead of Stefano. Each night they met up and headed off into the woods to make a camp. After four days, they reached the border of the Kingdom of Naples, a huge state that spread from the south of Italy to the mountains east of Rome.

Once across the border, Stefano decided to risk passing a night at a hostel in a small town to listen to any tales of searches for fugitives from the north. He needn't have worried: the hapless sergeant Gallo had returned to San Sepolcro after five days of fruitlessly searching most of the tracks that led generally in the direction of Verona, only to receive a severe reprimand from Archpriest d'Angeli.

To add to the archpriest's ire, word came back from Verona that far from being on her death bed, Luca di Stefano's aunt was still enjoying excellent health at the age of ninety.

With the threat of imminent capture receding, they considered their next move.

"Although the influence of Archpriest d'Angeli clearly doesn't reach this far, Nonno – sorry, Zio," said Gianni, "would it not be better to continue south to a place where we are not likely to be noticed? What better place could there be than Naples itself? I believe it is a huge and bustling city with people from many countries living there."

"An excellent idea, Gianni," agreed Stefano. "In a busy city, we'll have a chance to re-establish ourselves in our new identities without raising suspicion. What do you think, Nicchi?"

"I have heard much of Naples, Babbo. I think it will be the perfect place for us. I have no doubt that they have a need for gifted craftsmen from the north to teach them a thing or two."

Laughing, Stefano slapped a hand onto the log on which he was sitting.

"That settles it. Naples it shall be!"

# Chapter 5

## June 2009

Claudia felt exhilarated as she left the M6 motorway and directed her soft-top VW Golf towards the stark beauty of the Lake District. Summer had finally arrived and the three and a half hour drive from her tiny cottage in the Warwickshire village of Combrook had relaxed her, helping her to put the nagging doubts that had plagued her over the last ten days to the back of her mind.

She had taken two days of her precious annual holiday allowance, which, combined with the weekend, would give her four days to track down her quarry – the man with the rarest of rare DNA. She drove into Ambleside and parked the Golf in a 'Pay and Display' car park near the town centre and looked around. Directly across the road from the car park was a row of formal but attractive two-storey, grey stone houses, once private homes but now the offices of local solicitors, estate agents, dentists or doctors. However, the one that caught her eye had a dark-blue door with a blue sign above it: Police.

Claudia's confidence evaporated. She gulped, feeling suddenly nervous. Christ, she thought, whatever am I doing here? I should be back in the lab, not sitting in a car park in the Lake District. This whole thing is ridiculous, a fool's errand.

She closed the roof, got out of the car, fumbled with her keys and dropped them. She picked them up and went to lock the car, but then changed her mind and got straight back in, slamming the door. She checked out her appearance in the mirror, put her hair up with a couple of clips, looked again at her reflection and with a grimace, pulled the hair clips out. She put on her straw sun hat, decided she hated it, and took it off. She banged on the steering wheel in frustration.

This is stupid, she thought, I don't even have a plan. PC Roberts might not be here. He might be on holiday with Mrs R and Jeff junior.

She felt an urgent need for caffeine.

The Lakes Coffee Shoppe was about a hundred yards along the street from the police station, set back along a pathway that followed Stock Ghyll, the stream that rushed down from the hills behind the town and scurried urgently through it. It was eleven thirty and trade was brisk. As Claudia approached, she saw that all the outside tables were full. However, she was in luck. Just as she was thinking of trying another coffee shop, a well-dressed elderly couple got up to leave.

A couple of hikers weighed down with huge and bulging rucksacks arrived at the table at the same moment. The elderly man took one disdainful look at them and moved round to block their way. He held out a seat and smiled at Claudia.

"There you are, young lady, perfect timing," adding in a whisper, "they look ready for an assault on Mount Everest."

"You should try the buttered scones, my dear," smiled the elderly man's wife as she leaned over conspiratorially to Claudia. "They're freshly baked on the premises every morning. Quite delicious."

"Thanks, I will," stuttered Claudia. She wished she'd put on dark glasses and a very large sun hat after all.

If I eat, I think I'll throw up, she thought, studiously ignoring the still hovering hikers.

The waitress arrived. When Claudia ordered only a double espresso, she looked pointedly at her watch.

"Nothing to eat then? We're taking lunch orders."

"No, just coffee, thank you."

The waitress harrumphed and marched off.

As the coffee arrived, Claudia realised she needed the loo. There was now a short queue of customers waiting for tables and she didn't want to lose hers. She needed something apart from the coffee to show the table was taken. She retrieved her moleskin notebook from the depths of her handbag and put it next to her coffee cup. Still hesitating, she peered again into her bag, found an A-Z of the West Midlands, and placed it on her chair

On her way back from the loo, Claudia saw with dismay that the two hikers had decided to join her at her table: the removal of the mountainous rucksacks was underway. Just as they seemed ready to strike camp, their way was again blocked, this time by the arrival of a tall, good-looking man of about thirty wearing police uniform.

"Hi there," he smiled at Claudia, completely ignoring the hikers and seating himself at the table.

"Sorry I'm late, I was delayed at the station. Not the sleepy, crime-free place you'd think it might be," he added with a wink.

Claudia realised that she was staring at him with her mouth open. She closed it, blushing.

Ignoring her reaction, the police officer continued chattily.

"I expect you thought I wasn't coming. Sorry about that but it's not always easy to make definite arrangements, especially with the sarge off on a course. I'm the only one holding the fort today, apart from Joan, of course."

"Joan?" Claudia croaked a strangled whisper.

"Yes, she answers the phones, makes the tea and keeps the filing up to date," he smiled, very much understating WPC Joan Hunter's job description.

He turned to the hikers who were angrily struggling to put back on their unruly rucksacks.

"Careful with those, lads, you don't want to do anybody any damage now, do you? Why don't you go down the road to the Amble Cafe, there's much more room there."

They shuffled off, muttering.

Once they were out of earshot, the police officer leaned forward to Claudia and in a quieter voice said, "Sorry to intrude on your table, miss, but I could see that you wanted to be alone and those lads were likely to demolish the place with all that gear."

Claudia looked at his handsome, clean-cut features and stuttered, "You mean ... that is ... did you think I was someone else?"

"Not at all, miss. I normally take my morning coffee here and between you and me, I try to discourage these types who are carrying around half a camping shop. Nothing against them, of course, they are what the Lakes are all about, but they don't realise how much space they take up. When I saw them about to invade your table, I thought you wouldn't mind if I stepped in."

"No, no," said Claudia, still totally confused. "That's very kind of you. Can I get you a coffee, Constable …?"

"Roberts, miss, PC Jeff Roberts, and I wouldn't dream of taking a coffee from you. In fact I was going to offer you another, if you'd like one. Are you all right, miss? You look like you've seen a ghost."

Claudia realised her mouth had dropped open again.

"No, I mean, yes, I'm fine, thanks. I'm just, you know, a bit windswept after the drive up here."

Her head was spinning and she thought she was going to faint. She absent-mindedly dragged the West Midlands A-Z from under her thigh where she'd sat on it and put it on the table.

"Don't think that'll help you much around here, miss."

"What? No, it's … I got it out to put on my seat when I … when I popped to the loo."

"That where you've come from is it, miss, the West Mids? Did you decide on another coffee?"

"Yes, please, thank you. Actually, I'm not sure how happy she is serving coffee at lunchtime."

"Oh, don't worry about her, miss, she loves to tut and moan. No meaning to it."

He waved at the waitress.

"Two coffees, Janet. What sort did you want, Miss … er?" he added, turning to Claudia.

"Um, Reid. Claudia Reid. I'd love another espresso, thanks."

"Two expressos, Janet, my love."

Janet scowled at him.

"She loves me really," he laughed.

"So, Miss Reid, is that where you live, the West Midlands?"

"Yes, in Warwickshire, but I work near Birmingham."

"What line of work are you in?"

It crossed Claudia's mind that PC Roberts was being rather inquisitive, but then she decided it probably came with the territory.

"I'm a biochemist, a geneticist, really. My lab carries out DNA profiling of CJ samples."

"You're kidding me," said Jeff Roberts in apparent surprise. "Not that lab out near the airport? I was there about three weeks ago. Pity I hadn't met you before; you could have shown me round."

"Yes, I could," Claudia replied. She didn't believe she was having this conversation. "What were you doing at the lab?"

"Delivering some buccal swabs. I was going to Leicester to see my mum and my boss reckoned he could save a bit of money if I took them. So I took the batch from here and from Kendal."

"Kendal?" Claudia was worried. She'd assumed that he would only have delivered samples from Ambleside. Maybe her donor wasn't from the Ambleside area after all.

"Yes, well, we tend to get a few more samples from around there than here. I only had three from this area. One was a tourist who'd driven his car into a tree, and the others were from a couple of blokes having a good old ding-dong in the Green Man car park in Grasmere."

"Tourist?" whispered Claudia quietly. Things were getting worse by the minute. Not only could the person have come from somewhere else, if he had been a tourist, he could have come from anywhere.

"Yes, Miss Reid, a tourist. We get one or two of them around here."

As their coffees arrived, Claudia looked into what Sally had described as Jeff Roberts' 'doe-eyes' and found them rather cold. She had a nagging feeling that he wasn't quite as friendly as he was trying to appear.

Roberts poured three packs of brown sugar into his coffee, stirred it gently and took a sip. He returned her look and appeared to hesitate. Then he said, "Actually, there are one or two things about the profiling I'd really like to know a bit more about. My good luck, I reckon, a real, live DNA expert turning up on my doorstep. And a young and pretty one at that."

Claudia looked down, blushing, and then, looking up at him again, said, "What would you like to know?"

He looked over to the lengthening queue.

"You were right," he said, "it's close to lunchtime and the place is getting busy. Don't want to hog the tables. The station's only just along the street here. Would you mind if we popped in there? We can chat in peace and quiet. It won't take long, I'm sure."

Claudia felt her stomach turn inside out again. The police station. But she couldn't really say no.

"OK," she replied meekly, gulping down her coffee.

PC Roberts stood and pulled her chair out for her as she stood up. He waved to the waitress, indicating to her to put the coffees on his tab, and then led the way through the tables and out onto the pavement in the direction of the police station.

"Why don't we go into the interview room? It's a bit quieter there and there won't be any interruptions."

PC Roberts held up the flap in the counter, letting Claudia through to the business side of the station. He waved to Joan, who to Claudia's surprise was wearing the uniform of a WPC, and said lightly, "Just going to have a little chat with this young lady."

"'kay, Jeff," she replied, looking up to make a rapid appraisal of Claudia as she walked by.

Claudia's legs felt like lead. The short corridor seemed to be a long, dark tunnel to the dungeons.

PC Roberts opened the door to the interview room, turned on the light and indicated a chair.

"Take a seat. 'Fraid we don't really do comfort in here."

Claudia looked round the small room with its cream walls, single table and four upright chairs, thinking it looked more like an interrogation room.

PC Roberts didn't immediately sit in the chair opposite Claudia. Instead he walked over to the right of where she was sitting and leaned his back against the wall. He looked down at her.

"OK, Dr Reid, perhaps you'd like to tell me what's going on." He wasn't smiling.

Claudia stared at him, aghast. Dr Reid. He knew.

"W…what do you mean?" she stuttered, her stomach churning again.

"Well, we both know, Dr Reid, that you haven't come up here today to take in the sun-kissed scenery and rugged charms of the Lake District, don't we?"

"I don't understand," Claudia stammered again, her head spinning with confusion. "I… I…"

She sniffed, bit her lip and blinked rapidly. How could this smooth-talking PC know exactly why she was here? Had he been waiting for her?

"I don't know what you mean." She was suddenly defensive.

PC Roberts sighed.

"You've come up here to be a very stupid young woman, haven't you? You've come not only to potentially wreck your own career but also to try to persuade me to wreck mine."

He paused, looking at Claudia, waiting for a response. When there wasn't one, he added, "Dr Reid?"

Claudia rested her chin in her cupped hands.

"I don't understand," she repeated.

"What don't you understand?" Roberts seemed a bit more hostile now.

She cast her eyes down at the tabletop. "I don't understand how you know."

He sighed and shook his head. "I know, Dr Reid, because you have a very good friend who clearly loves you dearly and who is terrified that you're about to do something extremely stupid. As it happens, I also know your friend and she has persuaded me – much against my better judgement, I might add – to stop you before you make a very foolish mistake."

Claudia stared at him, horrified. "Sally?"

"Yes, Sally."

"What did she tell you?"

"She called me and told me what you were planning to do. I wasn't particularly pleased to hear from her, I can tell you – water under the bridge and all that – and I didn't like her tone. But she made it clear that if I at least listened to her, I'd never hear from her again. After she'd pleaded your case, I agreed that I'd stop you before you asked me to do anything you shouldn't ask me to do. Fortunately, you'd told her that you'd be coming up here this morning. She even told me the registration number of your car."

"She knows my registration number?" Claudia was amazed. "I don't even know it."

"She said she found a photo of you both lounging on the bonnet, and you can see the plates in the picture. Said her boyfriend took it."

"Ced," replied Claudia, absently, not really taking it all in.

"Yes, said. She said it."

Claudia looked up at him, not understanding. Then she realised his confusion. "It's his name. Her boyfriend. His name's Ced."

The light dawned in Roberts' eyes. "Foreign is he?"

"What?" Claudia frowned. "No, he's from … actually, I don't know where he's from. His name's Ced. It's short for Cedric."

PC Roberts realised they were digressing.

"So, Dr Reid, armed with all that info, even for a country bobby like me it wasn't too difficult to spot your car when you arrived this morning."

"You were waiting for me?"

"Yes."

"So at the coffee shop, you weren't being a knight in shining armour."

"No, I wasn't, not then. But I am now, thanks to Sally. You realise, don't you, how much trouble you could get yourself into. Breaking the rules of confidentiality of the database, attempting to coerce a police officer to do the same. I don't think there's likely to be any precedent as far as the database is concerned, and I think the powers-that-be would enjoy making a huge example of you."

He sat down opposite her.

"What did you think you could achieve? You don't even know that this person is from round here. He could be from anywhere."

"I realise that now from what you told me at the coffee shop. I hadn't thought it through. I thought that with the sample coming from up here, I had a lucky break, a chance to identify the donor and a chance that he might be interested in his own profile."

"I don't think many people are interested in their DNA profiles and they certainly don't like having them on the database. A lot of people would like to see the whole thing scrapped. If your 'donor', as you call him, didn't take kindly to your actions, he could make a huge fuss that could rock the database to its foundations. The whole thing could come tumbling down, just from your thoughtlessness."

He had meant to frighten her, but the last part had come out more forcefully than he intended and now Claudia couldn't hold back the tears. Roberts produced a pack of tissues from his pocket and handed them to her.

Once she had calmed down, he said to her more softly, "What I want you to do now is get up, walk away and forget you've ever thought about trying to be so stupid. You've not, as yet, asked me to do anything, and, as far as I can see, you've not got hold of any information that you're not entitled to during the course of your work. You seem a sensible and very committed young lady. It's good to be passionate about what you do, but it's stupid to break the law. So don't. And don't be angry with Sally Moreton; she's been a very good friend to you."

He stopped and waited for Claudia to speak. She stared at the table for several seconds and then raised her eyes.

"I really appreciate it that you've gone to this trouble. You could have just let me dig a big hole and waited while I threw myself in it. I'm grateful, really."

She paused, looking down again.

"But?" he said.

"But … look, can I explain why I'm so passionate about this? I won't ask you to do anything for me."

She waited, but he said nothing.

"You see there's something I haven't told Sally yet. I've done some more tests."

Roberts frowned.

"When we do the tests for the database," explained Claudia, "we use a testing kit that gives eleven sets of results. One tells us the gender of the subject, which is necessary in case someone who seems to be Jane is actually John, the other ten give us a DNA profile that is compared with the database for outstanding crime. You know all this, of course."

Roberts had no idea about the number of tests but he did know about the automatic comparison of new profiles with the outstanding crime database.

"If we need to get a more specific profile, we can use other kits that let us test the person's DNA in up to seven other places. The distribution we get then is usually pretty conclusive. Well, what I haven't told Sally is that I've done that and the results are all new too, every single one of them. So from this one person, we now have more rare variants than we ever dreamed existed."

"So this person really is different," said PC Roberts, pursing his lips.

"So different," added Claudia, "that it's hard to believe. While we can argue that we are all unique, this man is a true one-off."

"What does it mean?"

"It means we're dealing with someone we would never expect to exist. A statistical improbability."

"What I meant was, what does it mean about the person? Is he different in any way?"

Claudia thought about Sally's comment about criminality, but decided that would be sailing too close to the wind.

"No, and this is the problem really – at least it is for me and what I was hoping to do."

He frowned at her, not understanding. She continued. "As far as is known, the variations we see in the areas on the DNA that we test for the database tell us nothing about the individual. But I think they are significant and I'm doing some research into it. Which is why I'd love to meet him and find out a bit more about him, to test his DNA further. With such an unexpected profile, if there really is anything special about these areas we test for the database, this would be a big chance to find out."

"So why haven't you gone to your boss to explain? Surely he would be as keen as you to follow this up?"

"No. My boss is openly dismissive of my research. This is what I meant when I said it was my problem. You see, most geneticists believe that these areas are what they've been informally called – junk DNA. They believe they have no function. I'm pretty sure he wouldn't be willing to go against the rules of the database. As you pointed out to me so emphatically, it's too sensitive an area."

"Do you really think this person is likely to be very different from everyone else? I mean, we get more than a few weirdos hanging around here, but are they likely to have this rare DNA?"

"I don't think he'd appear any different from anyone else. But the way his body works might be different. He might have a better resistance to certain diseases, particularly genetic diseases. Who knows? He might be cleverer than most people, or more talented in some way. If he is different, in some beneficial way, and we could understand it better, it could be of value to other people. You see what I mean?"

PC Roberts drummed his fingers on the table.

"It's fascinating, and I can see why you're so fired up about it. If it was my DNA, I'd be happy to let you poke about a bit more. But you can't ask me for confidential information about someone. It's more than my job's worth."

"I'm not. I was going to try, I admit, but you've convinced me I can't. It would be wrong. I just wanted to explain it to you so that you wouldn't think I was some nutty scientist with a mission."

The drumming of fingers stopped. Claudia saw his eyes stare into the middle distance. They seemed to have lost the cold, formal look of a few minutes earlier; they were now somehow more vulnerable.

He suddenly sighed and focused his eyes on her. "Have you got the reference number of the sample?"

Claudia looked at him in amazement. "Pardon?"

"The reference number. Have you got it?"

She opened her notebook and showed it to him.

"Wait here a minute," said Roberts as he got up and walked out.

Five minutes later he was back.

"I thought I'd check it against the list of samples I took down to your lab," he said, sitting down.

Claudia waited. Clearly Roberts was finding it hard to make a decision, but despite that, his whole tone had changed.

"I can't tell you his name. That would be wrong, even if you haven't asked me. What I can say, even though I shouldn't, is that the sample came from here. It was one of the three I told you about from the Ambleside area. And it wasn't the idiot who drove into the tree."

"You mean it was one of the men who was fighting outside the pub?"

"Yes, and not the one from Liverpool."

"You mean he lives around here?"

"I really can't say anymore. I've said too much already and I'd absolutely deny this conversation if the shit hit the fan."

"Thank you, I appreciate it. I appreciate everything you, um, haven't told me."

Roberts pushed back his chair and stood. Claudia frowned, trying to remember exactly what she'd said.

"Before I go," she said, standing up as well, "can I ask you what made you change your mind? You were very adamant earlier."

"Doesn't matter," he muttered, rather embarrassed, "but I can assure you it wasn't those pretty blue eyes."

Claudia smiled and held out her hand. "Thank you, Jeff, I'll keep you posted."

"No. You won't. I don't want to hear anymore about it. But good luck with those scientific breakthroughs."

As Claudia walked past her, WPC Joan Hunter looked up inquisitively. Claudia smiled at her and stepped out into the sunshine.

# Chapter 6

## 1492-1517

By 1499, Stefano Crispi's studio in Naples was one of many in an area of burgeoning artistic activity inspired by the creative genius of the Renaissance. Looking out over the Bay of Naples with the gently smoking Vesuvius rising majestically in the distance, Stefano thought the view one of the most stunning he had ever seen, rivalling in its maritime splendour the rolling verdant beauty of the Tuscany he had left behind.

He loved everything about the city: the passion of the people; the sun-bleached colours; the rough and tumble of children playing in the streets; the unceasing babble of the many Mediterranean languages. They all combined to stimulate him, infusing his work with a new life that had been missing for many years.

Stefano had been sixty-five when he arrived in Naples with Niccolò and Gianni, but he had looked and felt thirty. He had reluctantly agreed that Niccolò, at forty, would be his elder brother by ten years and they had set up a studio and workshop. It was now seven years since their arrival and while there was still no change in Stefano's youthful looks and energy, Niccolò had aged beyond his years, his complexion in the winter months a sickly grey and his health fragile. Stefano slowly began to realise that he might outlive his son.

In the spring of 1500, Gianni announced that he had asked for the hand of Anna, the daughter of a successful cloth trader, Aldo Santini. The announcement was no surprise. The couple had met six months earlier when Gianni was assisting Stefano on a portrait

Santini had commissioned of his ageing mother. At seventy-one, Nonna Luisa was a year younger than Stefano's real age, but she would never have guessed it from the look of this handsome and energetic man who stood before her, brush in hand.

When Anna walked into the studio, Gianni was mesmerised. He had been blending some colours but was now reduced to a trance, absently stirring paints in the earthenware container he was holding as he stared at her.

"Gianni, if you stir that paint any more, you'll make a hole in the container," called Stefano.

Colouring to the roots of his hair, Gianni stuttered his apologies, then continued stirring.

"Gianni!" barked Stefano. "The blend?"

Gianni looked up at him. "Sorry, Zio. It's ready. Here."

"It's been ready for fifteen minutes," teased Stefano.

Then to Gianni's horror, Stefano turned to Anna. "Signorina Santini. I am remiss in my manners. I haven't introduced you to my apprentice and nephew, Gianni. I was forgetting that on the previous occasion you were here, he was absent."

Looking into Gianni's eyes, Anna took the sides of her skirts in her hands and curtseyed.

"I am very honoured to make your acquaintance, signore," she smiled coyly.

To Gianni's further confusion, she walked over to him.

"I am fascinated by the subtleties of the colours your uncle has been using. Could you show me how you make these blends? It must require a great deal of skill."

Forgetting every word of the Neapolitan language he'd become fluent in over the past few years, Gianni could only babble a few incoherent words in Tuscan, much to the amusement of both Anna and Stefano.

"Pray, signore, what language do you speak?" teased Anna, secretly thrilled that this handsome young man should be showing an interest in her.

Taking a deep breath, Gianni looked into Anna's eyes.

"Um, it's really very, um, simple. Really," he stammered. "You just need to know something about the colours of the properties."

He frowned at the quizzical smile on Anna's face.

"Um, I mean the properties of the colours. How they are affected by other colours, and the proportions required to blend them to the desired colour." Suddenly, he was in his stride and the two of them chatted animatedly until a loud cough from Nonna Luisa brought them up short.

"I'm coming, Nonna," said Anna meekly and turned to walk away, but not before catching Gianni's eyes in a look that told him his feelings were reciprocated.

They were married in the summer of 1501, their first child arriving a year later. Niccolò rallied on both occasions, but his decline was inexorable. As the winter of 1502 approached, the physician was a regular visitor, although there was little he could do.

"I fear, Signor Crispi, that your brother has a canker. His sputum is frequently very dark, indicating, as is well known, that an excess of black bile is the cause of this dreadful disease. There is, regrettably, no cure."

"Is there really nothing you can give him, Dottore? He is frequently in such distress."

The physician nodded. "There are preparations of arsenical compounds that I have sometimes prescribed. They might ease his suffering. But you must realise this is not a cure."

"I understand that, Dottore. This canker is a curse that seems to inflict much pain. If there is anything that can reduce his torment, it would be merciful." Stefano looked over at the emaciated form that was his son. "Anything, Dottore."

The treatment gave him some relief and for short periods he could talk to them. However, the illness followed its inevitable course and Niccolò died in early February 1503, a few days after his fifty-first birthday.

Anna's younger sister, Francesca, was no match for Anna in looks. While both were raven-haired and olive-skinned, Anna's subtle beauty was inherited from the women on her father's side; Francesca had her mother's far plainer features. Once Anna was engaged to Gianni, there were far fewer young men calling on the Santini household and Francesca knew her chances of marrying someone of her own age were now limited. Yet she had no intention of being palmed off on one of the ageing notaries her mother had in mind for her: Gianni's Uncle Stefano was a far better catch. Even though he was forty-two, he was youthful for his years, and very handsome. There was only one problem: Stefano appeared oblivious to Francesca's unsubtle advances.

She complained bitterly to her sister.

"The way he talks to me, Anna, it's like an old man would treat a favourite grandchild. Can't he see that is not the way I wish to be treated? I do not wish to be patronised. I am not a child!"

"I think he is finding the death of his brother very difficult to come to terms with, Franci," smiled Anna. "I'll talk to Gianni about it."

Gianni's opinion, although not one he could explain to Anna, was one of disgust. The thought of his grandfather, a man of now seventy-seven, becoming involved with a girl of twenty-two was repulsive to him. Anna was surprised by his negativity. "It's not that unusual, Gianni. Zio Stefano is only forty-two and he has the figure and stature of a man much younger. I know of many instances where men of that age take a young wife."

"Yes," replied Gianni angrily, "and what happens? I'll tell you what happens. The young wives are very quickly young widows, often with several children to bring up and with no father to support them. Is that what you want for your sister?"

"Of course not, Gianni. Nobody wants that. But I can't believe that a man as youthful and vital as Stefano would be leaving this world just yet."

"Perhaps you wish you had married him instead of me," pouted Gianni, folding his arms and turning his back to her.

Anna sighed to herself. Why were men so idiotic?

Gianni didn't leave it there. He visited Stefano the same evening to make his case, which he did forcefully.

Stefano was shocked: he hadn't realised Francesca's intentions. Gianni's indignation amused him, although he tried his best to mask his smiles.

"Gianni, Gianni! Don't worry; I have no designs on Francesca. She is a sweet girl, I grant you." He held up his hand as Gianni started to protest. "But I agree that I couldn't possibly take on a wife at my age, even if I wanted to."

"Mind you," he teased, "when she smiles, she can be rather pretty."

"Nonno!"

"It's all right, Gianni, I'm joking." He laughed and shook his head. "Imagine if she knew the truth; she'd run all the way from here to the top of Vesuvius!"

Francesca's solution was to insinuate herself into Stefano's company as often as possible. She started to bring him lunch, particularly when he was away from the studio on a commission. These were times she particularly enjoyed since he was often alone. On these occasions she would chatter away, always ensuring that there would be mention of one friend or another's recent engagement.

But the progress she hoped for was slow. Time passed and while Anna had produced a second child, Francesca had no choice but to live in hope. There were times when she felt Stefano might be weakening, but if ever he made any flattering comments to her, it seemed that Gianni was always there to interrupt and change the subject, increasingly short-tempered with his uncle.

In spite of having a loving wife and two healthy children, Gianni was unsettled. He was frustrated with his progress as an artist, knowing in his heart he could never hope to emulate Stefano's skill. Worse was the pressure he felt over Stefano's secret, a fear that one day they would be forced to leave, as they had left San Sepolcro.

"I'm thirty-one, Nonno, and I'm getting nowhere," he hissed at Stefano one morning in the late spring of 1508. He was working in an echoey church where he was reluctantly performing some restoration on a number of deteriorating frescos, work he felt was beneath him. Stefano had come to view his progress.

Stefano glared at him. "Keep your voice down, Gianni! You never know who's listening."

He looked around, but there was nobody within earshot.

"It's all very well, *Zio*," continued Gianni, sarcastically emphasising the word, "but I resent restoring some other artist's second-rate efforts; I should be moving forward. And I don't want to wait until I'm eighty-one like you."

"Gianni, that's enough. I've told you many times that you have a fine talent; you just need to be more patient. You are always in too much of a hurry to finish whatever project you're working on and move onto the next. You know that you cannot rush a painting; it has to come from the heart."

"I know all that, Zio." He was softer now, more reasonable. "But I live in fear that all this, all our work here, might suddenly come to an abrupt end; that some zealot from the Church will discover your secret and persecute you, forcing you to flee like last time. I should have to leave as well."

"It worries me too, Gianni, believe me. But I can assure you that if I were to be discovered, I should not expect you to leave with me. You have your family to consider. They are the most important thing in your life now."

"How could I stay behind, Zio? The Church would regard me as your accomplice."

Eventually, Gianni started to heed Stefano's advice, resulting in the improvement Stefano knew he was capable of. When the studio received a commission for a portrait of the Contessa di Salerno, Stefano rewarded Gianni by giving him the work. The sittings were in the Contessa's villa, an hour's walk across the city and early each morning, once Anna had approved his appearance, Gianni would set out with two assistants.

The painting progressed better than Gianni had dared to hope. The likeness was excellent and the contessa talked enthusiastically of further portraits of her family.

One evening, after the contessa had retired from the sitting, Gianni was completing some background detail. As the light outside began to fade, he became concerned that his assistants' families would be expecting them, so he dismissed them for the day.

"I think we should stay, Gianni," suggested Vittorio, the elder of the two. "The walk across the city is not safe these days after dark. It would be better if we were to accompany you."

"Nonsense, Vittorio, I know the route well; all the pathways I intend to take have torches burning. There is no danger. Off you go, both of you. I'll see you at the studio in the morning."

Gianni had not been entirely truthful with his assistants – he intended using a few short cuts that were far from well lit. As a young man, he had explored the city many times with Neapolitan friends and was confident he could find his way through the maze of back streets in the poor quarter. However, the darkness quickly confused him.

Entering a small square, he noticed a group of youths on the far side strutting around and shouting to each other. They called out to him as he emerged from the shadows, but he ignored them and set off down a narrow alley he thought he recognised, only to find a dead end. Turning back, he saw the youths were now blocking his way.

"This foreigner seems lost!" declared the loudest of the group, Gianni's northern looks immediately obvious to him. He peered forward at Gianni - he was a head shorter but a rise in the alley put their eyes level.

"Lost, are we, signore?" The words were spat sarcastically. "Can't. Find. Your. Way."

Gianni looked at him warily.

Another of the youths joined in. "The fool either can't speak or doesn't understand our beautiful language. I regard it as an insult that some turnip-headed foreigner should come to the greatest city in the world and refuse to learn our language."

A third youth, also short but more muscular than the others, curled his fleshy lips in a sneer. "I think this foreigner needs to be taught a lesson."

He took a step towards Gianni, who held up his hand. "I understand your fine language very well, lads. I roamed these streets too, when I was younger."

The youth who had been first to speak turned to his friends.

"What fine manners this foreigner has developed since coming here from the north. They don't have houses there, you know, they live with the swine."

"That would account for their looks," said the third youth, looking darkly at Gianni. The others laughed, snorting like pigs.

Gianni took a step towards them and put a hand on his bag. Five hands immediately went to the hilts of five short thrusting swords. But Gianni had no weapon. He lifted his hands and held out both palms.

"What is it you want, lads?"

"Lads? Lads, he says? How dare he talk down to us in such a way? Does the pig not know his station in life?"

The first youth drew his sword and waved it under Gianni's nose. Gianni, angry now, made to step towards him, but moved quickly sideways and grabbed one of the others, taking him by surprise. Holding him in a headlock, Gianni snatched a thin-bladed knife he had seen on the youth's belt and held it to his throat. Immediately, four swords were out and pointing at him.

"I mean nobody any harm, but I will use this knife if you don't drop your swords and let me leave," threatened Gianni, pushing the knife blade harder against the wriggling boy's neck and pulling the headlock tighter. The four backed off, lowering their swords a fraction. Gianni moved slowly along the wall towards the square, not taking his eyes off the group.

As he reached the end of the wall, he felt something sharp push against his back.

"Better let him go, pig, or I'll slice your insides."

Gianni spun round to see another member of the group who had hung back in the square. He was waving a sword at him. Gianni's grip on the small youth's neck had loosened as he turned and the boy wriggled free, falling over as he did.

"Did the pig push you over, Mario?" came a goading voice from the shadows.

"No pig pushes me," was the reply. "Hey pig, time to become ham!"

The boy stood up, drew his sword and thrust it in Gianni's direction. At the same moment, the youth behind Gianni pushed him hard and Gianni was impaled on the sword. The wide-eyed Mario looked in horror at what he'd done.

"Carmine, you fool, you pushed him! It wasn't my fault! I was only going to cut him a little, teach him a lesson. What have you done?"

He backed away in horror, pulling out the sword, and Gianni slumped to the ground. The blade had pierced his heart. The group evaporated from the square, leaving their victim dying on the cobblestones.

Gianni's death left his family numbed in uncomprehending shock. In his anger and frustration, Stefano took to wearing a sword and walking the streets of the poor quarters, heedless of the consequences. But the gang was never found. It wasn't until Francesca pleaded with him one evening that he finally came to his senses.

"Stefano, my dear, sad Stefano. To lose your nephew so soon after your brother, and in such a way, is truly terrible. But if you carry on like this, we shall lose you too. You are all we have now. Anna needs you. Her children need you."

She paused. "I need you," she added more quietly. "Can't you see that, you poor man?"

Stefano slumped into her arms and she guided him to a couch. Nestling his head against her breast, he wept like a baby. He wept for Gianni, for Niccolò, for Maria. He wept for his past life. He wept for himself. He was eighty-three years old. His world had turned upside down and he no longer understood anything.

Francesca let him weep. She stroked his hair with one hand while playing with the crucifix on her necklace with the other, a soft smile on her face.

God moves in mysterious ways, she thought.

Still suffering from the shock of Gianni's death, Stefano was easily persuaded by Francesca's careful arguments that it was their joint responsibility to take on the role of leaders and protectors of the family. They were married three months later.

Francesca was now twenty-eight and longing for a family. As with all her missions in life, she launched into this one with a passion that surprised and pleased Stefano – he had missed sharing his bed more than he realised.

Two years went by, then three. By 1513, Francesca was getting desperate; it seemed she was never going to be blessed with children. She blamed her husband: the youthful looks that increasingly puzzled her clearly meant nothing. "You're fifty-one, Stefano, even though you don't look it. Perhaps that's too old to father children. It's not fair; Anna was pregnant almost immediately after she and Gianni were married." She paused to cross herself. "Why not me?"

"I'm certainly not too old, Franci," replied Stefano, thinking to himself that maybe at eighty-six he was. Perhaps this was a sign that he was ageing after all. "I know many men far older than I who have become fathers."

In her quest for help, Francesca automatically turned to the Church. She prayed, she confessed. She sought and got an audience with the bishop who prayed with her, somewhat intimidated and embarrassed by her frank tales of Stefano's prowess. She became more devout. She tried but failed to get Stefano to attend church as regularly as she did.

"You spend so much time there that I'd have to stop painting and take up residence in the confessional, Francesca," he complained.

Francesca's failure to become a mother had a devasting effect on their relationship. She started to resent him. She felt she was wasting her life on this man who looked so young but who could not give her a child. She felt in her heart she wasn't barren, that it wasn't her fault. So it must be his.

Late in November 1517, a maid came to Francesca one morning as she was preparing to leave for church for the second time that day.

"There is a gentleman at the door, signora, a gentleman seeking Signor Crispi. He says he is an artist, signora, from Tuscany."

The mention of Tuscany caused Francesca to think he might be worth talking to.

"Send him to the front reception room, Maria."

She left him there for two minutes and then made her entrance.

"Signor…?"

The man bowed elaborately. His fleshy lips were unpleasantly moist as he addressed her. "Rossi, Signora, Enrico Rossi."

"I am pleased to make your acquaintance, Signor Rossi. How can I help you?"

"I was hoping to meet your husband, signora. I am an artist who has been working in various towns in Tuscany, but for health reasons I have come south to pursue my career in this warmer climate."

He coughed delicately into an elaborately embroidered lace handkerchief.

"I have heard that your husband paints in the style of the Tuscan masters. I was hoping to speak with him, perhaps gain some introductions."

"My husband has done more than paint in that style here in Naples, Signor Rossi, he was a prolific artist in Tuscany as a young man before he came south. You must be familiar with his work."

"Forgive me, signora, when did your husband come to Naples?"

"In 1492."

"Where was he working in Tuscany, signora?"

"In San Sepolcro, Signor Rossi."

Rossi paused and frowned, not wanting to cause offence or seem stupid.

"I regret, signora, that I only heard of your husband's name when I arrived here in Naples. I have never heard of a Stefano Crispi working in San Sepolcro."

There was an embarrassed silence. Rossi looked discreetly round the room at a number of paintings hanging on the walls.

"Are these your husband's work, signora? Would you be offended if I presumed to take a closer look?"

"Please do, Signor Rossi, please do."

For the next five minutes, Rossi walked from painting to painting, studying each one in detail. As he moved on from one to another, Francesca heard him muttering to himself. "Remarkable, quite remarkable."

Finally he turned and smiled at her. "This is indeed work of rare brilliance, signora. It is no wonder your husband has such a high reputation here in Naples: his style is very much that of the Tuscan masters. I can see the influence of the great Piero, but interestingly, these paintings are remarkably even more like those of a Tuscan artist who worked in San Sepolcro from the 1460s until 1492. His name was Luca di Stefano. The similarity is really astounding."

"1492, Signor Rossi? Is that when he died?"

"No signora, it would seem not. There were tales of witchcraft associated with him, a pact with the Devil. It seems he did not appear to age as the years passed; he always looked the same, like a young man of thirty."

Francesca gasped. "What happened to him?" she whispered.

"Apparently he disappeared, signora, along with his son and grandson. In late 1492. They simply vanished. Signora, is everything all right? You look pale."

"Do you know what they were called, his son and grandson?"

"I believe the son was Niccolò, signora. And the grandson Gianni."

Francesca burst into Stefano's studio, yelling agitatedly that he stop and listen while she told him what Rossi had said.

As he heard her story, Stefano felt sick to the heart, but he managed to stay calm.

"It's a strange tale, Franci," he said, rather too nonchalantly. "I've heard vaguely of this di Stefano, but I think your Signor Rossi is overstating his importance. As for the ageing, I heard that was a ploy on behalf of the city councillors to punish him for not attending church. They made it all up."

He continued. "Anyway, I think these tales of witchcraft are exaggerated. They are merely a device the Church uses to control people."

Francesca crossed herself. "Stefano, how can you speak such blasphemy? It is well known that some weak people become possessed by the Devil and that he then uses them for his own wicked purposes. The Church has a continuing fight against such evil. It has to resist before we are all conquered by Satan and condemned to an eternity of fire."

She paused, breathing heavily as her anger built.

"How can you mock the wisdom of the Church?" she yelled at him. "No wonder we are cursed with not having children!"

"Francesca, be reasonable. How can you believe tales of people who do not age? It's complete nonsense. We all get older and die. That's the way of life. Can't you understand that?"

"No, Stefano, I can't! I don't understand anything anymore. I'm totally confused. I don't know who you are or what you are. I need to talk to the priest. He is the only one who will be able to shed any light on it, to explain God's way in all of this."

"Franci, please," he continued, trying to reason with her. "I think it would be better if you calmed down before discussing this with the priest. You need to relax. If you relax perhaps you will be able to conceive. We're still not too old. As for me, you know who I am. I'm your Stefano, and I always have been."

Her shoulders sagged; she seemed to have given in. Stefano held out his arms but as Francesca looked into his pale grey eyes, she saw fear. She assumed it was fear of discovery, but of what? A pact with the Devil? Was she married to such a man? Then she remembered Rossi's mention of Niccolò and Gianni. She had to get away. She moved back from him, avoiding his arms. She wanted no more contact with him, but she needed to placate him.

"You're right, Stefano." She attempted a smile. "I'm overexcited. I need to think the whole thing over. Let's talk again this evening."

Stefano watched her hurry from the studio. He called to his assistant. "Vito, I'm concerned about the signora. Could you follow her discreetly to make sure she gets home without any mishap? Don't let her see you following, she would only get upset."

Stefano looked sadly around his beloved studio. He sighed and walked over to a large wooden chest under a window. The two travelling bags he withdrew were already packed – they had been for some time – he just added a set of brushes and a few personal items. Then he went to a bureau and took out three letters written on scrolls of parchment. He sat down and waited.

Some fifteen minutes later a breathless Vito burst into the room.

"Signore! Signore! I fear that something terrible is going to happen!" He paused, gasping for breath.

Stefano put a hand on his shoulder. "Take a deep breath, Vito, and tell me what you saw."

Still panting, Vittorio launched into his account.

"I followed the signora as you asked, signore, but she didn't go to your house. She walked in the opposite direction, towards the church. She went inside and I followed her, staying in the shadows. I assumed she was going to pray, but you'd said to make sure she got home all right, so I stayed."

"You did well, Vito."

"She went straight to the confessional, signore, but there was someone in it with the priest. Instead of waiting quietly, she marched up and down outside, coughing loudly. The priest came out and told her to be quiet. But she took his arm, signore, and marched him off into a corner. I couldn't hear what they were saying but the priest became very agitated, wringing his hands and crossing himself. At one point the priest even sank to his knees, on the bare stones, and prayed. After that, he raised his voice and I heard words like 'bishop' and 'militia' and 'cardinal' and 'burning in hell'. He then turned on his heel and rushed out of the church, leaving the signora crying on her knees in front of a statue of Our Lady. At that point, I thought I should return and tell you, signore."

"You did very well, Vito, better than you realise."

Picking up a quill, he signed and dated the scrolls and then sealed them with wax.

He paused and placed his hands on Vittorio's shoulders. "There is one more thing I need you to do. Vito, you have been a fine and trustworthy apprentice. I'm afraid I have to go away for some time, a long time, and I regret the studio will have to close." He handed the youth one of the scrolls. "I want you to take this scroll to Signor Marinello. He is a fine artist and I am sure that with my recommendation he will employ you. Take it, and take this purse."

He took a purse of coins from his belt.

"There are your wages and enough to keep you for a few months in case you can't find employment straight away. Now listen carefully. There are two other scrolls. One is addressed to Signora Anna. I want you to take it to her tomorrow, not before. The other is addressed to Signor Farrara, the notary. I need you to take it to him immediately."

Looking the youth squarely in the eyes, he said, "Vito, you will hear some terrible things said about me in the next few days. Whether they are true or not, you will have to decide for yourself. I can only say that I think you know me well enough as a man and a friend not be swayed by the crazed passions of the overzealous. Now go, Vittorio, there is no time to lose."

Vittorio turned to go, faltered and turned back. He threw his arms around Stefano, tears in his eyes.

"Signore, I … I shall not let you down. And I shall never forget you."

After one last glance around the studio, Stefano quickly gathered his things and ran to the next street where he kept his horse. He had already sent word for it to be saddled. He mounted up and left the city, taking a northerly road.

On a rise a few miles away that gave a commanding view of the entire city, the Bay of Naples and the ever-threatening smoke of Vesuvius, he stopped and looked back for one final time, wondering if he would ever return. He shook his head in disbelief. He was ninety years old and yet he felt and looked no older than he had sixty years before. How much longer was he going to continue like this?


The notary, Aldo Farrara opened the scroll with interest, raising his eyebrows in surprise as he read it. Stefano had instructed him to transfer immediately all titles for his property and possessions to Francesca's sole name along with all his investments and monies.

Aldo Farrara sat back in his chair in surprise and re-read the document several times.

"You saw your master prepare this document?" he said to Vito.

"I saw him sign it, signore."

"There was no coercion or threat?"

"None, signore."

"And where is your master now?"

"He has gone, signore."

"Gone where?"

"I do not know, signore."

"Then you may leave. There is no reply."


Farrara quickly retrieved the relevant papers. The task was straightforward and by early afternoon, shortly before the forces of the Church descended to search for the agent of the Devil and seize his property, there was nothing in Naples that now belonged to Stefano Crispi. And the man himself was gone.

One reason why Farrara was pleased to act so promptly for his client was that he was very attracted to the young widow, Anna Santini. With Stefano out of the picture, he was confident he would be able to charm her.

Five weeks later, Francesca arrived one morning at her sister's house. Her hair was dishevelled, her face blotchy and puffed. She had been up all night crying. As she sat down heavily in a chair, Anna took her hand. She was herself still confused over Stefano's departure, despite the reassurances she had received in his letter.

"Franci, despite all that has been said about him, I remain convinced that Stefano is a good and honourable man. There must be some other explanation for everything that has happened. He was a good husband to you. Perhaps once he has had time to think everything over, you will hear from him. I feel sure he will come back."

She knew her words were hollow. From what Stefano had written to her, she was in no doubt: he would never return.

Francesca stopped sobbing and looked painfully into Anna's eyes.

"He'll never come back, Anna, I know it. I'll never see him again, and that means he'll never know."

"Know what, Franci?"

Francesca's voice dropped to a whisper.

"I'm pregnant."

# Chapter 7

## June 2009

Claudia walked quickly back to her car. She wanted to leave before PC Roberts changed his mind, although thinking through the conversation, she realised that she hadn't broken any rules – the information he'd given her was unsolicited.

She picked up her map of the Lakes to check the road to Grasmere and was pleased to find the village was only four and a half miles away.

She turned left out of the car park. The road ran alongside Rydal Water. This was Wordsworth country and she could imagine the poet walking along its shores getting fired up about the scenery and the clouds. However her mind was far from poetry.

Distracted, Claudia missed the first turning from the main road into Grasmere, but there was a second road into the village for traffic coming from the north. She took this and to her delight, one of the first buildings she saw as she reached the village was the Green Man. Two of the samples Roberts had taken were from the men who'd been fighting in its car park.

She stopped outside the village store next to the pub.

As she got out, she saw a sign on the door: 'Fresh rolls and sandwiches made to order'. She suddenly felt very hungry.

The rotund figure of Gordon, the shop owner, turned towards her as he heard the door open.

"Lovely day, miss. How can I help you?"

"Do you have any crusty rolls, and some cheddar and tomatoes?"

"Fresh rolls every morning, miss, and I've this delicious crumbly cheddar, not too strong, and locally grown tomatoes. Would you like some ham in that too? Lots of folks do. It's locally cured, very lean, miss."

"Sounds great," smiled Claudia, picking up a bottle of sparkling water from a chilled display cabinet.

"What a fabulous day. How has the summer been up here? It's been rubbish in the Midlands."

"Same, miss. Been rotten until a couple of days ago. Doesn't do much for business, I can tell you. Are you here on holiday?"

"Just a long weekend."

While Gordon was engaged in a certain amount of theatre preparing her roll, she looked out of the window and across the pub car park to the village beyond.

"It's so lovely and peaceful up here; so quiet. It's such a contrast to where I live in the West Midlands. Go to a pub down there and there's always some lout looking for trouble."

She forgave herself the small lie – the village of Combrook where she lived couldn't be more peaceful.

"I'll bet you don't get much trouble around here."

"Pretty peaceful most of the time, miss. But we have our moments. Only a couple of weeks ago, no, more like three it was, there was quite a tussle in the car park right there, outside the pub. Not late in the evening either, but it was chucking it down. Seemed like the middle of the night. Came as a bit of a surprise, though."

"Surprise?" Claudia held her breath.

"Yes, I didn't see it so well myself 'cause I was looking this way, you see, like I am now, talking to a couple of tourists, like yourself. Standing right where you are, they were. They saw most of it. Reckoned that John's car took a knock from this other bloke who then got real stroppy. But that wasn't how our local bobby saw it, and he marched them both off."

"So why were you surprised?"

"Well, I'd always put him down as a peaceful sort, John, that is. Very quiet. But it looked like he gave the other guy a bit of a thumping, by the blood and all. Because it was raining so hard, we didn't go out, but after the bobby took them off, the tourists said that it looked like he was having more of an argument with John than the other bloke, whose fault it all was. They asked me where the police station was and said they were going there to tell the police what they'd seen; how the other bloke had driven into John's car and then picked a fight with him. As I said, bit of a surprise to see John defending himself so well. Who'd a thought it, eh? He'd only just popped in here for some pasta and wine."

Claudia stared at him wide-eyed. Trying to sound casual, she stuttered, "So, er, who's this peace-loving man called John? He sounds interesting."

"John Andrews? He's a local artist. Well, he is now. Not actually from round these parts. Don't know where he's from orig–"

Claudia interrupted him, "Does he show his work anywhere? I'm really interested in Lakeland scenes – I suppose he does that sort of stuff?"

"Beautiful pictures, miss, real works of art, if you know what I mean, not like some of the daubers who sling paint at their canvasses around here. No, John's a real talent. He's got a gallery down the road in the village, 'bout 300 yards down there, miss, on the left, near the village green. Lovely setting … Miss, don't you want your roll?"

Claudia found herself marching out of the shop. She stopped, embarrassed.

"Of course," she smiled guiltily. "I was just checking if I could see the gallery from here."

"There we are, miss," said Gordon, handing her his own work of art in the form of a crusty roll. "That'll be four pounds fifty-five."

Claudia looked up at the sign over the gallery: John Andrews. Fine Artist. Lakeland Views and Portraits. Some of the nervousness that she'd felt earlier returned, but, at the same time, she couldn't believe how much progress she'd made. Was this man really going to be the source of the unbelievably rare DNA?

There were several oil paintings displayed in the gallery window, with the largest placed centrally on an easel. All were beautifully detailed scenes of lakes and mountains in the area. On the left side of the window, there was a small portrait of an elderly woman which combined an almost photographic quality with a timeless air, as if the subject were really from another century. Claudia looked at it in awe, examining the exquisite translucency of the skin tones.

She took a deep breath and pushed open the gallery door. Inside, the walls were hung with numerous views like those in the window, while freestanding panels in the centre were devoted to portraits. The subjects were all modern, but the paintings all had that same combination of fine, photographic detail and incredible skin tones. Claudia went up to one of the medium-sized views and glanced at the price tag.

Rather outside my range, she thought, raising her eyebrows.

"Can I help at all?"

She turned towards the voice and found herself looking up into the olive-complexioned face of a lean man she estimated to be in his late thirties, perhaps younger. He was a little shy of six foot tall with short but stylish dark brown hair that showed no evidence of greying. He was wearing beige jeans-cut trousers and a mid-blue linen shirt, but what struck her particularly were his pale grey eyes. They seemed to be looking through her and reading everything about her.

He smiled. "Please, feel free to look around. If there's anything in particular that catches your eye, I can put it on an easel so you can see it on its own."

Claudia found herself staring at him. "They're all so beautiful," she finally stuttered in hardly more than a whisper.

"Thank you."

"Are you the artist?"

"Yes, I am. John Andrews." He held out his hand and Claudia extended hers to shake it.

"Um, Claudia Reid," she replied.

"Pleased to meet you, Miss Reid."

He turned, leaving her to browse, but Claudia wanted to talk.

"There are so many," she said, rather lamely. "Does it take you long to paint each one? There's so much detail. I can't imagine ..."

"Not as long as you might think," he smiled.

He tilted his head in question. "Is there something I can help you with?"

"How do you mean?"

"Well, you're staring at me, not at the paintings. I can assure you they are far more interesting to look at."

Claudia looked down, embarrassed.

"Sorry, I didn't mean to be rude. It's just that ... I was wondering, um, well, could I possibly ask you something?"

"Go ahead," he replied, amused by this rather flustered young woman.

"Well, I haven't come only to look at the paintings. Well, that is, I have, because they're brilliant and I'd love to buy one, but they seem a bit out of my price range."

"They're not all highly priced," he said, "I've some smaller scenes and portraits over here–"

"No. Yes. Good." Claudia was getting cross with herself. She took a deep breath.

"Look, can I ask you something?"

"You've already asked me," said John genially, raising his eyebrows and smiling at her.

"Yes, of course I did." Claudia took another breath.

"I'm a biochemist doing DNA profiling of samples taken by the police. One of the samples I analysed recently was incredibly unusual, very rare, so I did a bit of checking up and I'm pretty sure it came from you."

John frowned, now less amused. "Go on," he said cautiously.

"Well, could you confirm that you gave a sample to the police recently for profiling? Have I got the right person?"

John looked at her coldly.

"You sound more like some sort of journalist than a biochemist. How did you get this information? I thought these things were confidential. Do you go around interviewing all the people whose samples you analyse?"

"No, of course not. There are millions of them. And anyway, we can't. I mean, you're right; it is confidential. But since I work with the samples, there's a certain amount of information that comes with them."

"Like my name and address?" It seemed to Claudia he was getting more hostile.

"No, certainly not. I had to dig a little to find that."

"And why would you want to do that. Surely it must be against the rules?"

Claudia blushed. This wasn't going well. She ran her hands through her hair.

"Well, yes, it is, in a way–"

78

"In a way? It either is or it isn't. What is it you want?"

"Look, I don't care why you were asked to give a sample, I–"

"I wasn't asked. I was told I had no choice. Do you think I want to have my sample on your database?"

"Sorry, no, I don't suppose you do. A lot of people don't. But as I said, the reason why you were required to give a sample doesn't matter. The fact is, you have and I profiled it." She paused to look up into his eyes. "And the results are, frankly, incredible. You have a DNA profile that is unbelievably rare. I mean all profiles are rare, otherwise there'd be no value in them, in crime investigation, that is. But yours is off the scale."

"Well, I haven't committed any crimes, and I'm not about to, so whether my profile is rare or not doesn't matter. It's of no interest to me."

"Can I just explain it?"

Claudia waited, but John didn't reply. He merely stood and fixed his eyes on hers, his face unsmiling. She decided to plough on.

"When we test the samples, we look at bits of the DNA that vary from one person to another. These variations, some are more common than others; some are very rare. Obviously it's unusual to find someone with a rare variant; it's even more unusual to find someone with two. In your case, you have a whole host of rare variants. But they're not just rare; they are, for the most part, unique. We've never seen them before. And they're all together in your DNA."

"You must have made a mistake; there's nothing special about me."

John shrugged his shoulders, deciding it was really time that he sent this Claudia Reid on her way.

"There's no mistake. I checked the results and repeated the tests. They are correct. When your sample turned up, I realised it was a golden opportunity to find out if the areas we test have any particular function, whether you are different in any way. Of course, you might not be aware of any differences–"

Oh, I'm very aware of them, thought John, feeling increasingly alarmed.

"–it could be that all the differences are subtle ones, things that occur at a molecular level in your metabolism."

"It all sounds very complicated to me," said John dismissively.

"It would be fascinating to be able to make a few more tests. And perhaps to look at your family to see if they have many of the same rare variants."

"No, I certainly don't want you testing my family. It would be a total invasion of their privacy."

"Well, could I just ask about your parents, are they–?"

"No, they died a long time ago," he interrupted, emphasizing the 'long'.

"Look, Miss Reid, I can sympathise with you, but I'm really not interested in your research. It seems to me that you've very much overstepped the mark by tracking me down and talking to me. I don't know much about your database, but I imagine that you could find yourself in a lot of trouble if I chose to make a complaint about your behaviour. I think you are misguided and letting your enthusiasm get the better of your common sense. I'm right, aren't I?"

Claudia was mortified. She'd blown it. She'd come in half-cocked without thinking of a strategy and had alienated him. She wasn't to know that going to the authorities was the last thing John Andrews would do, that he had far too much to hide.

"Yes," she mumbled, "you're right, I'm sorry. I apologise. I shouldn't have come. I have no right to ask you these things. I hoped that you'd understand that this could have been a once-in-a-lifetime opportunity for me, whichever way any further research turned out."

She looked up sheepishly and saw John's pale grey eyes boring into her. After a moment his face relaxed.

"OK, Miss Reid, no harm done. I won't report you, but please, I don't want you or anyone else probing into my DNA, or my family's. So why don't you go and we'll leave it there?"

But Claudia wasn't ready to leave. She looked around the gallery and said, "Yes, of course. I'm sorry. Look, I really am interested in your work. Could I have a look at some more? You said that you had some smaller paintings that I might be able to afford."

John didn't want her in the gallery any longer. He was about to make an excuse for closing up when the door flew open and his two daughters rushed in.

"Hi, Daddy, we're back." Eight-year-old Sophie ran in, glanced at Claudia, and charged straight on past them both into the studio at the back. Her five-year-old sister, Phoebe, was close behind.

"I'm going to do some painting," called out Sophie as she disappeared. Phoebe's glance at Claudia had lasted a little longer, enough for Claudia to gasp quietly, not only at her resemblance to John, but also at her pale grey eyes.

"Sorry, darling," said Lola as she appeared at the door, arms full of books and shopping. "I told them to go quietly in case you had a customer, which I see you do."

She turned to Claudia. "Sorry. They can be so exuberant."

"No problem," smiled Claudia, glad that the tension had been broken. "I've been looking at these wonderful paintings."

"Buy as many as you can afford," replied Lola, ever the saleswoman. "They're a brilliant investment. Your grandchildren will thank you for it."

She turned to her husband. "I've got some lunch, John, I'll sort it out in the studio."

"OK," he replied, "I won't be long."

"Oh, take your time. If you sell a picture, I can pay the grocer."

"Well, that puts my paintings in their place."

"You haven't seen what we owe him," called Lola, disappearing into the studio.

Claudia browsed the portraits and located a few of elderly women, rather like the one in the window. She held one up. "This is beautiful. It reminds me of my grandmother." She looked at the price and did a swift calculation. She reckoned her credit card could just about take it.

"I can give you a discount," said John.

"After all I've said to irritate you? You're very kind." Claudia was delighted.

"Let's say it will close the matter, shall we?" John replied, taking the picture from her. "I'll go and wrap it for you."

John took the painting into the studio and left Claudia looking around. Taking advantage of being alone, she pulled out her phone and aimed its lens at a few of the pictures. She was about to move to another part of the gallery when she looked towards the studio door. Leaning against the doorframe, Phoebe was holding a large rag doll and looking at her, swaying slightly. Claudia smiled at her, rapidly putting the phone to her ear and pretending to talk to someone. Phoebe looked down and then disappeared back into the studio.

"Here we are," announced John, returning to the gallery and handing Claudia the now securely wrapped painting. She handed him her credit card.

He had also written out a brief description of the work, which he folded and put in an envelope. He licked the flap, sealed the envelope and handed it to Claudia.

"I like to give customers a brief description of a work along with their purchase for insurance purposes," he explained.

"Thank you," said Claudia, putting the envelope in her bag. "Are there any books of your work, you know, a coffee table art book or something?"

There are dozens of books, thought John. And you could take a look in the National Gallery, The Louvre, the Uffizi or the Metropolitan Museum of Art...

"No," he said, "only the odd exhibition catalogue."

"Well, I shall treasure this," said Claudia. "Thank you for being so understanding. I hope you appreciate my motives." She took a business card from her bag, scribbled on it and handed it to him. "If you ever change your mind..."

Later, as John was eating lunch in the studio, Phoebe looked up at him.

"Daddy, who was that lady?"

"She was only someone who bought one of my paintings, darling."

"Is she a nice lady?"

"I don't know. I haven't met her before. But she seemed to be a nice lady."

"I don't think she is."

"Why's that, sweetheart?"

"Because she taked photos of your pictures with her phone. Lots of photos."

John's face darkened. Once again, he felt threatened.

# Chapter 8

## 1517-1548

As Stefano Crispi galloped north from Naples and the uncompromising forces of the Church bent on putting him to death, he realised that for the first time in his life he was completely alone. His son and grandson were dead, as were all contemporaries from his early life, while his wife, Francesca, had abandoned him for her faith. He was a ninety-year-old man with the body, health and mind of a thirty-year-old. Illness and ageing passed him by, although he was well aware that he would die as quickly as the next man if run through with a sword or burnt at the stake. He didn't understand his 'condition' but he was learning to accept it.

Walking his horse into some woods, he stopped by a stream. He threw away the bonnet he had worn for several years to hide his hair and stripped off his middle-aged man's clothes, replacing them with a stylish set of travelling clothes from his saddelbag. Finally, he shaved off the beard he'd been artfully tinting grey. When he emerged from the woods, he looked every bit as youthful as he felt.

As he crossed from the Kingdom of Naples into the Papal States, he considered his options. Should he go to Rome? It was only a few years since Michelangelo Buonarotti had completed his work on the ceiling of the Sistine Chapel, and the city still buzzed with activity. Or should he head further north, putting more distance between himself and Naples?

He decided against Rome and headed northeast, intending to cross the Apennines and work his way up the coast to the Po Valley. In a hostel one evening in the town of Todi, he struck up a conversation with a trader from the Republic of Venice who was heading for Rome.

Without thinking, Stefano greeted the man in Neapolitan, but when the response was a frown of suspicion of a foreigner from the south, Stefano quickly moved into Tuscan.

His peace of mind restored, the trader felt at ease to air his prejudices.

"I find the south so alien to my tastes. It is very unsophisticated, so unlike the Republic where the influence of our superior language and manners is apparent even among the peasants."

He leaned towards Stefano and put his hand to the side of his mouth to prevent others from hearing, "Coming here is like returning to the dark ages."

He then leaned back and let out a huge guffaw.

Stefano looked in mild amusement at this pompous but jolly man of around fifty. He was expensively dressed in a fine burgundy velvet doublet and white silk blouse with matching silk hose, his shoes soft pale-brown leather. His greying hair was a mass of unruly curls.

The trader was still talking. "But I have to make this annual trek. I have clients, very wealthy clients," he pulled on the lower lid of one eye and winked, "who are desperate for my unequalled choice of rare and magnificent goods."

He gave a world-weary wave in the direction of his entourage.

"The money pays their wages and keeps my wife and daughters in the finest fashions that their place in Venetian society demands."

There was another guffaw and he shook his head at the folly of women, failing to remember that the cost of his present outfit alone would have kept more than a few local families in food for several months.

Stefano asked him more about Venice and for the next hour he was regaled with descriptions of fine palaces, sumptuous feasts, a cultured populace and a cosmopolitan atmosphere unparalleled anywhere in the world – all punctuated with gales of laughter.

On hearing that Stefano was a portrait painter the merchant immediately adjusted his stance.

"Are you any good?" he demanded forthrightly, guffawing loudly once again.

Taken aback, Stefano thought quickly about an answer.

"Well, when I was younger, I was apprentice to one of the finest artists in Naples and since establishing my own studio, I have had many commissions from the nobility."

As he was talking, Stefano took a sheet of paper from his bag and made a rapid sketch. No more than a few lines, it captured the man's features perfectly. He handed it to the trader who slapped his hand on the bar in surprise.

"My God, if your paintings are half as good as this, you'll have people falling over themselves for your work. Some of them very pretty young things too." He winked at Stefano and dissolved again into hoots of laughter.

Having mopped his eyes with a huge embroidered lace handkerchief, the trader frowned. "If you had such a fine reputation in the city, no matter how barbaric the place is, why have you left it?"

Stefano feigned a slight coyness.

"It's a little embarrassing," he replied. "There was a certain noblewoman, a very attractive lady. Her portrait involved my often being alone with her and ..." He paused and shrugged. "Unfortunately, her husband became suspicious and paid one of her maids for information that proved a little compromising. I had no choice but to leave."

The merchant laughed heartily and slapped Stefano on the back. "Ah, the pleasures of the flesh. So difficult to resist."

Bursting out laughing again, he banged on the table and called for more wine.

"You should go to Venice," he continued. "It's attracting some of the finest of this new age of artists. You could do well. You've probably heard of this Tiziano Vecellio fellow, calls himself Da Cadore. Making quite a name for himself. Very fine painter. What's your name, my young friend?"

Stefano had been musing on this question over the last few days but so far had decided only upon a new Christian name.

"Giovanni," he said, and then wondered what should come next, but he could only think of his original Christian name. "Giovanni di Luca," he stammered.

"Pleased to meet you, Signor di Luca. Giacomo di Roberti is delighted to make your acquaintance. I'll arrange some introductions for you in La Serenissima."

Venice was a city unlike any Giovanni had ever seen or imagined. Originally a group of more than a hundred islands in a marshy lagoon, it had for several centuries been a city on the water, its buildings, streets and alleyways never far from one of the maze of canals that crisscrossed and segmented it. All aspects of the city's life revolved around the canals. Transportation of people and goods was largely by gondola, the sheer number of which all busily plying their way through the complex network of aquatic streets – some no wider than alleys – giving the impression of a colony of giant insects each working as part of a grand plan.

Giovanni found the Venetians to be a proud people, as proud as the Neapolitans had been of their chaotic city, but with a cultured edge that their centuries of trade with the East had honed into an aloof sense of superiority over not only the rest of Italy, but the entire world. Their language was closer to Spanish than Italian, making it as foreign to Giovanni's ears as Neapolitan had been twenty-five years before. But Venice was a cosmopolitan city and he found his Tuscan dialect was easily understood by most of the locals. Even so, he resolved to learn as much of the Venetian tongue as quickly as his improving linguistic skills would let him.

In the richer area of the city, close to the Rialto Bridge, sumptuous palazzos vied for position along the canal edges, their owners keen to outdo their neighbours in the originality of design and decoration. Here were the homes and places of business of the traders and merchants whose family fortunes had for generations, like the waters of the lagoon, ebbed and flowed with the fortunes of the city.

By the spring of 1522, thanks to di Roberti's contacts, Giovanni di Luca was well established in a studio in the heart of the city, all worries of Naples and exposure by the Church pushed to the back of his mind. He was working on a portrait of the Duke of Verona's stunningly beautiful eighteen-year-old daughter, Cecilia. During one of the final sittings for the portrait, Giovanni's assistant interrupted him with a message that there was a gentleman to see him. The youth was rather agitated, knowing that Giovanni discouraged interruptions.

"Send him in, Umberto," he reluctantly told the boy.

Umberto opened the door and in swept a tall and imposing man in his early thirties wearing a flowing emerald green cloak over a matching doublet and hose. His eyes darted around, taking in everything. He took off his pointed green hat, bowed politely to Cecilia's chaperones and then rather more elaborately to Cecilia herself, his eyes remaining on her with great interest. He then turned to Giovanni.

"Signor di Luca, I must seek your forgiveness for this intrusion. May I introduce myself? Tiziano Vecellio."

He bowed again, this time towards Giovanni.

"You need no introduction, signore," replied Giovanni, "your reputation precedes you. I am honoured that you should wish to visit me."

"You are too kind, Signor di Luca. I wonder, as a fellow artist, would it be presumptuous of me to ask permission to view your portrait of this exquisite young lady."

"Please." Giovanni gestured towards the painting.

Vecellio, who would be known to future generations of English-speakers as Titian, moved round the easel to study the painting. After several minutes, he stood back.

"Remarkable work, Signor di Luca. I had heard that your portraiture rivalled mine, but this work, it's breathtaking in its delicacy and subtlety of tone."

"You are very generous, Signor Vecellio," said Giovanni, bowing his head.

"Not at all, signore. But I am intrigued by your style. It is reminiscent of works of the last century; I can see some of the sfumato technique of the great da Vinci. One sees it less often these days. Have you not been tempted to experiment with more vivid colour?"

Giovanni smiled and walking over to a leather portfolio, pulled out two carnival scenes.

"I love the use of rich colour in certain situations, Signor Vecellio, as you can see from these drafts, but for portraits, I prefer to keep my tones more muted."

Vecellio took the two paintings and studied them.

"I underestimated your versatility, Signor di Luca. I apologise. But these are no drafts; they are masterpieces. Who has commissioned them, may I ask?"

"No one, signore, they are solely for my own amusement."

Vecellio shook his head. "They should be adorning the walls of a fine palazzo, or the council chamber of the Signoria, not hidden away in your portfolio."

Giovanni smiled. "When the series is completed, signore, perhaps I shall offer them for sale. But there is much I still want to try with them."

Vecellio put the paintings down and offered his hand. "Signor di Luca – may I call you Giovanni to my Tiziano? – would you do me the honour of visiting my studio in the very near future? I should be humbled to show you my work."

Giovanni was delighted. He knew of Vecellio's reputation and how he preferred to be called Da Cadore from the name of the town where he was born, reserving the use of his Christian name for close friends and the very few people he considered his artistic equal.

He grasped Vecellio's hand firmly.

"Tiziano," he smiled, "I should be greatly honoured to visit you at the earliest opportunity."

The two became firm friends, meeting to discuss new ideas and projects whenever Vecellio was in Venice. Giovanni found him a very adventurous artist, his use of colour innovative and exciting. It influenced his own work, taking him out of the fifteenth century into the more experimental sixteenth. Nevertheless, despite their close friendship, Vecellio made no attempt to persuade Giovanni to expand his horizons beyond relatively small canvasses. Whether this was from respect for his stated preferences or from a perceived threat to his own position, Giovanni never knew, but he was more than happy with the status quo.

In early June 1530, a few days after his hundred-and-third birthday – to his Venetian friends it was his fortieth – Giovanni received a note from Giacomo di Roberti inviting him to dinner the following evening. He had scribbled on it 'Someone interesting I should like you to meet'.

"Di Luca!" cried di Roberti, clapping his hands in delight as

Giovanni was shown into a third floor reception room of his vast house. "Let me introduce you to my esteemed guest. This elegant gentleman is my very good friend, Signor 'Enery Marka-ham."

The tall, slim and silver-haired Markham, a man in his late fifties, stepped towards Giovanni and bowed his head. Speaking in good but accented Italian, he looked Giovanni in the eye and smiled warmly.

"Henry Markham at your service, signore. I am delighted to make your acquaintance. Your reputation as an artist is, might I say, second to none. I hope that following this most fortunate meeting I might be able to request your undoubtedly highly sought-after services."

Giovanni bowed his head and began to reply. "Signor Markham, I–" But Markham interrupted him, pointing at di Roberti.

"You see, Giacomo, my language is not as impossible as you make it!" He turned to Giovanni, "Bravo, Signor di Luca! That was a perfect rendition of my name. Please be so kind as to attempt my Christian name."

Giovanni smiled. "Henry," he said, "Henry Markham."

"Bravo! Bravo!" exclaimed the delighted Markham. "You have an excellent ear, signore. You must give our tone-deaf host some lessons!"

Di Roberti hooted with laughter. "That's exactly like I said it. 'Enery. 'Enery Marka-ham."

Later, during the dinner, Giovanni continued the thread of conversation they had started earlier.

"Signor Markham, you mentioned that you might want to engage my services. I should be delighted to attempt your likeness."

"Oh, it's not my likeness I seek, Signor di Luca, I wouldn't waste a piece of canvas on my ageing and uninteresting features. No, it is my daughter, Beth, whose portrait I desire. She will be arriving here soon from London. The fortunate girl inherited my late wife's beauty, and there is nothing I should like more than to see that beauty captured on canvas."

When he heard mention of Markham's daughter, di Roberti bellowed down the table at Giovanni.

"I believe Signor Marka-ham's daughter will be a challenge even for your exceptional skills, di Luca. If she is like her dear late mother, she will have a beauty unsurpassed in this city."

Noting the slight bristling of the ladies at the table, and wincing from a kick from one of his daughters, he added, "Present company excepted, of course," and guffawed all the more.

Markham lost no time in visiting Giovanni's studio and buying several of his paintings. They quickly became friends, with Markham even attempting to teach Giovanni some English. Whenever di Roberti was around, Giovanni noticed he and Markham would retreat into whispered conversations. He wondered what they were plotting.

Once Beth Markham arrived in Venice in late August 1530, her father wasted no time in introducing her to Venetian society. Giovanni di Luca was among the guests at the first dinner held in her honour.

Although normally self-assured, Beth felt nervous as she made her entrance to the reception room of her father's newly rented house, knowing that all twenty-two pairs of the guests' eyes would be upon her. The buzz of conversation filling the room suddenly hushed as the guests appraised her looks. A beaming di Roberti marched forward to greet her, breaking the spell.

"Signore e Signori," he cried, "may I take the opportunity of introducing my esteemed friend 'Eneri's charming and beautiful daughter, Betta."

Beth curtseyed demurely to the room, smiling in amusement at di Roberti's rendering of her name. Giovanni, standing at the back of the room, felt his breath catch involuntarily as he saw her. With her rich blonde curls drawn back by an elaborate set of combs to emphasise her angular features and high cheekbones, Beth's Anglo-Saxon beauty was like none he had seen before. He waited impatiently to be introduced.

"My dear," said Markham to Beth, "this is Signor Giovanni di Luca, the artist I have been telling you about and whose work you have already seen adorning my offices."

Giovanni bowed his head and lifted Beth's hand to his lips. He was aware of her looking into his pale grey eyes.

"Signorina Markham," he said, "it is a great pleasure to meet you. Your father has told me much about you."

Beth smiled at him playfully and replied in English. "Signor di Luca. It seems my father has been talking about us both, since after all he has told me, I feel as if I already know you. He has told me you have a natural ear for languages."

Slightly taken aback at what was clearly a need to reply in English, Giovanni stammered, "Signorina Markham, I, er, think-a that your father has been-a too generous. My English eez, I am-a sure, of-a very poor quality."

"Bravo, Signor di Luca," cried Beth, clapping her hands in delight. "Your English is excellent. With a little more instruction, you will soon be speaking like an Englishman."

He smiled at her and switched back to Italian. "For the benefit of the other guests, I think we should use Italian. I know you are very comfortable with the language and everyone here can speak it as well as they can Venetian."

"Ah, Venetian, Signor di Luca," replied Beth, her Italian excellent. "Is it really a difficult tongue?"

"It is not too difficult, Signorina. I myself could not speak a word when I arrived here some years ago, but now it is second nature to me."

Later that evening, when the guests had gone, Henry Markham relaxed on a balcony overlooking the Grand Canal, his beloved daughter sitting beside him.

"A very successful evening, Beth. You had these Venetians eating out of your hand. Do you think you will be able to live among them?"

"I have no doubt, Papa. Your friends were all charming people."

"And the dashing artist, di Luca, how did you find him?"

"Oh I found him very well, Papa, a delightful man. But I am surprised by his youthful looks. Did you say he was forty years old? He really does not look it."

"Yes, he could certainly pass for someone much younger. And what an artist! I don't think I have ever seen such skill. In my opinion he rivals this Da Cadore fellow. But he does seem to lack ambition. He's content with only taking commissions for portraits from private families."

"I hope that I can see a lot more of him, Papa. He seems to me to be a very interesting man, despite his lack of ambition."

"We can certainly arrange that, my dear," smiled her father, relieved that she appeared to like his choice of potential husband for her, not that he thought he had made it too obvious.

Beth smiled softly at him, fully aware of his thoughts and intentions. She was very pleased that this man her father thought worthy of her had turned out to be both handsome and charming.

In the weeks that followed, it was clear to Beth that Giovanni liked her very much. He would call at the Markham house frequently, altough he often remained rather distant and formal, as if he were suppressing his emotions.

For his part, Giovanni was worried. His feelings for Beth were growing stronger by the day. But he was, he assumed, still married, albeit as Stefano Crispi in another city. He could not make a commitment to Beth without knowing the situation in Naples. He decided to employ an agent to make discreet enquiries.

During the two months following the agent's departure, Giovanni waited impatiently. Beth and her father noticed he was more distracted than usual, but they put it down to an artistic temperament and the heat of an unusually hot summer.

When the agent finally returned in the first week of August, Giovanni bustled him quickly into a back room of his studio and sat him down.

"Tell me everything, Alfredo, everything. What have you discovered? How are the two Santini ladies?"

"Both ladies are well, signore. Signora Francesca is living in the same household as her sister, Signora Anna, and her husband—"

"Husband! Francesca Santini has a husband?" interrupted Giovanni.

"No, signore, it is Signora Anna Santini who has a husband. Quite an elderly one, a notary called Aldo Farrara."

"Farrara! The scheming devil!" muttered Giovanni under his breath.

"It seems, signore, that Signora Anna has two children from an earlier marriage to an artist, a Gianni Crispi, who was murdered in a street brawl. Both are now adults and indeed married with their own children."

Giovanni was stunned: he was a great-great grandfather.

"And she has two more children from her marriage to Signor Farrara," continued the agent.

"And you say that the Signora Francesca lives with her sister?"

"Yes, signore, she does, together with her daughter, Paola."

"Her daughter!" Giovanni felt a chill run down his spine. "How... how old is this daughter?" he whispered.

"She is twelve, signore; she was born in August 1518."

Giovanni sat down hard in a chair. A daughter. Paola must be his daughter.

"Tell me about this daughter, Alfredo. What did you find out? How does she look?"

"She will, I think, signore, be a woman of great beauty. She is already very handsome, and she has the most striking pale grey eyes."

He paused to look up at Giovanni. "Rather like yours, I should say, signore."

"Yes, yes, quite a coincidence, I'm sure, Alfredo." Giovanni looked away hurriedly.

"I found out a little more about the child, signore. It appears that she enjoys the most exceptional health. It is reported that she is indeed never ill, not even with the usual childhood coughs and sneezes."

"Did you find out anything about the child's father, Alfredo?" asked Giovanni hesitantly.

"He was called Stefano Crispi, signore. He was Signora Anna's late husband's uncle and an artist, like yourself. He disappeared suddenly, long before the child was born and the child has since taken her mother's name. She is Paola Santini. Her mother insisted on this after the annulment, signore."

"The annulment?"

"Yes, signore. Signora Francesca had her marriage to Signor Crispi annulled on the grounds that he was in league with the Devil. When the child was born, there were many ceremonies of exorcism to remove any influence her father's curse may have had on her."

Once the agent had left, Giovanni leaned forward and buried his head in his hands. A daughter! And very likely one who was like him. Paola. A daughter he would probably never see.

When he finally stirred from his introspection, he got up and walked over to a mirror to take a long look at himself. He was a man of a hundred and four who had no idea why he had lived so long, nor how long he would live. Was it not wrong, absurd, immoral even, for a man of his age to have feelings for a woman born when he was in his eighties? He looked again into his eyes in the mirror and made a decision. If he was going to ask Beth to marry him, he would have to tell her everything, even though it would run the risk of her rejecting him and perhaps even denouncing him.

That afternoon Giovanni called at the Markham house. Henry was out on business so Beth was alone. He was shown into a third-floor sitting room with a commanding view of the Grand Canal. As Beth entered, she saw that Giovanni was preoccupied, staring out of the window. She sighed to herself, wondering if this was going to be another difficult afternoon where she had to do most of the talking.

To her surprise Giovanni walked over to her and took both her hands in his.

"Beth, you look radiant in that wonderful dress. Please come and sit by me. There is something I need to discuss with you."

Beth's heart leapt. Was he finally going to make a declaration of his love for her?

"Beth, I think it must be obvious that I have very strong feelings for you, feelings that I hope might be reciprocated." He held up his hand to stall her when he saw she was about to interrupt him, her eagerness showing in her eyes.

"My dear Beth, please, there is something I must tell you about myself. Something that you are going to find very hard to believe."

She frowned, her heart pounding. "Tell me, Giovanni. Whatever it is, I'll try to understand."

"Beth, what I am about to say will probably make you think I have lost my senses, that I am mad. However, I can assure you that I am perfectly sane."

He took a breath. "Beth, you know me as a man of forty-one—"

"And a very youthful forty-one," she interrupted eagerly.

94

"But what if I told you that I am not that age, Beth, but much, much older."

She put her hand to her mouth to suppress a laugh. "But how could that be, Giovanni? If you were to confess that you were younger, I should not be surprised, but older? I cannot imagine such a thing."

She saw he was looking very serious, his whole demeanour that of a man consumed by worry. She turned her hands in his and gripped his fingers tightly. "I apologise. I shouldn't interrupt. Pray continue."

"It is true, Beth, but I cannot explain it. I am telling you because if you were to consider me worthy, as … as a possible husband, I think you should know the truth about me, as difficult as it might be to understand."

"A husband!" she gasped. Letting go of his hands, she clutched her own together to her breast, "Giovanni, are you–?"

"Beth, please, hear me out. Once I have finished, you might no longer think me suitable. You might, instead, find me repulsive."

She was shocked. "Giovanni, what have you done? Is it something terrible?"

"I have done nothing, Beth. It's, well, it's my age. It seems I have a strange and inexplicable condition. No, do not look concerned; I am not ill – far from it. Not only am I not ill, I have never been ill, not once in my life. Not a single cough, cold, fever. Nothing. Not as a child, not as an adult. Not in a hundred and four years, Beth."

"A hundred and four years! Giovanni, what are you saying? That you are a hundred and four years old?"

She laughed dismissively. "Giovanni, don't be absurd. Nobody lives that long, and if they did, they would not look youthful as you do. They would look horribly wrinkled! This extreme summer heat must have affected your mind. You are delirious, my dear. Let me fetch you some water."

He put his hand on her arm. "Beth, I am not delirious. What I have told you is true. Since I reached the age of about thirty I simply have not aged. I have maintained perfect health despite having been exposed from time to time to the most fearful of diseases." He paused, seeing she was beginning to look worried. He held her hands tighter and told her about his lives in Naples and San Sepolcro, his two wives and his son. And then he told her about Paola.

He studied Beth's face to see if she seemed to be genuinely believing him or whether she was simply humouring him. He took her hands again.

"Beth, I have only today been told the information about my daughter in Naples and about the annulment. I could not possibly have asked you to marry me if I knew I was still married, even if it were in another lifetime and another city. Now, having heard my tale, I doubt you would want to consider me. But please, dear Beth, if you reject my tale and think me mad, before you go to your father and declare me so, please give me a chance to escape this city."

"Escape this city? I could not possibly allow you to do that! No, Giovanni di Luca – for that is the name I know you by and the name I shall use – you came here this afternoon, I believe, with two intentions in mind. One was to tell me this amazing, unbelievable, incredible tale of your life, a tale that will require some time to absorb. You have told me your tale. I have not rejected it since you seem so earnest, so ... believable. So pray tell me, what was your second intention this afternoon, assuming you were successful in your first?"

She looked at him mischievously, raising her eyebrows in question.

Giovanni stared back at her, hardly daring to believe what he was hearing. Had she really accepted his story?

"Beth, my second intention this afternoon, was to ask if you would possibly consider being my wife. Will you marry me, Beth?"

"Well, knowing my feelings for you, my friends have teased me about the possibility of marrying an older man. Little do they know," she laughed.

She suddenly sat back, withdrawing her hands from him and tilting her head slightly sideways.

"Kind sir, I sincerely accept your proposal. But you shall, of course, have to seek my father's permission."

Giovanni tooks her hands again and pressed them to his lips. "Beth, I am so happy. But, could this —"

"This incredible tale you have told me?" she interrupted. "Could it remain our secret? Of course. It must. No one must know, not even my father. Although I'm not sure that I like the prospect of catching you up in age and then overtaking you. Becoming old while you remain as you are. You might be attracted by another young woman."

"Never, Beth, on my life. As for my staying like this, surely it cannot last. I must start to age soon. I simply don't believe I can carry on like this forever."

"Well, don't start yet, my love, I want our marriage to be a long one."

The following fifteen years were a time of continuing happiness for them both. In 1542, Beth produced a boy, Piero, followed two years later by a girl, Sofia. Both children were healthy, although neither appeared to have Giovanni's 'condition'.

Giovanni called on Vecellio whenever the now famous man was in Venice. Like Piero della Francesca before him, Vecellio's keen artistic eye saw through Giovanni's attempts at disguising his youthfulness. It puzzled him greatly, but unlike Piero, he never discussed it.

In June 1548, two months after Beth had announced that she was pregnant with their third child, Giovanni returned one morning from Vecellio's studio with news of a grand unveiling of his friend's latest masterpiece.

"It was commissioned by that fat and pompous merchant from Rome, Alvise Baldissera. The one who is always trying to ingratiate himself with the cardinal. It was only the size of the purse that persuaded Tiziano to take it on. He cannot stand the man."

At the ceremony two weeks later, Beth and Giovanni were watching in amusement as Tiziano held court to a gaggle of priests when the huge Baldissera waddled up to them, his tiny eyes staring piercingly at Giovanni's from his bloated, porcine features. Ignoring Beth and any niceties, he said,

"Signor di Luca, I believe. Heard all about you. Been meaning to chat. Come with me; something I want to show you."

Giovanni raised his eyebrows in surprise. "I won't be long," he said quietly to Beth.

Baldissera led him to a large room separated from the reception hall by two corridors. On the way, Giovanni noticed the now eighty-year-old Giacomo di Roberti in full flood to a crowd of his attendants. Giovanni caught his eye and waved.

"In here, di Luca," said the still unsmiling Baldissera.

The walls of the room were packed with paintings.

"Something of a collector," said Baldissera, with the sweep of an arm. "Thought you'd like to see my latest purchases."

He waddled to one corner, pointing at two portraits that Giovanni recognised in surprise. They were his own work. He frowned. "These were commissioned by–"

"Conte Ludovico Contarini. I know. Died recently, family eager for money. Sold his collection."

"I didn't know," said Giovanni, glancing around the room uneasily.

"Reminded me of these," said Baldissera, waddling over to the opposite corner.

As he followed, Giovanni's eyes fell on two large portraits mounted at head height. He gasped.

"Recognise them?" said Baldissera, his face a sneer.

But he didn't wait for an answer. "Stefano Crispi, as you well know, Signor di Luca, or should I say, Signor Crispi."

He turned and stood close to Giovanni.

"Couldn't believe it when I saw those other two," he said, sneering. "Just like these. Identical. It had to be you. I'd always wondered where you'd gone."

Giovanni said nothing, his mind racing.

"You don't remember me, do you, Crispi?" continued Baldiserra. "Not surprised. Thirty years ago I was an altar boy in the church in Naples your wife prayed in almost constantly. I was a skinny young lad then. Unrecognisable now. But not you. You're exactly the same. Those eyes are unmistakeable. Well your pact with the Devil has just expired. He can't help you now."

A noise from the door caused Giovanni to turn in panic. Four burly guards had quietly walked in.

"Seize him!" ordered Baldissera. "Take him down the back stairs and bind him. We'll let the cardinal decide on his fate later. But I've no doubt what will happen. Burning is the only way to free his miserable carcass from the Devil!"

# Chapter 9

## June 2009

Claudia was despondent as she walked back to her car from John Andrews' gallery. Through her lack of planning, she had blown it. She flopped into the driver's seat and stared gloomily at the package she was still clutching. The only outcome of her otherwise fruitless journey was a huge dent in her credit card.

She needed somewhere quiet to sit and think. Looking at her map, she decided to go to Thirlmere, a few miles to the north.

For the next three hours she sat by the lake, staring across the water to the dramatic ridge of fells that rose behind it and the 950-metre peak of Helvelyn, a popular spot with hikers in all seasons. However, walking was the furthest thing from Claudia's thoughts. She kept turning over the events of the morning in her mind, wondering how she could have gone about it in a better way. From what she'd seen and experienced of PC Jeff Roberts, she realised that Sally's intervention had probably saved her career. But why had he softened? What had she said that had persuaded him to point her in the right direction?

Checking her watch, she was surprised to find it was five o'clock. She shivered and looked around. Clouds were increasingly disturbing the sky and adding to the lengthening shadows of the hills surrounding her on all sides. A breeze was starting to blow along the lake and the heat was rapidly going out of the day.

Tired and hungry, she couldn't face the long drive back so she decided to find somewhere to spend the night. She'd head home in the morning. She took the road back into Grasmere and driving past the 'Green Man', she saw that as well as claiming itself to be a fine example of an English country pub, it offered 'B&B'. She checked in and had an early dinner in the restaurant next to the bar. After, she sat idly sipping a glass of Sauvignon Blanc and tried to lose herself in a book.

As she got into her car the following morning to head home, her phone pinged to indicate an incoming message. It was from Sally: 'what r visitg hrs in ur prison? xxS'

Claudia smiled and touched Sally's speed dial number. She'd meant to call her the previous evening, but when she'd got back to her room, early though it was, the events of the day had caught up with her and she'd fallen asleep almost immediately she'd lain on the bed. She hadn't even undressed.

"Claw, are you OK? When you didn't call, I imagined Jeff Roberts had locked you up. Didn't strip search you, did he?"

"No, he didn't," laughed Claudia. "I'm fine. I don't know whether to shout at you for spoiling my chances with PC Doe-Eyes or thank you for saving my bacon."

"Saved your bacon whichever way you look at it, given it was a choice between his roving hands or time in the clink. What happened?"

Claudia outlined her meeting with Roberts and then her visit to John Andrews' gallery.

"Got any idea why he might have changed his mind, Sal?" said Claudia, referring to Jeff Roberts. "I mean, he was all ready to send me unceremoniously on my way, for which by then I was grateful enough, when he suddenly asked for the file number."

"No idea. Most unlike him," was the reply. "So this John Andrews doesn't have two heads."

"No, he's just a quiet and seemingly gentle artist. He does have an amazing talent though. I'd be interested to know what Ced thinks about his work."

"Well, why don't you drop by and ask him? He's at home today doing some work on his project. You could call in on your way down. Better still, stay for the weekend. We haven't seen each other for a while. And there's this friend of Ced's you should meet–"

"Sal, I'd love to see you both, but I don't need any more matchmaking. That last bloke you lined me up with was a complete jerk. But yeah, I'll head off now and be down at your place in a couple of hours."

"OK, I'll call Ced and tell him you're coming. He'll have the coffee ready and the Chablis chilled for when I get home." She paused, and then added, "I'm pleased you're all right, Claw. I couldn't stand by and let you jump in with both feet the way you were going to. I love you too much to let you do that. You understand, don't you?"

"I'll forgive you, Sal. Eventually."


Claudia lightly tooted the horn as she pulled into the driveway of Sally and Ced's modern terraced town house on the outskirts of Knutsford. Ced appeared at the door in running shorts and vest, a hand towel round his neck. He loped over to the car, his long legs ready for another sprint, despite having already run ten miles along country lanes at a blistering pace.

"I thought you were supposed to be working," said Claudia leaning back from him, trying to avoid the sweating six-foot-four-inch body that was towering over her diminutive frame.

"Hi, Claw," he grinned. "Yeah, well, I was feeling cooped up so I left a couple of programs to run and got some air. Tell me all about your trip." He grabbed her bag from the back seat and they went into the house.

At thirty-two, Ced Fisher had carved himself an unusual career. Following a first in art history at Cambridge, he had surprised his tutors by registering for a second bachelor's degree, this one in computer studies. Excelling at this, he'd gone on to complete a one-year masters in image analysis and programming and then joined Forefront Forensics. Once he'd learned the basics of forensic science, he focused his skills on developing programs for analysing paintings for evidence of forgery. It was a smart move: while many large galleries and auction houses had their experts, the non-subjective approach to image analysis that Ced's work offered was becoming increasingly valued in the art world. It wouldn't be long before all insurance companies would require a computer-based assessment of art works as part of their background analysis before determining premiums on art works – the world was simply too full of forgeries.

Ced's spare time was spent on a research project on the computer analysis of paintings to identify the styles of artists. His art history studies had made him very familiar with the techniques of the old masters from the thirteenth century onwards. He was fascinated by the communal approach that had been used in the studios, the use of apprentices still honing their skills to undertake the routine parts of a painting – the backgrounds, parts of the clothing, shoes. It depended on the whim of the artist, but it was known that for many paintings, large parts were not painted by the master himself. He would have concentrated more on the most important areas: the face or faces, the pose, the use of light, the hair. The old masters, Ced knew, were like film directors. They controlled all the steps of production of a masterpiece and determined the final form of their work, using their brilliance to fine tune all the way. However, the number of hands contributing to the production of a painting could be many. Ced's passion was to develop his image analysis program to identify and distinguish those different hands. Did some of them later become masters in their own right? How had their techniques changed, evolved and matured? Could the innate style of an artist seen in his early work still be seen at the end of his career, even though it may appear to have changed profoundly?

In the world of art forgery, the more highly skilled artists could change their technique to mimic that of the original artist. Such was their brilliance at doing this that experts relying on visual examination had often been fooled into attributing a work to a major artist when in reality it was a copy. Ced was impressed with the amazing skill of a forger to analyse a painting and adapt his hand – the ability to make instinctively the sort of assessments that took his program untold millions of complex operations to achieve. His goal was to fine-tune his image analysis software to see through a forger's mimicry and detect the man's hand: his style signature.

"Coffee, Claw?"

"I'll make it, Ced. You go and shower and return your body to some sort of acceptable human condition." Claudia shooed Ced from the kitchen while holding her nose.

"Hey, it's not that bad. I think Sal finds it rather sexy."

"Yes, well, I'm not Sal. She's never happier than when she's pumping iron and pouring with sweat." Sally had met Ced when she joined Forefront Forensics and found they had a common interest in triathlons.

Ced loped off to the shower while Claudia organised coffee, rolls, butter and marmalade, all organic since Sally's arrival into Ced's life.

Ten minutes later, Ced returned looking fresh, wearing tracksuit bottoms and a T-shirt that would have reached Claudia's ankles. He tucked into the rolls like a man possessed.

"Hungry, were you?" said Claudia, after a couple of minutes.

"Ravenous, Claw," replied Ced through a mouthful, missing her sarcasm.

Ced wiped his mouth on a paper napkin. "Sal told me what you were up to, in strict confidence, of course. You worried her, Claw. Me too. You were really sticking your neck out, what with the confidentiality of the database and all that."

"Yes, I know, but please don't give me another lecture. I had a hard enough time from the PC in Ambleside yesterday."

"It was lucky that Sal knew him and could get him to cut you off at the pass."

"Yes, it was odd really. He was all for sending me off with a stern warning when he suddenly softened and gave me a bit of information that helped me track down the person I was looking for."

"He didn't give you his name, then?"

"No, but what he told me was enough to locate him, with a bit of detective work of my own."

"And this guy with the rare DNA? Sal said he's an artist. Sounds interesting. Is he any good?"

"Good? I think he's brilliant. I know I'm no expert, but I found his work breathtaking."

"What's his name?"

"Andrews. John Andrews."

Ced rubbed his chin. "John Andrews. Yeah, I've heard the name. Landscapes, I think, mainly of the Lake District. Don't think I've ever seen his work, but these little specialist cliques do appear at exhibitions and auctions from time to time. They normally produce fairly standard views that appeal to the masses."

"Don't be such a snob, Ced. He could be a Turner or a Constable waiting to be discovered. And he doesn't only do landscapes; his portraits are amazing. In fact, I was so taken that I bought one."

"You bought one!" Ced's eyebrows shot up. "How much did you pay? You should have talked to me about it first. These guys normally overcharge, you know."

"Well, it wasn't cheap, but I was very taken. It reminded me of my Gran. It's really beautiful. Quite small. Do you want to see it? It's in the car. I'll go and fetch it."

"Yeah, I'd like to. If it's a load of derivative rubbish, we'll take it back and demand a refund."

"We certainly won't! Just because you're an art snob doesn't mean we mere mortals can't enjoy a work we really like, derivative or not."

"I absolutely agree, with the personal taste thing, I mean, not with me being an art snob." Ced pretended to look offended. "But liking it is one thing, paying over the odds is another."

"I didn't pay over the odds. I thought eight hundred quid was a good price, especially compared with some of the prices there."

"You paid eight hundred! Christ, Claw, have you won the lottery? That's a lot for a miniature from some unknown artist."

"It's not a miniature and he gave me a good discount. It was marked up at a thousand. And you said that you've heard of him, so he's not unknown."

"Claw, I've heard of an awful lot of the artists working in this country. I don't necessarily know their work, but I know their names. So the fact I know the name 'John Andrews' doesn't mean that he's anything special. Why don't you get the painting?"

Claudia got up and went to the door. "Not sure that I want to show you now; you'll only rubbish it." She pouted at him, turned and walked towards the front door.

"You'll get an objective opinion, Claw, that's all," he called after her, clearing away the coffee mugs and plates.

As Claudia came back into the room, Ced sat down on the sofa and rubbed his hands. "OK, let's have a look at this masterpiece."

She handed it to him without a word and watched while he pulled at the knot and removed the string. Taking it from the wrapping, he held it up so that it caught the full light from the window behind him. He frowned, tilted it, put it close to his eyes to look at the fine detail and then held it at arm's length. He pursed his lips as if he was going to speak, but didn't – he merely continued to study it, his eyes darting around every detail.

Finally, Claudia couldn't wait any longer. "Ced, speak to me. If you really think it's a load of rubbish, say so!"

Ced still didn't speak for a moment, but when he did, he slowly raised his eyes to her and whispered, "Load of rubbish?"

Claudia missed the questioning tone. "I thought that's what you'd say. Well, I like it!"

She made to snatch the painting back from him, but he moved it to one side.

"Hey, careful, Claw, you don't want to damage it."

"What does it matter to you? You think it's rubbish." Claudia was beginning to get upset with him.

"I didn't say that, Claw, I was questioning what you'd said, not agreeing with you." He paused. "This portrait, Claw, is one of the most stunning of its type that I've ever seen. It's really quite remarkable. The skill, the mastery that has gone into this is extraordinary. This man has a real talent, a gift. I'm amazed that he isn't more well known, amazed that he's working away quietly up there in the Lakes and that people aren't beating a path to his door."

Claudia looked at him suspiciously. "You're having me on, right? You don't mean all that; you're winding me up. Christ, Ced, tell me what you really think!"

Ced looked adoringly at the painting and then he turned his head to Claudia. "I swear to God, Claw, I'm not taking the piss. I mean it; this work is amazing. Can't you see it – the subtlety of these tones, the delicacy of the skin? The technique he's used is like that of the old masters. A lot of people try it, you know, but only a few succeed. I'd bet he could copy anything. I'd love to see his landscapes."

"Why do you assume that because he's a good artist, he's going to be a crook, forging other people's work?" Claudia was indignant.

"Coz that's where the easy money is these days, Claw. It's really difficult to make serious bucks as an artist in your own right."

"Well, some make it. Look at Hockney! Look at Hurst!"

"Yeah, but for every Hockney and Hurst, there are hundreds, no, thousands, who are probably as talented, possibly more talented, who never get more than a pittance for their work."

"I've just remembered something," interrupted Claudia.

Ced looked up at her.

"You can look at his landscapes, or at least a few. I snapped some on my iPhone. Probably another reason he doesn't like me; his daughter caught me in the act. I don't know if she realised, but if she did, I expect she's told him."

"I doubt it's the first time it's happened, Claw. Let's have a look."

Claudia took her phone from her bag and called up the photos.

"Here, they've come out quite well. There are, um six, no seven." She passed the phone to him. "You swipe the screen, like this–"

"I know how it works, Claw."

Ced looked quickly through the images and then again more slowly.

"Would you mind if I downloaded these onto the computer? The resolution of photos on this model is only 2 Meg, which isn't brilliant, but we should be able to see more on a bigger screen."

"Go ahead. Oh, I haven't got the cables with me."

"Not a problem," said Ced, heading off to the study to connect the iPhone to his computer.

Two minutes later they were looking at the twenty-seven inch screen of Ced's iMac. He enlarged the photos to their limit, enhanced them and then sat back to take a look. Claudia looked from Ced to the screen and back again, expecting a comment or two, but all she heard were a few 'mmms' and grunts.

Finally, Ced rubbed the back of his neck and sighed.

"Amazing, Claw, quite amazing. It's not so easy to see the detail on these photos; I'd need to see the real thing, but even from these, it's clear that this man's talent isn't only in his portraits. I'm sorry if I was dismissive earlier. It's just that you see a lot of mediocrity, especially on sale to tourists. But this stuff. Wow! The style is really interesting. There's a huge number of influences, from Renaissance art onwards, you can see it in here." He pointed at one of the images. "Where there are figures, the attention to detail is there like it is in the portrait. But the overall style of these is quite modern, the last century anyway. The style reminds me of someone I've seen, but I can't quite place it."

106

"So you think I haven't wasted my money?"

"On the contrary, Claw," replied Ced, missing the mockery again, "I reckon you've quite an eye. Listen, tell me about this guy's DNA. Is it really super rare?"

"Yes, Ced, it is. This man is his own collection of unique alleles. He shouldn't exist. That's why I was so excited about wanting to follow it up. It's a real shame that he doesn't want to play. Odd really, don't you think? I mean, if I came to you and told you that quite by chance I'd examined your DNA profile and found it to be very different from anything that's ever been seen before, wouldn't you jump at the chance to find out more? I mean, who knows what further research might lead to?"

"Course I would, Claw, but I'm a scientist, of sorts. This chap's an artist and they tend to have no interest in science. I can understand where he's coming from. I mean, he's probably very embarrassed about the fact that the police took his sample in the first place. And to be frank, it doesn't sound like you gave him a great sales pitch."

"No, I could kick myself. I could've explained it so much better."

"Interesting that he's got this rare profile and that he's also a very talented artist. Reckon there's a connection?" mused Ced.

"Who knows?" replied Claudia. "Perhaps I should follow it up. Test a few artists. You haven't got a sample of Michelangelo's saliva secreted away somewhere, have you?"

"There's a whole rack of his swabs in the freezer. Seriously, Claw, there could be a future in looking at some of these old paintings. They must have handled them a lot – they'd have their DNA all over them."

"Theirs and a million other people's," shrugged Claudia, "I think we'd better establish a stronger link before we start taking swabs from old masters."

They heard the front door slam. "Hi guys!"

Sally burst into the room and gave Claudia a huge hug. "I took the afternoon off. Didn't reckon I should leave you two together with Ced showing you his etchings. You look great, hon, considering you've been through the mill with our friend PC Roberts."

"Oh, he's a pussy cat really," said Claudia dismissively.

"Yeah, right. One with sharp claws."

"Wanted to get his claws into Claw, did he?" said Ced, laughing at his own joke until he saw the withering look the two girls gave him.

He looked back at Claudia's painting.

"Claw," he said. "I was wondering. I know you've only just bought this, but before you give it pride of place in your cottage, would you mind if I ran it through my latest imaging routines? All nondestructive, I promise. I'd need to take it to the lab, but it would only be for a week or so."

"You put one mark on it or damage it in any way and I'll feed that six-foot-four frame through the mincer, Ced Fisher. Understand?"

"Deal," said Ced, picking up the portrait and staring at it again. "Look at this, Sal."

"You bought a painting, Claw?"

"Yes, a John Andrews."

"A John Andrews, huh," said Sally, taking the portrait from Ced. "Wow, even I, with the artistic appreciation of a prune, can see that this is really something. It's beautiful, Claw. I didn't know you were into art."

"It's the first piece in what one day will be my extensive collection," said Claudia, with mock haughtiness. "Actually, I wanted to keep him talking because he was trying to kick me out of the gallery. Fortunately his family came in and his wife gave me a sales pitch. I'm glad she did, even though I'll be surviving on bread and water for a few months to pay for it. I'm thrilled with it."

Ced announced that he wanted to study the portrait a bit more and to see if he could find anything about John Andrews' work online. "I'll leave you two to natter and then we could go down the pub for a late lunch."

"Great idea, hon," said Sally, reaching over to peck him on the cheek.

Back in the living room, Sally sat down with Claudia.

"Look Claw, I want to explain again about me interfering. I know you told me not to talk to Jeff Roberts but after you called, I got really worried about you just turning up there and trying to appeal to his better nature. Apart from the fact I don't think he's got one, I thought there was a great chance that he'd arrest you on the spot. So

I called him. I told him what you were after and how important it was to you and the pursuit of knowledge etc, but he didn't really listen. All he heard was that you wanted to break the confidentiality of the database. I didn't think it was worth pulling the threatening to tell his wife trick so I tried a different tack. I told him that in my heart I didn't want you to go ahead with it coz I was so worried about the possible consequences. I turned a bit soft on him, muttered a bit about what a good time we'd had and said that what I really wanted was for him to stop you before you got in too deep. Ced doesn't know all of this, of course, even though what happened was before his time. Anyway, that seemed to appeal to his control freak nature and he agreed that if you turned up, he'd read you the Riot Act and send you on your way. Fortunately, you called to tell me when you were going."

Claudia nodded ruefully. "Yes, well, he certainly read me the Riot Act and all its appendices and annexes. One thing that really puzzles me though, as I said on the phone, is why he softened?"

"What did you say to him?"

"I can't remember exactly, but I mentioned genetic diseases and that there was always a possibility that these alleles could have some significance."

"I see," Sally nodded. "That could explain it."

"What do you mean?"

"As it happens, there was a PC in from Carlisle this morning delivering exhibits. I was chatting to him about his case and then we got talking, you know, about people we knew and so on. I casually mentioned that I'd met Jeff when he'd been on a course in Chorley some years ago and the PC gave me a real knowing look. Anyway, he then said that Jeff was a really nice guy at heart and that he was worried about his son."

"What's wrong with him?"

"It seems that there's Huntington's disease in his wife's family and that his son might have inherited the gene."

"That doesn't mean that he'll automatically get the disease."

"I know, but there's a chance. It seems he only found out recently and they haven't finished all the tests. You know what the NHS is like. So when you mentioned genetic research, maybe he thought that it could help."

"Christ, I wouldn't want to get his hopes up."

"Of course not, but if these alleles do have some significance, then it's not beyond the bounds of possibility that it could help PC Roberts' problem. Anyway, you didn't mislead him; he made that decision off his own bat."

Claudia looked glum. "Well, whatever it was, it hasn't worked because John Andrews isn't playing ball. So that's the end of it."

Although she understood her friend's frustration, Sally was sure that this was the right outcome. The risks to Claudia's career had been too great – both PC Roberts and John Andrews had been quick to bring up the possibility of reporting her. It was only luck that Andrews had chosen not to. Or so she thought.

# Chapter 10

## 1548

"**D**i Luca! Been looking for you everywhere!"

Giacomo di Roberti bellowed down the corridor as Giovanni was being hurriedly escorted from Baldiserra's gallery by the four guards. Everyone stopped, the guards confused by the unexpected interruption from this important man. Giovanni turned to di Roberti and saw the man's ancient eyes hurriedly assessing the situation.

Di Roberti took a step towards them. "I thought I'd… arghh!"

He stopped, clutching his chest. "God! What's happening?"

He sank to his knees and rolled onto the floor, his legs kicking and his arms thrashing with the agony of the sudden pain. There was a scream from behind him as his entourage caught up and rushed to his aid.

Giovanni made to run to his friend but the two guards holding his arms stopped him.

He turned angrily to them. "For God's sake, Signor di Roberti is one of the most important men in the city. He needs help!" He shrugged their arms away and pointed at them. "Don't just stand there! Run! Fetch a physician or you will be held responsible for his death. Go!"

The two guards turned to Baldiserra who waved at them to do as they were told. His eyes burned into Giovanni's as he called the two remaining guards over to him. Giovanni ignored them and ran to di Roberti's side.

"Stand back! Give him some air!" he yelled at the confusion of hands grasping at their master. He leaned over di Roberti and cried urgently. "Giacomo! Giacomo! Lie still. Help is coming."

Di Roberti groaned and thrashed his arms around some more. "Air," he gasped. "Arrgh!"

He grasped his chest again as Giovanni waved his own arms to move the entourage further way. Turning back to di Roberti, he gently cradled the man's head.

"Giacomo," he whispered, his voice breaking with emotion.

Di Roberti slowly opened his eyes, took a sly look around and then focussed on Giovanni and winked.

"I don't know what that zealot Baldiserra is up to, but I can see you are in danger," he whispered, his hand rising to pull Giovanni's head closer to his mouth. "You must get out of the city now. Fetch Augusto, my attendant. I'll instruct him. And get those two guards to carry me somewhere. Anywhere. But go. Now!"

Di Roberti's head sagged back and he let out a huge scream of apparent pain. Giovanni was stunned into a moment's inaction, but then felt di Robert's hand push at him. He turned to the remaining two guards.

"You two! Come here. Carry Signor di Roberti to a bedroom. Signor Baldiserra, please, guide them. He needs more comfort than this hard floor."

The guards rushed over and attempted to pick up the enormous di Roberti. Four of the entourage came forward to help them and together they carried off their still writhing burden, a fuming Baldiserra leading the way.

Giovanni beckoned Augusto, who was following di Roberti. "Go to your master," he whispered. "He needs to speak to you urgently."

Augusto proved remarkably efficient, arriving at Giovanni and Beth's house only a few minutes after they did.

"There is no time to lose, signore. My master says we must leave immediately. Fetch your children and follow me. All arrangements for your belongings will be made later."

An hour later, having crossed the lagoon and climbed into a waiting coach, they were racing across the countryside away from Venice.

112

Two weeks later, an increasingly frustrated Giovanni was pacing the grounds of a substantial villa set in the foothills of the mountains north of Verona, one of several retreats that di Roberti kept very secret from his friends and associates in Venice. Augusto and the staff of the villa had provided Giovanni and Beth with every comfort, while at the same time insisting they remain within the grounds.

"We are effectively imprisoned here, Beth," grumbled Giovanni for the tenth time that day. "We have no news from Venice. Nothing. For all we know, Baldiserra might come charging through those gates at any moment."

"Augusto has assured us that this house is secret, Giovanni," replied Beth, trying as ever to calm her husband. "No one in Venice knows about it."

"There must be some who know. And while there are some, we are not safe. I do not want to put you and the children at risk. We should be far away from here."

Just then they heard the sound of hooves thundering along the track below them, the only path up to the house. As the hooves got closer, the galloping was overlaid by the grinding of a coach's wheels spinning and complaining along the rough terrain. Five minutes later, the gates opened and a coach and four horses burst onto the drive.

As the coach pulled up in front of the house, there was a bellow from inside it.

"Augusto, where are you! This old man needs an arm. Two; more; as many as you can spare!" The guffaw that followed meant the coach's occupant could only be di Roberti himself.

Giovanni rushed up and opened the door.

"Di Luca!" bellowed di Roberti. "Help me out of here. My insides have been shaken to pieces. And there's plenty of them to shake." He roared with laughter again as Giovanni eased him through the coach's door and guided him into the villa.

Later, after a substantial dinner, di Roberti dismissed the servants and called Augusto to bring him his document case.

"Giacomo," began Giovanni, "I–"

"Stop thanking me, man. It's getting tedious," roared di Roberti. "You've been a wonderful friend these past thirty years. Kept me alive, wondering what your next masterpiece is going to be like. Glad to be able to help."

His eyes fixed on Giovanni's, his expression uncharacteristically serious.

"I've always known there is something different about you, di Luca, something very special."

Giovanni started to speak, but di Roberti held up a huge hand.

"No, don't even try to explain, I could never understand it, and anyway, there are some things that should remain unexplained. I only know that your life is in danger from the zealots who hound you. But unlike them, I have known you for many years and I know you are a good man without an evil bone in you. When I heard that Baldiserra was making enquiries about you, I made enquiries about him. When I discovered he was from Naples, I put two and two together and got a mystery."

He paused to laugh loudly, irrepressible as ever.

"Didn't know when he was going to act, but he was behaving very strangely that evening of the reception for Da Cadore. Caused me all sorts of palpitations."

He guffawed again, clutching his chest theatrically.

"No matter. You need to move on and I have, on your behalf, made some arrangements. You do not have to accept them, but I think they will be to your liking. Now, that property of yours in Venice. I should like to acquire it for one of my grandchildren. Getting married soon. So I'll buy it from you. As it happens, I have a place, rather like this one, in Arezzo. Picked it up years ago. Don't need it, so what I propose is that you move there. Take over the ownership in return for the Venice house. The notary can sort out all the details. What do you think, Signor Perini?"

"Signor Perini?" frowned Giovanni. "I don't understand. Who is Signor Perini?"

"Why, you are, my friend. Tommaso Perini. Can't keep your present name, any of you. So I've created a new one for you. Got all the papers. Lot of opportunity in Arezzo for a talented artist. Not been one there for over a hundred years, unless you like Vasari's stuff. No, there's been no real talent since Piero della Francesca walked that town's streets."

Giovanni smiled. "Yes, you are right." He paused. "I knew h–"

"No, di Luca." Di Roberti held up a hand. "I told you, I don't want to know. Too much for my ancient brain to understand."

By the time the ebullient di Roberti died ten years later at the age of ninety, his creation, Tommaso Perini, and the Perini family were well established in Arezzo, the young artist attracting many clients from the town's merchant and noble classes. Tommaso and di Roberti met up at the villa outside Verona on a number of occasions during those years, when Tommaso was pleased to revert to being Giovanni di Luca for a few days. Di Roberti stubbornly refused to discuss anything about the past of the young man who shared his company, the young man he knew to be at least sixty-eight.

Tommaso waited until his three children were adults before telling them about himself. When he did, with Beth's agreement and support, their overriding concern was for their half-sister Paola in Naples. Tommaso had sent several agents to check on her over the years and he was satisfied her mother, Francesca, was not hounding her. As the first agent he'd sent in 1530 had predicted, she had grown into a beautiful woman and she had married well. She had only one child, a son, whom the various agents reported had been sickly as a boy but who later grew to be fit and strong. Then an agent sent soon after Beth died in 1580 returned with distastrous news. Aged sixty-two, the youthful-looking Paola had come to the attention of the Church, ancient priests among its ranks remembering her devil-worshipping father. Paola was interrogated and it was only with the quick thinking of her son that she managed to escape Naples. No trace of her could be found and enquiries from more agents sent by Tommaso were treated with hostility and suspicion.

After Beth's death, Tommaso became the itinerant artist he had determined not to be in his San Sepolcro days. However, there was a difference: every move from one town to another included a change of name and the need to re-establish himself. Moving on frequently, he was restless for many years, his only real comfort coming from visits to his children: Piero, a now highly successful artist in Rome; Sofia, the wife of a Florentine consul to Venice; and Gianna, married to a notary in Florence.

Piero died young, a victim of cholera, while Sofia lived until she was over seventy. Gianna, always a favourite, lived well beyond her husband and always delighted in her father's visits. Her final moments were a strange scene that no outsider could possibly have understood. A frail, eighty-year-old woman took the hand of a man who was seemingly in his thirties and looked lovingly into his eyes.

"Babbo," she whispered hoarsely. "Babbo, I don't want to leave you but I feel it's time. Promise me, Babbo, promise me that you will try to find my sister. Try to find Paola."

"I promise, my dear, darling daughter."

He continued to search, but there was nothing. By the time he left Italy for France in the mid-1630s, Paola would have been a hundred and seventeen. Her trail had been cold for fifty years.

# Chapter 11

## June 2009

"**H**i, Claw, it's Ced."

"Ced, I thought you'd never call. It's been ten days since you hijacked my painting. How are the tests going?"

"Been busy, Claw. But I've just finished working on it and the results are really interesting. This guy's got more than just talent, he's bloody incredible."

Claudia chewed her bottom lip in delight, her eyes sparkling.

"Wow, that's praise indeed coming from you. How's my painting? Not suffered too much from the slings and arrows of outrageous x-rays?"

"I'm not using x-rays, Claw! Just a few scalpels and a wire brush. But, yeah, it's stood up pretty well, really. No major damage. Nothing a good restorer can't fix anyway."

"What! Ced, you promised nothing would happen to it!"

"Come on, Claw, don't be daft. I've treated it like a baby. Now listen, I think the easiest way to show you all this stuff is for you to come here. Friday's a holiday, so why don't you come up Thursday evening and stay for the weekend? I can explain it all to you, and we'd have the added bonus of seeing you again. How does that sound?"

"Brilliant, I can't wait! I'd come now if I could. But, Ced, as much as I'd like to, I can't stay the whole weekend; I've promised Mum and Dad that I'd visit them. They're off on a Caribbean cruise soon and they want to see me before they go. Gosh, Ced, I'm desperate to hear what you've found."

The following Thursday evening, after a frustratingly slow journey up a rush-hour-congested M6 motorway in pouring rain, Claudia turned into the driveway of Sally and Ced's house. Five minutes earlier, the sun had pushed a few teasing rays through the clouds, offering the prospect of a dry summer's evening. Claudia didn't care if it snowed.

She pushed open the front door, which Ced had left on the latch, and called him.

"Hi Claw," he yelled back from his study. "Just setting up the link to the lab. Almost done. Pour yourself a drink and come up."

Claudia dropped her overnight bag on the living room floor and went into the kitchen. She took a glass from a rack over the breakfast bar and poured herself some wine from a bottle sitting in an ice bucket on the counter top.

"Can I get you one?" she called.

"I've already got one, thanks. Can you bring that large book that's sitting on the coffee table?"

Claudia looked into the living room and saw a substantial art book resting among some others on the glass surface of the chrome-framed table: 'The Works of Piero della Francesca'. She picked it up, nearly dropping her wine glass in the process, and headed upstairs.

Ced was tapping on his keyboard as she entered the room. He hit the return key with a flourish and sat back to look at the screen of the large monitor. "Bingo!"

He stood up, waited for Claudia to put down the book and her wine, and gave her a hug. "Hiya. Good trip?"

"If you enjoy pelting rain, nose-to-tail traffic and huge lorries slinging oceans of water at you, then yes; it was great!"

Claudia's eyes were riveted on a high-resolution image of her portrait on the screen. After a few moments, she shifted her gaze to Ced's eyes.

"Well! What are you waiting for? Explain, please."

He grinned at her mischievously, "Actually, Claw, I'm a bit tired really. Had a knackering run this morning. Could we wait until tomorrow?"

She punched him on the upper arm. "Get moving, buster!"

"OK," he said, running his hands over the keyboard. "This is a super-hi-res image of your painting."

He clicked on it a few times with the mouse to enlarge a tiny section below the left eye.

"First thing that's really interesting, as I mentioned before, is that this guy has quite a mixture of styles. Here, on the cheeks and around the eyes, there's an amazing delicacy. He has built up the layers very slowly which give a translucency that most artists these days simply don't have the patience for. With oils, he would have to wait at least a day, often several, between each application of the paint to let it dry, sometimes applying a very small amount on a given day. The early masters like Leonardo, Raphael, Titian, etc., were brilliant at this. Andrews has got it down to a T. Look, I've got some details of a few well-known works from that time to compare."

He clicked a few times on the keyboard and some smaller images showing close-up of face detail appeared. He pointed at them to emphasise the similarities.

"But for other parts of the painting, it's more like he's moved into the seventeenth century to give depth to areas that the Renaissance lot didn't bother with. Parts of the hair and the background are very Rembrandt-like. Not so much in the use of colour, but the brushwork. You'd think it would end up looking like a patchwork but he's so competent that it really works."

Claudia moved in closer to look at the screen. "Is it similar overall to any works from those early periods?"

Ced paused. "Yes and no. I mean, there are thousands of paintings that use this pose. It's fairly standard because it works. The trick is bringing it to life which he does incredibly well. Those eyes are captivating; there's a superb sparkle to them without using any cheap tricks. It's really got a dynamism about it."

"So what are you saying about Andrews?"

Ced scratched his head absently. "Well, you know that a major part of my work is checking out paintings to see if they are genuine. There are loads of painters out there who can knock up a quick Constable or Rembrandt or whatever and many are very good at it. Almost all of these guys are totally above board and don't try to hide the fact that they are copying an old master. People pay good money for a known copy because having a proper painting hanging on your wall is more satisfying than having a print. While they can switch styles and easily fool the untrained eye, it's not that difficult to differentiate them from the real thing. Whatever, it's a legitimate market and everybody's happy. What interests me, and the people who send me work, is when an artist's making copies for fraudulent purposes. Perhaps it might be to fool a collector into thinking he's bought something rare and valuable. There are rich people out there with a passion to own a masterpiece that they can guard jealously, possibly never showing it to anyone. It's the power, if you like, of being able to own, say, a Picasso, or preferably something much older. These are the guys who the crooks will try to prey on. They will appeal to their greed, run a long, slow con to build up trust and then sell them a fake for a huge sum. Obviously these crooks need access to accomplished artists who can deliver."

Claudia looked horrified. "You're not saying that John Andrews is doing this sort of thing, are you?"

"No, of course not. But part of what I'm doing is looking at paintings that are known to be modern forgeries and trying to cut through the style mimicry to get to the real, innate style of the artist. Some of these guys are so good that it's incredibly hard. There have been many so-called experts over the years who have been fooled by good forgers. And most of the buyers themselves aren't dummies; they know their stuff. So to fool them and the rest of the art world, a forger has to be very good. What I'm doing is accumulating data on the styles used in known forgeries, focusing on the occasional slip-up by the forger that gives him away, and developing programs that will do the analyses automatically. It's very subtle stuff. Looking at this portrait by John Andrews, what I'm saying is that if he wanted to be in the business of art forgery, he would be very good at it. I think he could mimic almost any style. So he's an interesting find."

Claudia continued her defence. "But just because he's a brilliant artist doesn't mean he's a crook!"

"Of course it doesn't. I'm merely saying that if he wanted to be, he could be. It's certainly good to know about him and, assuming he is legit, he could turn out to be a very valuable source of advice. I really want to meet him."

"I hope you have more success than I did."

Claudia stood back and her eye fell on the large book she'd

brought upstairs. She pointed at it. "How does that fit in with your analysis?"

"Well, as you know, Piero is a particular favourite of mine. His forte was fresco painting which interestingly didn't really suit his style because he was a slow worker. You see, for frescos you get one shot at applying the paint to the section of the plaster you're working on before it dries. He was, apparently, often experimenting with ways of slowing down the drying process."

Claudia had started to leaf through the large book on Piero as Ced was talking. "I'd never really heard of him before you mentioned his name. Some of these paintings are very powerful, don't you think?"

"I agree; they're amazing. It's interesting: for centuries after his death he was largely ignored and only really came back into prominence about a hundred years ago. These days, if you go to Tuscany, you'll see his name everywhere. They're really cashing in on it.

"Anyway, I was talking about his style. Even though his works are in a very different medium from this portrait by John Andrews, who's using modern, manufactured oils, the influence on Andrews is there. It's almost as if Andrews is applying the oil in a tempera-like way. Your painting is of an elderly woman and we don't have direct examples from Piero of the same subject matter. But you can see similarities in the expressions in some of the female figures in Piero's work. Andrews must have studied him in great depth and tried to emulate his style."

Claudia had paused to look at a large print in the book of the painting: 'The Resurrection.'

"The eyes in this figure of Christ – I assume that's who it is – are mesmerising. They seem to be staring straight through you."

"Absolutely. The central figure is Christ who has just emerged from the tomb. It's quite a political painting when you look at all the symbolism but what it's also famous for is that one of the figures at the bottom, the one to Christ's right with his back to the tomb, is thought to be a self-portrait of Piero."

Claudia looked at the face. "Strong features. He looks like he was a powerfully built man. He could have been a triathlete like you."

"I don't think they were really into physical fitness. And sadly for them, the bicycle hadn't been invented. Or running shoes."

Claudia turned a few pages of the book. "Presumably, the artists would have used models for all these paintings."

"Without question," nodded Ced. "They did it all the time. They used friends, family members, anyone willing to pose. I reckon the female figure Piero used in his famous Madonna del Parto, the so-called pregnant Madonna where she looks about to pop, has the same face as women in a number of other paintings he produced. Could have been his wife, or mistress, I suppose."

He looked down at the painting Claudia had turned to. "That's a fascinating painting. It's a fresco called 'The Awakening' and was only discovered relatively recently in an obscure church in the Tuscan hills. It had been plastered over, but fortunately with a plaster that didn't wreck the painting underneath. Caused quite a stir in the art world when it was attributed to Piero. It's an allegorical painting set in the fifteenth century, but it really depicts Christ counselling some of his disciples. I've examined it in some detail and tried to do a comparison between the faces in it with those in the Resurrection. I reckon Piero's there again in the figure of this one: St. Paul. Bit cheeky really, putting his own face on a saint."

He noticed Claudia's hand was resting on another part of the picture with her fingers pointing at one of the shepherds, a background figure but, nevertheless, quite a large one that was painted in great detail.

"No, not that one, Claw, he's a shepherd. I mean this one, on the left."

She ignored him and masked the figure's hair with her finger.

"Do you have a hi-res image of this painting, Ced?" she asked quietly.

"Um, yes, I should have. It'll be in the library file in the lab. Hang on a sec."

He hit a few keys and the image appeared.

"Could you zoom in on the figure of the shepherd?"

Ced looked puzzled. "Sure, if you like."

He hit some more keys and the face of the shepherd filled the screen. Claudia stared at it, her mouth open.

"Can you … could you … um, can you isolate the face, so that the hair isn't so dominant?"

"Easy." Another few keys were pressed. "There. Wow! It's very detailed for a minor figure. I hadn't really taken much notice of it before."

There was a bump as Claudia sat down hard in the chair she'd been standing in front of.

"You all right, Claw? You look pale."

"Ced," Claudia gasped in a whisper, staring at the face on the screen. "Ced, it's him. Look at the eyes."

Ced looked in puzzlement at the image. "Who?"

"It's John Andrews. I know it can't be, but it's him!"

# Chapter 12

## 1677

Gisèle Prideaux slipped silently through the door in the high garden wall into the pitch darkness of the alley. She strained her ears for any sound, but all she could hear was her heart pounding. She pulled her cloak tightly around her and crept slowly towards the street. She paused. Before stepping into the light from the torches burning high on the walls, she touched the hilt of the knife in her belt. Reassured by its presence, she hurried along the street and darted down another alley. The streets were the dangerous parts, places she might be spotted by one of the squads of militia still searching Marseille four nights after the killings. Searching for her and the three men.

She was about to break cover to cross the next street when a sixth sense stopped her. She held her breath and listened. Two militiamen were heading in her direction. She pressed back into a doorway, forcing herself to breathe slowly and silently. The men were complaining noisily about the extra hours they had been ordered to spend patrolling.

"What's the point? Those murdering scum will be long gone. Steal some horses and head inland to the hills, that's what they'll've done. Only a fool would stay. It's not as if we don't know who they are. One step from their hidey holes and we'd have 'em."

"Me," said the other, "I hope they're still around. I'd like to catch that Prideaux girl lurkin' in some dark alley. I'd enjoy forcing her to confess."

He laughed lewdly and thrust his pelvis forward a few times.

"Mind, if we catch her, we'd better get our fill of her first before we turn her in. Once the officers get hold of her, she'll be passed around their mess for days before she's given back. She'll just be a lump of battered meat by then."

Gisèle shuddered. But the militiamen's talk encouraged her. If they were still searching, they hadn't caught Henri, Michel or their father, Philippe, since they too had left the house. She waited until they'd gone and ran to the last alley.

She stopped in the shadows near the far end and forced herself to relax. She didn't hear him approach and she jumped as he whispered close to her ear.

"Gisèle!"

"Henri," she sighed in relief, leaning back onto him. "Any sign of him?"

"No. The bells have yet to ring."

"The others?"

"Safe. They're where we agreed and waiting for your performance."

She smiled grimly to herself. Turning in the darkness, she caught a glint from his pale grey eyes. "Can you hear my heart thumping? You must be able to."

"Not over the noise of mine."

She'd found the man, Louis Brochard, the previous day and followed him. She had wanted to kill him there and then but Philippe had forbidden it. Now it was time.

The cathedral bells chimed and Henri felt Gisèle tense as he held her shoulders. She removed her cloak and undid the tie at the top of her blouse, slipping the short sleeves down over her shoulders.

"I'm ready," she said.

He turned his head towards her. "It's time, cherie. For God's sake be careful."

"I'm not sure God would look kindly on us tonight, Henri." She kissed him once, hard on the lips, and was gone into the street.

A door slammed and she heard the man spit noisily into the gutter. A shudder went through her and she wondered if she could go through with it. Then she thought of Arlette. She crossed herself and leaned back against the wall. She was only a few feet away from the alley where Michel and Philippe stood in wait, but it seemed like a mile. She raised one knee and pressed her foot against the wall, hitching up her skirt to show her thigh. She pulled her blouse down a little more and turned her head downwards, casting a shadow over her face in case he recognised her.

She tried to say something to attract his attention, something coarse she knew a whore would say, but her throat had frozen in fear. She needn't have worried – the man had seen her and was now strutting towards her with a leer on his sweaty face.

"Well, wot have we here? You're new, ain'tcha darlin'? Not seen your pretty little face around here before."

He was very close and she could smell his foul breath as he leaned over her. She thought she was going to vomit.

"I'll give yer two, since you're a nice fresh little piece." He grasped one of her breasts. "Yeah, very nice and fresh."

She pushed his hand away. "Keep yer hands to yerself, mister, until I seen yer money. And it'll be five. I got me pride."

The man laughed, coughed hard and spat on the ground. "So, you're a fiery one. I like 'em when they fight a bit. I'll give you five darlin' but you better wriggle nice for me." He pushed himself up against her.

"Christ, mister, not here," she said, taking the five franc coin and looking up into his face, her eyes burning with hatred. She saw the scar that ran from above the bridge of his nose down one cheek to the corner of his mouth. An image from four nights earlier of this same foul face flashed across her mind, a face that had looked her in the eye for a fleeting moment as he stood back from Arlette, the knife in his hand dripping her blood. She would never forget that face.

He grinned and grabbed her arm, pushing her towards the alley.

"Bit shy are we, darlin'? You'd better be good or I'll take that coin back."

She knew she had to get at least ten feet down the alley, past the deep doorway where Michel was hiding. She tried to walk on but he had hold of her shoulder.

"This'll do, it's dark enough here."

She reached behind and grabbed at his crotch, finding he was already hard. "Bit further, there's a nice comfy spot down here," she spat through her teeth as she pulled him along.

"This'll do," he said. "Right, down on yer knees."

126

He was aware of Gisèle letting go of him, but he couldn't see her in the darkness.

"Open wide, darlin," he grunted, reaching out for her head but not finding it.

"You're the one who's going to open wide."

The man spun round to the voice and saw the silhouette of a tall figure against the light from the street. He reached for the knife at his belt, but a firm hand took hold of his wrist from behind him and twisted it up his back. He struggled but his arm was wrenched harder and he yelped with pain.

"Wot the fuck! You lit'le slut, I'll rip yer —"

"You'll be doing nothing to her or any other woman. Ever again." Philippe's voice was quiet and cold.

The man felt a shiver run through him.

"Look, I ain't got no money, so wot d'yer want? Yer can have this little slut, take her. She's only a tramp. You two boys can have some fun."

"It's three," said Henri as he entered the alley from the street. "And you should be careful what you say, you murdering bastard, or I'll make your death a lingering one."

"Wot the fuck you talkin' about? You think three against one is fair? Wot d'you lot want?"

It was Philippe who answered. "Think back to four nights ago when you killed Arlette. Was that fair, when you stabbed her out of temper? Killed her without a second thought?"

For a moment, the man didn't understand. Then he remembered.

"That was an accident. She got in me way."

"The first wound maybe, but the thrust that killed her was pure malice. A woman had spoilt your fun and you killed her without a second thought."

"And you'd already killed her son." It was Michel's voice that now came at him from the darkness.

"Wot's he to you?" The man was defiant.

"He was my half-brother," said Michel. "And the woman you murdered was my mother."

The man was silent but his eyes were darting around, trying to gauge where his attackers were in the darkness of the alley. The grip on his wrist had been released and he was standing with his back against the alley wall. As he moved a hand to reach for his knife, he caught a glint of light from the pale grey eyes of the man who had been behind him and then he caught the glint of steel as it flashed past the man's side. There was a whispered cry of "Bastard!" and Gisèle's knife sank into his chest.

As he slumped to his knees, he heard the sound of three swords being drawn and saw the flash of more steel. But as the three blades pierced his body, a blackness descended on him and he felt nothing more.

Henri turned to Gisèle. Her hands were pressed against her open mouth, her face a mask of horror.

"Gisèle, it's over," he said. "It had to be done. Now we must go."

Michel moved to the alley entrance to check the street. He signalled to them that it was clear. They were going to the harbour where they would board one of Jacques Bognard's ships. The arrangements had been made. They were leaving on the next tide.

Philippe Laurent stood against the starboard rail of the ship, staring into the gently rolling waters, but the beauty of the full moon reflecting off the silver sea was lost on him. The ship's captain and Philippe's friend of the last thirty-three years, Jacques Bognard, walked up to him.

"Philippe, you should try to get some sleep."

"I'm not interested in sleep tonight, Jacques."

"I understand, my friend. These last few days have been more than any man should have to bear."

Philippe turned to him. "Jacques, I... We couldn't have... completed everything without you."

Jacques smiled warmly, holding out his arms. He was a large, muscular man, some five inches taller than Philippe. His almost black eyes always had humour in them, reflecting the confidence that came with knowing he could handle himself well in any of the threatening situations that frequently arose on a ship. He was sixty-one, the same age Philippe was claiming and like Philippe, he looked nothing like his years. His skin, although weather-beaten from years at sea, was smooth. He claimed this was the result of his wife Mathilde's wonderful cooking padding out his body and smoothing the creases.

"Philippe, you're my oldest and dearest friend. And I loved Arlette like a sister." At this, Philippe sagged into Jacques' chest, his body shaking with grief.

Jacques sat him down on a sail locker and let him weep.

After some minutes, Philippe straightened up and ran his hands through his hair. He sighed wearily. "I didn't imagine four nights ago when we were sitting in my studio that we should be here tonight. That Arlette and Georges would be dead and the boys, Gisèle and I would be fugitives."

"We never know what fate has in store for us, old friend. And sometimes she delivers a bitter blow. I wish with all my heart that I hadn't left so early that night. Maybe things would have been different."

Philippe rubbed a medallion hanging round his neck.

"Arlette gave me this. She said it would bring me luck. I should have bought her one."

"It wouldn't have saved her; that scum was bent on murder. At least he's now rotting in hell, and good riddance to him."

"Would they were both still alive and none of this had been necessary. I have committed murder, Jacques. My sons have committed murder. We shall have to live with that for ever."

"I don't believe that killing such a dog counts as murder. He killed more than a few people in his time and I am sure never felt the slightest twinge of remorse. And don't think you would have got justice out of the militia. They would happily string you up for the other deaths that night. They were baying for your blood."

The first mate came up to Jacques. "Beg your pardon, cap'n, would you like a blanket?"

"No thanks, Louis, but Monsieur Laurent would appreciate one if he's going to remain out here on deck."

The sailor produced a blanket and Jacques threw it over Philippe's shoulders.

"I need to check the watch, Philippe. Try to get some rest."

Philippe pulled the blanket tightly round himself. His thoughts drifted back to the evening of four nights ago. Jacques had come to review progress on the latest portrait of his wife, Mathilde, who at seventy-three was still a very good-looking woman, her fine, distinguished features framed by her pure white hair. Jacques had met her soon after his arrival in Marseille in 1643 when she was a childless widow of forty. They had married the following year. Jacques ran a small fleet of trading ships and after the wedding Mathilde had insisted on accompanying him on his trips. Being superstitious about women on boats, he had agreed only because he assumed that one voyage would be enough for her. He couldn't have been more mistaken. By the third day of the voyage, Mathilde had developed a love of the sea that would remain for the rest of her life.

Jacques was delighted with the portrait. Philippe's remarkable talent had never failed to impress him and he had often tried to persuade him to move elsewhere to establish a wider reputation. Philippe had always resisted, saying that although he wasn't married to Arlette, they were effectively man and wife and that it wouldn't be fair to take her away from the tavern she loved.

Philippe had met Arlette and her husband, Pierre, some years after his arrival in Marseille, by which time he had added the strong Marseille dialect to his repertoire. He had been looking for a new studio and was delighted when Pierre had offered him rooms above the tavern he ran in the docks. When Pierre was killed in 1652 in a fight in the tavern, leaving Arlette with a young son, Georges, Philippe immediately offered his help. He loved the tavern's wild atmosphere and often when he had finished for the night, he would spend two or three hours rapidly sketching or painting one figure after another.

Arlette's mother had been a Spanish gypsy and Arlette had inherited her looks and fiery character. She was a strong-willed girl and not afraid to solve an argument with a well-aimed punch.

After a year, the bond between Arlette and Philippe had developed into more than a friendship, although neither of them was willing to face their feelings head on. One noisy evening as Arlette carried an armful of mugs to a table, a young sailor had put his hand on her thigh and tried to pull her onto his lap. She thumped the mugs onto the table, whirled round and hit him hard on the jaw, knocking him out cold. His friends rounded on her. She smashed a mug into the face of one, but two others grabbed her from behind. Another was raising his fist to strike her when Philippe yelled from the bar. The man turned and as he did was laid out flat by a punch from one of the regulars. Philippe ran from the bar and threw himself at the sailors still gripping Arlette. Arlette struggled free and between them they quickly dispatched them. They took hold of the sailors' feet, dragged their unconscious bodies to the door and threw them down the steps to the filthy gutters. Arlette leaned back against the doorframe, wiped her forehead with her arm and laughed.

"Well, Philippe Laurent, it's good to see you have a brawny side."

He took a step towards her and brushed her hair from her face. "I learned all my fighting skills from watching you. I now need to learn how to put all that energy into a painting, to portray it."

"Do you never think of anything but your work, man?" she replied playfully, as she wiped a smear of blood from beside his eye where one of the sailors had tried to head-butt him.

He looked into her dark brown eyes and she held his stare. He was holding her waist with both hands and as he tightened his grip, she put both her hands round his head and kissed him fiercely. Breathless, Philippe pulled back.

"Arlette, I–"

She stopped him with a finger on his lips. "It's been more than a year, Philippe," she said quietly. "I miss Pierre every day and I still love him dearly. But he's not coming back and I have to move on. I am still young and I have feelings, Philippe. I have desires." She kissed him again, first gently and then passionately.

Their relationship moved easily from that of good friends to passionate lovers. Philippe had been in no long-term relationships since Beth died in 1580 and he had resolved that he would never marry again. But within three months of sharing Arlette's bed, he had changed his mind. To his surprise, Arlette refused him, saying that although she loved him with every fibre of her body, she would not marry again. She said she was still angry with God for cutting short her husband's life and she didn't want to give Him the opportunity to take away another husband. She reasoned that if they didn't marry, God would not be tempted to cause her such heartbreak again since taking away a lover wasn't the same as taking away a husband. Even when eighteen months later she became pregnant, she remained immovable on the subject and rather than fire up her temper, Philippe avoided the subject of marriage thereafter.

Philippe and Arlette's son, Henri, was born in late 1655, a second son, Michel, arriving three years later. Both boys had Philippe's pale grey eyes and both enjoyed perfect health, unlike Georges who caught his fair share of childhood illnesses.

The difference in the boys didn't escape Arlette's attention.

"Those pale grey eyes of yours must have magical powers," she often told Philippe. "I didn't realise it at first, but you are never ill, are you? You never even get a cold. Nothing."

"Oh, I don't know, I get pretty hot when you're around," he laughed, trying to make light of it.

"Well, your passion certainly seems to know no bounds," she smiled, kissing him, "but you must admit it's strange. I've never known anyone who was never ill. And you're pretty fit, given your age." She punched his stomach lightly.

"Well, I'm only forty-five and you work me so hard it's not surprising that I'm lean."

She studied his face. "My God, Philippe, you are forty-five, aren't you? You're almost as old now as Pierre was when he was killed, but you look so much younger. You haven't got a grey hair on your head, nor any wrinkles on your face."

"You keep me young, cherie," smiled Philippe. He wondered, as he often had, if he should tell Arlette, but her gypsy superstitions worried him.

Gisèle Prideaux had come into their lives in 1670. With similar gypsy origins, her mother and Arlette had been close friends and it was only natural that Arlette took the girl under her wing when her mother died. Gisèle was fifteen at the time, the same age as Henri, and the two had quickly become inseparable.

By his mid-twenties, Georges was the image of his father and had his mother's quick temper. When the sailors who started what would be his last fight started to throw their weight around after two hours of heavy drinking, it was natural that Georges went over to them. But despite his size, two of them pushed him away. He pushed back angrily and one of them produced a knife. Arlette, serving at the bar, looked up to see what had caused the sudden silence as the men confronted each other. She sighed when she saw the knife and turned to Michel.

"Go and get your father. I have a bad feeling about this group."

As Michel rushed off, Arlette called out to the men and made her way over to them.

"Let's not get overheated boys, just back away from each other and calm down."

"Mind yer business." A man older than the others had staggered to his feet. He spat on the floor and gesticulated drunkenly at her.

Georges moved towards him but the sailor holding the knife pointed it at him and he stopped, looking warily from him to the older man and back.

"What's the matter, flat nose, worried about yer mummy, are you?" the older man laughed derisively at Georges.

Seeing the sailor with the knife was distracted, Georges grabbed his wrist and twisted it hard, bringing it down onto a table. The knife fell from his hand and slid across the floor. He pushed the man away into his mates, but they shoved him back and he stumbled, falling across the table in front of Georges. As this was happening, the older man had pulled his own knife and lunged at Georges. But instead of stabbing Georges, the knife plunged into the neck of the falling sailor as he crashed across the table. A spurt of blood hit the older man in the face as his unwitting victim screamed in terror.

"Yer'll pay for that," screamed the man and lunged across the table again. Georges stepped back out of reach but the man jumped onto the table after him. He was about to launch himself at Georges when Arlette grabbed a bottle and swung it at the man's knees as hard as she could. It smashed across its target and the man crashed down onto the body of the dying sailor he'd stabbed.

"You bitch!" he snarled, clawing himself to his feet, his eyes fixed on Arlette. She saw the large scar that ran across his face and was surprised she didn't recognise him. She thought she knew most of the troublemakers in Marseille.

Georges rushed forward to grab the man but he wasn't quick enough. The man saw him out of the corner of his eye and swung his knife round in a large arc, slicing into Georges' throat. Georges collapsed, clutching at the wound as the blood spurted around his clasping fingers.

Henri and Gisèle had heard the commotion from a back room and came rushing through in time to see Georges' fatal stabbing. Henri ran at the group, taking his own knife from his belt and screaming at the top of his voice. As he drew near, the older man lunged at him but succeeded only in stabbing Arlette's arm as she tried to protect her son.

The dying sailor's mates, wanting revenge, decided to make the tavern's owners pay. One of them kicked a table out of the way from in front of him and with his dagger held high, rushed towards Henri. But he suddenly stopped in his tracks as a knife flew through the air and landed up to its hilt in his chest. He looked down in disbelief, dropped to his knees and died.

Moments earlier, Michel had run into the room, closely followed by Philippe. Seeing that Henri was in danger, Michel had withdrawn his knife from his belt and in one continuous movement had thrown it at the sailor. Without a pause, he and Philippe advanced on the group, their swords now drawn.

Realising the odds were now stacked against him, the older man grabbed one of the young sailors and, using him as a barrier, pushed him ahead towards Henri. As they passed the wounded Arlette, the older man shoved the sailor hard, making him stumble forward. Then he turned to Arlette. "Bitch!" he snarled and plunged his knife into her chest. Pulling it out, he looked across the room, a victorious sneer on his face. Then he vaulted over a table, ran for the door and was through it before anyone could react.

The remainder of the group of young sailors shrank away from the scene, apart from the one the older man had pushed at Henri. In his drunken fury he decided to make a go of it and lunged at Henri. He missed but in sidestepping out of his way, Henri tripped on a fallen chair and fell onto his back. The sailor raised his knife, ready to plunge it into Henri. But that was as far as he got. As his arm reached its highest point, two swords pierced through his body almost as one as Michel and Philippe charged at him.

As Philippe withdrew his sword from the dead sailor, he heard Gisèle's urgent cry. "Philippe! Quickly!"

He rushed to Arlette. She looked up at him through half-closed eyes. "Cheri," she whispered.

"Don't try to talk, Arlette, I'll fetch a physician."

"No, cheri, it's too late." She coughed, blood oozing from her mouth.

"Philippe, my strange, wonderful man …" She died gazing into his eyes.

The tavern had fallen silent, the customers frozen to the spot. Then suddenly everyone was trying to get out of the door at the same time. Philippe lifted Arlette's lifeless body and carried it into the back room where he lay it on a table. Henri and Michel followed with Georges' body. His face haggard with emotion, Philippe grasped the edge of the table and bowed his head.

"Michel," he said quietly. "We need some help, and quickly. Go to Jacques' house. Tell him what's happened. He will know what to do."

He paused and then looked up, his eyes cold. "Did anyone recognise that man?"

It was Gisèle who voiced what they were all thinking. "No, but I'll search this town until I find him. And then kill him."

Ten minutes later, Jacques arrived with three menservants and two maids.

"My men will carry the bodies to my house, mon ami," he urged Philippe. "We don't want the militia dealing with them. And you must take whatever you need from this house; you cannot come back."

He turned to the others.

"Quickly now, there is no time to waste!" He sent one of the maids with Gisèle and the other with Henri and Michel. He virtually dragged Philippe up the stairs. "Collect your things and what you need of Arlette's. I'll get your paintings."

To Philippe it seemed that no more than a few seconds later Jacques was standing at the bedroom door holding a huge pile of portfolios, brushes, books and papers. "Hurry, Philippe! The militia will be here any minute. They'll delight in stringing you up."

Philippe threw what he could onto the bed, gathered up the

corners of the blanket and followed Jacques down the stairs. The others had already arrived in the back room. Jacques opened the door that led onto the rear lane, looked cautiously up and down it, and nodded to them to follow.

As they disappeared into the shadows, they heard the thudding of a squad of militia's boots decending the hill towards the tavern's front entrance.

The following evening, soon after nightfall, they stood in a secluded churchyard on a hill above the town. The priest was an old friend of Jacques and Mathilde who had needed no persuasion to perform the burial rites. Earlier, Philippe had dressed Arlette's body in her finest gown while Mathilde arranged her hair. When they laid her in her coffin, she looked completely at peace.

Once the two coffins had been placed in the ground, all the men took turns replacing the earth, after which they stood in silent reflection. Their thoughts were finally interrupted by a sigh from Gisèle. They looked over to her as she pulled her cloak around her.

"I have business to attend to," she said quietly. "There is no time to waste in case that brute decides to leave Marseille."

"Gisèle, I'll go with you," said Henri.

"No, Henri. They know you too well. I am the one they know least; I can pass through the town with relative ease." She tried to make the words sound convincing, but she knew that she too would be in great danger.

"Gisèle," Philippe's voice commanded. "If you find him, do nothing. We shall all deal with him together."

Gisèle nodded. "I'll find him," she said and slipped into the night.

As the sun rose over the hills of Italy, Jacques walked over to his friend and sat on the sail locker next to him.

"There is little in this world to match the beauty of a sunrise over those hills when seen from the sea."

Philippe followed his gaze and nodded. Another day, he thought. Another day in two hundred and fifty years of days.

He turned to Jacques and saw him gazing at him with a strange, knowing expression on his face, as if he had read his thoughts.

"Jacques, I–"

"I understand, mon ami."

If only you did, thought Philippe, realising that he'd almost started to tell him his secret.

He stood up and stretched. "I think I should take some breakfast and then rest a while."

After he had eaten, Philippe went to his cabin where he dozed fitfully for a couple of hours.

There was a knock on the the door. It was Henri.

"Papa," he called, "are you awake?"

He came in and sat down on the bed. He was agitated, playing with his hands. "Papa, have you decided yet where we are going?"

"Not yet, Henri. We all need to discuss it."

He saw the distraction on his son's face and frowned, trying to read his thoughts.

"It has been a very difficult time, Henri. There has been so much tension that we have had little chance to think about Maman. I still can't believe she's gone. I feel so lost."

"We all do, Papa. But at least I have Gisèle. She's a wonderful girl and she has been so strong. She loved Maman as if she were her own mother."

"She was the daughter Maman would always have liked along with the three of you."

Henri fell silent, still playing with his hands.

"There's something else, Henri, isn't there?"

Henri turned his eyes briefly to Philippe's, and then looked away again, chewing his lip.

"I don't know how to say this, Papa." He paused. "There's something I … we, Michel and I, have been wanting to discuss with you for some time. The last few days have made me think about it again."

Philippe said nothing.

"Papa. I know Maman was concerned about this as well."

Another pause.

"Papa, are we different, Michel and I? Are you different?"

"Different?"

"Well, it's just that we've always been so healthy. You know, never ill. You too, even as you've got older. That's one thing. The other is, well, Papa, you are sixty-one but you don't look it. And in the fight in the bar and when we were searching for Brochard you seemed so young. Not like a man of your years at all. When I look at you, Papa, you don't look much older than I do. You certainly don't look like other men of your age."

Philippe touched Henri's arm gently. "Henri, I'm not even sure there are other men of my age."

There was confusion on Henri's face interwoven with fear.

"What do you mean, Papa?" he said quietly.

"Henri, I think perhaps you should fetch Michel. And Gisèle. It's about time I explained something to you."

# Chapter 13

## July 2009

Claudia and Ced were still staring at the image of the shepherd on the Piero della Francesca painting when Sally returned home. They told her what they'd found but having never met John Andrews, she could only take Claudia's word on the resemblance.

"I'll search the internet for a photo of him," said Ced. "He's probably got a website."

But there was nothing. The only time John Andrews' name appeared was among lists of exhibitors in minor exhibitions.

"I can't believe it," frowned Ced. "He's an artist; they all want to put themselves out there."

He scratched his head as he stared at the screen. "You know, I can't help but believe this is important. I mean, he's got a DNA profile that's off the scale; he's an amazingly talented artist and now we've found his face in a famous Renaissance painting. And then there are those landscapes."

He turned to Sally and Claudia. "Listen, tomorrow's a holiday, I think I'll drive up to the Lakes to get a look at him. Do you want to come along, Claw?"

Claudia pursed her lips. "I don't think he should know we know each other. I don't want to tempt fate; he might change his mind and report me to the police."

"Yeah, you're right, Claw. Don't want to risk your career any further than you have already, although I think you'd look pretty sexy in prisoner's uniform."

"Oy, Fisher, watch it!" said Sally, throwing a cushion at him.

"Hey," she added, "I've got an idea. Why don't you see if you can get a photo of him with this new digital toy you bought me?" She turned to a cupboard and retrieved a camera.

Ced looked skeptical. "Oh yeah, Sal, he's really going to agree to a snap of him posing next to one of his paintings."

"You're a forensic scientist, hon. I'm sure you'll think of something."

The following morning Ced set off early, and by ten thirty he was standing outside John Andrews' gallery looking at the paintings displayed in the window. He was immediately struck by their quality as he carefully assessed each one. One of the landscapes showed a country house set in a valley among formal gardens. He remembered one of the images on Claudia's phone – it had reminded him of something. This painting did the same and after staring at it for some moments, he realised the something was the work of another artist. What was his name? Frustrated, he pulled out his Blackberry and opened the web browser. He trawled through a number of sites, his eyes scanning the images on each. Then he tapped the screen and smiled. "Got it!"

The gallery was busy, giving him the chance to explore the paintings undisturbed. He walked towards a central display from where he could see a middle-aged woman in earnest conversation with a man casually dressed in beige chinos and a red and white checked shirt who was showing her a small, framed painting. As the man looked up to explain a point, Ced stopped in his tracks. He had to be John Andrews: his face was straight out of the painting he had been examining on his computer the previous evening.

Ced slowly worked his way around the gallery, taking in both the landscapes and the portraits, occasionally looking over to where John was continuing to explain a number of his paintings to the woman. After some minutes, he lifted one of the landscapes from the wall and took it and a smaller work to the back of the gallery. The woman followed brandishing a credit card. After wrapping the paintings and bidding farewell to its new owner, John turned his attention to Ced.

"Are you interested in a landscape or a portrait? I couldn't help noticing that you were looking at both." He walked up to Ced and held out his hand.

"I'm John Andrews," he said. "Please, take your time to browse my work."

"Thanks," replied Ced, shaking his hand and staring rather more intently into John's pale grey eyes than he intended. The features were even more remarkable now that the man's face was close to him.

"Ced. Ced Fisher. I'm, er, I'm very taken by your work; it's very unusual."

"That's normally a polite code for people saying they either don't like it or it's too expensive," smiled John.

Ced laughed. "On the contrary, I think your work is, well frankly, I think it's stunning. I'm amazed that I haven't come across it before. And as for the prices, given the quality, I think these are bargains."

"That's very kind," said John.

"I'm fascinated by your style," continued Ced. "Your portraits seem to have more than a little of the Renaissance about them. Is the Renaissance a strong influence for you?"

John looked at him thoughtfully, not replying immediately. Then he said, "Yes, I suppose it is. I've always liked the work of the Renaissance artists and that seems to come through in my work. It doesn't help, I'm afraid, since many people find it rather old-fashioned — stereotyped, if you like. However, that's the way it is."

Ced's thoughts were still focussed on art forgery.

"I was wondering," he said, "if you undertake commissions?"

"Certainly I do," nodded John. "If there's a particular view in the Lakes that you like, I'd be delighted. Alternatively, if you're thinking of a portrait of yourself, or your wife, girlfriend, kids. I don't normally need to arrange many sittings. But I prefer not to work from photographs; they simply don't have the dimensional depth."

Ced nodded. "I know what you mean. Paintings based on photographs always look exactly that: paintings of photographs. What about other work? Say I'd like a copy of a famous painting, do you take on that sort of commission as well?"

John smiled and shook his head. "No, not any more. Not since I was a student."

He paused and it seemed to Ced that his eyes were looking through him to somewhere else. Another place and time. John continued talking. "I have more than enough work to keep me occupied full time. I don't have the need or desire to copy other people's work."

While they were talking, Ced had picked up a framed portrait of a young girl who bore a strong likeness to John himself.

"Was this a commission?" he asked.

"No, that's one of a number I painted earlier in the year of my younger daughter. I didn't need to keep them all so I decided to sell some of them. They've been rather popular. That's the last of them."

"It's beautiful," replied Ced, scrutinising the painting closely and nodding in recognition. "That Renaissance influence is really there. I'm a big fan of the Italian painter Piero della Francesca; I take it that you are familiar with his work."

More than you could ever know, thought John.

"Yes," he said, "I think Piero's work is brilliant. He was a true craftsman and a revolutionary in his time."

Ced looked up from the painting. "I hope you don't mind me saying, but thinking of Piero has answered a question for me. When I first walked in here and saw you, I thought that perhaps we'd met before, but now I realise that your face is similar to one I've seen in one of Piero's paintings. How incredible."

John tried to hide his concern. "A number of people have said the same. I often wonder if one of my distant ancestors was a friend of Piero's."

"You know, it could be more than one painting," continued Ced, as he looked more intently at John's face. "I'd need to look again through the Piero catalogue, but…"

He stopped, realising that John was looking somewhat uncomfortable. He thought it would be better to make light of it.

"I suppose it's not that surprising that the same face would appear in a number of works by an artist. After all, once you've got a good model, why not use him or her."

John didn't reply. He felt suddenly ill at ease with this man asking him questions. While he couldn't avoid it from time to time, he still didn't like associations with the past being noticed.

Ced looked from John to the portrait of his daughter and back again, noting her pale grey eyes. "Well, whatever the explanation, judging from your daughter's features, the genes in your family must be pretty strong."

John decided to change the subject. "How did you develop an interest in Piero? Have you been on holiday to Tuscany? I hear there's a so-called Piero della Francesca Trail now."

Ced smiled. "Yes, I've been there and followed part of it, seeking out the original works. Amazing stuff. I've been interested in Piero's work for a long time. My work is connected to artists' styles. I studied fine art at university and then computing. I'm doing some research into the image analysis of paintings to see if it's possible to identify what's called a style signature for a specific artist."

Ced thought it best to avoid mention of art fraud.

John raised a skeptical eyebrow.

"Style signature?"

"Yes, I think that once an artist has developed his style, it should be apparent in all his work. It's what art experts are looking for when they visually examine paintings. What I'm trying to do is computerise it."

"Personally, I'd doubt that you're going to get a computer to achieve what art experts often get wrong. I agree that all artists develop a style, but whether you could always see it is another matter. An artist's style isn't that difficult for another accomplished artist to copy, you know. Look at the huge number of copies that are produced of famous works. Some of them are brilliant. And good artists can mimic different styles if they want to. There have been many occasions when top experts have been fooled by copies and I'm sure there are many paintings out there still fooling them."

"I'd agree that it's difficult," replied Ced, "but where the computer has an advantage is that it can perform any number of endless comparisons of the minutiae of a painting, stroke by stroke; something that ultimately you couldn't do with a visual examination. What I'm talking about here goes further than an artist's style, which I agree can be copied. The style signature is a subconscious thing, not something the artist is in control of. I believe that once an artist has developed his style signature – has matured if you like – it will be there in all his work, albeit very subtly. Tell me, as a skilled artist, how easy do you think it would be to copy a work from, say, five hundred years ago? Copy it so well that it couldn't be detected?"

"You mean make a forgery?"

Ced saw that John had raised his eyebrows at him in surprise.

"Um, yes and no, I don't mean for criminal purposes necessarily," he lied. "I mean for someone who might want to own a very special work, one truly produced in the way an old master produced it."

"That would involve using all the relevant materials from the period, but I really don't think that people who commission top copies of old masters care whether the materials used are the same, as long as the painting looks like the original. In fact, they would probably want to be assured that their money had been spent on something that was likely to last; that the colours wouldn't fade and the painting wouldn't separate from the ground layer. However, if you mean forgeries that are intended to fool the art world, there have been countless attempts. But it's very hard to outwit a modern scientific analysis. It wouldn't only be the paint that was used, but also the substrate for the painting — the canvas, or for early Renaissance work, the tavola. You'd have to get hold of genuine fifteenth century pieces of wood. As for frescos, they are painted on walls and ceilings, so you couldn't just produce one out of a hat. Those that remain are well known. It's very unusual for a new work to emerge, as happened with 'The Awakening' a few years ago. And that went through a huge barrage of tests for authenticity. No, I don't think it could be done; there would always be differences."

"I tend to agree with you," nodded Ced, "but not everyone has the resources to pay for a detailed analysis. Of course, there have been cases where a copy has been produced to replace an original. More than one museum or gallery around the world has paintings on display that are thought to be valuable old masters when the truth is that what they have adorning their walls are copies, the originals being in some rich and crooked collector's treasure trove.

"You know," he went on, hoping to steer the conversation towards his eventual goal, "it would be fascinating to compare the work of someone with your skill with the old masters. I wonder, would you agree to me using my computer analysis techniques on your work and comparing your style with Piero and his contemporaries to see how much of their technique comes through in yours?"

John was horrified, realising that if such an analysis were successful, it would reveal more than a connection with Piero; it

144

would link him with many of his own paintings over the last five hundred years. Feeling increasingly uncomfortable with the way the conversation was going, he thought it was really time to get rid of this persistent young man.

"What would be the point?" he said, looking at his watch. "Do you think I am forging old masters?"

Ced saw the unsubtle hint but chose to ignore it.

"Not at all. As I say, it would be fascinating to see if the various influences can be identified."

"I really don't see any value in it." John was dismissive. "Surely it would be better to compare the contemporary works of the period with each other to see how much influence one artist had on another at the time, all assuming, of course, that your approach works."

"Well, for the older works," countered Ced, "it's harder than you might think. For the more minor artists, there is often great debate about the authenticity of a painting, so it's difficult to establish a starting point. Even for a well-known artist like Piero, there is still a lot of debate over exactly when he lived and was painting. It seems fairly certain that he died in late 1492 but his birth date isn't known precisely."

He was born, thought John, on June 1, 1412, fifteen years to the day before I was. We were always amused by the coincidence.

Ced continued. "To have a modern painter who paints very much in the style of the old masters would give a very valuable reference point since there would be no doubt over the origin of his works, while at the same time they couldn't be confused with older works since the artist clearly couldn't have been involved in painting them."

Oh, how wrong you are, young man, thought John.

"The whole process is really very straightforward," continued Ced, "and would cause you no inconvenience. Since I normally can't move the paintings I'm examining, the imaging equipment is designed to be totally portable."

John held up his hands and shook his head.

"I'm sorry, but I'm really not convinced by all this. Supposing I were to agree to this imaging and supposing, just for a moment, that my technique is as good as you seem to think it is and you can't find any difference between my style and Piero's. What's that going to prove? Simply that your method isn't working since, as you have so rightly pointed out, I cannot have been involved with paintings by a man who has been dead for several centuries."

"It would mean that my technique wasn't sensitive enough, that it needed refining further. In fact it would be a great test for the analysis."

"Perhaps," said John, "but it seems to me that your idea of what research is all about is wrong. Surely the point is to develop a theory, test it thoroughly and if it fails the test, then reject it. You shouldn't develop a theory and then mould the testing to prove it; that would be bad science as well as being a waste of time and money. Who is funding this wild goose chase anyway?"

"I couldn't agree more about the principles of research," replied Ced. "Every researcher should keep an open mind and be prepared to see his theory collapse. I just don't think I'm at that stage yet. As for my research, it's funded using money – a very modest amount I should add – from an Arts Council grant. The equipment is all fairly standard and not very costly in the scheme of things. The complicated part is the development of the software and I do that largely in my own time. I'm prepared to do so because I think my research could have long term benefits to the art world."

But not my world, thought John.

"Well, I'm afraid you haven't convinced me and I don't want my gallery cluttered up with scientific equipment. We're coming into the summer season when I sell most of my work. I'm sorry, but that's the way it is. There must be other artists out there who are less busy and who could help your research."

Ced felt that he'd really gone far enough. He didn't want to alienate Andrews completely. He'd prefer to try to leave a door open so that he could return later. As he was musing on this, he realised that he'd picked up the portrait of Andrews' daughter.

"I don't think there are artists with your skill, particularly in the techniques from the early Renaissance. However, it's your decision and I have to respect it."

He held up the portrait.

"I've been looking again at this wonderful portrait of your daughter. What price are you asking for it?"

Taking the portrait from him, John turned it over and pointed to a label.

"It's marked up at two thousand pounds, but I've been thinking about it too. My wife was very reluctant for me to put it on sale even though we have others," he lied. "I think I'm going to accede to her wishes, so I'm afraid it's no longer on sale." He gave Ced a cold smile and put the painting to one side.

He must be well pissed with me, thought Ced. What has he got to hide?.

Ced decided on a parting shot.

"I was wondering if perhaps you are familiar with the work of Francesco Moretti, the wartime artist? He produced many paintings of the bomb damage in London, but he also specialised in works showing lakes, gardens and large country houses."

He was surprised at the effect this seemingly innocent question had on Andrews. The colour drained from his face and he became distinctly agitated.

"I've, er, I've heard of him, of course, but only vaguely. I'm not really familiar with his work," he stuttered, looking around as if he was suddenly desperate to escape.

John's reply surprised Ced. Moretti was quite well known. And now he was dead his work had increased substantially in value. A landscape artist should certainly know his work.

"Why do you ask about Moretti?" John's question was guarded.

"Well, it's just that while we've been talking, I've been looking at those paintings over there."

Ced pointed to two large pastoral scenes, the central focus of each of which was a fine country house with a lake and gardens. "There's also one in your gallery window."

"I've studied Moretti's work quite extensively," he lied, "and all three of these works could have been painted by him."

As John watched Ced Fisher turn on his toes and walk from the gallery, his mind was spinning furiously.

Francesco Moretti. If Fisher had noticed a link, how long would it take for him to recognise links with other artists he had been? He clearly knew his art and the computer analysis was potentially a serious problem.

Ced Fisher was unaware of John Andrews' dilemma. He was

angry with himself for having alienated the man, as well as being even more confused by him. Why did he have such an attitude? He was a professional artist who lived by selling his paintings. Not only that, he was an exceptional artist in a world full of talented artists. Why wouldn't he want to participate in a comparison with the old masters? OK, maybe not participate, but why so negative? What had the man got to hide?

Perhaps he is involved in the forgery game after all, mused Ced. Perhaps he has a lot to hide. Maybe I've struck gold and found a master forger hiding away in the innocent recesses of the Lake District.

He returned to his car. Having now more or less convinced himself of Andrews' criminality, he decided that a photograph of Andrews would be very useful, although he wasn't quite sure what he was going to do with it apart from compare it with faces in five-hundred-year-old paintings. He drove the car to a spot on the other side of the road from the gallery, parked and waited, feeling extremely self-conscious.

After an hour, he saw John coming out of the gallery with his wife, who must have returned while Ced was fetching his car. Ced fired off half a dozen shots zoomed in on John's face. He was about to drive away when he remembered the photographs Claudia had taken on her mobile phone of the landscapes in the gallery window. Their quality wasn't good enough for serious comparison work and although Sally's camera was still only a point-and-shoot, it had a far better image quality than a mobile phone. But to get some half-decent shots, he would have to get closer and to do that he needed to wait until the gallery closed and Andrews had left.

He sat up and looked around at the hills stretching up behind Grasmere. He had his running shoes and some kit in the boot of his car. What better way to pass a few hours than pounding the paths and hills of the Lake District?

# Chapter 14

## 1677-1701

Gisèle thumped her fist hard onto the map table that she and the three men were squeezed around in the tiny cabin.

"I cannot believe you, Philippe!" she yelled, her eyes flashing with anger.

Henri and Michel's heads shot up as they were jolted from their introspection. They had been struggling to understand what Philippe had been quietly explaining to them about his 'condition' and how he thought they were the same. It was beyond anything they had ever imagined, and yet their father had laid out a convincing case. Over the last hour there had been many questions, mostly from Henri, the more outspoken of the brothers. Occupied with their own thoughts, none of the men had noticed Gisèle's whole demeanour darkening with a growing anger.

Philippe wasn't too surprised at Gisèle's outburst – he had seen her temper before – but he wasn't expecting the reason for it.

"I know it's hard to believe, Gisèle. Perhaps if I showed you some of my earlier work, you might be more convinced."

He picked up one of his leather portfolios and started to open it, but Gisèle wasn't interested. Her eyes burned into his and she laughed scornfully.

"It's not your story I cannot believe!" she screamed. "Although I think you might well be completely mad. What I can't forgive, if your story is true and not some nonsense dreamed up to upset me, is that you didn't tell Arlette!"

She stood up, knocking over her chair. She whirled around in frustration, wanting to pace the floor but unable to in the small space. Tearing at her hair, she turned again to the table and thumped the middle of it with her fists.

"How could you not tell her?" she shouted. "She was living with you all those years. She looked after you, cared for you, loved you. And you kept this secret of yours from her? Weren't she good enough to know the truth about you? Sweet Jesus, she was the mother of your two sons, who you now say are the same as you!"

She leaned over, her face inches from Philippe's. "She had a right to know!" she screamed, even louder than before. "A right!"

She kicked at the fallen chair, picked it up and sat down hard on it.

"It would have changed everything if you'd told her. She might have given up the tavern and still be alive. But instead she's dead, and it's your fault, Philippe! Your fault! I can never forgive you! Never!"

She let her head fall onto her arms, her body convulsed with sobbing.

Philippe reached out a hand, but Henri grabbed his wrist. "No, Papa, I'll look after her."

Gisèle looked up and recoiled in her chair.

"Don't touch me!" she screamed. "I never want you to touch me again!" She paused, turning her wild eyes to Henri and Michel.

"You're both in league with him, aren't you? You suspected this, didn't you? You're all crazy heartless bastards. If this is what being immortal does to you, I don't want nothing to do with it!"

She stood up, tore open the cabin door and stormed out.

Philippe sagged in his chair.

"Henri," he said quietly, "I think you'd better follow her. In this mood, she could blurt out all sorts of nonsense. She clearly didn't understand when I told her we are anything but immortal. I'm concerned about what she might say to the crew. It's bad enough for them having a woman on board. If they think she's mad, who knows what they might do?"

"I'm not surprised she didn't understand it all, Papa; it's very hard to believe. And I think she has a point. Why didn't you tell Maman?"

There was a hard edge to Henri's voice.

"I don't know, Henri; I meant to, I wanted to. I nearly told her on a number of occasions. But Maman was always very volatile, like Gisèle is. I was afraid that she'd reject me, that she'd throw me out. We had many fierce arguments, you know."

"Yes, Papa, I know. It was quite difficult not to overhear them."

Philippe's lips formed a thin, humourless smile.

He sighed wearily. "Listen, Henri, I really think you should go after Gisèle. We can discuss this later."

Henri nodded. "Yes, I've never seen her like that." He stood, turned to his father as if he was going to say more, but then he shook his head and marched out of the cabin.

Philippe turned to his younger son. "Do you have anything to say, Michel? It was Henri who asked the questions and who seemed to have all the doubts."

"Do you mean about your not telling Maman, or about us having the same 'condition' as you?" Michel's tone was harsh, accusing.

"Any of it, Michel, all of it. I know how difficult this must be for you to accept. It was hard to tell you even though I wanted you to know. In all my ridiculously long life, this is the first time that I have been able to tell a child of mine that they're the same as I am – the first time in two hundred and fifty years. For the others I've told, it was different – they weren't the same as me. What they had to understand, which was difficult enough, was that their father was not only going to outlive them, but in their old age he would look like their son or grandson. For us, Michel, we shall always look like brothers."

Michel frowned. "Do you think we are the only ones, Papa? What about the daughter in Naples?"

"She is the only other person like us I have ever known of. And I don't know for certain because I have never met her."

He paused and reached for Michel's hand. "But I am certain about you and Henri, and that is now the most important thing in my life. Memories are one thing, and I have a lot more than other people, but that's all they are – memories. It's the present that's important and we need to decide where we are going from here."

Michel nodded wearily. "I'm so tired, Papa. The last few days have been terrible. I still can't stop thinking about Maman and wondering if there is more I could have done; if I could have saved her from that madman."

"You saved Henri with a remarkable piece of quick thinking. You couldn't have done more. None of us could have predicted that Brochard would have killed Maman in cold blood like he did. We are all tired, Michel, but we have avenged Maman's murder, even if the price we must pay is exile. I suggest you try to get some sleep."

Soon after six in the evening, there was a knock on Philippe's door. It was Henri.

"Papa, are you awake?"

"Yes, Henri, come in."

The door opened and a stern-faced Henri entered followed by Gisèle, her whole body still radiating anger.

Philippe did his best to ignore their faces and smiled at them. "Sit down, both of you. Have you had anything to eat?"

"The steward brought us dinner, Papa, which I've eaten, but Gisèle wasn't hungry."

Philippe looked at the girl. "You need to eat, you know, Gisèle. You must keep your strength up."

"I know what I need, Philippe, I need to get off this ship. We both do, Henri and me. We don't wanta stay any longer. We'll get off at the first port in Italy and take our chances."

Philippe sighed. "I really don't think that's the best idea. We should stick together. I know how angry you are with me, and I can understand it, but I can't change the past, no matter how much I might want to."

"Don't matter," pouted Gisèle, "we just wanta get off. We wanta stop at Genoa."

"Have you spoken to Michel about it?"

"Yeah. He don't agree. Thinks we're stupid. Don't wanta come wiv us."

Philippe noticed that as the girl's sullenness increased, so did her Marseille accent. A thought occurred to him about their destination.

"How's your Italian, Gisèle? Or at least the Genovese dialect?"

"What?"

"The language, Gisèle. I don't think you speak any Italian, do you? I know Henri doesn't. How are you going to manage? No job, nowhere to live, no money."

"We'll soon pick up the lingo; can't be that difficult. Anyway, it'll be the same for you, so goin' our own way won't make no difference."

He looked into her eyes and saw confusion amongst the anger. He smiled.

"What's so funny, Philippe, don't yer think we can do it?"

Philippe sat back in his chair. His mouth twisted into a sneer while his eyes flitted from one of them to the other. After a few seconds, he stretched out his arms as if in greeting, but his eyes were cold.

"My dear young friends, welcome to our wonderful city of Genoa. These are my companions, slit-throat Mauro and cut-purse Tito. They'll be pleased to relieve you of any valuables you have about your person and you won't even feel a thing. And what else have you got to offer, young lady? I'm sure that Mauro's roving hands would like to find out. Let's take you down this alley and Mauro can teach you the ways of Genoa before he passes you round his friends."

Their mouths dropped open. Philippe had spoken to them in rapid-fire Italian dialect.

"It isn't the same for me, Gisèle," said Philippe, reverting to French. "Didn't you realise from what I told you this morning? I am Italian, not French. I speak the language and a number of dialects. And believe me, you won't simply pick it up overnight. As for Genoa, it makes Marseille look like a peaceful country village; you wouldn't last a few minutes."

He told them what he'd said and their eyes opened wide in shock.

"It would be madness to try to make it on your own," he continued. "And, Henri, you have your apprenticeship to think about. Neither you nor Michel is ready to make a living as an artist yet."

They decided they would head for Siena. Philippe had worked there nearly a hundred years before and was confident he could establish a studio. For their new identities they chose to be French-speaking Italians from the north of Piedmont, the Lorenzini brothers. Only Philippe changed his Christian name; to Claudio. The boys saw no reason to change theirs, while Gisèle steadfastly refused to change at all, although she did agree to be their cousin.

153

However, Gisèle did change in other ways. Always volatile, her involvement in the killing of Arlette's murderer played increasingly on her mind. She became sullen and moody; always short-tempered. And she never forgave Claudio, despite his best efforts to win her over. Ever restless, once Henri had established a reputation for himself, Gisèle urged him to move elsewhere.

"Siena's so dull," she would repeat daily. "You should be working in a more exciting city like Rome. We could have much more fun there."

By 1685, there was no longer any reason to delay. They were now totally fluent in Italian, Gisèle with a strong Sienese accent that could match the rough nature of her street Marseille dialect when she chose, and they were confident that they could survive.

Claudio was sad to see them go, but he knew, as he had with his son Piero more than a hundred years before, that it was what Henri needed. He had also had enough of the constant attrition of Gisèle's moods.


For Henri, it was a successful move. He had matured well as an artist and he quickly found acclaim in The Eternal City. He wrote regularly, regaling Claudio and Michel with glowing tales of his success. But for a long time he said little about Gisèle. It wasn't until after a rare letter from Michel that Henri admitted that Gisèle had fallen in with a dissolute crowd and had started to drink heavily. However, he insisted that he still loved her and would support her for as long as she wanted him.

In June 1694, the now very successful Henri visited Siena for the first time in several years. After the initial euphoria of recounting his many commissions, the conversation inevitably turned to Gisèle. Claudio was pleased to hear that she and Henri had gone their separate ways for most of the previous year. She was still in Rome but had moved in with a sculptor, a bear of a man from Sicily who liked his drink as much as she did. The separation had not been Henri's idea: he felt as protective and drawn to Gisèle as he ever had, despite her temper, abuse and drinking. The problem had been Gisèle. Her lifestyle had aged her and she had found the burden of living with a man who was looking increasingly like her son too hard to bear. Her jealousy over his never-changing youthful looks and health had consumed her and turned into a sour hatred.

"You must be careful, Henri," cautioned Claudio. "She could be dangerous. When she is the worse for drink, her tongue will become very loose. "

"You are right, Papa, and rest assured, I do take care. But I miss the girl I used to know, even though she was always hotheaded. It's the drinking that has turned her mind."

In May 1701, Claudio was eagerly preparing for his first trip to Rome for four years. Henri had arranged a full calendar for him to meet other artists and view many new works. Michel was accompanying Claudio and excited to be seeing his brother again. Claudio was, therefore, totally shocked when on answering a knock on the studio door, he found Henri's apprentice Enrico standing before him, mud-splattered and tearful, his mouth opening and closing as he tried to speak. Claudio took the young man by the shoulders and guided him into the room.

"Enrico, my boy, whatever is it?" he said, the deep sadness in the boy's eyes causing him to shiver in apprehension.

Finally Enrico shuddered and looked down. "Signor Lorenzini..." He gulped some air. "Signore, it is Henri."

"Henri!" cried Claudio. "What has happened? Is he injured?"

"He is dead, signore. Murdered by that woman he used to live with. His cousin."

Claudio stood clutching the almost-collapsing Enrico, unable to take in what he had heard.

Michel stepped forward to them. "Murdered, Enrico? By Gisèle? I cannot believe it."

He took Enrico's arm and guided him to a chair. He fetched a glass of wine, but the young man waved it away.

"I just need some water."

Enrico took a deep breath to gather his thoughts.

"Oh, signori, it was so terrible. Henri was in his studio along with a young client whose portrait he was painting, Signorina Daniela d'Alemo. Her sister, Rosanna, and cousin, Portia were also present. I was out buying materials for the studio. According to the cousin, the studio door was suddenly kicked open by a giant of a man, a huge ogre with a long black beard. With the giant was the woman, Gisèle. She immediately pointed at Henri and screamed wildly that he was the one, the one who was immortal. The giant sneered that if he was immortal then he wouldn't worry about a little nick of his sword. Henri, being immediately protective of the ladies, pushed them behind himself, his arms outstretched to shield them. He yelled at the giant to get out, that he should take no notice of the ramblings of a drunk. But that only angered the man. He pulled his sword and cut Henri on the arm. At the sight of blood the giant sniggered that perhaps Henri wasn't immortal after all. As he turned to say this to the woman, Henri rushed forward to grapple with him, but the giant swung his arm round, knocking Henri to the ground. Then he jabbed again at his face and arms."

Enrico paused and Michel helped him to some more water. He glanced up at Claudio and was shocked. The only other time he had seen his father's eyes so cold was when Arlette had been murdered. It was as if a thundercloud had descended on him.

Enrico continued. "The giant was now taunting the almost helpless Henri and laughing and sneering at Gisèle that Henri was no more than an ordinary man. Gisèle screamed that it was impossible to kill Henri, even if he ran him through. She ran at the giant and tried to take the sword from him, screaming that she'd show him. At this point, Daniela tried to intervene but she hadn't noticed that Gisèle was carrying a knife. As Daniela grabbed her by the hair, Gisèle turned and plunged the knife into her heart, yelling that if she was Henri's whore, she could die with him. Her language, signori, was apparently so appalling that the cousin couldn't bring herself to repeat the actual words."

"I can imagine," Claudio replied in a hollow whisper.

"Having witnessed this terrible incident, Henri was attempting to get to his feet when the giant turned and lunged at him with the sword, piercing his chest and his heart. As he collapsed, Gisèle threw herself on him, screaming his name. This enraged the giant. He screamed obscenities and ran her through with his sword so forcefully that the blade also pierced through Henri and became firmly fixed in the floor. The giant was trying to withdraw it when Rosanna bravely smashed a large clay jar over his head, knocking him unconscious. Rosanna and Portia were found in each others arms when two neighbours, aroused by all the noise, came to investigate."

"And the giant?" Claudio asked.

"He was arrested by the guard and has been thrown in gaol. There is little doubt he will hang."

"What of the young women after this terrible ordeal?" asked Michel.

"Rosanna is in total shock. She has not spoken since and the physician fears for her sanity. Portia has a stronger constitution and although terribly shocked, is able to speak."

Claudio sat down on a stool and bent over, his head in his hands. Several minutes passed before he looked up. "Enrico, when did all this happen?"

"Yesterday, signore. I would have come earlier but my father thought it safer to leave at first light rather than ride part of the way in the dark."

"We are indebted to you, Enrico. To leave so quickly when you yourself must have been overcome with grief, we are truly indebted. You must have ridden like the wind."

"When do you want to leave for Rome, signore? Since I assume there will be three of us, we could risk riding through the night."

Claudio was deeply touched by the boy's earnestness. "While my heart yearns to be there immediately to deal with my s ... er my brother's body, a few hours will make little difference. I think it would be better to leave at first light. By then you will be refreshed."

Henri's funeral passed in a blur. They had wanted a small, private ceremony, but Henri was famous and several hundred friends and clients expected the right to display their grief. After, when Claudio and Michel were at Henri's studio sorting through his belongings and paintings, Claudio came across a number of sketches of Gisèle. They portrayed an altogether calmer, happier woman, her captivating smile the one they remembered from when she was a girl in Marseille.

Claudio passed them to his son. "What shall we do with these, Michel?"

Michel looked through them, his face emotionless. Then, without a word, he tore them to shreds.

They took two days to ride back to Siena. Neither of them was in a hurry and they said little, both still coming to terms with their pain. On the second day, they stopped for lunch in a field by a stream not far from the hill town of Montepulciano.

Michel took a bite from an apple and chewed on it reflectively.

"You know, Papa, now Henri is gone, I don't think I want to stay in this country any longer. The language has always been a problem for me, and the people, well, they are not like us." He paused, remembering his father's history. "Well, they are not like me, anyway. They're not French."

He took another bite from his apple. "I'd really like to return to France, perhaps to Marseille. It's where I'm from and where I know I'd feel at home. What's more, I can communicate with people there. What do you think?"

Claudio smiled at him. "I agree, Michel. We should go somewhere we are both at ease. As to where, there are many places to choose from, but I don't think we should return to Marseille. Not yet. I know it's been twenty-four years now since we left, but memories can be long; it would be better to wait a few more years. However, it's been nearly sixty years since I was in Paris and you've never been there. It's an exciting city and I know our talents can bring us some success there as they did before for me. I think you'd like it. Shall we go to Paris?"

# Chapter 15

## July 2009

Ced's run around the hills near Grasmere look longer than he'd anticipated, largely because he'd set off without a map. He eventually jogged back into Grasmere at seven in the evening, by which time even he was tired. He tucked into a large steak and three fried eggs at the Green Man, photographed the Andrews landscapes through the gallery window and left to negotiate a congested M6 motorway. Arriving home at midnight, he was asleep within seconds of climbing into bed.

The next morning, he awoke with a start at eight. Saturday mornings were a time when he and Sally would pound the country lanes. That morning, Sally had left him to catch up on his sleep.

He showered, made himself his usual breakfast of scrambled eggs and bacon and headed for his study to upload the images from his camera. As he finished, he heard Sally moving around downstairs.

"Sal! Come and look at these!"

Sally came upstairs with a towel draped over her shoulders.

"That's it, is it, marathon man? You disappear for the day, come home shattered at midnight and go straight to sleep, and now you're buried in your computer without even a 'Hi, good morning, Sal, my love, did you have a good day yesterday doing all my washing?'"

He stood up and gave her a kiss. "Yeah, sorry, Sal. It was quite a day."

He sat down again, his eyes on the screen.

Sally shook her head in resignation and put the cup of coffee and yoghurt she was carrying on the desk next to the monitor. Ced's hand automatically reached out to the yoghurt, only to receive a slap.

"Oy, Fisher, you've just had your breakfast, judging from the mess in the kitchen!"

"Forgot about the yoghurt, Sal," he said, swallowing a large spoonful.

"Look at these. What do you think?"

She bent to look at the three of the images he'd taken of John Andrews and the face of the shepherd in the Piero fresco.

"'The Awakening' was painted when?"

"Probably sometime in the 1470s. Certainly no later than 1485."

"Well, either John Andrews is very well preserved for his age or his gene line is surprisingly strong. The similarity is incredible. It's a fifteenth century John Andrews."

Ced nodded. "Amazing, isn't it? He said that people had commented on a similarity between his face and faces in Piero's paintings – presumably he meant this one – and he was right. I wonder if he's ever tried to trace his ancestry. He could easily be Italian, don't you think?"

"It's the eyes that spook me, Ced," replied Sally, looking from the painting to the photographs and back. "Eyes like that are pretty unusual. To see them in a Renaissance painting and on the face of a twenty-first century man whose other features are also identical is mind-blowing. But what does it mean?"

"Dunno, really, other than 'Genetics Rules!'"

"Have you looked at any other Piero paintings to see if he used the same man? Perhaps this guy came from the local modelling agency."

Ced laughed. "I don't think they had quite the same set-up in those days. He will have been a friend or a relative. I'll have a look around the other Pieros I've got on file."

Sally kissed the top of his head and ambled off downstairs to continue her chores.

Ten minutes later, she became aware of the sound of Ced's fingers flying over the computer keys. He was normally fast, but this sounded frenetic. The sound was accompanied by grunts, oohs and gasps.

"Sal! Come up here again!" he yelled.

She put down the clothes she was folding and returned to the study.

"Twelve, Sal! I've found twelve faces that could all be the man from 'The Awakening'. Five of them are from the Legend of the True Cross cycle, mostly profiles, but one almost full face. Look! The similarity is incredible."

Sally looked over his shoulder at the screen.

"Wow! Are these the five from the 'Legend'? When was it painted?"

"It was painted over a period of more than twenty years, so in some of these the model should have been quite a bit younger. But he looks much the same in all of them."

Ced paused to call up the shepherd again.

"I've just realised. We've been studying the face and ignoring the hair. Here in 'The Awakening' it's quite grey, unlike in the 'Legend'. But if you ignore the hair, the age of the face appears to be no different from those in the 'Legend'. Curious, huh?"

Another thought occurred to Ced and he tapped manically on the keys. The image from 'The Awakening' filled the right half of the screen alongside a set of images on the left side from the 'Legend' that he'd placed one on top of the other. Keeping the image from 'The Awakening' visible, he flicked through the 'Legend' set, enlarging portions of each one and moving around them, studying the detail.

Finally he sat back.

"You know what, Sal? I think I've sussed it."

He stared at the images, concentrating hard. Nodding to himself, he then called up the remaining images from the twelve faces he'd found and ran his eyes over each of them. "Yeah," he muttered.

"Well, genius, are you going to keep me in suspense much longer? I don't know what I'm supposed to be looking at and all that clicking is making me dizzy," said Sally, bending over him and nuzzling his neck.

He pressed his head against hers affectionately.

"Look at the detail in the image on the right, Sal, and compare it with the others. They're all good, but there is much more in the one from 'The Awakening'. I reckon for that painting, Mr Andrews' ancestor was present; he actually modelled for the painting. But for the others, I reckon Piero did them from memory."

He turned his head to her and grinned. "There could be a paper in this, Sal."

"Wow, marathon, man, I'm impressed! That's quite a conclusion."

Ced spent the following two hours refining the images and comparing details from one image to the next. Then he stretched his arms above his head. A good morning's work and it was still only eleven thirty. Time for a run.

After two hours of pounding the country lanes near their house and racing each other on their bikes, Ced and Sally returned pleasantly weary and, in Ced's case, ravenously hungry.

Ced returned to his computer at around four in the afternoon and opened the hi-res image of Claudia's painting, just to look at it and marvel at its detail and technique. Leaving the portrait on one side of the screen, he called up one of the landscapes from Andrews' gallery window. It had reminded him of Francesco Moretti's work and out of curiosity he wanted to run a Moretti against the Andrews to check the similarities and differences. From the online library, he retrieved a Moretti with a similar setting and placed it on the screen alongside the other two paintings. However, in his late afternoon weariness, he hit the wrong preset key and set the computer to work comparing all three images. The routine would take about ten minutes so he went to make a cup of green tea.

Twenty minutes later, the program was still churning the numbers and Ced was drumming his fingers on the desktop, wondering what was taking it so long. A window finally appeared giving him a number of options. He hit 'Cool' – he had created his own buttons – and the screen filled with a complicated table of numerical results.

He studied the data and frowned. They made no sense. Having accidentally included the portrait in the comparisons, he was expecting the results to indicate the same artist painted the Andrews landscape and portrait. They did – he couldn't expect a complete match since the landscape image wasn't hi-res and the two subjects were very different. What he hadn't expected was that the data from the Moretti image indicated that it too was painted by the same artist as the other two, the match being stronger for the portrait than for the landscape.

He entered the data into another statistical comparison program he had written to refine it further, and came up with the same answer. A cold feeling of panic crept over him. He had been writing, refining, testing and rewriting his basic comparison program for over a year. It was now at a very sophisticated level and he had run a huge number of test comparisons with paintings of indisputable origin. Only in the very early days, when the programming was much cruder, had anomalous results such as these occurred. It could no longer happen. But it had.

He stared at the screen. Something had gone wrong, a glitch in the programming. He decided to run the comparison again, but this time using only the two high-quality images – the Andrews old lady portrait and the Moretti landscape. He added a few extra parameters to highlight differences where they occurred and to place emphasis on brushstroke technique.

This time he waited by the computer, willing it to hurry up, his fingers drumming impatiently on the desk. As he hit 'Cool', he wondered if it would be. It wasn't. He ran his practised eye down the columns of data and saw immediately that the results indicated the level of certainty that the paintings were by the same artist was even higher than earlier.

Absently tapping a thumbnail against his front teeth, he considered what to do next. An idea occurred. If the program was faulty or corrupted, a different comparison should show it. He called up the online library for the work of an English landscape artist, Philip Johnston, a contemporary of Moretti's who had produced similar paintings. He located a scene similar to the Moretti and set the comparison program running, this time using the Andrews portrait and landscape, the Moretti and the Johnston. He paced the floor waiting for the result.

When it appeared, he slumped back in his chair. "Shit!"

"Something wrong, hon?"

Sally had noticed the long silences in between the frantic key pounding and come to investigate.

"Yeah, there's something seriously wrong with the program."

"That can't be right, hon, you've tested and tested it a million times. It's always come up trumps."

"I know. But while it can differentiate a contemporary of Moretti's and Moretti, as you would expect, at the same time it says the Moretti and both the Andrews are painted by the same artist."

"It said that?"

"Yeah, makes no sense at all."

"Have you run other Morettis against Andrews' paintings?"

"Good idea. I'll dig some out."

An hour later, a despondent Ced appeared at the bottom of the stairs. Sally looked up from her book and saw him standing there, head and shoulders drooping. She rushed over to him and threw her arms around his neck, hugging him tightly.

"Come on, hon, it can't be that bad. It's gone too far and been too successful to fail now. You'll find what's causing the problem."

He laid his head on her shoulder. "What if I can't, Sal? This sort of program has to be bulletproof. If it can't distinguish between the work of two painters whose lives only overlapped by a couple of years, then it's no good."

"Tell me what you've done."

"Well, I've run the two Andrews paintings against all the Morettis I can find and I get the same ridiculous results, basically that Andrews painted the Morettis, or vice versa. I've also run the Johnstons, and other Moretti contemporaries, all landscape artists, and none of them compares with either Moretti or Andrews, which is what you'd expect. And, of course, they differ from each other."

"So the only anomalous result is when you run Moretti against Andrews; for everyone else, you can distinguish them?"

There was a silence.

"Hon?"

Ced was shaking his head.

"No. I thought that was the case, but then I went a bit further."

"What do you mean?"

Ced sighed wearily; he could feel his world collapsing around him.

"You know the case I've been working on recently, the eighteenth century forgeries?"

164

"Yes, but I thought they were portraits."

"They are, most of them. But some of the artists also produced landscapes with country houses, grand homes, that sort of thing. Well, I thought they might be a useful alternative control. They've all behaved as expected so far, so if the program's suddenly become corrupted somewhere, running them again might show it. So I linked up with the computer at the lab and called up a selection. There were ten artists in all that I had been comparing with the alleged forgeries. I ran all the genuine eighteenth century paintings against the Andrews, the Morettis, the Johnstons, and a couple of others. All was fine, all very distinguishable except one, and that one I can't distinguish from either Moretti or Andrews. It's ridiculous, Sal. How can that be?"

"Who's the artist?"

"Jean de la Place. He's a fairly obscure French artist who worked in England for twenty years or so, mainly in London and then, apparently, just disappeared."

"Never heard of him."

"No, well, he was hardly big time. But it gets worse. De la Place specialised mainly in portraits; landscapes were a bit of a sideline. So I looked for what I had in the libraries on his portraits and found one good hi-res image. It's of a middle-aged woman, semi-profile, rather like the Andrews old lady of Claw's. When I called it up, I couldn't help noticing how similar it was in style and technique to Andrews' portraits; it's got that same Renaissance feel about it."

"How did it compare with Claw's painting?"

"That's the crunch. The analysis says the two portraits are by the same artist."

"Christ."

"I really don't know what to do, Sal. Well, that's not true. I'm going to dissect the program line by line, look at all the assumptions, routines, algorithms, etc., to check them. But you know, in my gut, I don't think the program's corrupted. Why should it go wrong for only some artists?"

Ced worked on through the evening and into the night, checking and re-checking the code.

At four in the morning, a bleary-eyed Sally wandered into the study.

"Hon, don't you think you should give it a break? You need to get some rest."

"I know, Sal, but it's driving me crazy, I can't find anything. I'm convinced that all the underlying principles I've used are sound; the algorithms were all very carefully crafted."

"I've been thinking about the quality of the images," said Sally. "How many of the images you've been using have you made with your top notch kit, and how many are images from the libraries?"

"The only one that I've made is the one of the portrait that Claw bought. All the others are from libraries, apart from the photo I took of the Andrews landscape, and I accept that that one is of limited quality. Why?"

"So you have no control over their quality."

"No, but I allow for it. That's one of the prime factors written into the program. I know that I won't always be able to get direct access to an original painting to photograph it under controlled conditions with ideal lighting, so I've allowed for that in the programming. It affects the confidence factor of the result, but unless the image is total crap, you get something."

"Suppose there is something in the images that's screwing the results, something you're perhaps assuming is right that isn't. Do you think it might be an idea to get access to some of these paintings and use your own kit? At least then you'd be comparing like with like; one potential variable would have been eliminated."

Ced rubbed his chin thoughtfully. "Well, I suppose it could be worth a punt, but I really thought I'd got that one covered. There are several Morettis in the National Gallery, and some Johnstons. I could call Lawrence Forbes tomorrow – he owes me a favour – and go down to London."

Sal smiled at him as she saw his features relax. There was a glimmer of hope, a faint chance that the problem could be solved, and he had jumped at it.

"Good, then I think it's time you took your mind off computers and put your boundless energy to better use."

She took hold of his arm and led him from his chair into the bedroom.

Ced awoke with a start at seven-thirty, looked at the clock and started to get out of bed.

"Where are you going, marathon man?" mumbled Sally sleepily. "I was on the podium accepting my Olympic gold medal for the pentathlon. You've ruined my moment of glory."

"It's seven thirty, Sal, time for my run."

"Forget it, lover boy, it's Sunday. Alternative sport day." She yanked him back down and pulled the duvet over them.

It was noon before Ced finally staggered out of bed, heading straight for the kitchen. He prepared them both some breakfast, put it on a tray and took it back to the bedroom.

"Wow, breakfast in bed!" smiled Sally. "You must be feeling well relaxed this morning."

"It's actually afternoon," grinned Ced. "I've been thinking about what you said about the hi-res images. You could have a point."

"I have some of my best ideas at four in the morning," smiled Sally.

Lawrence Forbes was an old friend from Ced's Cambridge days. They had studied fine art together and when Ced went on to study image analysis, Lawrence had taken a doctorate in European Art of the eighteenth and nineteenth centuries. Now an assistant curator in the National Gallery's European Art division, he was responsible for maintaining the Gallery's extensive collection of works from that era.

Forbes was one hundred per cent behind Ced's project and had already used early versions of the program to confirm his doubts about several very good forgeries he'd been offered. He would be as devastated as Ced if it failed.

Ced called him at home that afternoon and described the problem.

"Gosh, Cedric," replied Forbes in the clipped tones of his public school accent, "that's jolly worrying news. There's got to be some sensible explanation, you know. The fundamentals of your thesis are rock solid. Nevertheless, it's a jolly good idea to get your own images. We've got plenty of Morettis stashed away and a few de la Place's. Picked up one myself from a private sale not long ago. It's a remarkable work too. De la Place was something of an enigmatic character. Not a lot known about him before or after his time in England. But from the little I've seen of his work, I'd say he's very underrated."

"That's brilliant, Lawrence, thanks," replied Ced. "I knew you'd understand. Listen, I'm not going to be able to concentrate on anything else until I've got this sorted. D'you think I could come down in the morning?"

"No problem, Cedric, old chap. I'll dig around the store and get out the paintings you want. How's the lovely Sally?"

"She's great, thanks, Lawrence; sends her love. Harriet and the kids OK?"

"All wonderful, Cedric. Mind you, the kids can be a bit of a handful. Talking of which, old chap, got to dash. Little Algy's yelling for something and Harri's taken Jane to the park. Nanny's day off too. Bit of a war zone in the sitting room."

With train delays, it was closer to noon by the time Ced arrived at Forbes' office in the National Gallery the following day.

Forbes looked pleased with himself. "Dug through the shelves for you, Cedric, and guess what? We have eighteen Morettis. Several are from his 'Blitz' series, but there are six sizeable landscapes with grand houses and so on. Found a similar bunch of Johnstons, too. Sort of stuff you're after?"

"Brilliant, Lawrence! That should put the program through its paces, although I'm afraid the only Andrews landscape I've got is a photo taken on a point and shoot. However, I do have an excellent image of a portrait – the painting the program matches with the Morettis and the de la Place portrait."

"Well, the other good news, Cedric, is that I've unearthed seven de la Place portraits."

"That's brilliant, Lawrence. Where are they?"

"Over here," replied Lawrence, pointing to a large table in the corner of his huge office. "Come and take a look."

He walked over to the paintings, picked up the first one and handed it to Ced. It was a half-profile of a young woman in her early twenties in mid-eighteenth century clothing. Her pale brown eyes were looking back at the artist and her lips slightly parted as if in conversation. Ced held the picture spellbound.

168

"How come I've never seen this before; it's truly amazing. She looks as if she's about to walk off the canvas into the room."

"So many artists, so little time," replied Lawrence.

"You know, Lawrence, it's incredibly like the Andrews portrait. Take a look on my laptop."

Ced hit a few keys and Forbes peered at the screen.

"Good heavens!" exclaimed Forbes. "How remarkable. Better get your stuff out and run some image comparisons."

Ced set up his equipment on the table. It comprised an impressively compact set of lights together with a high-resolution large-format camera boasting scores of megapixels.

Once he'd recorded his images and transferred them to the computer, he set the comparison program running. While he was waiting, he studied the details of each of the paintings. He found himself spellbound by the de la Place portraits, most of them of aristocratic-looking women of various ages. He shook his head and wondered. Suddenly he no longer felt confident his program would distinguish these paintings from the Andrews portrait; he was certainly unable to do it by eye.

An hour later, the analysis was finished. Now there was no flourish when Ced hit the 'Cool' button, only a sinking feeling in the pit of his stomach.

A glance down the column of raw data was all that he needed to confirm his thoughts. The results were as before, but worse since there were more paintings. All the de la Place portraits showed a very close match to the Andrews portrait and the Morettis. By contrast, the Johnstons that Forbes had provided as controls showed no similarity.

Ced was on his own when he reviewed the results, Forbes having excused himself to search out another painting the de la Place portrait reminded him of.

When he came back into his office, Ced was despondently packing up his equipment.

"How are the results, Cedric?" asked Forbes, not registering the look of despair on Ced's face.

Ced glanced up at him. "Shattering, Lawrence, completely shattering. I don't know why, but I'd become convinced that if I took my own hi-res images and compared them, the problem would be solved. Well, it wasn't. It's got worse."

Forbes nodded sympathetically. "There's got to be an explanation, Cedric, we're just missing it. I absolutely do not believe your program is flawed."

"That's as maybe, Lawrence, and I'm grateful for your confidence, but I can't use the program any more for my work until I've solved the problem. God, if this lot all goes pear-shaped, I'll be a laughing stock. I've put so much store by this work and I've convinced a lot of people of its capabilities. I don't know what to do."

He turned and continued to pack his cases.

"Oh, before you put all that away, Cedric, you might want to take a look at this. I'm not trying to add fuel to the fire, but I suddenly remembered it and I think you might find it interesting."

He handed Ced the small painting he was carrying.

Unbeknown to him, it was a portrait of Beth Markham painted by Tommaso Perini some years after their arrival in Arezzo.

"It's exquisite, Lawrence, and you don't need to point out the similarities. But it's old, much older than the de la Place portraits. You can see that from the clothes this woman is wearing, and from the overall condition of the painting."

"Do you know who it's by?" asked Forbes.

Ced looked up at him with a bitter smile. "John Andrews?"

Forbes laughed. "Come on, Cedric, we'll sort this out. It's Tommaso Perini. Heard of him?"

Ced thought for a moment. "Sixteenth century. Italian. Rome wasn't it? No, that was another Perini. Um, Piero, I think. Let me see, Tommaso. Tuscany somewhere."

"Very good, Cedric. He lived and worked in Arezzo. Although, like our friend de la Place, his life is shrouded in a certain amount of mystery. His early years, that is."

"It's beautiful, Lawrence. Must be worth quite a bit. Where did you get it?"

"Colleague of mine picked it up in Rome recently. Got it for a song. Quite a coup. The Italians would be hopping if they knew, even though it was a perfectly legitimate purchase."

"All's fair in love and art, eh, Lawrence."

"Do you want to add it to your comparisons? When I saw the de la Places, they reminded me of it. It would be another good test for your program. It surely can't match these others as well. When the program says it's by a different artist, it will renew your confidence. Let's do it."

"OK, Lawrence, if you insist, but I have a funny feeling about it."

Thirty minutes later, the program finished churning.

"Moment of truth, Lawrence," said Ced dryly as he clicked the 'Cool' button. He felt like a prisoner facing a firing squad.

"Well?" asked Forbes as he watched Ced scan his eyes over the numbers. Ced scrolled down the screen to a results summary and the words: Match. Degree of confidence: 95%.

Ced sat back, shook his head and uttered a brittle laugh. "You know what this means, Lawrence?"

Forbes shook his head slowly, still stunned by the result he had been sure would be negative.

"It means, my friend," he said as he started to close the computer down, "that Tommaso Perini is alive and well and living in the Lake District."

Forbes smiled thoughtfully. He was silent for a few moments, and then a light seemed to switch on in his eyes.

"There's another explanation, Cedric, certainly with the Perini and I think with the de la Places," he said slowly, his head nodding as he developed the idea in his mind.

Ced waited.

"You know, these paintings' provenances aren't really known too well. This Perini has appeared out of nowhere and while I was fetching it just now, I checked the records on the de la Places. They've all come out of private collections in the last ten years."

"Andrews," whispered Ced.

"Exactly. This John Andrews is a most accomplished artist, and consequently he could be a brilliant forger. We could have here the most remarkable set of forgeries discovered in modern times. And this could be the tip of the iceberg."

Ced's mind raced with the possibilities. "What about the Morettis? Could he have produced those as well?"

"It's stretching things a bit. You've seen Andrews. How old would you say he is?"

"Hard to say really. He could be a lived-in thirty, but he could also be a well-preserved forty-five."

"So let's say he's forty-five. That would mean he was born in nineteen sixty-four. The first of these Morettis came out of a private collection in nineteen eighty. He would have been sixteen."

"Mmm," considered Ced. "Pushing it a bit, but not beyond the bounds of possibility. Child prodigy and all that."

"Well, let's leave the Morettis aside for now; they're too modern." Forbes was now getting excited with his theory. "But we can certainly test the Perini and the de la Places. Andrews must have made a mistake somewhere. I'll get our lab onto it. Sort of challenge they love."

Ced stood up and put his hands on his friend's shoulders. "God, Lawrence, you've made me feel better. Listen, while your lab is doing that analysis, there's something else I can do. You know Corrado Verdi in the Rome Art Academy, don't you?"

"Certainly. He's the ultimate fount of all knowledge for Italian art from the Renaissance onwards; a mine of information. Name an Italian artist and he'll list his works and tell you where they are, what condition they're in and not only whether they're available for sale, but also how much to pay for them."

"That's Corrado. Well, it occurs to me that Andrews can't have produced every Perini available everywhere, especially in the museums of Italy. Some of them must have been there since long before John Andrews was born. If I were to go to Italy, talk to Corrado, I'm sure he could arrange for me to make my own hi-res images of a number of Perinis that are one hundred per cent genuine. They must turn out to be different, even if the differences are subtle. That's what this program's designed to do: spot the subtleties to beat these buggers at their own game."

He slapped Lawrence on the back, nearly knocking him over.

"Christ! No wonder Andrews was so reluctant to play ball. The man's a master forger!"

# Chapter 16

## 1780-1794

Pierre Labreche sighed with relief as the coach scraped along the cobbles of the Pont de Saône toward Presqu'île, the peninsula in the centre of Lyon formed by the confluence of the Saône and Rhône rivers. The ride from Paris had taken nine spine-jarring days; the earlier journey from London even longer.

He had spent the last thirty years in London as the portrait painter, Jean de la Place. Now he had moved on. A change of name, age and location. He was returning to Florence, but first he was visiting his son, Michel.

Michel had kept the surname, Laroche, that they had both adopted on their arrival in Paris in 1701, although in 1730, he had adjusted his age when he had met and married Marie Gravoix and they had moved to her home town of Lyon. Michel had told his wife about himself and his father, and later, when they had grown, Michel and Marie's three children, François, Paulette and Pascal had also been let into the secret. For the Laroche household, a father who never aged was accepted as a closely guarded secret, as was the subterfuge involved when he adopted disguises to age himself.

Now, in 1780, Michel acted the part of an old man, a widower since Marie's recent death. However, once behind the closed doors of Michel's house, the two men could relax and swap stories without fear of suspicion. They looked like brothers; their pale grey eyes striking, although Michel also bore a strong resemblance to his long-dead mother Arlette.

"I am changing my name, Papa," announced Michel, "and, of

course, my age. Michel Laroche is old and it's time he met his maker. I am to become his cousin's grandson, Charles Landry, a young artist recently arrived from Paris."

"I am pleased to make your acquaintance, Monsieur Landry. Pierre Labreche at your service, also recently arrived from Paris and en route to Florence to establish a portrait studio!"

"I hope to visit you often, Monsieur Labreche; Florence is such a cultured city."

"Can I not tempt you to join me, Michel? I should dearly love us to work together again."

"In Italy, Papa, no. My poor language skills would be as much a hindrance as ever."

His father smiled. "But will you at least accompany me to Marseille? I want to visit your mother's grave. And when you visit me in Florence, we shall travel to Rome to Henri's."

Two months later, on a crisp October morning, the two men opened the gate of the churchyard on the hill above Marseille. It had been more than a hundred years since they had set foot there and they were relieved to find it well maintained. They made straight for the secluded corner near an ancient olive tree where they had laid Arlette and Georges to rest, finding to their delight that the crude wooden crosses they'd left behind on that sad evening had been replaced with engraved headstones.

"Jacques," said Pierre, as much to himself as to Charles. "He wrote to me in Siena to tell me he had arranged these. After that, I lost touch with him. He was getting old by then; I regret I don't know what happened to him."

"Well, I know what happened to Mathilde," said Charles, pointing to the next headstone along. "Look, Papa. 'Mathilde Bognard, 1604 - 1686. Much beloved wife of Jacques Bognard'."

Pierre looked at the stone and then at the others nearby, but there was no indication that Jacques was also buried there.

"These gravestones are very well maintained, Papa. It's as if they are new, not a hundred years old. There's a priest just leaving the church; I'll see what he knows."

When he returned, he was smiling softly.

"Papa, the priest told me that Jacques left a considerable sum in the hands of the Church with instructions that it be invested and the profit used to keep all three graves tidy with fresh flowers put on each weekly; these instructions to be carried out in perpetuity."

Pierre smiled incredulously. "I'm delighted the Church decided that 'perpetuity' should last this long."

Charles smiled. "I think I'll fetch some flowers," he said.

"An excellent idea, Charles. After so long, it will be good to lay our own flowers on their graves. I'll stay and talk to your Maman for a while."

Half an hour later, Pierre was in earnest conversation with Arlette's headstone when the priest interrupted him.

"Forgive me, m'sieur, I couldn't help overhearing. Your discussion with the deceased lady was quite agitated at times. Your ancestor must have been an important person in your family's history."

Dragged back into the present, Pierre looked round at him, embarrassed. Then he laughed at the priest's words.

"Forgive me, Father, I didn't mean to disturb the peace of this tranquil spot."

He started to walk away, but stopped and half-turned. "But Father, she wasn't my ancestor. For more than twenty years we lived together as man and wife."

The confused priest spun round to look at the headstone to confirm what he remembered of the dates carved on it, his mouth dropping open as he did. Turning back, he was in time to see Pierre disappearing through the gate.

Arriving in Florence three weeks later, Pierre immediately set about exploring the city that he had first visited some three hundred and forty years before as a very young man with Piero della Francesca. He was astounded how much of the city was still as he remembered it: although there were many new buildings, the essence of the Renaissance remained. He suspected it always would.

A week later, he found the perfect studio – a ground floor premises with a terrace bordering the south bank of the Arno, two hundred yards from the Ponte Vecchio. His apartment was just two blocks away.

As he was moving into the studio, on a freezing morning in early January 1781, he was interrupted by the yapping of a small terrier that had run in from the street. A small urchin of a girl followed in hot pursuit.

"Arno!" her young voice piped. "Come 'ere!" The dog ran at her and with a deft swoop, she gathered him into her arms. But she misjudged the dog's speed and the impact knocked her backwards. She sat down with a bump, still clutching the struggling dog.

"You naughty dog, Arno! I've told you not to run into other people's houses, ain't I?"

She struggled to her feet and started towards the street door, but Pierre was blocking her way.

"Just a minute, young lady."

He looked at the shivering girl. Her dress was little more than rags, her long black hair a matted mess of curls, her face and body filthy. Her eyes darted around the studio, looking for the opportunity to run. There was no fear in them; simply caution and cunning.

Pierre thought of Sofia and Gianna, his daughters born in the 1540s and smiled at her. "This is no weather to be out on the street, especially in those flimsy rags. Come and warm yourself and your dog by the stove; I'll warm up some broth for you."

The girl eyed him suspiciously, but it was too good an offer to miss.

"Can me bruvver have some too?"

"Of course. Where is he? Outside?"

"Yeah, in the street."

"Why don't you go and call him?"

The girl, Tella, was seven and her brother, Fausto, nine. They had been on the street for as long as they could remember, but Pierre knew that their chances of survival among the ruthless gangs that ran the urchins were slim. They were both painfully thin and if hunger didn't take them, the cold weather surely would. He watched them thoughtfully while they wolfed down the broth, along with cheese and bread, and he knew he couldn't turn them out. He struck a bargain with them that they simply couldn't believe. They could stay. He would clothe and feed them and give them a roof over their heads. In return, they would help him around the studio and accompany him on the streets when the weather improved so that when he was sketching in the more dangerous areas of the city, he would remain unmolested by other beggars and street urchins.

Six years later, in the late summer of 1787 when Charles finally found time to visit Pierre, the underfed urchins had transformed into well-spoken and refined young teenagers. Tella, now thirteen, had taken to literature with a passion, seeking out books and devouring them in every spare moment. She also had a natural flair for languages, speaking French and English at every opportunity with Pierre. Fausto, less academic, was very skillful with his hands and was now apprenticed to a local master carpenter.

Pierre had not told Tella and Fausto about himself. As far as they knew, he was a thirty-one-year-old Frenchman who had previously lived in Lyon and Paris; Charles was an old childhood friend. He had warned Charles in more than one letter that he must be very careful not to call him 'Papa' in the children's presence, and preferably not at all.

When Charles arrived at the studio, he knocked lightly, whispering his name to Tella when she answered the door and touching his fingers to his lips. He stepped quietly into the studio where Pierre was engrossed in his work. He walked up behind him and peered over his shoulder.

"You've left that wart off the end of her nose; I'm sure she'll be delighted."

Pierre spun round, almost colliding with him. "Charles! My dear Charles! How wonderful! You are here!"

They hugged and greeted each other with a warmth that surprised Tella: even to her young eyes they seemed more than just friends. While Pierre and Charles launched into animated conversation in French, she looked closely at this man with the strange French accent – she was unfamiliar with the Marseille dialect – and she was struck by how like Pierre he was, especially the eyes. Their mannerisms too were similar. If they were related, brothers maybe, why hadn't Pierre told her?

She realised Pierre was introducing her. "This, Charles, is my lovely Donatella, but she's Tella to everyone, the sweetest child, and one who is growing into a beautiful young lady."

Charles held out his hand to the blushing Tella. "I'm delighted to meet you, Donatella," he said. "Pierre has told me so much about you in his letters."

"I'm very pleased to meet you too, monsieur," she replied in French as she curtseyed to him.

Laughing loudly, Charles replied, "Brava, my dear, you have a good accent, I could almost imagine you are French. Pierre, you have taught her well. But Tella, you must call me Charles. I am not one for formality; we must all be like one big family."

Pierre picked up one of Charles' bags. "You must be exhausted after your journey, Charles. We'll close up the studio for the day and return to the apartment where you can soak your aching bones in a tub of hot water while Tella and I prepare you some luncheon."

Tella had never seen Pierre so animated. As she hurried ahead of them to prepare the fire under the water for Charles' bath, it occurred to her that the man she thought she knew so well had a hidden side and a history she knew nothing about.

"So tell me, Charles, what is the political situation now in France? One hears so many rumours of discontent spreading around the country."

They had finished their lunch and they were sitting on the apartment's small balcony.

Charles' face darkened. "The situation is not good, Pierre. The king continues in his excesses while the lot of the poor and even the middle classes gets worse. Lyon is royalist at heart, but there are many of us who are worried that if the king continues to ignore the needs of his country, the undercurrent of discontent could swell into a raging river of revolution."

"Have you ever considered leaving?"

"Well, I–" started Charles, but his eye caught Tella's and he remembered that she knew nothing of their history. "I have thought about it, but France is my home and despite its problems, I have no wish to leave. And I really do not have an ear for other languages."

Pierre laughed and turned to Tella. "What do you make of this man's French, Tella? Is it difficult to follow?"

"It's different from yours. Pierre. Which region is it from?"

The two men laughed and broke into a broad, street version of the Marseille dialect.

"I spent much of my youth in Marseille, Tella," explained Charles. "The accent there is strong and although I have lived away from the city for many years now, I fear I cannot lose it altogether. I'll teach you some of the words and expressions."

"Thank you, but I fear it might confuse my rather limited French."

"Nonsense, your French is excellent. Maybe when you're a little older, you should persuade Pierre to let you come to Lyon. A couple of months there and you'll be speaking French like one of the locals."

Charles' departure two months later left Pierre dispirited and Tella decided he needed a diversion. With fewer commissions as the season changed, she suggested one of her own.

"I'm afraid I cannot afford to pay you, signore," she said to Pierre, fluttering her eyelashes, "but if I am satisfied that you have been able to apply a likeness of me to a canvas in a competent enough manner, I can offer recompense in the form of a number of expertly prepared dinners."

"For which I buy the food," chuckled Pierre. "It's an excellent idea, Tella, I haven't painted your portrait for a couple of years now, and I should like to capture the last vestige of your childhood before the woman that is blossoming daily before me has replaced the little Tella I love so much."

She gave him a hug. "I'll go and find my finest dress."

"No, I shall have plenty of opportunity to paint Donatella the beautiful woman. It's the still-present child I want to capture. Come, sit over here so this soft afternoon light can play onto your hair. I need to start sketching."

Tella used the opportunity of sitting for Pierre to probe more deeply into his past with Charles. As he gave her what sounded like details, she realised he was being evasive. His account was insubstantial despite being wordy; there were episodes in their lives that didn't really add up: neither of them was old enough to have spent so much time in the places Pierre described. As for the Laroche family to whom Charles seemed so attached, where did they fit in?

Such a bond could not have resulted from a brief visit to Lyon; he must have lived there for years. Tella was frustrated: if she started to make what she thought was progress in her questioning, Pierre would shush her on the excuse that her face needed to be still.

Charles' regular letters started arriving again a month after his departure. Pierre would read and reread them, smiling warmly, sometimes laughing out loud. He would recite small passages, but Tella never got sight of them. Whenever she tried to position herself to see them, Pierre would artfully move away, folding them and putting them back in his jacket pocket.

He kept the letters in a locked box under his bed, the key always somewhere about his person. Tella had carefully retrieved the box and studied the lock on a number of occasions. It wasn't a simple one, but then again, it wasn't overcomplicated. With the right skills...

Tella and Fausto still had a few contacts from their early childhood on the streets, although they kept them well away from Pierre's eyes. One, Federico, now a gangly youth of twenty, was an expert lockpicker. She found him and for the price of two hearty meals he taught her what she needed to know. The opportunity to use her new skills arose when Pierre travelled to Siena to discuss a commission with a wealthy family who wanted a number of portraits. Once she'd seen him off, Tella went to Pierre's room and gently removed the box from under the bed. Taking great care not to scratch the lock mechanism, she gingerly applied the picks, feeling the tension in the springs and balancing their resistance. It turned out to be remarkably easy. With a deft twist, she turned the larger main pick and the lock opened. She lifted the lid. Inside were the dozens of letters that Pierre had received from Charles over the last seven years, all neatly stacked in two piles of bundles of about ten letters each, each bundle tied with cord.

Tella felt her heart racing. She had never felt so guilty about anything in her life. But she had to continue. She waited for her heart to settle down while she stared at the contents of the box. After memorising the layout of the letters, she lifted out the top bundle and pulled out the first letter. It was dated one year earlier and she gasped as she began to read.

'*Cher Papa,*'

Papa! Why would Charles call Pierre 'Papa'? It made no sense. Then her eyes fell on the signature.

'*Your loving son, Michel.*'

The letter was not from Charles!

She was now thoroughly confused. Pierre had a son? He was only thirty-one years old; how could he have a son who was old enough to write in such an adult hand? He would have to be at least fifteen.

She chose another letter. Dated six months earlier, it started and finished in the same way. She pulled out others: same greeting, same ending. Eventually she found one dated April 1781. It too was the same!

She started to read the letters to see if she could make any more sense of the puzzle.

Fifteen minutes later it had become clear that all the letters, while signed Michel, were from Charles. He spoke extensively and with great affection about the Laroche family; he talked about how much he still missed Marie, his wife; and about someone called François who appeared to be his son, but who himself had children. There was someone called Arlette whom he also called Maman and who seemed to have been murdered many years ago, and a brother, Henri, who had also been murdered.

She read and reread the letters but could make absolutely no sense of them. Finally, she replaced them all, locked the box and placed it carefully back under Pierre's bed.

Tella spent the rest of the day in a daze, trying in vain to make some sense of the letters. Finally, she realised that nothing about them affected her personally. Pierre clearly loved her and Fausto as a father would love his children. He trusted them totally and she had betrayed that trust. That thought reduced her to tears.

By the time Pierre returned home that evening, full of amusing tales of the family commissioning him, Tella's thumping heart had settled down and her outward appearance was one of her usual calm. Pierre noticed nothing odd in her behaviour, even though she scrutinised his face far more than was her normal practice.

In late July 1789, news started to reach Florence of the storming of the Bastille in Paris and of riots throughout the French countryside where the estates of the nobility were attacked. The revolution Charles had predicted had started and France would never be the same again.

Although the flow of letters from Charles was less regular, he had a merchant friend who made occasional trips to northern Italy who agreed to carry his letters across the border and dispatch them to Florence. Pierre was therefore able to keep track of events in Lyon and the rest of the country. With each successive letter, Pierre became increasingly concerned. Charles, his son, François – now a senior figure in the administration of the city – and Paulette's husband, Bertrand, had all taken up with the royalist cause, a move Pierre considered to be potentially dangerous.

In early 1792, Charles' increasingly infrequent letters stopped altogether. Pierre was beside himself with worry and it was only Tella's persistent reasoning that dissuaded him from heading for Lyon. Then, suddenly, after six months of silence, a letter arrived. He and the family were safe. His merchant friend had been attacked and murdered on the road south out of Lyon and Charles had not been able to find an alternative courier. However, there were to be no more letters.

In mid-1793, the so-called Reign of Terror started and continued until the execution of one of its principal leaders, Maximilien Robespierre, in July 1794. During this dark period, following fighting in Paris among the rival factions – the Jacobins and the Girondists – the administrators of Lyon sided with the Girondists, effectively setting themselves apart from the main revolutionary rulers in the capital. Such action could not be tolerated and a force was dispatched to bring Lyon to heel. The siege of Lyon that ensued lasted over a month, after which the city's civil authorities surrendered. Paris had had its way.

The end of the siege of Lyon on October 9, 1793, also marked the end for Charles, François and Bertrand, together with François' eldest son, Jacques. Identified as being among the leading players in the Girondist movement in the city, they were arrested and summarily executed by firing squad, along with several dozen others from the city's administration.

When Pierre heard of the siege of Lyon and its bloody aftermath, he became desperate for information and was only prevented from going by Tella who insisted that if he was fool enough to risk his life while the terror stalked the length and breadth of France, she was going with him.

It was not until early in a typically hot August in 1794 that Pierre finally learnt the awful truth about Charles. He was alone in the studio when the knock came on the door – Tella, now twenty and in charge of the business side of the studio, was out interviewing a prospective client. It was no more than three sharp blows, but it conveyed a sense of urgency and foreboding that caused Pierre to stop in his tracks. He opened the door without a word. Facing him was a young man in his early twenties, his travelling clothes far too thick for the August heat, his long hair lank with sweat and his face grimy. Pierre recognised him immediately, even though the boy had only been seven when they last met. The look in his eyes confirmed all that Pierre had feared.

"You are Étienne," said Pierre in French. It was a statement, not a question.

"Yes, monsieur, and I believe you are Monsieur Pierre Labreche. But my mother insisted that you state the name by which she knew you. She is very conscious of the need for security."

Pierre shrugged. "The name you seek is Jean de la Place." He showed him in.

"You look exhausted," said Pierre as he fetched him some water.

"My horse lost a shoe a few miles away, so I have had to walk the rest of the way."

"My groom will deal with it," replied Pierre.

He sat opposite the young man. "I am indebted to you, Étienne. You have come far on what I have no doubt was a difficult and dangerous journey to give me news that I fear I can read in your eyes and in your stance."

"You owe me nothing, monsieur. I did not wish to come; it was only at my mother's insistence." His voice was angry, strained.

Although disturbed by the youth's words and tone, Pierre said nothing, giving him time to gather his thoughts.

After a few moments, he lifted his eyes. Pierre was shocked at how cold and empty they appeared. "You will have heard about the siege, monsieur, I am sure. It started in–"

Pierre held up a hand and said very quietly, "Please, Étienne. Tell me about Charles. And about your father."

Étienne held Pierre's eyes. "They are dead, monsieur. All dead. Charles, Papa, Bertrand and Jacques."

"How?" Pierre's voice was scarcely audible.

"A firing squad. They were herded with many others from the city's administration and lined up against a wall. They were taken from their homes by force, marched to the square, and shot. I only escaped because my father had pushed me into the cellar with my mother, insisting I take care of her. I should have died with them."

"And the bodies?" asked Pierre in a whisper. "What happened to the bodies?"

"That was the final insult, monsieur. They were slung onto a cart and taken to a mass grave outside the city. It was not even consecrated ground."

Pierre stood and walked out onto the terrace to stare at the Arno, its waters listless and sluggish in the summer heat. Why hadn't he gone?

After some minutes, he returned to the studio.

"How is your mother, Étienne?"

"How do you expect, monsieur? She is heartbroken. And yet, monsieur, her thoughts have always been with you. She has kept saying that you must be told, as if everything depended on it. Why should that be, monsieur? I know you are my great-grandfather, although I do not understand how you can be, but why was it so important that you be told? You were not part of our lives. You were not part of the cause. You chose to remain here in the safety of this city in another country. You never visited. You had no relevance to our family. So why was it so important?" He was angry now, accusing.

"I had every intention of visiting, Étienne, especially after Charles' visit in '87. We wrote regularly; he kept me informed about your family. Please believe me, I meant to come, but then the Revolution started. Charles insisted that I wait. As did Tella and Fausto."

He was startled by a snort from Étienne. "Ah, the famous Tella. Is she your wife yet? I hear she is very beautiful."

"My wife! Whatever are you talking about? Tella is my … well; she's like a daughter. And Fausto like a son. What do you think you are saying?" Pierre had to fight the anger welling up inside him.

There was another dismissive snort from Étienne. "From my grandfather's behaviour, I assume that age has been of no consequence to either of you. I do not know how old he was, only that he was very old. You are aware, I assume, that in the last five years of his life he took up with a girl younger than I am. It disgusts me even to think about it."

Pierre was genuinely surprised. Charles had told him nothing of any relationship in his letters.

"I knew nothing of this. What did your parents have to say about it?"

"They didn't seem to think it odd; if anything they encouraged it. But for me it was a betrayal of the memory of my grandmother. An old man like that. No matter how young he looked, it was sinful."

For the first time, Pierre noticed the thick chain around Étienne's neck. He suspected there was a substantial cross hanging from it tucked out of sight in his clothes.

"Étienne, you must remember that life was very different for your grandfather, as it is for me. We are not like ordinary people, as I am sure your father will have explained. Your grandmother, Marie, understood this and when she died, one of her main concerns was that her husband would be able to start a new life with someone else. He was very resistant to this idea, so devoted was he to her. If he eventually did find someone else, it is not for you to judge him. He was an honourable man with a strong sense of duty to his family, all of whom he loved dearly, including you."

"I think you are all making excuses for him," snapped Étienne. "I think–"

He was interrupted by a shout from Tella as she came rushing through the street door. "Pierre! Pierre! Guess what? I … oh, sorry, I didn't realise you had a visitor." She turned to Étienne. "My apologies, signore."

Étienne didn't respond – not speaking Italian, he hadn't under-stood. He was also angry to have been interrupted.

When Tella registered his disdainful look, she frowned and looked more carefully at him. It only took a moment for the light to dawn. The eyes weren't the same, but otherwise there was a strong family resemblance. She turned to Pierre and registered the pain in his eyes. Without a word, she put her arms around him.

"Oh, Pierre, I am so sorry."

As Pierre finally reacted to the news, his legs buckled and he almost pulled Tella over. As they fell, she guided him onto a sofa where his head sagged onto her shoulder and he wept, huge gasps of grief shuddering through his body.

After some time, Pierre recovered enough to suggest they go to the apartment. As they left the studio, Tella tried again to speak to Étienne, but he replied in French that he didn't understand her. Apologising, she switched immediately into French, which, although accented, was now fluent.

"Your French is good, mademoiselle," he said humourlessly. "Where did you learn it?"

"Pierre has been teaching me since I was little. We speak it together often."

"I imagine my great-grandfather has picked up a number of languages," replied Étienne, his tone still cold and aloof.

"Your great-gra...? Er, yes, I think he has." Tella tried hard to hide her shock as the pieces of the puzzle fell into place in her mind. Charles had not been a friend of the Laroches; he was one of them, as was Pierre. She would tuck this piece of information away until she judged the time was right to confront Pierre with it.

Despite their attempts to break down Étienne's reserve, he remained uncommunicative and distant, answering their questions briefly and factually, but never expanding on any theme. A serious doubt about him dawned in Pierre's mind and he tried to draw out the young man's views about the Revolution. For someone who had lost his father, grandfather, uncle and cousin to the bloodlust of the Jacobins, he remained remarkably unemotional and noncommittal. It was only when Pierre touched on religion that Étienne became more animated. He was clearly devout and although he tried to hide it, there was a zealousness to his words that worried Pierre.

The one message that Étienne did reiterate was the request from his mother, Yvette, for Pierre to visit as soon as it was safe to do so.

But he made it clear that he had no interest in whether Pierre complied or not: he was merely the messenger.

After four days, Étienne declared he had no wish to stay longer. He left with a carefully sealed letter from Pierre to Yvette saying he would come as soon as possible.

After he left, Tella turned to Pierre. "What a dreadful man. I didn't trust him an inch. There was something about him. He has a secret, a guilt that made my skin crawl," she said, shuddering.

Pierre nodded. "I agree, Tella. I need to get to Lyon as soon as possible."

"Not on your own, Pierre. I insist that I come with you."

"Tella, we've discussed this endlessly. It will be a hard and dangerous journey. I cannot allow it."

"The choice, Pierre, is that I accompany you, or I follow behind on my own. Which would you rather I do – travel under your protection or pit my wits against the perils of the road alone?"

They arrived in Lyon three weeks later after a long but uneventful journey. While on their way, Pierre had cautiously broached the subject of Charles, finally admitting that Charles was his son and that they were both considerably older than they'd admitted.

"How old are you?" she asked quietly.

"I'd rather not say, Tella. Not at the moment, it's too difficult. After Lyon I'll tell you?"

She thought of the letters and once again felt guilty. Could he really be a great-grandfather? It seemed ridiculous; he looked so young. She'd heard of illnesses where children looked very old when they were still children. Perhaps there were also illnesses that made you look young when you were really very old. Was Pierre like that? If he was very old, was he about to die? The thought sent a shiver through her body. She couldn't imagine a life without him.

Pierre was aghast as he entered Lyon. The once bustling city, so full of life, colour and gaiety, had transformed into a sombre, forbidding place. The streets were almost deserted. What citizens there were scurrying from one shadow to the next, like rats seeking refuge in dark corners, afraid of the dangers of being exposed. There were soldiers everywhere, constantly checking papers and eyeing everyone suspiciously.

However, they arrived at the Laroche house without incident and were shown into a drawing room.

"Jean!" exclaimed Yvette bustling into the room and throwing her arms round him. "Oh, Jean, I've waited so long for this moment. Look at you; you haven't changed one jot. But then, why should you?"

Pierre was shocked at the change in Yvette in the fifteen years since he had seen her. She was old before her time, her face a maze of lines etched by the strain of the past few years.

But the old fussiness was still there as she held onto Pierre's arms, touched his jacket and stroked his face. She pressed her hands together in front of her lips. "I cannot tell you how wonderful it is to see you." She studied his face as if not believing he was real.

Pierre was lost for words. Then he remembered Tella. "Yvette, let me introduce Tella."

"Of course, of course, how rude of me. My dear child, welcome to our home. My, you are every bit as beautiful as dear Michel described you." Registering the look of confusion on Tella's face, she added, "I'm sorry, you will have known him as Charles. It's all so bewildering at times."

Over the following days, Pierre talked extensively with Yvette and Paulette about the events leading up to the awful day of the executions. Sometimes Tella was with them, others not. Pierre took the first opportunity to explain to Yvette that Tella had a limited understanding of his and Charles' secret.

"Then it's about time you told her the whole truth, Jean. She strikes me as a determined young woman. If she wants to, she won't find it difficult to extract the truth from you. It's only fair that she knows, anyway."

With every snippet Tella gained about Pierre, the more incredulous she became and the more determined to get to the bottom of his story. She found the Laroche family all totally unlike Étienne, who was very noticeable by his absence – he had moved out of the family home and was living in a hostel run by Dominican monks outside the city.

In describing the events leading up to the arrest and execution of the Laroche men, Yvette explained how surprised they all were to have been discovered so quickly. The details were not as Étienne had described them. François had been among the party surrendering to the besieging forces and he and other senior members of the administration had been quickly dealt with. However, they had all arranged for their immediate families to be protected or hidden, knowing the reprisals would be merciless. Expecting some delay in the searching of their homes, the families of the administration were surprised to find that their homes were clearly targeted, as if on a list. When the soldiers were about to enter the house, Étienne had taken the women to the cellar, telling them that he would protect them, while the other men remained upstairs. The soldiers made no attempt to search the cellar.

When Pierre told Tella, she was first shocked and then as she realised the significance of the story, her face darkened. "The murdering bastard!" She spat the words rather than spoke them. "You realise, Pierre, that Étienne must have been a spy for the Jacobins, an informer. He knew that the cellar of his house would not be searched: the soldiers had a list of houses where this was not to be carried out. But instead of getting everyone down there, he let the men remain to be captured. No wonder he behaved as he did in Florence. He must be racked with guilt. He knew his father would be executed; there was no choice. But to deliberately allow, encourage, the deaths of his grandfather and the others … where is the bastard? I want to kill him with my bare hands!"

Pierre took her hands. "Tella," he said, his voice trembling. "Yvette and the rest of the family have no knowledge of this. They think that Étienne is a hero, that he helped to save them. They must not know otherwise, it would destroy them."

"Hero!" yelled Tella. "He deserves to burn in hell!"

"Tella, there has been enough killing, I–"

"Pierre! That traitor was responsible for the murder of your son. He allowed it, cold-bloodedly and deliberately. And then he had the barefaced nerve to come to us in Florence and tell us a pack of lies. He cannot go unpunished!"

Pierre looked into Tella's eyes and saw the same cold determination he had seen long before in Gisèle's eyes when Arlette had been killed. Revenge.

"Tella, you cannot. We cannot take the law into our own hands."

"Pierre!" she yelled. "Are you crazy? The law is on his side. The law condoned what he did and will permit him to do it again. How safe do you think Yvette and her other children and their children are? Paulette and hers? Étienne is as mad and as twisted as any zealot can be. He will betray the entire family."

She stopped as another truth hit her.

"And he will betray you, Pierre. Don't you see? Whatever he says about you will be believed. He has won their trust. Étienne is no fool, Pierre. You are Charles' father. He will realise that once you have spoken to the family, you will guess the truth and want revenge. He will try to act more quickly than you. You are not safe here. We must leave without delay."

"So we must flee like cowards while Étienne continues in his treachery?"

"No, he will not continue in his treachery. I'm going out, Pierre. I'm not sure when I shall return. It might be a few hours. When I do, you must be ready to leave. So make your excuses to the family. We are going."

"Tella, you can't … it's too dangerous."

"You forget that I grew up on the streets. I was only young, but there are things that I learned then, things that I know. You probably do not realise that I have kept in touch with some of my street friends over the years. It's in my soul, Pierre, no matter how much of a lady you've made me."

"But that is Florence, Tella. This is Lyon."

"The streets are the streets, Pierre, as long as you speak the language, which I do, thanks to you." She smiled and kissed him on the cheek. Then she turned and left.

Two nights later they were in the foothills of the western Alps. They had ridden hard for two days and now felt they could relax. Not that Tella was seriously concerned about them being linked with Étienne's death. She had been thorough, even paying witnesses to swear they saw two hooded men pounce on and slay the youth as he made his way from a meeting with the city's occupying forces. At the meeting, he had woven a web of lies around Pierre and Tella's names.

They had escaped the city by a matter of hours.

After dinner at the inn where they were spending the night, they sat in Pierre's room. Pierre was staring at the logs burning in the fireplace.

"Don't look so worried, Pierre, we are safe here. You know that it had to be done. For Charles' sake and the others."

Pierre turned his head to her. He wondered how she could appear so calm. He took in her delicate features, her face radiant in the soft firelight, finding it impossible to imagine how the same person could have sought out and killed a man with such determination.

"You know, Pierre, in the talk of the streets, you owe me."

He nodded. "You're right, Tella, how can I ever repay you? I don't know where I should be without you."

"Your debt can easily be settled, signore," she smiled, her eyes sparkling. She had him.

"Name your price, signorina."

"It's a very simple thing, really, Pierre. I want to know your story. All of it. From start to finish."

Pierre looked into the fire. "It's far from simple, Tella, far from simple. As for the finish, who knows? I can only tell you what there is to tell so far. And you are going to need a great deal of imagination."

# Chapter 17

## July 2009

A week after his visit to Lawrence Forbes in the National Gallery in London, Ced Fisher found himself in the very different surroundings of Corrado Verdi's office in the Accademia di Ristauro e Conservazione, two streets from the Piazza Navona in the historic centre of Rome. He had spent the past few days champing at the bit, desperate to follow up on his theory of John Andrews as a master forger. Finally, he had escaped his work schedule and taken an early flight from Heathrow to Rome's Fiumicino airport and then a taxi into the city, arriving shortly after eleven-thirty.

The Accademia was in the Palazzo Leone, a fifteenth century five-storey villa that had always been associated with painting and sculpture. It had an international reputation for conservation and restoration, employing some of the most skillful and knowledgeable minds in the world of Italian art to be found anywhere, Corrado Verdi pre-eminent among them.

Ced gazed around Verdi's vast office. Originally a grand dining room, it had walls and ceilings decorated with frescos dating back to the mid-fourteen hundreds, the vaulted ceiling disappearing into the poorly lit gloom some thirty feet above him.

"Fascinating, aren't they, Cedric?" laughed Verdi, pronouncing the name as 'Chey-drick'. "And yet we still don't know who painted them. They are Giotto-like, no? But the building isn't old enough. Maybe you should photograph them and run them through your comparison program. It might give us an answer."

Ced shook his head in amazement. "You mean, Corrado, that I am sitting here in the vast office of a world-renowned art scholar surrounded by Renaissance beauty the world never sees and you don't know who the artist is?"

Verdi shrugged. "Cedric, you must understand, Italy is full of buildings like this one that are covered in such works. There simply isn't time to examine them all. Neither is there the money. We need your program to help us, Cedric. It will save so much time."

Ced looked at his host. He blended so well with his surroundings it was hard to imagine he hadn't occupied his office since the fifteenth century. He even fitted the building's name – his studiedly casual but immaculately styled mane of long grey hair brushed back to half-cover his ears. A lion in the Palazzo Leone. Ced wouldn't have been surprised if Verdi had greeted him in a long velvet cloak fastened at the neck. Instead, he was wearing crisply pressed light-grey designer trousers, an open-necked, blindingly white, long-sleeved cotton shirt and black leather shoes polished to a dazzling shine.

"As I mentioned on the phone, Corrado, I've hit what seems to be a big problem and I really need to take my own very hi-res photographs of some authenticated works as controls for comparisons with other paintings. I have images of a Tommaso Perini and a number of de la Places that my program says are painted by an artist who's currently alive and working in England. The only explanation that makes any sense is that I've stumbled across possibly the most accomplished art forger of all time. I need more paintings of undisputed provenance from these artists; it's the only way to solve the problem."

"Ah, yes, Perini and de la Place. Both highly accomplished and underrated artists. Well, I can certainly help you with some Perinis, we have a number whose provenance is unquestionable. In fact, a couple of them had never been out of the hands of the family for whom they were painted until they sent them to us for conservation. But de la Place ..." he shrugged. "He was French, and this is Italy." He shook his head sadly and Ced expected the worst. "I'm afraid, Cedric, I can only lay my hands on three."

"Three!" beamed Ced. "That's brilliant, Corrado. And their history?"

"No problem, my friend," replied Verdi nonchalantly. "Bought by my mother's great-grandfather in London."

"Corrado, you're a genius. I have a good feeling we'll get this sorted today. When can I start?"

"Cedric, it's lunchtime and you're in Rome. We can start about three-thirty once I have introduced you to the most divine pasta you have ever tasted accompanied by a white wine so delicate you would kill for it. Come, life in Italy is all about priorities, and there is no higher priority than food."

He paused as he slipped his suit jacket over his shoulders, his arms remaining outside the sleeves, and looked mischievously into Ced's eyes. "Well, perhaps there is one. That's what the siesta is for, but my lady friends are all out of town this week."

By three o'clock, Cedric had finished his third plate of linguine alle vongole followed by two helpings of saltimbocca alla romana, all helped on their way with a fine, dry Frascati, perfectly chilled. For dessert, Verdi suggested some cantucci biscuits for dipping in Vin Santo. "It's not a Roman dish, Cedric, but I think it will be to your taste. The 'Holy Wine' is from Tuscany. It's exquisite, and by making it the Tuscans justify their claim to be Italians, even if they are otherwise a little primitive."

Ced sat back in his chair and caught the eye of the restaurant owner. The small, almost round man was standing by the door to the kitchen beaming in delight. Ced raised his glass to him, "Grazie, signore! Ottimo!"

Verdi laughed and, turning to the owner, launched into a lengthy monologue in Italian that appeared to be all about Ced. An equally lengthy reply followed, accompanied by much chortling, after which, the owner left to get them some espresso.

"You understood, Cedric?"

"Not a word, Corrado."

Verdi smiled. "I was telling him that you are a brilliant art expert who is going to weed out all the world's forgers. He was very impressed. He thinks you should marry his daughter and come to live in Rome."

"I'd better run that one by Sal, I think, Corrado."

"Ah yes, your new girlfriend. I am very disappointed she did not accompany you. Lawrence told me on the telephone that she is a great beauty."

"Lawrence said that?"

"Not those words, exactly, but I could tell from his tone of voice it is what he meant. You have her photograph?"

"I do, as a matter of fact." He took a photo from his wallet, one taken of Sally and him crammed into a passport photo booth after a triathlon.

Corrado took it. "Madonna e tutti i Santi, Cedric, she is a goddess! No wonder you left her at home. She would have hordes of men stalking her in this city. You must promise me you will come to Rome for your honeymoon. I shall lend you a villa in the hills. It is the most romantic spot you could imagine."

"It would be idyllic, Corrado. I've always wanted to run the hills of Lazio."

"Cedric!" Verdi was aghast. "It will be your honeymoon!"

Verdi had collected twenty Tommaso Perini paintings for Ced to process.

As Ced worked through them, totally absorbed with adjusting the lighting and angles for each of the shots, Verdi looked on in admiration and not a little wonder.

"This is the miracle of modern technology in action, Cedric. Each of these beautiful portraits submitting gracefully to the caress of expert hands gliding gently over them, like a shy young maiden in the arms of her first adoring lover."

Ced smiled. "I sincerely hope they prove to be more willing to reveal their mysteries than some I've been dealing with lately, Corrado. My program is feeling rather emasculated at the moment."

At six that evening, as Ced completed his imaging, Verdi moved to a stack of a dozen paintings in a corner of his office.

"I thought these might interest you, Cedric," he said picking up two of the pictures. "They are also portraits, but by Piero Perini, Tommaso's son. It would be interesting to see what your program makes of them. It is known that Piero learned his trade from his father, so the styles should be similar."

Ced agreed and set to work.

As he finished, he checked his watch. Seven thirty.

"Corrado, the next stage is going to be slow because I only have my laptop with me. I can continue at my hotel and have the results by the morning."

"An excellent idea, Cedric. Shall we meet here at eight-thirty?"

"So your results show that all the Tommaso Perinis were painted by one person, and all the Piero Perinis were painted by one person, but the same person could not have produced both sets of works. And, as you found in England, the Tommaso Perinis cannot be distinguished from the John Andrews portrait."

It was the following morning and a bleary-eyed and despondent Ced was sitting across from Corrado Verdi, today wearing immaculate blue jeans and a pale pink shirt.

Ced nodded. "Exactly. The program has performed perfectly in distinguishing the two Perini men. As you pointed out yesterday the styles of Perini father and son are very similar, although Tommaso Perini's is definitely more sophisticated. A layman would not be able to tell many of the paintings apart but the program distinguishes them with no problem at all. Which is what it's designed to do. So why can't it distinguish Tommaso Perini's work from John Andrews'? There's no way he could have painted them."

Verdi shook his head. "I can offer no explanation, Cedric, but like Lawrence, I am convinced there is something you are missing."

Corrado Verdi scratched his head delicately with the little finger of his right hand. "Dare I suggest we look at the three de la Places? If nothing else, it would give you more good image data for when you do solve this problem."

Cedric reluctantly agreed, knowing in his heart what the result would be.

While they were waiting for the comparison program to churn through the numbers for the de la Place paintings, Cedric looked around the walls of Verdi's office. Verdi walked over to join him, handing him a pair of binoculars.

"Try these, Cedric; without a stepladder to get close, it's the best way to study the detail."

Ced took the binoculars and focused on various details of the frescos. But his mind was elsewhere.

"You know, Corrado," he said as he looked absently from one area to another, "I can accept the fact that Andrews is so good a forger that he is able to defeat my program when he reproduces the work of any particular painter. That would be a very exciting discovery which would necessitate a further refining to find the subtle differences that must be there but which are currently escaping the program's attention. It would result in a better program. What I simply can't understand is why the program can't distinguish the works of a number of painters coming from completely different eras, works that we know are genuine."

"It's a complete mystery, Cedric," replied Verdi. "I can offer no solution. I am not an expert in your computing methods so all I can suggest is that you expand the number of paintings you test from these artists you cannot distinguish. Perhaps by doing that you will find one you can tell apart from Andrews' work, and by finding what it is that distinguishes that one, you might discover the way into solving the problem."

"That's what I thought was going to happen by coming here to Rome. I thought I'd be going back with a set of images from genuine Tommaso Perinis and Jean de la Places, and then hit Andrews with the results, with the fraud squad waiting outside to arrest him."

"It will happen eventually," smiled Verdi in an attempt at reassurance. "He will slip up. Now, I have another idea. While you are attempting to coax your clever program to be even cleverer, I could use my brain, my eyes and my experience to become a little smarter. I intend to scrutinise in every way I can the originals of these mysterious works by Perini the elder and de la Place, to cast my so-called expert eye over them and see if I can find something that shows me they were painted by different painters."

"That would be brilliant, Corrado. If anyone can do it by eye, it's you."

Verdi nodded, pleased to have thought of another potentially constructive approach. "It will be a very interesting exercise, not normally something one would think of doing. After all, apart from saying that artist A from one century paints in the same style as artist B from another century, one would never consider that artist A could be artist B. It is not logical."

They worked on through the morning, took a light lunch and continued into the afternoon. Around four, Verdi excused himself to search for some paintings by another artist he had thought of. He returned with three portraits.

"Claudio Lorenzini, Cedric. Seventeenth century. Like these others, very underrated. Please, try your program on them."

An hour later, Ced thumped his hands on the table and slumped back in his chair, close to tears in frustration. He waved a hand at the laptop screen.

"It gets worse by the minute, Corrado. The program can't distinguish these Lorenzinis either. Where's it going to end? I don't understand it. It's not as if the program is coming up with only a possible match. On the contrary, it couldn't be much more definite, whether it's when I compare one of these artists with another or with the John Andrews portrait of the old woman."

Corrado Verdi paced the floor, his arms working furiously as he tossed arguments around in his head. He stopped, turned to Ced, his shoulders and arms lifted in an emphatic Italian shrug.

"You are convinced, Cedric, that this man Andrews is some kind of master forger?"

Ced nodded.

"If that is true," continued Verdi, "suppose he has recognised another series of forgeries from long ago."

Ced frowned, not understanding Verdi's line of reasoning.

"Think about it, Cedric, we think that we know the provenance of these Perinis, the de la Places, even the Lorenzinis. But do we? The Perinis are from three hundred and fifty years ago; much could have happened in that time that we are totally unaware of. There could have been copies made, the originals switched."

Ced pulled a doubtful face. "It's possible, but why? Tommaso Perini was a relatively minor artist. I doubt that one or two hundred years ago very many people had even heard of him. Why should anyone want to copy his works and make off with the originals?"

"Who knows, Cedric, but it's possible, yes? The question is: who would do it and when was it done?"

Ced thought for a moment. "Well, so far, we have Perini painting in the middle to late fifteen hundreds, Lorenzini in the late sixteen hundreds, and de la Place in the mid seventeen hundreds. But he was painting in Paris and London, while the other two were here in Rome and somewhere else in Italy."

"Siena," said Verdi, "Lorenzini and his sons worked in Siena."

Ced shook his head. "Is your brain permanently logged into Google search, Corrado? There seems to be nothing about Italian artists you don't know."

Verdi smiled and tapped his head knowingly. "Signor Google downloads from me, not the other way round, you know."

Ced laughed. "OK, given we can't distinguish one from the other in style signature, that would make de la Place, as the most recent of them, the forger. Unless there are others we have yet to discover who are even more recent."

He hit his forehead with the palm of his hand.

"Moretti! I'd forgotten about Moretti. But he was working in England in the nineteen forties and fifties. I don't think he left England apart from when he died."

"He died in Venice, didn't he?" said Verdi.

"Yes," replied Ced, "he drowned. Look, Corrado, this theory of a master forger replacing all these paintings, it doesn't really work. It can't have been Moretti; he's too recent. And what about John Andrews' work? Andrews can't have had the opportunity to creep into all these Italian museums and galleries in the dead of night and swap a pile of paintings for no known reason."

"You're right, Cedric. It makes no sense."

He went back to his examination while Ced returned to scrutinising his results.

After about half an hour, Ced sat back, his mind unable to focus further on the numbers, He was thinking about the artists whose work he had now spent many apparently fruitless hours studying. Who were they? What was known about them? What did they look like? He turned to Verdi.

"Corrado? May I interrupt you for a moment and ask you to dig into that encyclopedia of a mind? Do you know much about the lives of these artists who are tormenting us? Are there any paintings of them? Do we know even what their faces were like?"

Verdi stretched his arms above his head and cracked his knuckles. "Interesting questions, Cedric. Let me think. No, I am not aware of any paintings of the artists themselves. You know, 'Self-portrait of the artist as a young man' and so on. As for their lives, now you mention it, it's strange. There are distinct gaps in what is known about them. OK, for an artist in Tommaso Perini's time, that is not too unusual; it was a long time ago and records weren't always good. From what I remember about him, he turned up in Arezzo as a relatively young man with a wife and young family. It isn't known where he came from."

He frowned, thinking about what he'd just said.

"That in itself is rather odd, you know, Cedric. Artists moved around in those days, for commissions and so on, but for a whole family to move, that is strange."

"What about the Lorenzinis?" asked Ced.

"The Lorenzinis? Well, Henri Lorenzini worked here in Rome for a number of years until he was murdered."

"Murdered? I didn't know that."

"Yes, it was a tragedy: he was maturing as an artist very well. Certainly he was a lot more accomplished than his younger brother, Michel. But the older one, Claudio, as we now know from what we've seen today, he was brilliant and yet hardly recognised then or now."

"And they were from Siena?"

"Yes and no. They worked in Siena, Claudio and Michel, but like Perini in Arezzo, they just appeared there. They certainly didn't originate from Siena and after the death of their brother, Henri, they returned there briefly and then disappeared. I'm not aware of anything by them after Henri's death."

"So we have two Italian artists we can't distinguish who both led enigmatic lives. And then de la Place?"

Verdi shook his head. "Yes, he was French and, as far as I know, never set foot in Italy. But his life was equally shrouded in mystery."

"So," mused Ced, "we have three artists linked in their style signature to such a degree that we can't distinguish them and all of them led lives we know only fragments about. You know, come to think of it, Moretti wasn't that different either."

"Moretti?"

"Yes, he turned up in London from obscure origins in the US, son of Italian immigrants, worked in England all his adult life, largely as a recluse, and then upped and left on a whim in his sixties only to drown in Italy. I wonder if there are any others."

"Perhaps you should ask Mr Andrews."

"After my meeting with John Andrews, I doubt he'd be too

willing to answer any of my questions."

Verdi nodded thoughtfully. "You say his likeness is in some of the Piero della Francesca frescos."

"Yes, that's what crossed my mind when I asked you if there were any paintings of the others. Although why that should be relevant, I don't know."

"May I have a look, Cedric, at the photographs of Andrews and the faces in the della Francescas?"

"I'll call them up now," replied Cedric.


"So this is John Andrews."

Corrado Verdi was studying the images Ced had called onto his computer screen. "He has an interesting face. Those eyes are very unusual."

"Yes," agreed Ced, "it's the first thing you notice about him."

"And here they are in 'The Awakening'. How strange."

Verdi stared at the images for some minutes, then turning to Ced, he asked, "Have you ever seen it in the flesh, so to speak?"

"'The Awakening'? No, I haven't. It wasn't on view to the public when I was a student and I haven't been back to the San Sepolcro area since."

"You should. It's a very powerful painting, as powerful in its way as 'The Resurrection'. Do you want to go and see it? We can get there and back in a day."

"If there's time, Corrado, I'd love to."

"It will be my pleasure. We'll drive up first thing in the morning. My little car needs to stretch its legs on the autostrada."

# Chapter 18

## 1877

Stephen Waters leaned on the port rail of the steam ship Eastern Star and stared at the grey waters of the South China Sea. It was late March and as the ship moved steadily north towards the British Crown Colony of Hong Kong, the temperature was dropping and the swell rising.

He had no intention of remaining in Hong Kong for longer than necessary; he had heard little to recommend it during his time in Sydney and Angus Jackson, the wiry Scottish captain of the 'Star', had reinforced what he'd heard.

"The place is one big slum, laddie. There are legions of Chinamen floodin' into it; shacks geyin' up everywhere. And today's shack is tomorrow's cess pit. There's a putrid sorta stink that hangs o'er it mosta the time. And my God, the heat! It's hotter than Hades in the summer. You'll best be leavin' as smart as ye can, laddie."

Stephen would nod in agreement. His goal was India, the mystical land he had read so much about in the past few months.

Musing on India, he remembered the fine woollen shawl made from goat hair from Kashmir that he had bought in London for Tella before his return to Florence in 1870. He had been in mourning for his wife, Millie, who had been killed in a riding accident at the age of seventy. He had been Robert Trenton when he married Millie in England, but to Tella he was still Pierre, the man who rescued her from the gutter and who later introduced her to the Conte di Clemenza when he was commissioned to paint the family's portraits. She had married the conte's only son, later becoming the Contessa di

Clemenza and mother to their seven children.

Millie and Robert had been married for over thirty years and he was shattered by her death. Inevitably, he returned to his Tella, who, at ninety-six, seemed as enduring as himself.

"She would have felt nothing, Pierre," whispered the frail old woman. "Her life was extinguished as quickly as a pinched candle flame loses it life. You poor man; it's only now in my ridiculously old state that I can appreciate how difficult things must be for you. I have lost so many loved ones, not just my beloved husband, but children and even grandchildren, while this old body still carries on. God alone knows how it does; I'm nothing but skin and bone. I am worried that one day all that will be left is my soul. With nothing to hold it in place, it will fall out of my clothes and lie helpless on the floor."

He laughed. "Your soul will always be with me, Tella, part of it anyway, since there are many claims on it. My part will never leave me."

Tella's face became serious. "Do you find it hard, Pierre? Too hard at times?"

"It's always hard to lose loved ones, Tella. But I am not like an old man outliving his children. I have never been old. The only time I thought I felt old was when I was Luca di Stefano. I knew no different, so for a while, I thought as an old man. Then I finally realised that not only was I not old, I was young. My mind worked, and still works, as a young mind. My body stays strong, fit, active and healthy. Although that doesn't stop the sadness when I lose someone. I shall miss Millie as much as I miss Beth or Maria or Arlette. Still miss them. But they are always with me; I can remember them so well. It's as if they are parts of a whole; parts of wives who have yet to be. Is that strange, Tella? I doubt I am making much sense."

She smiled at him lovingly. "You are making perfect sense, Pierre. And you are such a strength to me, surrounded as I am by my huge and ever-changing family. You are the constant in my life, Pierre. You have been for almost ninety years."

He stayed in Florence until finally, five years later at the age of a hundred and one, Tella simply did not wake up one morning. There was no fuss, no illness. The night before he had visited her and they had talked as ever of their lives, their loved ones. She had kissed him goodnight, smiled and gone to sleep.

Three weeks after Tella's death, Pierre, as the family also knew him, had set out for Genoa and a new start. On the way, he prepared a set of documents for his new persona: Stephen Waters, a twenty-seven-year-old Englishman.

In Genoa, he roamed the shipping offices; he'd decided to go to the Americas. Lacking inspiration for one of the many possible destinations, he wandered at dusk to the docks where he found both steamers and sailing ships. He had never been to sea on a steamer and compared with the majesty of the sailing ships, he thought the modern craft lacked elegance. He loved the graceful lines of the three-masters, the creaking of their mooring ropes, the smell of pitch, and he thought of voyages in the Mediterranean in Jacques Bognard's boat two hundred years before.

In his reverie, he hadn't noticed a group of youths prowling the docks. As he turned at the corner of a warehouse, he almost bumped into the largest of the group, a swarthy, greasy-haired youth who had detached himself from his friends and silently approached him.

"My apologies, signore," said Stephen, "I was daydreaming."

"Well, you should be more careful, signore," replied the youth loudly, an arrogant sneer lifting his top lip. "Your actions could cost a man dearly on this dangerous dock. It would take very little for a man to end up in these oily waters. I feel you owe me more than a few easy words that I doubt have sincerity. No, signore, since I have come close to drowning at your hand, I consider a substantial payment as recompense for your foolhardy actions is obligatory."

Stephen stared at the youth in confusion. "You exaggerate, signore. I did not even touch you."

"But you caused me to step backwards, signore, such was the shock of your uninvited proximity! One more step and I should have plunged into the blackness and found my life extinguished."

Stephen snorted derisively. "We are at least ten good steps away from the dock's edge. You were never in any danger."

The youth squared up to him. He had the face of a prize-fighter, the skin around his eyes scarred from many fights.

"So, signore, first you threaten me with death, second you refuse to compensate me and finally, you insult me by branding me a liar!" As he spat the words, the youth pushed his face within inches of Stephen's.

"I think this creature needs a lesson, boys!" he yelled to his friends.

He pulled his right arm back, his large fist clenched ready for the punch he intended to deliver.

But it never arrived. Instead, the youth was suddenly lifted vertically from the ground, his body rotated and then projected sideways towards the dock's edge with great force. As he hit the ground, his left foot caught in a mooring rope and he stopped abruptly, his body hanging half over the water.

Stephen looked back to where the youth had been standing and saw what appeared to be a giant standing there grinning at him.

"Hey, you ox, you've got a lesson to learn for that!"

The giant turned towards the voice that had come from behind him, watching in amusement as two of the other youths charged across the dock towards him, followed closely by their three friends. One of the front two was brandishing a knife. As he launched himself at the giant, the knife suddenly separated from his hand, bouncing onto the dock with a clang. The giant's left arm had chopped down on the youth's wrist so fast that Stephen saw only a blur. In one fluid motion, the giant grabbed the two youths, one in each of his massive hands, and swung them through a sweeping arc so that their heads crashed heavily into each other. He then pulled them apart and swinging his arms up and back, tossed them over both his own head and Stephen's.

The remaining youths skidded to a halt and turned on their heels to run. However, they hadn't gone two steps when the middle one flew backwards, launched in the direction of the giant who cuffed him aside as if swatting a fly. The youth had run straight into the fist of another man, this one very much shorter but packed with muscle. Echoing the actions of the giant, the second man spun round and grabbed the remaining youths as they ran at full tilt. He hauled them back towards him and closing his powerful arms like jaws, crashed their heads together and tossed them aside.

The giant grunted in satisfaction and ambled over to the youth who had been threatening Stephen. He looked down on the foot that was still caught in the rope. He raised his own massive boot above it.

"Don't!" screamed the youth. "I can't swim."

"All vermin can svim ven zey needs to," said the giant, and stamped on the youth's foot.

Stephen winced at the crunch of bones as the youth disappeared over the dock edge with a scream. The giant looked around, found a large piece of timber and tossed it after the youth.

"Hold zat while you are learning to svim, vermin."

He walked over to Stephen and took hold of his coat. Stephen flinched but the man was only straightening it for him. There was a laugh from behind. "Don't worry, my friend, he's only helping to tidy you up. Doesn't do for a gentleman to look rumpled."

The smaller man walked up to Stephen and held out his hand. "Johanne Van der Merwe."

"Stephen Waters," stuttered Stephen, still shocked at the action of the last few seconds.

"You are English?" said Van der Merwe, switching from his heavily accented Italian.

"Yes," nodded Stephen. Suddenly aware of a huge presence behind him, he turned to see the giant holding out a hand the size of a leg of pork. Stephen extended his own hand hesitantly, expecting it to be crushed. But the giant shook it gently and smiled, his white teeth sparkling. "Lars," he said, his voice so deep that the word was like the rumbling of distant thunder.

Stephen gazed at him in awe. He was all of six foot ten, and two hundred and eighty pounds of muscle. By contrast the other man was no more than five foot six, but his equally muscular body made him seem larger.

Van der Merwe laughed. "Big bugger, yah! But a mouse really, eh Lars!" He punched the giant lightly on the arm. The reply was another distant rumble.

"I must thank you, gentlemen," said Stephen, coming to his senses.

"No thanks needed, Englishman," replied Van der Merwe. "We saw that group of louts strutting through the dock. They were clearly up to no good, so we followed them."

"Well, it was my good fortune you did," said Stephen.

Van der Merwe laughed again. "I think, Englishman, you need a few lessons in the art of self-defence. Come, buy us some dinner; we can talk, yes?"

"So you want to go to sea, Englishman?" said Johanne through a mouthful of the meat he'd just torn from a pork rib with his teeth.

"In a sailing boat!" he added, laughing. "Did you hear that, Lars? This Englishman's a traditionalist; he wants to sail."

There was a reverberation from Lars that could have been laughter, but it could equally have been a register of the satisfaction he was feeling from the massive meal he had almost finished.

"You have sailed before, Englishman?" continued Johanne.

"From Marseille to Genoa, yes, and I have taken the boats that run across the English Channel on many occasions."

"But you have never been on the ocean." It was a statement, not a question.

"Well, the Mediterranean–"

"Is a puddle; it is not the ocean. I will tell you Englishman, in the past twenty years, me and Lars, we have sailed all the oceans and we have been round both Capes many times. There are storms in the Mediterranean, yes, and they need respect, but the ocean; that is different."

He looked Stephen in the eye, his own twinkling with a perpetual amusement that Stephen would get to know very well. "Do you know the difference between a steamer and a sailboat, Englishman?"

"Of course, I–"

"No, I don't think you do." He tore the meat off another rib and raised his tankard to the bar for more wine. "I will tell you. A sailing boat is at the mercy of the wind, the currents and the weather, while a steamer – just the weather. A sailing boat cannot travel in a straight line, it must zig and zag all over the ocean, sometimes travelling backwards. A steamer will always travel forward."

He paused for a swig of the fresh wine.

"A sailing boat bobs around like a cork. It pitches and rolls and is very uncomfortable, unless it is going fast, when it is magnificent. But when you are becalmed in a steaming hot ocean – no wind, running out of water, the heat blistering your skin – you don't care about magnificence. No, all you care about is moving, and you don't care how. If you could tie the boat to Lars and whip him to tow it through the water, you would do it."

He paused as Stephen smiled at the thought.

"Believe me, Englishman, I have thought of trying it more than once."

Stephen nodded thoughtfully.

"I have heard, Johanne, that steamers are noisy, the vibration from the engines and propellers always present, and the odours most disagreeable."

Johanne nodded. "It is true there are some steamers that are not pleasant, but most are comfortable enough now the designs are improving. After a while you do not hear the engines, and as a passenger you will get food that is fresh and edible and a cabin you can move in. I tell you, Englishman, for the past three years now, me and Lars, we have worked on steamers, some big, some small, some agreeable, some not. But we would never go back."

He stopped to let Stephen digest his words.

"Anyway, Englishman, you need to come with us if you are going to sea. You must learn to box, to defend yourself. I shall teach you. It is not something even a young man like you can learn overnight. It takes time and patience. Of course, I cannot teach you on board and anyway, I should not have time. Me and Lars, we are stokers, shovelling coal all day. When a stoker is not working, he is sleeping. But we do not depart for a week, so you can learn the basics, heh! And then when we get to our destination, you can learn some more. You will soon have the skills to protect yourself. Tell me, Englishman, why do you want to go to sea? Are you a naturalist?"

Stephen smiled, amused at the thought. "No, Johanne, I am an artist, a painter of portraits and landscapes. And there is so much of the world I should like to see, so many places and peoples."

"An artist! Well, well. That, then, is another challenge. I shall need to teach you to box without damaging your hands."

"What is your destination, Johanne?" asked Stephen. "Indeed, our destination. Where are we bound?"

"Why, to the Brazils, Englishman! To Rio de Janeiro!"

The lessons went well. Johanne was old friends with the master of a fencing academy who let them use his premises. Stripped to the waist and wearing tight white cotton knee breeches, Johanne and Lars were a fearful sight. Johanne was an expert bare-knuckle boxer, having learned the art in Amsterdam in his youth. He practised almost daily with Lars who, while less expert, had the huge size, power and lightning reactions to counter any opponent.

When Stephen stripped off his shirt for his first lesson, Johanne complimented him on his physique. "While you clearly do not work on your muscle, Englishman, your lean frame tells me you treat your body with respect."

Stephan smiled to himself at the irony of this. He wondered what Johanne would say if he knew he was about to throw punches at a man almost four hundred and fifty years old.

"Let's see if we can't tone that frame and tune those reflexes," added Johanne. He raised his fists in a defensive stance and, without warning, threw three punches to Stephen's face in rapid succession, each of them stopping just short. Before Stephen could even move, Johanne was back in his defensive stance while Lars stood in the background chuckling quietly.

Johanne put his hands on his hips and rocked back on his feet, laughing. "Oh dear, Englishman, you are already unconscious and we have barely begun! Never mind, I guarantee that within a short time you will not only be swaying and ducking in more than ample time to avoid those punches, you will also have replied with punches of your own. Now let's get to work. First, raise your arms like this and I shall explain how you can defend yourself."


Stephen proved to be a good student with a natural ability. Once Johanne had explained the basic steps, the positioning of the body, the need to be constantly adjusting his feet, it started to make sense to him and he became hungry to learn.

Once he had cooled down and got his breath back, Stephen would sit down with his sketchpad while the two Dutchmen continued to spar. To Stephen's eyes, they were like Roman gladiators circling each other in deadly combat. Seeing him sketching on the first day, the two were keen to discover what he could possibly be putting on his paper. When he showed them, they shook their heads in amazement. "These drawings seem alive, Englishman, like they are moving pictures. Can you turn them into paintings?"

"That's what I'm planning for the voyage," said Stephen.

Four months later, they landed at Port Jackson in Sydney, the capital of the British Colony of New South Wales, having changed ships in Rio de Janeiro and Valparaiso in Chile. Every morning they went to 'Joe's Boxing Gymnasium' where Stephen's skills were honed until Johanne was satisfied his reflexes and abilities were sufficient for him to give a good account of himself if the need arose.

After a few weeks, Johanne announced that he and Lars needed to go back to sea. "But we shall be back in a few months, Englishman. You will still be here, yes?"


It was six months before the pair appeared again, arriving unannounced one evening at Stephen's small apartment. By this time he was impatient to leave, his research for his trip to India complete.

"Englishman!" exclaimed Johanne, as Stephen opened the door. "Surprised to see us?" he said, throwing his arms round Stephen and hugging the air out of him.

"Surprised and delighted," gasped Stephen, once Johanne had put him down.

The pair followed him into the apartment, filling it immediately with their bulk, their bags and their delight at seeing him again. Johanne was full of tales of their travels while Lars grunted along in deep resonating agreement.

"You have arrived at an opportune time, my friends," Stephen told them finally. "I am ready to leave. I was hoping that perhaps you would like to accompany me."

He told them of his plans to go to India and how he wanted to spend some years there. He was so full of enthusiasm that Johanne kept his doubts to himself.

"How are you planning to get to your mystical land, my friend?" Johanne asked.

"By way of the Straits Settlements; it seems the most direct route," said Stephen.

Johanne nodded. "The most direct, yes, but not the best."

Stephen frowned. "What would you recommend?"

"Hong Kong," said Johanne. "There are even more sailings to Hong Kong and far better services in better vessels from there to India."

Stephen shrugged. It made little difference to him so long as he departed soon.

"I shall make enquiries for you tomorrow, Englishman."

During the days that followed, Johanne and Lars enjoyed themselves in the bars in the dock areas, teaming up with other Dutch seaman. Stephen left them to carouse while he sorted out his extensive portfolio of paintings. He was leaving most of them with a dealer, but there were still a number he intended to keep and they needed careful packing.

At one o'clock one morning, he was surprised to hear a quiet but urgent knocking on his door. He opened the door to a worried-looking Johanne.

"Stephen, can I come in?" he said.

Stephen was shocked: Johanne had never used his first name.

He closed the door as Johanne slumped in the chair.

"What has happened, Johanne? Is it Lars?"

The Dutchman shook his head. "Lars? No, Lars is fine. He didn't come with me this evening. Can't take the pace." He paused.

"I have a problem, my friend. A big problem." As he said this, he peeled off his scarf. Stephen saw that his face was cut and bruised. He looked down at his hands; they too were bleeding from the knuckles.

"You have been in a fight, Johanne?"

The Dutchman nodded. "Yes, a bad one. It was not my fault, Englishman, I didn't start it, and I didn't finish it. But I shall be blamed."

"Blamed? Blamed for what?"

"There were three of them. They were waiting for me in an alley. It was going well; I had them. Then one of them produced a knife and charged at me. But at the same moment, another one rushed at me from a different direction. I ducked and the two of them collided. The knife went straight into the other one's heart. He was dead in seconds."

He stopped, the events playing back in his eyes.

"The one with the knife, he threw it at my feet. Started yelling that I'd killed his friend. Yelling loudly. Yelling for the constables. Two of them appeared out of nowhere. There was pandemonium.

One of the constables said that it was the gallows for me, that they didn't tolerate drunken foreigners killing their citizens."

"So what happened? You escaped?"

Johanne nodded. "They had hold of me. Big fellas but not fit. I suddenly swung them both together. It's a trick I've used a lot. Crashed their heads. They went out like lights, Englishman." He shrugged. "I then hit the one with the knife. Only once, but he won't wake up for a while and his jaw is busted. Then I had to do the same to the other one, because he had pulled a knife as well. Then I ran. I didn't know what to do, but then I heard a lot of commotion and those whistles the bobbies blow, so I kept to the shadows and came here. They didn't see me. No one did."

Stephen rubbed his chin thoughtfully. He removed the scarf from Johanne's neck and pulled off his woollen hat. The single cut on his face was very superficial, as was the bruising. He studied the Dutchman's hairless head and face and pursed his lips, nodding to himself.

"The trouble is, Johanne, you have a very distinctive head. Your baldness is unusual and people remember it, but that could be to our advantage."

"I don't understand, Englishman."

"Johanne, we have got to get you out of the country. The constables will be looking everywhere for you and if they catch you, they will hang you, for sure. Any trial will just be for show. They will get plenty of witnesses to say you killed the man. Until you leave, you'll have to stay here. You are sure that no one saw you?"

"Quite sure."

"Then let me clean you up and tomorrow I'll make some arrangements."

In the morning, Stephen was up early. He made some coffee and woke Johanne.

"Johanne, help yourself to some breakfast. I need to go out for a while. I'll first go to warn Lars and then fetch your things. Then I'll need to go out again."

"Where to, Englishman?"

"The theatre, Johanne. I'm going to the theatre!"

212

When Stephen returned, he was carrying two parcels. He put the smaller on a table in front of Johanne and unwrapped it to reveal a number of packets, pots and brushes.

He looked up at Johanne and studied his face. Then he turned to Lars, who had arrived while Stephen was out.

"Lars, I should like to introduce you to Mr Waters."

Lars frowned, not understanding "But you are Mr Waters, Englishman," his voice rumbled.

"I am indeed, Lars. But this is also Mr Waters." He nodded his head towards Johanne. "Mr Ernest Waters. My father."

A series of disconnected vibrations emerged from the region of Lars' throat, while Johanne cocked his head in question.

Stephen waved his hand across the goods arrayed in front of him like a conjuror.

"I told you this morning I was going to the theatre. Actors work in theatres and actors are very skilled at altering their appearances. At the theatre, I asked for the names of suppliers of theatrical costumes, props, wigs and so on."

He stopped in amusement at their frowns.

"I am not an actor, but I am skilled – very skilled, in fact – in the application of false hair, wigs and make-up. I can turn you, Johanne, from your forty-something fit and vital self into Ernest Waters: aged, bent and grey-haired."

Stephen picked up the larger parcel.

"Here, old man, are your new clothes. Actually not so new, I picked them up at a second-hand store. The jacket is rather too large for you. It will disguise your muscular frame and droop on you when you adopt the stoop I shall teach you. Your walking stick I left by the door."

Johanne nodded slowly.

"That is amazing, Englishman, if you think you can really do it. But what about papers? The officials at the docks are very particular about papers – passports as they are sometimes called. They will be looking for me and scrutinising all papers."

Stephen stood and walked over to a drawer and pulled out a large envelope. Removing some papers, he passed them to Johanne.

"Take a look at these."

Johanne flicked through them.

"These are your papers," he said, puzzled.

"That's right."

"I don't understand."

"Well, I know they are my papers because I made them. From scratch. There is nothing genuine about any of them."

Johanne stared back at the papers in his hands, checking them and holding them up to the light.

"You made these, Englishman?"

"I am an artist, Johanne. It is not too difficult."

"So you are not really Stephen Waters?"

"No, I am not."

"Are you on the run from the law as well?"

Stephen laughed. "Technically, I suppose I am."

Not wanting to dwell on the subject, he clapped his hands. "So, Ernest Waters, you are going to have to forego the pleasure of stoking coal on this forthcoming voyage; the work is far too strenuous for a man of your age. You will, for a change, be a passenger. As far as the authorities here are concerned, we shall be father and son, returning to England by way of Hong Kong and India."

Johanne touched Stephen's arm, his eyes moist.

"If we can get away with this, I shall be indebted to you for the rest of my life, Englishman."

"Nonsense, I am merely repaying my debt to you. Of course, if we don't get away with it, the rest of our lives will be rather short. They will hang us both."

Stephen found a steamer heading for Hong Kong, the SS Eastern Star, due to depart five days hence, and booked a first class cabin with two berths. Returning to the apartment, he sent Lars to sign on as a stoker. Lars was back within the hour. "All done, Englishman. I know the captain, Angus Jackson. He wanted to know where Johanne is. I told him Amsterdam with his sick mother."

The next morning, Stephen started the laborious task of applying hair and whiskers to Johanne's face, laying them down in strands until he had a full but neat beard and a moustache. The head hair took longer but the result was astounding. After applying some fine make-up to give him a sallow, grey-yellow complexion and finishing off with a number of liver spots on his temples and forehead, he handed Johanne a mirror.

"There, Johanne, I don't think your own mother would recognise you."

Johanne stared at himself in awe, shaking his head. "I wouldn't recognise me if I bumped into me in the street. This is incredible, Englishman. Who taught you how to do this?"

"Someone I met a long time ago, Johanne. Come, put on the clothes and I'll show you how to walk."

When they got to the shoes, Stephen pulled a pebble out of his pocket. "Slip this inside the left shoe. It will be a constant reminder to you to limp."

As Johanne hobbled around the room, practising using the walking stick, he quickly transformed into a man of seventy.

"You shouldn't smile like that, Johanne."

"Can't help it, Englishman. I'm too happy."

The slow half-mile walk to the docks on the evening of their departure passed without incident. Arriving at the immigration desk, they joined the small queue of passengers waiting to board. Stephen handed over their papers and the official took them away to check them against a list.

"Mr Waters?"

Stephen turned to the voice. The official was pointing to Johanne. "No, Mr Waters senior."

Stephen touched his ear to indicate that his father was a little deaf.

The official smiled understandingly. "I was wondering if your father would like to sit down while we process the papers."

"Thank you," said Stephen. "Come, Father, let's sit over here."

Ten minutes later they were on board. "This is not going to be the easiest of times, Johanne, You are going to have to wear that disguise for the whole voyage. It will get itchy and uncomfortable, and you must always be on your guard."

"If it's a choice between an itchy neck and a stretched one, I'll take the itchy one every time," smiled Johanne.

Low cloud covered the hills of Hong Kong Island as they moored in the harbour. A small armada of sampans arrived to take the bags to shore, the sampan boys jostling for position in the choppy water. The chief steward was directing operations, yelling instructions at everyone, his words being interpreted into screeched Cantonese by the shipping company's head boy.

A larger steam-powered vessel came alongside. A gangplank with railings on either side was set up, and the captain arrived to bid farewell to his guests, shaking each one by the hand. When it came to Stephen and Johanne's turn, Stephen walked forward.

"Goodbye, Captain Jackson. I should like to thank you for all you have done to make this voyage a most pleasant experience for my father and me."

The captain bowed his head courteously.

"Ma pleasure, Mr Waters, ma pleasure. Ah hope to see you on board again. You too, Mr Waters," he said, nodding towards Johanne.

Johanne bowed his head, saying nothing.

They started across the gangplank.

"Good luck, Mr Waters!" called out the captain. "And good luck to you too, Johanne!"

Stephen and Johanne stopped in their tracks and turned their heads, their eyes wide. But the captain was already saying his farewells to the next passenger.

# Chapter 19

## July 2009

On the same Monday morning that Ced was flying to Rome, Claudia was driving to London to keep an appointment with Professor Frank Young at Kings College. The professor had been Claudia's supervisor for her doctoral studies when he was head of genetics in the Biochemistry Department at Manchester University. Since then he had taken up a more lucrative appointment in a private institute affiliated to Kings that enabled him to pursue his research interests into gene structures and functions without the distraction of teaching commitments.

For Claudia, the previous week had seen the mystery of John Andrews' DNA profile deepen further. Following her trip to see Sally and Ced, she had carried out further tests with new probes and obtained more baffling results. She was hoping her trip to London might help her learn more about this mysterious man.

She'd called Sally at the beginning of the week to ask about Ced's visit to Grasmere. Sally told her that having met Andrews, Ced agreed how strongly he resembled the face in the Piero fresco. She went on to explain Ced's problems in not being able to distinguish Andrews' work from first Moretti's and now other long-dead artists.

"This gets weirder and weirder, Sal," said Claudia, once Sally had finished. "Whatever's going on?"

"I simply don't know, Claw, but I'm increasingly coming round to your way of thinking that junk DNA isn't junk at all. There's got to be something different about this man and I'm sure the answer's in the DNA."

"It must be," replied Claudia. "I've got thirty-eight new alleles now. The frustrating thing is that another testing kit arrived last week that will enable us to run tests on ten more loci, but I've already used up all of Andrews' sample."

"Mmmm," mused Sally. "Couldn't we get some more of Andrews' DNA from somewhere? What about the portrait you bought?"

"It's a thought, Sal, but it will have been handled by several other people apart from us. Who knows how many customers have picked it up?"

"Maybe we should go and raid his dustbins, snaffle his hairbrush. Hey, we could take a swab of the door handle of his car–"

"That his wife also drives," interjected Claudia.

"OK, I could always rush into his gallery screaming 'Darlink!' at him very dramatically in my best Russian accent, kiss him passionately on the lips and then rush out again. You can be waiting outside to swab my lips for his saliva. And take the hair from my hands."

"Hair?"

"I'll grab a handful of his hair as I kiss him. He'll be so overcome with passion for me that he won't notice."

There was a pause on the line. Then Sally heard Claudia whisper 'saliva' very quietly.

"Yes, Claw, I'll make sure his saliva is all over my lips."

"Saliva!" Claudia said it louder now.

"Keep saying it, Claw, and it'll start to sound yucky."

"Of course! Sal, you're a genius!"

"Er, Claw, you're not seriously thinking of trying this, are you?"

"Don't need to, Sal, I've got some of his saliva."

"Where? From what you told me about your meeting with Andrews, there wasn't much kissing going on."

"No, of course there wasn't, but there was licking."

"Licking? That's an interesting approach to interrogation."

"Of the envelope, Sal!"

"What envelope?"

"He wrote me a description of the painting I bought. He put it in an envelope which he sealed by licking the flap. I saw him do it."

"And you've kept it?"

"Of course I have. And it's still sealed, which means it's uncontaminated."

"That's brilliant, Claw."

"I'll get on with the profiling with the new kit in the morning."

"Actually, Claw, do you think it's a good idea to commit all the sample to more loci profiling?"

"Well, it's important, and anyway, we're not equipped to do anything else."

"I know that, Claw, but since this isn't a CJ sample, you don't have to worry about carrying out tests on it elsewhere."

"You mean testing for gene-related properties? What are you suggesting, Sal?"

"Well, first you should estimate how much sample you have. If there's enough, run it against your new kit; the results will certainly be grist to the mill if they continue to be as odd as the others. But make sure that there's plenty left. What I was thinking was that you could ask your old supervisor, the potty Professor Young, to have a look at it. His field's immune systems, isn't it? Maybe he could give you an opinion on whether these odd alleles are likely to affect them in some way."

"Brilliant, Sal. These rare alleles have got to influence something. I think the prof would be up for it, especially if I sweet talk him a bit."

Two days later, she called her old mentor to explain her findings and to ask for his help.

The professor was cautious.

"You know, Claudia, what you have done and what you're now asking of me is really quite unethical. There's a huge amount of accountability in this game; the whole field is tottering under the weight of red tape that ties it up to the point of strangulation. I always have to get permission from donors to carry out my research work. And if I start a new line of investigation using their samples, I go back to them and explain what I'm doing so they know I'm not using their samples or their gene structures for anything underhand. DNA research is such a sensitive area that if we are found wanting in our procedures, it could be closed down. If that were to happen, it would be left in the hands of unscrupulous scientists from elsewhere in the world where governments aren't very interested in the rights of the individual."

"So what you are really saying is that I should stop. Call a halt here." Claudia was defensive.

"No, I'm not saying that, Claudia. Something these fool administrators can't legislate against is the spirit of innovation; but it is important that you understand where this could lead you. You are playing with fire here conducting tests on a sample taken without the donor's permission."

"But it was freely given."

"Not for scientific research. The man licked the flap of an envelope he gave you. That doesn't give you the right to try to clone him, for example."

The professor paused while he thought over the problem. He then continued.

"OK, this is what I propose. My research interests are mainly in the field of immune systems. We're looking at the differences some people have in certain genes that increase or decrease their chances of contracting a disease or an illness. It's a huge area and there are researchers worldwide in the field. That said, there are certain standard tests that everyone carries out. I'm prepared to submit part of your sample to a simple test that will tell us if this man's DNA confers upon him anything out of the ordinary regarding disease resistance. It's a very basic test, but it's a good starting point."

"And you think that this is the right avenue to go down?" asked Claudia.

"It's as good as any, Claudia. The immune system is of fundamental importance to our bodies. It's very heavily affected by our genetic make-up and mutations to our genetic make-up that can occur during our lives. I think it's a very good line to follow.

"Now, if the results do indicate anything interesting, we have got to go back to this man to ask his permission to carry out more tests and request some more sample from him. We have to explain to him what we're doing, why we're doing it, why it's important and how we've got to where we've got so far. That last point could prove a stumbling block because we're coming at this from the wrong direction. Normally people are asked to volunteer samples having been apprised first of our research interests."

"Then we might as well stop now. I've already spoken to him and he simply wasn't interested."

"That's unfortunate, given his number of rare alleles," answered the professor.

"There's something else I haven't explained about this man, Prof."

"Really? What's that?"

Claudia described the similarities between Andrews' face and the face in the Piero fresco, and then told him about the problems Ced had subsequently had with his program.

"Ced's convinced that man's a master forger, possibly the best that's ever existed. That he can replicate any style he wants."

The professor wasn't convinced.

"My first question would naturally be whether your Mr Fisher's program is really as good as he thinks it is. He is really asking a lot if he expects a computer program to differentiate the subtleties of style between two artists, especially if one artist is trying to copy the style of the other."

"Oh, he's good, Prof, really good. He's got a brilliant mind when it comes to programming. When you combine that with his knowledge of art, he has written something the art world has been dreaming of ever since the first computers were built."

"OK, I'll have to take your word on that, but there's another point that nags at me. If this man is such a good forger, why would he allow his style to be so similar to others? You'd think he would have developed a style specifically for his own work that was distinct and separate from artists whose work he was copying so he could ensure that the finger of suspicion wouldn't be pointed at him. And why would the work of certain artists turn out to be indistinguishable when they worked centuries apart? That part really doesn't make any sense."

He paused to think the problem through further.

"Off the top of my head, I'd say that Fisher's program is flawed in some subtle but fundamental way that neither he nor anyone else he's consulted has discovered. I say 'subtle' because it would appear that until he started looking at Andrews' work, everything was hunky-dory. But Andrews' work and the work of the other artists that it has led on to have turned out to be the exception that proves the rule, that is, tests the rule; and now the rule has been found wanting. My advice to Fisher would be to go back to revisit every single assumption he has made."

"He's already done that, Prof. He's no slouch when it comes to thoroughness."

"OK, let's leave that little problem in the pending box, shall we? I'll give it some further thought when I'm reflecting over a glass or two of single malt this evening. It doesn't in any way change the results you have for this man Andrews' DNA. I can see you next Monday afternoon, Claudia. Why don't you get down here in time for lunch? I'll treat you to the delights of this institute's catering and, if you survive, we can run the test I described. After that, we'll take a view, as they say. Oh yes, could you please bring all your results with you? I'd really like to see them for myself."

"Claudia, how delightful to see you."

Frank Young was a tall, avuncular man in his mid-fifties with a mass of unruly grey hair that he constantly ran his fingers through in a vain attempt to keep it in place. He had small, smiling eyes and a small, amused mouth, the two features kept well apart by a large, bulbous nose that showed strong evidence of its owner's weakness for malt whisky.

Although their lives had inevitably moved apart since Claudia's post-graduate days, they had remained in contact. It was always a special pleasure for both of them to meet and catch up with each other's lives.

Lunch, which Young had been teasing her about, was excellent, and they found an hour and a half flew by in tales, reminiscences and laughter.

Young looked at his watch. "Good heavens, Dr Reid, look at the time. Enough of this idle chatter; we have work to do!"

He stood and strode off in the direction of his laboratories, the diminutive Claudia trotting along in his wake.

Two hours later, a tiny portion of the precious sample from the envelope had been extracted, separated and run through Professor Young's instruments to test for enhanced or reduced immunity to a number of diseases and conditions.

The results were displayed on various computer monitors attached to the instruments. Young flitted from one screen to another like a honeybee darting among flowers for pollen.

"There, Claudia, that's the last of them. Now let's press this key here … and a summary of the results should appear on the monitor next to where you're standing. It's your sample so I think you should interpret the result. What does it say? Anything interesting?"

Claudia turned to study the data that had appeared on the screen and frowned. She said nothing.

"Come on, Dr Reid, I know it's been a while, but you must remember your basic immunology. Speak to me!"

Claudia shook her head. Still staring at the screen, she said, "Sorry, Prof, it really has been a while. Could you remind me what you normally see when someone has some sort of enhanced immunity?"

"Certainly, Claudia. What we see for the various conditions we've included in this broad-spectrum screen is that some people will have a greater or reduced immunity to one, or perhaps two, of the factors we've covered. Very occasionally three, but never more than that. So, how does your man measure up?"

"Prof, you need to look at this. I don't understand these results."

Amused that his ex-student was confused by what he regarded as a routine interpretation of data, the professor took two steps forward to look over Claudia's shoulder.

"Good heavens!"

The prof's amused smile was replaced with a puzzled frown. His eyes darted over the figures as he muttered to himself, running through a mental checklist and comparing data from the controls with the data from Andrews' sample.

He stood up straight, spun around and walked three circuits of the laboratory, his hands tented to his face as he considered the result. He returned to the screen and checked all the data again.

He turned to Claudia. "This is quite remarkable, Claudia. Unprecedented. These results indicate this man doesn't simply have an enhanced immunity to all ten factors in this test; he has immunity at a level I've never before seen."

He sat down heavily on a laboratory stool. "I'll need to conduct some more tests, Claudia. There are five specifically that I'd like to do, but I think from your sample, there will only be enough material for three. I'll think very carefully about which three."

Claudia said nothing; she could almost hear the cogs whirring in Young's mind. Then she thought back to their phone conversation.

"What about the ethical considerations, Prof? You said on the phone that if this test proved interesting, we'd have to contact Andrews for permission to continue."

A cloud of doubt passed briefly across the professor's brow. Then he made a decision.

"Bugger that, Claudia, I haven't even begun to digest the implications of what this might mean, but I have to get more data. We could be looking at one of the most fundamental discoveries made about DNA since the elucidation of the double helix. We'll worry about ethics later. We're not hurting anybody by carrying out these tests, and it would be utterly irresponsible not to continue, just because some bunch of idiots in Brussels spend their lives worrying about privacy and the rights of the individual. This could be above all that, Claudia, way above it."

He paused for a moment and then he looked into her eyes, his own sparkling with delight.

"Oh, Claudia!" he said as he took both her hands, surprising her with an uncharacteristic gesture of affection. "Diminutive, clever, tenacious, wonderful Claudia!" His smile filled the laboratory with its joy. "This is so exciting! But we must keep it between ourselves. Not a word to anyone, at least until I've conducted the other tests. Then we'll worry about what we do next."

"Not a word, Prof," grinned the elated Claudia.

# Chapter 20

## 1880-1900

Three years after his arrival in Hong Kong in 1877, Stephen Waters' business as a portrait painter to the colonial dignitaries and their families was flourishing. However, despite his success and his ever-increasing fascination with Chinese culture and traditions, the high-handed attitudes of his clients towards him as an artisan and to the Chinese in general was beginning to wear him down. He had reluctantly moved his studio to a premises near the Anglican cathedral of St. Johns in an area less likely to offend the sensibilities of the colonial wives and daughters than the lower class Western District where, with Johanne's help, he had initially set up shop in the Hostel Da Rosa where he still lived. But increasingly, his thoughts turned to India and he had started to revisit his plans.

In the meantime, his escape was to take himself off to the mainland to sketch and paint the dramatic landscapes and rural life whenever he could find the time, his rapidly increasing fluency in Cantonese acting as a passport to the village communities.

Then he met William Trevelyan and his daughter, Fiona.

Trevelyan was the founder and head of Trevelyan & Company, a large and successful business that had been trading in India, China and the East Indies for the past twenty-five years. Although he lived in a grand mansion in the Hill District that surrounded the Peak – the imposing two thousand foot mountain that dominated the island of Hong Kong – Trevelyan had none of the haughty cynicism of so many of his peers. The Far East was his adopted home as well as his place of business, and he had absorbed much of its culture as well as its languages – he was fluent in Urdu and Hindi, as well as Cantonese.

"Trouble with these colonials is they think they're here to civilise a bunch of natives," he confided in Stephen once they knew each other better. "Might be the form in Africa, but it won't wash with the Chinese. They were civilised while we were still painting woad on our faces."

Trevelyan had turned up unannounced in Stephen's studio in the late spring of 1880 to commission a portrait of his daughter.

"Wilful gell. Absolute mind of her own. Tried to marry her off but she's having none of it. Twenty-six now and seems to be well settled on the shelf. Thinks of nothing but that damned hospital of hers."

"Hospital?" asked Stephen, somewhat taken aback at this man's forthrightness.

"Yes, she works voluntarily in one of the disease-ridden hospitals in the town. Insists she wants to help the poor women who pass through its doors. Told her we could build our own hospital, but she insists she wants to work as a nurse, not an administrator. Worries me, all that disease."

Fiona Trevelyan proved to be very different from any of the colonial women Stephen had met in Hong Kong. She was lively and engaging and, although not beautiful, she had a grace and charm that made Stephen immediately wonder why she was 'well settled on the shelf.'

Three months later he found out. Soon after the portrait William Trevelyan had commissioned was given pride of place in Trevelyan House, William departed to India on business. The morning after his departure, Fiona arrived at Stephen's studio with a very different commission.

"As you know, Stephen, I am fascinated by Chinese culture, particularly the costumes and clothing which I often wear in private. What I should love is for you to paint a series of studies of me wearing my collection. Could you do that?"

"I should be delighted, Fiona," smiled Stephen.

"Of course, the sittings will have to be at Trevelyan House. Would that be terribly inconvenient?"

"Not at all. It will be my pleasure."

As he worked on the paintings, Stephen talked to Fiona of his frustrations and his plans to move on to India. He was surprised that instead of appearing enthusiastic, she laughed dismissively.

"Oh dear, Stephen, if your reason for this move is the hope of finding a more enlightened crowd, I fear you will be disappointed. The British have been in India far longer than they have in Hong Kong. And believe me, apart from considering themselves terribly 'pukka', they have developed the manners you abhor to an art form. It would be out of the frying pan into the fire."

On the day Stephen arrived to put the finishing touches to the final study, Fiona greeted him by taking both his hands, a sparkle of conspiracy in her eyes.

"Stephen, there is someone I want you to meet, someone very dear to me. Come, he is waiting in the sitting room."

Still holding his hands, Fiona led Stephen through. To his surprise, waiting for them was a young Chinese man in his mid-twenties. He was tall for a southern Chinese, as tall as Stephen, and he had a proud bearing. He was plainly dressed in a long silk coat buttoned to the neck over a pair of baggy silk pantaloons. He had white silk socks and black soft slippers on his feet. A round silk cap hid the front of his head, which was shaven, while his hair was worn in the queue all Chinese men were required by royal decree to wear, regardless of their social status. From the style and quality of his clothes, Stephen could see he was from a wealthy family.

"Stephen, I should like you to meet Kwok Fu-keung. Ah Keung, this is Waters Sin Saang – Mr Stephen Waters."

The young man half crossed his arms and bowed to Stephen.

"I am very pleased to meet you, Mr Waters. Fiona has shown me your work. It is truly remarkable."

Stephen was surprised by the man's rich deep voice and excellent English.

He bowed his head in return and replied using the Cantonese 'Sin Saang' for 'Mr'.

"I am honoured to meet you, Kwok Sin Saang. You are too kind about my paintings."

"It is not kindness, Mr Waters; it is admiration. I doubt a skill such as yours has been matched in China by more than a very small number of artists over the centuries." He smiled, his face relaxing to reveal fine, handsome features, his jet eyes warm and intelligent.

Fiona walked up to him and took his hands. She turned to Stephen. "Keung is my secret, Stephen. My oh-so-special, wonderful secret."

She turned and leaned up to kiss Keung on the lips, holding the kiss for a few seconds.

Looking back to Stephen, she smiled and said, "Do I shock you, Mr Waters?"

"You delight me, Miss Trevelyan," laughed Stephen, "you absolutely delight me."

Keung was the fourth of six sons of a wealthy Chinese merchant, Kwok Fu-ming. Although a traditionalist, Kwok senior was far-sighted enough to understand the value of trading with the foreign devils and had insisted all his sons become fluent in English and conversant with the Western ways of business. However, a liaison such as Keung's with Fiona could only ever be that; marriage was unthinkable.

"So you see, Stephen," smiled Fiona wickedly, "I am a concubine, and a secret one at that."

Keung's father's concubines were another matter: they were all Chinese and it was perfectly acceptable that he should have them, although naturally they were kept separate from the family, as were the numerous children he had with them. However, he was a good father and none of his illegitimate children wanted for much. He had a particular love of music and painting and any talents his offspring showed in either direction were actively encouraged.

Learning of Stephen's skills, he commissioned him for a series of portraits of various members of his legitimate and illegitimate family. While negotiating the terms of these with Stephen, he told him that one of his illegitimate daughters, Ho Mei-ling, was talented in Chinese painting.

"She is only a child, Waters Sin Saang, just sixteen, but I think she has promise. I was wondering, would it be too much of an imposition to request she observe you while you are painting the various studies of my family?"

"It would be my pleasure, Kwok Sin Saang. If she has talent, with your approval, I could give her some instruction in the techniques of Western art."

The arrangements were made. As the eldest of Kwok Fu-ming's concubines was arranging herself and her six daughters in Stephen's studio, Ho Mei-ling and her two servants were standing quietly in the corner. As a daughter of Kwok's third concubine, she had to remain subservient.

Stephen walked over to where she was standing and smiled at her. "Siu-je," he said to her, using the Cantonese for 'Miss', "you must be number four daughter of Honourable Kwok's number three concubine."

Mei-ling bowed her head deferentially to him.

He said nothing, waiting for this diminutive girl to look up. As she turned her face upwards to his, he caught his breath – Mei-ling was stunningly beautiful. Her face was oval with high cheekbones and almond-shaped eyes, her hair drawn back into a single plait that hung down her back, emphasising her long, slender neck. She wore no make-up on her flawless skin while her mouth was a small rosebud that needed no rouge or lipstick to enhance it. She stood before him, holding his eyes with hers and willing him to say something. Anything.

Stephen bowed his head to her. "Mei-ling, I am honoured to meet you," he said, and heard a faint titter of amusement from the maids. "I have been told much about your gifts as an artist and I should very much like to see your work."

Stephen pointed to Mei-ling's portfolio. "May I?"

She took it from the maid holding it and handed it to him. Placing it on a table, he untied the strings. Taking out the top paintings, he nodded in approval at the quality of the work.

He smiled. "You have a remarkable talent, Mei-ling. What I should like you to do this morning is take your sketchpad and a charcoal stick and watch me sketch these charming ladies and their elegant mother. When you are ready to copy my strokes, start your own drawing."

Pulling up a stool, Stephen sat in front of the group of women and started to sketch. He worked fast as usual, all his concentration going into the drawings.

After an hour, he sat back and congratulated them all on their patience. He turned to Mei-ling. "May I see?" he asked holding out his hand for the sketchpad. She turned it towards him and he saw that she had only drawn a few lines.

"I am sorry, master," she said, bowing her head. "I have failed to draw anything. I shall leave now and not waste your time."

"There is nothing to be sorry about," smiled Stephen, "take all the time you need."

"I started to draw," she explained, "but I was enthralled by the speed with which you work, the confidence of your strokes. I have never seen a true artist at work before. My tutors were always so hesitant. I do not think I could ever approach a drawing with such confidence."

He smiled in reassurance at her. "You underestimate your ability, Mei-ling; I can see from your portfolio that you have great potential. Confidence will come with time."

Stephen sent a note to Kwok Fu-ming to request she be allowed to attend his studio every day so he could develop her skills. The request was granted and Mei-ling quickly became a permanent fixture, her confidence growing around Stephen's natural informality.

Neither Mei-ling nor any of her sisters or their mothers had been subject to the crippling practice of foot binding. Kwok Fu-ming was very much against it and had deliberately chosen concubines whose feet had been left to develop normally. Mei-ling was as light and agile on her feet as she was graceful and elegant in her movements, and Stephen took every opportunity to watch her.

Gradually, over the next three years, the two became very close. Hidden under the veneer of subservience and humility convention insisted she maintain, Mei-ling had a lively sense of humour. Whenever he was sketching or painting one of his European clients, she would take every opportunity to reach across Stephen to fetch some paint or distract him by asking him something about a sketch. At the same time, she would whisper quietly in the Cantonese she knew the foreign devil facing her would not understand, passing comments on their looks, smell or clothes. Stephen had to work hard to keep a straight face and not to incorporate into his paintings some of the uglier features Mei-ling would point out and put in her own sketches.

In the early autumn of 1883, after a difficult day's work with a spluttering, florid-faced captain from the garrison who, despite the relatively cool day, had produced pools of sweat that soaked visibly into his thick uniform, the pair were alone in the studio, Mei-ling having sent both her maids out on errands.

They had been laughing about the man's digestion – he seemed incapable of uttering a word without belching.

"When you mimicked him behind your hand, Ling, I thought I was going to burst. You are very naughty and will get me into trouble with my clients," chuckled Stephen.

He paused as she handed him some brushes to clean, noticing she was studying his features.

"What is it, Ling?"

She smiled. "You are not like the other gwai lo, Stephen; you do not pour with sweat or smell like rancid meat. You are kind and gentle, polite and considerate. And you do not order me about like Chinese men."

"That's because I respect you as an equal. You are not my inferior; you are a beautiful and talented young woman whom I admire more than any other woman in Hong Kong."

"More than Fiona?" she asked coyly.

"More than anyone, Ling."

He took her hands in his. "You, Mei-ling, are not like your sisters, half sisters nor most of the Chinese women I meet. You have an independent spirit; you are witty, clever and …"

As he spoke, she had inched closer to him, her eyes burning deeply into his. He could hear her breathing faster.

"And?" she said softly.

"And I have fallen in love with you."

She reached up and, standing on tiptoes, kissed him gently on the lips.

"I have loved you for a long time, honourable master," she whispered.

When Stephen told Fiona about his feelings for Mei-ling, she took him in her arms and kissed him.

He smiled at her. "Do I not shock you, Miss Trevelyan?" he asked.

She laughed. "Do you think you are telling me something I didn't know, Waters Sin Saang?"

"Was it that obvious?"

"I'm a woman, Stephen, and I'm also in love myself."

"And in the same forbidden way."

"Not at all. Mei-ling would not be forbidden to you. She is the daughter of a concubine; she doesn't count for much. I doubt that old man Kwok would have any objections to your marrying her if you wanted to. Of course, the European community would look down their noses, but who cares about them? You have the upper hand with them, Stephen. They want your work and I have no doubt they would accept a certain amount of eccentricity in you. Just don't expect to be invited to too many more of their dreary parties."

They were married in the spring of 1884. Mei-ling was twenty years old and, as far as she knew, her husband was thirty-four. Stephen thought long and hard about whether to tell Mei-ling his secret, trying to assess how she would react. He remembered Henri and Michel's admonishments, and Gisèle's, and how he had been determined thereafter to tell everything to any woman he was asking to share his life. But for Mei-ling, there were complicating factors. She was Chinese and despite having a distinctly free spirit, her character and beliefs were firmly based in the traditions of Chinese culture and philosophy. She believed strongly in the spirit world, in the existence of multiple gods, of good luck, bad luck, omens and superstitions. He respected all of these and he loved her for it. And he knew she loved him, but he was worried she might consider his tale simply too hard to believe, or, if she did believe it, that he was cursed in some way, possessed by devils.

When a year after their marriage, she delivered him a baby daughter, she cried because it wasn't a son. She felt ashamed that she had let him down. She simply could not accept that for him it made no difference whether a child was a son or a daughter, that the only matter of importance was that the child was alive and healthy. When

Stephen looked into the little girl's eyes, he was pleased that he had held back. Lei-li had pale grey eyes, exactly the same as his. Mei-ling thought this was a wonderful sign, that their daughter had strength and vision like her wise husband. Stephen wondered what she would have thought if she knew what other rare traits the child had inherited from her father. He wasn't prepared to risk finding out.

As Lei-li grew, Mei-ling felt truly blessed that she had produced such a healthy daughter. The child was simply never ill, not even contracting any colds when all around her, apart from Stephen, were suffering from them. Mei-ling had noticed this robust healthiness in Stephen and marvelled at it. It was also clear that Lei-li not only had her father's good health, but also his artistic talents. By the age of nine, she was producing paintings that showed a remarkable skill in capturing form and colour on her canvasses or paper.

In May 1894, there was an outbreak of bubonic plague in Hong Kong. The authorities attempted to control its spread by rapid removal of the dead and dying, by disinfection of houses where infected people had lived and by isolation of the sick in temporary hospitals. The Chinese community, resentful and suspicious of Western approaches to medical treatment, responded by hiding their dead or dumping them away from their houses and by leaving the Colony in droves, bringing commerce to a virtual standstill. Of those admitted to a hospital, most would eventually die, but this did not stop many futile attempts at treating them.

Knowing he was under no personal risk from infection, Stephen offered his help in disinfecting houses. At other times he would help either Fiona or Kwok Fu-keung, who was skilled in traditional Chinese medicine and worked voluntarily at the Tung Wah hospital. Initially it was thought that the disease only affected the Chinese – there had been no European deaths in the early days of the plague. But when deaths started to occur in June among members of the garrison involved in disinfection duties, panic spread among the European community and people were desperate to leave.

Although Stephen was not among those panicking, he worried about Mei-ling, insisting that she and all other members of the household remain behind its closed walls, maintaining minimal contact with the outside world. He was therefore shocked one afternoon at the height of the plague to see Mei-ling walk into the ward at the Tung Wah hospital where he was helping Kwok Fu-keung remove the bodies of five victims who had died earlier that day.

"Mei-ling, what are you doing here? I left strict instructions that you remain at the house; you are putting yourself at great risk."

"No more than you, husband," she replied, looking in horror around the ward at the pitiful state of the victims lying on flimsy matting on the floor. "I had to come at once. Lei-li is ill and I fear that it is this pestilence. I do not want the authorities finding out and taking her to one of these dreadful places where she will surely die."

Stephen stopped in his tracks.

"That's impossible, Mei-ling. Lei-li cannot possibly be ill."

"Why not, husband? She's the same as us all."

"No, she cannot be ill. What are her symptoms? Does she have a fever? Is she sweating?"

"No, she has no fever. She is vomiting and she has pains in her stomach. She has been clutching her body with the pain."

"I will come at once," replied Stephen, in panic. This went against everything he had assumed about Lei-li; everything he knew about himself. Was this plague so virulent that it might defeat even him?

He went to a table to pour water from a jug to wash his hands. As he did, an elderly female patient called out, delirious with pain from the swollen glands in her body as the disease devoured her. Mei-ling walked over to her. The woman's mouth was frothing, her eyes staring starkly at Mei-ling in terror. Mei-ling poured her a glass of water and put it to her mouth, lifting her head slightly to help her swallow it.

"No Mei-ling!" cried Stephen, as he turned to look for her. "Get away from her! It isn't safe!"

Mei-ling was confused. She opened her mouth to speak, but as she did, the woman's body convulsed, sputum spraying from her mouth onto Mei-ling's face.

Mei-ling dropped the glass of water and wiped her face with her sleeve. Stephen rushed to her and pulled her away. He grabbed a jug of water and threw it onto her face. Then he wiped her face in a cloth soaked in disinfectant.

"You didn't swallow anything, did you?" he asked, his concerned eyes studying her face for any remnants of spittle from the woman.

"No, husband, I spat it out, do not worry. You are here every day and have suffered no ill effects; one small incident cannot hurt me."

They rushed back to the house, where, even given the urgent need Stephen felt to see his daughter, he insisted that they remove their clothes, dropping them in a tub of disinfectant. Wearing clean clothes, they ran to Lei-li's bedroom to find her groaning and clutching her stomach.

"Lei-li, what is it?" cried Stephen, his hand checking her forehead. He was relieved to find that she had none of the normal plague symptoms, but he was still confused that she should have anything wrong.

He sat down on the bed. "Tell me when this started, Lei-li."

She told him, in between spasms of pain, that it had started that morning after her breakfast, which had included a special broth her amah, Ah Ho, had prepared for her.

"Special broth?" Stephen turned to Mei-ling. "Fetch Ah Ho immediately, Ling. We must find out what it was."

Two minutes later, he heard a shuffling outside as Mei-ling returned with the maid. "Tell me what was in the broth!" he shouted at her as she entered the room.

Normally, he would never raise his voice to any of the servants; it was unseemly and showed them great disrespect. However, he was in a panic as he saw the pain on his daughter's face.

"It was a preparation my brother obtained for me, honourable master," stuttered the maid in fright. "He said it would prevent the young mistress from catching the disease, that it would strengthen her body."

"Prevent her from catching it by poisoning her!" yelled Stephen, furious at the maid for giving anything he or Mei-ling hadn't sanctioned.

"Do you have any left?" he yelled again, ignoring the fear on the maid's face.

"Yes, honourable master."

"Then fetch it at once!"

She returned a few minutes later with a pouch of herbal material.

There was a label tied round the neck with minute, handwritten Chinese characters written on it.

Stephen looked at it, but it made little sense: his knowledge of traditional medicines was limited. "How much of it did you give her?" he said sternly to the cowering maid.

"Only one dose, as it says on the label, honourable master," she replied.

Stephen took the pouch and ran from the room. It had crossed his mind to send a runner but he decided that it would be quicker to go himself.

Within ten minutes, he arrived back at the Tung Wah hospital where he quickly located Kwok Fu-keung and breathlessly explained what had happened.

Keung took the pouch to the pharmacy where he consulted an ancient handwritten book, leafing through it rapidly.

He went to the medicine cupboard, removing several bottles containing powders. He weighed different amounts from each bottle and ground them together.

"Don't worry, Stephen, she will be fine. The stupid maid must have given her quite a dose, but it is not enough to cause her any permanent harm. Dissolve this in water and let Lei-li drink it. It will ease the pain. Tomorrow she should be fully recovered."

The crisis over, the next day Stephen returned to the hospital to continue with the gruesome duties of dealing with the dead and dying. He was later home than usual that evening and, having changed his clothes at the entrance, he walked into the main courtyard of the house expecting to find Mei-ling waiting for him. However, the courtyard was deserted apart from two servants skulking in the shadows.

"Where is the mistress?" he called, seeing them whispering quietly to each other.

"In her room, master," one of them replied.

Puzzled, Stephen went to their bedroom to find the gaslight turned down and Mei-ling stretched out on the bed.

"Mei-ling, what is it?" he asked, sitting on the edge of the bed and taking her hand. Her hand was cold and clammy. He felt her forehead; she had a fever.

236

She opened her eyes to look at him. "I am sorry, honourable husband, not to meet you downstairs. I have not been feeling well today. It will pass, I am sure. I shall be fine tomorrow."

She told him that her body had been aching, that she'd had a severe headache all day and that in the last hour she had developed pains in her groin.

He gently placed his hand at the top of her legs and found the glands there were starting to swell. A shiver of fear passed through his body: Mei-ling had all the classic symptoms of the plague.

He stared at her, remembering her visit to the hospital the previous day when the old woman had coughed in her face. He chewed his lip, trying to remain calm, not wanting to panic Mei-ling, his sweet, young, beautiful wife. He had been around the plague for two months now and had seen its mercilessness. Almost everyone who contracted it succumbed, and he knew that anyone in whom it had advanced as rapidly as it had in Mei-ling stood no chance. His only course of action was to try to make her remaining hours as peaceful as possible.

He heard a gentle knock at the door. It was Lei-li.

"How is mother, Papa? I left her sleeping earlier."

When he didn't answer, Lei-li looked into his eyes. When she saw the look of helplessness there, she knew at once what was wrong.

"Oh, Papa, is there nothing we can do?"

"I fear there is not, Lei-li," he whispered. "I will send for Kwok Fu-keung. He has medicines that ease the pain and the fever."

An hour later, Keung arrived with Fiona. They both examined Mei-ling and shook their heads.

"It is out of our hands, Stephen," said Fiona, swallowing back her tears. "We can only pray that she might be spared."

Keung had brought a number of potions. He took Stephen aside and passed one packet to him.

"Towards the end, Stephen, when the other potions will lose the battle at controlling the pain, there is this one that will deny the pestilence the satisfaction of inflicting its final fearful torture on Mei-ling. You must be brave when that moment comes; giving her this potion will be the only humane thing to do."

Stephen slipped the packet into his pocket and returned to the bedside.

When Stephen told Lei-li that they were going to look after Mei-ling together, that none of the servants would be placed at risk, Lei-li misunderstood his intentions. "I understand, Papa," she replied, trying to sound brave. "If we all die from this disease, we shall be in heaven together. We shall remain with mama."

He held her tight, trying to fight back the tears.

Later in the night, when Lei-li was fast asleep in a chair, Mei-ling awoke from her fever and called softly to Stephen for some water.

After a few sips, she leaned her head back against the pillow. "Husband," she whispered, "do not look so sad. You will have a good life with Lei-li. She is a wonderful child and she will learn so much from you. I am sure the gods will let me watch you from time to time until you both join me in Heaven."

"Mei-ling," he stuttered, "there is something I should … something that I have meant…" He couldn't go on. It was too late for her to know the truth about him.

He stared into the eyes of this woman he loved, remembering the other women like her he had also loved, wondering how much longer his heart could stand the torment. Then he thought of Lei-li, and he knew that his life was now with her. She was like him and when she was old enough, he would tell her everything.

The medicines Keung had given Stephen for Mei-ling were good, natural sedatives that left her sleeping through her remaining hours. She died in her sleep the following evening with both Stephen and Lei-li holding her hands. The final preparation Keung had given Stephen had sat like a lead weight in his pocket; he didn't know if he would have had the courage to use it.

Two hours after Mei-ling died, Kwok Fu-ming's eldest son, Kwok Fu-on, arrived at the house to talk to Stephen. Fu-on had taken over most of the everyday running of the family business from his ageing father.

"Waters Sin Saang, my father wishes, and I am sure you will agree, that Mei-ling's body should not be subjected to the indignity of being disposed of in one of the mass, limed graves that the authorities insist on for plague victims. She is worthy of more respectful treatment. We still have boats sailing along the coast. Some fifty miles east of Hong Kong, there is a family property where many of my ancestors are buried. The graves are on a hill facing the sea, as is only proper. It will be easy to arrange for Mei-ling's body to be transferred to a boat. My father is too frail to accompany us, but he would like you to know that arrangements can also be made for you and Lei-li to attend. You will have to be in disguise, naturally."

It was some months before Stephen could summon the enthusiasm to resume painting. He had stopped during the plague because he was too occupied at the hospitals or helping out with disinfection, and now, with many of his Chinese clients having disappeared into China in the vain hope of escaping the plague and many families of European clients fleeing anywhere they could, the demand for his work had decreased. Following Mei-ling's death, he and Lei-li clung to each other for support. Lei-li missed her mother terribly. They had been very close, particularly since she had no siblings. Mei-ling had adopted the traditional maternal Chinese role of advising her daughter on everything she could about the world, even things she knew nothing about. She had understood that life wouldn't necessarily be easy for Lei-li: she was a half-caste in societies that tended to subordinate anyone of mixed blood. She had hoped that one day, for her daughter's sake, Stephen would agree to move somewhere else in the world where their marriage would be more readily accepted and their mixed-blood daughter would be treated more fairly.

Stephen was also aware that the years were passing and before long, both he and Lei-li would have to move on. Before that happened, he would have to tell Lei-li the truth about himself and about how he was sure she was the same. It was a difficult subject. He had broached it before with Henri and Michel when they were that age. The memory of that, coloured with the memory of Gisèle, caused him to hesitate – it would be better, easier, for Lei-li to accept if she were older.

As Lei-li moved into her teenage years, her talents as an artist blossomed, encouraging Stephen to spend more time coaching her and honing her skills. By her fifteenth birthday, a few months into the new century, she had developed a maturity in her art well beyond her years.

Lei-li also became very close to Fiona, who would call almost daily to see her, becoming in many ways a substitute for the mother she had lost. The three were in Stephen's Hollywood Road studio late one morning in May 1900 when a messenger arrived with a note from the Hostel Da Rosa. The note respectfully asked if Mr Stephen Waters was available to receive four Dutchmen. No litter would be required – they would prefer to take the air by walking along the Queen's Road.

"*Four* Dutchmen!" exclaimed Stephen. "I hope the two extras aren't as big as Lars, they will never fit in the studio."

They weren't as big as Lars; they were bigger.

When the men arrived, Johanne came in first and threw his arms around Stephen. "Englishman! It has been so long. My wife refused to allow me to come to Hong Kong when the plague was at its height and–"

"Your wife, Johanne? You are married at last?"

Johanne grinned. "Well, when a man gets to my age, he starts to need a few home comforts. After my dear mother passed away ten years ago now, I became lonely. Brigitta is a wonderful woman, but she orders me about and boxes my ears if I fall out of line. It is wonderful, Englishman."

"Have you a photograph of her, Johanne?" asked Fiona. "We must see her."

He pulled a small sepia-toned photograph from his wallet and passed it proudly to them.

"She is very beautiful, Johanne," said Stephen, "you are a lucky man."

"Thank you, I am indeed. This is to be my last trip and I can look forward to settling down on dry land with great anticipation. But Englishman, I am rude. I have only just heard about Mei-ling. I am so sorry. I should have written to you if I had known."

"Thank you, Johanne," replied Stephen, hugging him again.

Johanne looked around the studio and saw Lei-li for the first time – she had been busying herself in a side room when he first arrived.

"This must be Lei-li. My heavens, how can such a miserable Englishman have so beautiful a daughter?"

"I am delighted to meet you, Johanne," smiled Lei-li. "Papa has told me so much about you and Lars."

"Talking of Lars," said Stephen, "where is he? I assume he is one of the four Dutchmen. Who are the other two?"

"You shall see," replied Johanne. "They are trying to get through the doorway without knocking the building down."

"Lars!" he called. "Come in and bring your boys. And try not to break the place!"

There was deep rumbling from outside that grew louder as Lars came into the room. He was as huge as ever, but at sixty-five, his face was deeply lined, his skin a deep weather-beaten brown. The rumbling continued after him as he walked in, coming from two giants behind him who were even taller than he was.

"Stephen," growled Lars, holding out his arms. As he enveloped Stephen, Lei-li was convinced her father would disappear entirely. Lars let go and turned, holding out a huge forearm.

"May I introduce my boys?"

The boys, who were the twenty-seven-year-old identical twins, Otto and Pieter, ducked through the doorway. They were Lars of forty years before – shaven-headed, massive men packed with muscle. Suddenly the room seemed full of people. Having introduced everyone, Lars told his boys to sit on the floor since he was concerned they might break any chairs that were offered. They sat meekly like a couple of obedient puppies.

It was Lars' final voyage as well. He and Johanne had decided that they had to visit one last time to introduce his boys to their Hong Kong friends.

Later, after they had swapped stories and Lei-li had prepared them all some tea, Johanne turned to Stephen.

"You are looking very well, Englishman," he said. "Do you remember that crazy trip we made when you made me look like an old man?"

"I do indeed, Ernest Waters," laughed Stephen.

"I wondered at the time about those skills of yours. Have you been applying them to your own hair? There is something about it that reminds me of that trip."

"I don't need to apply anything to my hair," smiled Stephen, "nature does her work perfectly well on her own."

Johanne persisted. "I thought perhaps you had made that trip to India you were so intent on and picked up an elixir of youth. You really don't look much different from when we first met."

"It's the company of beautiful women, Johanne," declared Stephen. "Look at you, sixty-nine, but now you've got yourself a wife, you don't look a day over forty!"

Stephen told his Dutch friends that he hoped to take a trip to Europe when Lei-li was a little older – he wanted to show her the galleries in London and Paris and to take her to Italy, where she could immerse herself in the world of the Renaissance. He promised that the trip would naturally include Holland, where they would visit their Dutch friends and meet their families.

It was with these happy prospects that the friends all parted at a landing stage in Central District two weeks later, not knowing that circumstances would prevent them from ever meeting again.

# Chapter 21

## July 2009

When Corrado Verdi mentioned his 'little car' that needed a spin up the autostrada, Ced Fisher imagined he would be spending an uncomfortable day with his six-foot-four frame folded into a Fiat 500. He couldn't have been more surprised when Verdi greeted him in his hotel lobby and guided him across the car park towards a Maserati GranTurismo S, its powder blue bodywork exactly matching the colour of its owner's Ermenegildo Zegna suit trousers – the jacket was carefully folded on the back seat.

"Would you like to drive, Cedric?" asked Verdi, dangling the keys from his index finger.

"Thanks, Corrado, I'd love to, but the steering wheel's on the wrong side for me. I'll think I'll just sit back, relax and enjoy the ride."

"Perhaps later," smiled Verdi, stowing Ced's equipment boxes.

Putting his problems to the back of his mind, Ced soaked up the luxury of the feisty sports car as the one hundred and eighty kilometres of autostrada between Rome and Arezzo disappeared in a blur. Verdi knew exactly where the speed checks would be and in between them, he opened up the throttle. The ride was so smooth that a hundred and eighty kilometres per hour seemed like fifty in any other car.

"She's a sweet little lady, eh, Cedric?" laughed Verdi as he flashed his lights at yet another slower moving car ahead of them in the fast lane.

"Magico, Corrado, pure magico," replied Ced.

After taking the exit for Arezzo, they skirted the city and headed off in the direction of Anghiari.

"We'll see 'The Awakening' first, Cedric," explained Verdi, "and then pop into San Sepolcro itself to see 'The Resurrection'. After that we'll call into Arezzo in time for my old friend Giorgio Bonazzi, the superintendent of fine art, to take us to lunch in one of his favourite Tuscan restaurants. Peasant food really, out here in the sticks, but it will be tasty enough I'm sure."

A few kilometres into the hills beyond Anghiari, they turned right on the crest of a rising curve through a newly built stone gateway that led onto a gravel road. A high stone wall topped with razor wire and security cameras disappeared into the trees on either side of the gateway. A sign announced that the site was the home of the chapel containing the Piero della Francesca painting 'The Awakening'.

"The discovery of this masterpiece caused the fine art authorities all sorts of headaches," laughed Verdi. "It is in the middle of nowhere and cannot be moved. Well, it could, but it would be madness. After standing abandoned and neglected for centuries while it slowly decayed, this crumbling villa with its very special chapel is now protected by the latest high-security technology and a squad of guards patrolling twenty-four hours a day."

"I'm surprised not to see more tourists here," remarked Ced as they drove down the gravel road and pulled up outside a large fourteenth century villa surrounded by scaffolding.

"There will be once the conservation work is finished," replied Verdi. "The authorities need to recoup the millions they are spending on this treasure."

A young man of about twenty-five was waiting for them near the chapel doors. Verdi introduced him to Ced as Luca Spinelli, one of his protégés from the Accademia working on the conservation work of 'The Awakening'.

Spinelli was full of questions about Ced's program that he hurled excitedly at him as they walked towards the chapel. Normally, Ced would have been pleased to discuss his work with a like-minded art expert, but the setbacks of the past few days had left him feeling more than a little insecure about the whole project. He caught Verdi's eye with a plaintive look. Picking up on it immediately, Verdi put an arm around Spinelli's shoulder.

"Luca, your enthusiasm is, as ever, a delight to see in this cynical world. May you never lose it. But you must remember that Cedric is about to experience a special moment, a moment that can only occur once. He is about to stand before a truly magnificent work of art for the first time, to have its beauty flow over him and caress him with its wonder. You must remember the awe you felt when you first laid eyes on this creation, Luca. It is a magical, religious moment, like speaking to God. Such moments deserve tranquility, peace. I am sure there will be time later for you to discuss technical matters."

The young man bowed his head in submission.

"Certainly, dottore, I sometimes forget how privileged I am to be in the presence of this work every day. I shall leave you in peace."

He nodded his head at them and walked away in the direction of the site office.

Verdi threw a conspiratorial wink at Ced.

"Thanks, Corrado," nodded Ced gratefully. "He's a good lad but it's hard to get enthusiastic about something that I'm seriously thinking might have to be binned."

Verdi shook his head. "It will never come to that, Cedric; your program is too good. I have every confidence you will solve your little problem."

They walked into the chapel. Inside was a rectangular nave with a small chancel at the far end. The only natural light came from two round windows in the wall above the main doors.

The open space of the nave was divided into two: a working area of tables and benches for the conservationists cordoned off by red ropes, and a public area behind for viewing. Verdi had called ahead to announce their arrival and the workers who would normally be quietly carrying out their tests and applying their pastes and solutions had disappeared for coffee.

The fresco was large, about twenty feet by fifteen, and covered much of the wall behind the chancel. The whole chapel was dominated by it. The two round windows let in a surprising amount of light, and, augmented by three floods left on by the team of conservationists, 'The Awakening' stood before them bathed in light.

Ced walked to the centre of the nave and let his eyes roam over the fresco.

"What do you think, Cedric?" asked Verdi quietly after a few minutes. "Is it worth all the fuss?"

"It's truly magnificent, Corrado," replied Ced. "No photograph or poster can ever do it justice. It has to be experienced in the flesh."

"Yes," agreed Verdi, "and to think it was lost for so long. It has sat in this room hidden behind a covering of plaster for maybe five hundred years. It is a miracle that the building survived, a true miracle."

Ced pointed to a small assembly of scaffolding on one side of the fresco.

"Would it be OK if I used that rig to look at it a bit closer?"

"Go ahead, Cedric, that is why we are here. Have you noticed the pale grey eyes of that shepherd, the one that looks like your Mr Andrews?"

"First thing I saw, Corrado; they hit me immediately."

He wheeled the scaffolding in front of the fresco and climbed onto its platform. From this vantage point he could study every inch of the detail. Taking a large magnifying glass from his pocket, he scrutinised the figures in the painting, looking first at the faces and then at the clothing. After that, he turned his attention to the bucolic scenery of the background.

Scratching his head and frowning, he moved back to the figures, specifically the faces, using his magnifying glass to study one area, then another, and then back to the first.

After about fifteen minutes, he called down to Verdi, who was using his binoculars to conduct his own study. "Corrado, have you looked in detail at the faces on these figures? Not the shepherd; the others, I mean. I assume they are the disciples from their clothing and the way they are looking directly at the Christ figure."

Missing the tension in Ced's voice, Verdi chuckled in amusement. "So you've spotted the Piero self-portrait. It's on the figure that is generally agreed to be St. Paul. Like many of his contemporaries, Piero included his face on a figure in a number of his paintings, Cedric. The famous one is the figure in 'The Resurrection'."

Cedric sat down on the platform, his legs dangling over the edge.

"I know, Corrado, I've seen it." His voice was distant, distracted.

He paused and clasped his hands in front of him in his lap, his head bent downwards as he gathered his thoughts. He looked up and fixed his eyes on Verdi. He spoke slowly and deliberately.

"I'd agree, Corrado, that the face on that saint, St. Paul, is Piero's face. The features are the same as those in the other self-portraits he produced. But," he continued, his voice dropping to a whisper as he shook his head in disbelief at what he was saying, "I don't think he painted it."

"What?" cried Verdi, in shock. "What do you mean, you don't think he painted it? Are you saying that this fresco isn't a Piero? I cannot agree with you, Cedric!"

He looked around in panic in case anyone else had come into the church.

Ced put up a hand to stop him.

"I'm not saying that, Corrado, not at all. I think that Piero painted quite a portion of this work. But the portrait of himself, and … well, it's difficult to say without a much more detailed examination, but I'd say that about forty per cent is della Francesca, and sixty per cent is another artist. Not a group of his apprentices, Corrado. Just one other artist."

Verdi rushed forward to the scaffolding. "Help me up, Cedric, I need you to show me exactly what you mean. I have studied this work in great detail and so have many other art experts. It's agreed that there is some minor variation in style, but it's also agreed that it is substantially the work of Piero."

"I should have formed the same opinion until I started to look for all the nuances that are searched for in my program. I think whoever painted alongside Piero was not only influenced by him – a gifted apprentice, say – but he actively tried to copy his style, to use Piero's own style signature."

"You mean more than simply painting in Piero's style because that is the way he had been taught, he was deliberately trying to disguise the fact that Piero wasn't creating the whole work? He was forging part of a Piero della Francesca fresco while the man himself was working alongside him?"

"Exactly, although I'm not sure that it would constitute forgery."

He paused, sighing. "That's my first conclusion, Corrado. But my second conclusion is more ... worrying."

Verdi turned to face him. "What do you mean, 'worrying'? That sounds like a piece of very British understatement."

Ced stared at the floor of the platform, gathering his thoughts. Then he lifted his eyes to Verdi's.

"Corrado, I've spent the last few days in London and here in Italy poring over paintings that have confounded my comparison program - the Perinis, the de la Places and the Lorenzinis; and there were also the Morettis. Not only have I checked every damn line of that program a hundred times, but I've studied the brushstrokes it examines, tried to get my eye to distinguish the subtleties that it can pick up, although it's designed to do it far better than I or anyone else can. I haven't been able to distinguish the works of those artists one from the other any more than my program can, or any more than you have so far, I regret to say.

"It hadn't really occurred to me before how much of Piero della Francesca's techniques are in those paintings. They are not by his hand; they are distinguishable, although they are very influenced by him. When I started to look around this fresco this morning, Corrado, I nearly fell off the scaffolding. I'm either delusional or I'm seeing the same technique here as well."

Disbelief clouded Verdi's face. "You mean you can't distinguish some of this painting from the Perinis and ... and the others?"

Ced nodded. "I can't by eye. What I need to find out is whether my program can. If it can't, we have yet another nail in its coffin."

"And in ours, Cedric," muttered Verdi. "We are supposed to be the experts. If we can't tell one artist from another, who can?"

Ced climbed down from the scaffolding, his heart heavy. He went outside to Verdi's car and retrieved his imaging equipment. He had no interest in photographing the entire fresco; that had been done many times. What he wanted were images of small sections of the painting that the program could analyse in the greatest of detail.

He clamped the scaffolding and set up his tripod, camera and lights. Meanwhile, Verdi was pacing the chapel. He would occasionally stop, raise his head and turn in Ced's direction, as if he were about to raise a significant point, but then his head would drop, his hands clasp each other behind his back, and he would continue pacing.

After an hour, Ced had what he considered to be enough images. He packed away his equipment and climbed down from the scaffolding.

"I'm done, Corrado. I can't do anything more until I get back to Rome; I didn't bring my computer with me."

Verdi reached up and put a hand on Ced's shoulder. "Cedric, listen," he said quietly. "What you have discovered this morning is potentially shattering. Its implications would reverberate all the way up to the President of the Republic. It's not so much that less of the fresco might have been painted by della Francesca than we thought, although that is bad enough. The more difficult matter is this confusion over styles. Until that is explained, we must keep this to ourselves. Do you agree?"

He looked around as he spoke, still worried that somebody might be listening to their conversation.

"I agree absolutely, Corrado. If we're not careful, we could become totally discredited."

"Along with the Accademia and all the experts who have deliberated over this painting," added Verdi.

They walked out to the car.

"Do you still want to see 'The Resurrection'?" asked Verdi.

"I've seen it on a number of occasions before, Corrado, and there are enough hi-res images on line for me to check it later. I'd rather get lunch over with and head back to Rome," replied Ced morosely.

As the tyres of the Maserati threw up gravel from the drive, Luca Spinelli rushed from the site office. He had been hoping for a long and detailed discussion with the English expert. As it was, he had to content himself with watching the sleek sports car disappear through the trees towards the gate.

Arriving in Arezzo, they went straight to the Piazza Grande in the heart of the city's historic centre where they found the superintendent of fine art for the Arezzo region, Giorgio Bonazzi, waiting for them in his chosen restaurant. By contrast to Verdi, Bonazzi was a harrassed-looking overweight man in his late forties crammed into a suit that had been bought when his girth carried far fewer kilos. He wore thick glasses and he spoke with an Italian accent that even to Ced's untrained ear was very different from what he had heard in Rome. To Ced's relief, he also spoke no English – Ced could leave Verdi to hold court and drift in his own sea of worries.

The lunch, for which neither Ced nor Verdi had any appetite, was delicious. Bonazzi had gone to a great deal of trouble in his ordering and both men tried their hardest to appear appreciative. Verdi refused any wine on the grounds he was driving, but Ced had no choice but to join Bonazzi in sampling the local red wine that he eulogised at length to Verdi, insisting he translate. Verdi kept it short.

"He says it is from a local boutique vineyard – one with a very low production but which lovingly cares for its grapes and then monitors the fermentation, bottling and storage with more attention than you would give a patient in intensive care. Look suitably impressed even if you just want to spit the stuff onto the floor."

Ced laughed and swirled the wine round his mouth. "It's actually delicious, Corrado, you old cynic, even though it's not from Lazio. There are hints of several fruits, blackberry being the strongest, but there is something else. It's like a plum, but it's very delicate."

"Madonna, you sound like the writer of some pretentious wine magazine!" snorted Verdi as he turned to Bonazzi to repeat what Ced had told him, embellishing it with his own floweriness.

Bonazzi beamed in delight and told them the subtle fruit Ced had detected was a special wild plum that grew in the area that affected the flavour of the grapes. He poured Ced another glass.

Keen to head back to Rome, the two men tried hard to leave, but Bonazzi was having none of it. He knew of Ced's program, and he wanted to show him a painting he had recently acquired as well as discuss several paintings housed in the city's art museum.

In his heart, Ced knew this was an important opportunity to gather more information since three of the paintings in the museum were Tommaso Perinis, but he was desperate to follow up his morning's imaging.

Bonazzi's office, a short walk away in the  fourteenth-century Palazzo del Comune, was a large room heavily panelled in dark wood. A huge antique desk dominated one end while a more modern display table occupied the other. In the centre were two sofas and a coffee table where he entertained his visitors.

With a certain amount of theatre, Bonazzi walked over to the display table and picked up two medium-sized paintings. He spoke rapidly to Verdi who translated for Ced.

"As he said earlier, he has three Tommaso Perinis from the art museum to show you – here are two and the other is on its way."

Ced took the first of the paintings. It was a portrait of a middle-aged man in the clothing and bonnet commonly worn by merchants in sixteenth-century Tuscany. He could see immediately that it was typical of Tommaso Perini.

He smiled at Bonazzi. "This is a stunning example of Perini's work, signore," he said, to which the superintendent nodded eagerly and passed him the second painting.

While Ced was studying this, there was a knock on the door and a young woman entered carrying the third painting. She appeared to have arrived straight from the catwalk of a fashion show. Assistant curator Maria di Laurentis cast a practised eye around the room, singled out Ced and smiled seductively at him. She walked over to the coffee table.

"Shall I leave the painting here, dottore?" she purred softly in English. When it was clear her boss hadn't understood, she barked it again at him in rapid Italian.

"Uh, grazie, Maria," replied the embarrassed Bonazzi.

Maria di Laurentis leaned over the coffee table and handed Ced the painting she was carrying, displaying to him as she did the substantial contents of her cream silk blouse.

With great difficulty, Ced raised his eyes to hers.

"Thank you, er, grazie," he stuttered.

"Prego, Dottor Fisher," she replied, smiling coquettishly.

"Grazie, Maria, that will be all for now," said Bonazzi in Italian.

The girl stood up straight and tossed her head at the director, her smile evaporating. She walked slowly from the room, turning once more to catch Ced's eyes as she closed the door.

"Cedric."

There was no reply.

"Cedric!" smiled Verdi insistently.

"What?"

"Mind your tongue. If it hangs out any further, you're going to damage that painting."

Ced grinned sheepishly at him, shook his head and turned his attention to the third painting.

A few minutes later, Ced turned to Verdi. "These are all superb examples of Perini's work, Corrado. Does Dottor Bonazzi know of their provenance?"

"He told me it is beyond question. These paintings have not left Arezzo once in four hundred and fifty years."

"I'm itching to get back to Rome to work up the images from this morning, but I really would like to add these three to my library, if that's possible. It's too good an opportunity to miss. Do you think the dottore would agree?"

"I've already asked him and he would be delighted to oblige."

"I'll need to pop to the car and get my stuff. It won't take a moment."

Verdi explained this to Bonazzi, who replied in Italian.

"The superintendent says he will send his young assistant curator to help you, Cedric," said Verdi. Then he laughed, seeing the look of panic in Ced's eyes. "Don't worry, he has more than one assistant curator and this one's a perfectly harmless young man."

Bonazzi lifted his phone to call the man and then walked to a cupboard beyond his display table. He unlocked the door with a key from a bundle attached to his trouser belt and took out another painting. He turned to explain something to Verdi, staring lovingly at the painting as he did.

"The superintendent has another painting he'd like to show you, Cedric. This one he bought for the museum recently when he was in Venice."

Ced stood and walked to the table where Bonazzi had set the painting on a small easel.

It was smaller than the other three, a portrait of a woman in her twenties, again in clothing typical of the early or mid-sixteenth century. Ced studied the style and brushwork; clearly another Tommaso Perini, he thought. He immediately recognised her as a younger version of the woman in the portrait Lawrence Forbes had shown him in London. He looked up into Bonazzi's eager eyes.

"An exquisite portrait, dottore," he said. "Really beautiful. How interesting that it travelled all the way to Venice only for you to bring it back here again."

Bonazzi waited while Verdi translated and then frowned as he replied.

"He doesn't understand Cedric. He's asking what you mean," said Verdi.

"Well," smiled Cedric, it's a Tommaso Perini, clearly, but from earlier in his life since I've seen this same model painted by him in middle age. What I meant was that he obviously painted it here in Arezzo, which is where he worked, and at some stage it was bought or taken to Venice. Now it's come back."

Verdi repeated this in Italian to Bonazzi, who started to shake his head furiously. There followed an intense conversation in rapid Italian between the two men that finished with Bonazzi turning on his heel and marching over to the cupboard where he kept the painting. He pulled out a large white envelope and retrieved a certificate from it. He marched back to Verdi and thrust it into his hands. Verdi read it carefully and shook his head.

He sighed deeply and turned to Ced.

"Cedric, you are not going to like this."

Ced eyed him warily.

"Cedric, Dottor Bonazzi says you are mistaken and with this document he can prove it. He says this painting is not by Tommaso Perini, although he agrees the style is similar and he can understand your confusion. He says, and this document confirms, that it is by a little-known Venetian artist called Giovanni di Luca who worked exclusively in Venice in the first part of the sixteenth century."

He paused, noting the shock in Cedric's face.

"It's another one, Cedric; we've found another one!"

# Chapter 22

## 1905

In March 1905, Stephen Waters received a note from Miguel la Torres, founder, owner and chairman of the Macao-based La Torres Shipping, instructing him to present himself at la Torres' office in two days' time to commence work on his portrait. He showed the note to Fiona when she called in that afternoon with Lei-li.

"The impudence of the man!" she cried. "Miguel la Torres is a snake, Stephen. An evil man not to be trusted. Keung hates him. That shipping firm of his is a front for all his criminal activities. He's nothing more than a jumped-up pickpocket, a gangster from the back streets of Macao."

"I assume he only wants his portrait painted," replied Stephen. "I can't see much harm in that. In my line of work, I can stay removed from all the intrigues that businessmen and criminals tie themselves up in knots with."

"Don't be so sure of it, Stephen. My advice would be to turn him down if you can. I'll talk to Keung and see what he thinks."

However, when she consulted her lover, he reluctantly advised it would be prudent for Stephen to comply.

"To turn him down, Stephen, would only provoke him, and that is best avoided, believe me."

When Stephen arrived at la Torres' company headquarters at the appointed hour, he was shown into a large office decorated in heavy lacquered blackwood furniture. Thick red rugs with patterns of intertwined golden dragons covered the floor and ornate gas lamps hung from the ceiling.

La Torres was sitting cross-legged at a low table in front of a window, sipping tea. He was wearing the black gown of a mandarin, buttoned to one side of the neck. Glancing swiftly around the dark room, Stephen became aware of two huge men dressed entirely in black standing motionless and almost invisible in the shadows.

"Mr Waters," said la Torres in an impeccable upper-class English accent, "how good of you to come. Sit. Take some tea."

He clapped his hands and a servant shuffled hurriedly into the room from a side door to pour some tea into a tiny cup, bowing continuously as he did so.

La Torres was Eurasian, his main features Portuguese, but his almond-shaped eyes pure Chinese. He would once have been handsome, but years of underworld activity had left his face hard and humourless. There were deep lines etched into the corners of his mouth and his narrow unsmiling eyes while his skin was lightly powdered in an attempt to hide large areas of pockmarks on his cheeks and forehead. His dyed black hair was combed straight back and pomaded.

"I have chosen a setting, Mr Waters. I shall sit on the chair by the window so that the light accentuates my features. I require a semi-profile portrait, head and shoulders, that shows my regal bearing. I realise that time has been good to me, that I appear ... youthful. I am often complimented for it, Mr Waters."

Stephen fought to maintain a neutral expression: la Torres looked considerably more than his fifty years.

"I trust you can portray this on your canvas, that you can achieve a balance between the handsome ruggedness of a mature man and the youthful, virile masculinity of a male still in his prime."

Smiling thinly in self-satisfaction, la Torres stood and walked over to his chosen spot. Stephen was surprised to find he stood no more than five feet five inches tall. He was even more surprised when the man told him he did not wish anyone, himself included, to see the painting until it was officially unveiled three weeks hence.

The work started immediately and a week later, back in his studio, Stephen discussed progress with Lei-li and Fiona.

"It's one of the hardest portraits I've ever painted. He has an evil, harsh face that exudes malevolence. It's very hard to exclude that from the work because that's what I am seeing. I'm doing my best to ignore it, to soften what I see and make him appear the way he thinks he looks."

"I told you it wouldn't be easy, Stephen. It's not just any portrait," said Fiona, concerned.

"I don't think I've ever met such a terrifying man. How does he get away with all the criminal activity he is clearly connected with? The shipping company is a façade, a thinly disguised cover for his illegal activities. You should hear him talking to his minions; he has them all shaking in their shoes."

"He has the police in the palm of his hand, Stephen. They are paid very poorly and he can supplement their income substantially. The only thing he requires for his money is that they turn a blind eye to whatever he is doing."

Stephen nodded. "It will always be the way of the world, I fear. However, I'm concerned about this portrait; what will happen if he doesn't like it?"

Lei-li took his hand. "I think that is most unlikely, Papa. Has there ever been anyone who has not liked your work?"

Stephen smiled enigmatically. "No, not really. It's been fairly well-received so far."

Neither Fiona nor Lei-li was invited to the reception la Torres had ordered for the unveiling. The guests were very much from the shadier side of Hong Kong's entrepreneurial traders, both Chinese and Western, together with a number of government officials, police and garrison who owed la Torres favours.

La Torres surpised Stephen by inviting him to join him on the stage where the painting stood on an easel, covered with a red velvet cloth. Stephen stood behind and to one side of him, trying in vain to look as insignificant as he could. He felt a trickle of sweat run down his back under the European clothing he had become unused to wearing.

"Good evening, dear friends," smiled la Torres, his arms out in welcome to the sea of faces before him, although the smile looked as if it would slash each of their throats.

"I am delighted to see so many of you here this evening to mark this very special occasion. As you know, I have commissioned Mr Waters to use his considerable skills to produce my portrait to record the completion of the first fifty years of my life."

A round of applause broke out which la Torres allowed to flow over him for a few seconds, then held up his hands. "I can see from the shocked look on your faces you are surprised by my age." He smiled in false modesty, holding one hand over the other in front of his chest and nodding smugly.

"What can I say? Nature has blessed me with youthful looks, and my constitution has rebuffed the ravages of age often shown by lesser men."

The remark caused some uncomfortable shuffling of feet. Stephen was finding it very hard not to laugh out loud at the self-congratulatory nonsense this criminal was spouting. He half expected him to wave a bejewelled hand at the crowd like a bishop beatifically saluting his flock.

After a pause, la Torres continued.

"Mr Waters has told me that never in his career has he had such strong features, such perfect symmetry, such fine lines in so well-balanced proportions to copy onto his canvas."

He half-turned to Stephen, his eyes piercing coldly in his direction as if daring him to contradict.

"During the production of this work, I have refrained from viewing its progress," continued la Torres, turning back to the crowd. "I, like everyone else here, have not laid eyes on this work. My reasons are simple. I want to share the same moment of revelation with you so we can all say with one accord that we witnessed together, as a group of dear friends and comrades, the first glimpses of what I have no doubt will be a portrait like no other, a portrait that will be admired and revered for generations to come."

He half-turned to Stephen. "Mr Waters, if you would be so kind as to remove the cloth and satisfy the anticipation that has been buzzing around the room."

He turned back to the crowd, wanting to savour the moment of seeing the adoration, the delight and wonder in their eyes at this tribute to him.

He was not disappointed. As Stephen pulled the cloth from the painting, the crowd gasped as one in appreciation, bursting into spontaneous applause as they surged forward to take a closer look. There were cries of "Bravo!" "Brilliant!" "A masterpiece!" followed by even louder applause.

Overcome with the moment, la Torres turned to Stephen to congratulate him and finally to lay his eyes on what he had convinced himself would become a famous work, perhaps as famous as the Mona Lisa.

Stephen, who had started to relax as the clamorous praise from the room enveloped him, saw the closest thing he had seen to a smile on la Torres' face as his eyes fell briefly onto him. He then saw that smile contort and twist as the eyes above it widened in reaction to their first sighting of the portrait. La Torres stood in stunned silence as he faced the image of himself, his mouth working slowly, his shoulders hunching as his whole body started to shake. Stephen saw the colour rise through the man's short neck and up through his face until his entire head was a pulsating deep red. Spittle started to form at the edges of his mouth.

The roar of the crowd faded away in an instant. Then in the ensuing silence, another roar grew. It was from la Torres and it was fearsome. Stephen instinctively took a step backwards as the roar turned into a scream. La Torres' arms both rose slowly until they were extended high above his head, his hands and fingers the claws of a vulture waiting to pounce.

His head started to turn from side to side as his breathing became laboured. His eyes bulged in their sockets, revolving and searching until they fell onto Stephen. His right arm shot out, his index finger pointing accusingly.

"You traitor!" he screeched. "You incompetent! You European dog! How dare you! How DARE you portray me like this! This … this … caricature of a human being! This egregious mockery! This is obscene! An insult! You have ridiculed me, abused me with this … this worthless trash!"

As he spat the final words, he pulled a short double-bladed knife from under his jacket and held it up threateningly in his right hand. Then without warning, he turned to the painting and slashed it, cutting it from top to bottom. His whole body shaking in rage, he repeated his attack again and again until the painting was a series of fine ribbons hanging from the frame. His arm dropped and the knife fell from his hand. He turned again to Stephen and pointed at the door. "Get out of my sight, you worthless dog, before I inflict the same treatment on you!"

There was a rumbling of protest from the crowd. Even for la Torres this was going too far.

As Stephen watched in shock and horror at the vicious destruction of his work, his reaction turned from incredulity to indignation, and then to anger. La Torres' final words were the last straw. Stephen turned on him.

"You accuse *me* of being worthless, you low-life scum. You have less worth than a piece of excrement floating in the sewer you crawled out of. You are nothing but a narcissistic, self-important, jumped-up nobody. If you didn't surround yourself with these thugs for protection, you'd be trampled to death by a crowd baying for your blood on the first street you ventured out on. You might live by threats and brutality, but I can assure you that you and your threats mean this much to me!"

He spat on the floor. There was a gasp from the crowd, but he hadn't finished.

"You, sir," he continued, his eyes half-closed and his voice trembling slightly as he fought to control his emotions, "you have had the privilege of having your portrait painted by a master craftsman. That portrait showed you in as favourable a light as it would be possible to portray a demon who has gone so far down the road of evil that his every foul thought and deed is etched into his face. If I had painted you as I really see you, as everyone in this room sees you, then you would have had the horns and blood-red eyes of the Devil himself. You disgust me, sir!"

With that, Stephen turned on his heel and walked from the stage, expecting la Torres' bodyguards to grab him and beat him to a pulp. The crowd parted as Stephen strode for the door. From somewhere in its depths he heard a cry of "Hear! Hear!" and another of "Bravo, Waters!"

As Stephen reached the door, he heard another shout from the stage. La Torres had recovered from the shock of someone speaking to him in such a manner. In coarse street Cantonese, he yelled, "Stop him! I want him back here!"

Stephen felt the crowd close around him, but he suddenly realised they were on his side – la Torres' underworld rivals had sensed an opportunity to rebel against him, while for the Europeans in his sway, his actions had been a step too far. They physically blocked the bodyguards, allowing Stephen time to disappear from the building.

"Stephen," said Fiona, "I am worried. La Torres will not take this quietly. You have caused him the most incredible loss of face and he will not rest until he has had some form of retribution."

They were sitting in a drawing room of Stephen's house with Lei-li, who had poured her father a whisky to calm him down. She was now seated next to him as he sipped it, her hands on his arm.

"I have sent word to Keung to ask for his advice and help," continued Fiona. "I think you are in considerable danger, and probably Lei-li as well."

Stephen frowned. "I probably shouldn't have said what I said, but I couldn't stop myself. That rat is so used to riding roughshod over everyone, getting his own way through threats and coercion, that I simply couldn't allow myself to become another one of his spineless lackeys. I had already gone far enough down that route by painting the picture."

There was a light knock on the door and a servant entered followed by an anxious-looking Keung.

"I came immediately I received your note, Fiona," he said, bending over to kiss her.

"Stephen," he said, smiling and shaking his head in admiration, "you have certainly ruffled some feathers tonight. Word is already out on the street that la Torres has been thoroughly trounced by the English artist. There will be some blood spilt before the night is over as the rival factions taunt each other."

He sat next to Stephen. "I have taken the liberty of posting guards outside your studio. It is the first place la Torres would go to inflict retribution. He would have it torn down. I have also posted some guards here, outside your house. They will remain in place until the matter is resolved."

Stephen nodded slowly, staring at his own glass of whisky. He had no real understanding of the extent of Keung's dealings, nor whether they were entirely honest. He did know that besides the work he undertook on behalf of the Kwok empire, Keung had numerous other business interests, many of them carried out quietly and discreetly behind closed doors.

Three days later, Stephen was again in the drawing room with Keung and Fiona. They had just arrived and Fiona was pouring them some tea from a tray a servant had laid on the low table.

Keung's face now showed serious concern. "Things are grim, Stephen. I said there would be bloodshed and I was right. That in itself is nothing to worry about – it's just one group of low-life fighting another. It happens all the time and your run-in with la Torres is merely a convenient excuse."

He paused as the door opened. It was Lei-li, dressed like a servant and in the process of removing a headscarf and woven cane hat from her head.

"Lei-li," cried Stephen in surprise. "What are you doing dressed like that?"

"Papa, I have been into the city, disguised as a servant going about her business, but listening wherever I could to gossip and talk on the street. I have heard a disturbing story, Papa." She took his right hand and kissed it.

"You went alone, Lei-li, without the guards?"

"Yes, Papa, I had to. I can hardly slip around the city unseen if I have two fearsome guards trailing along behind me. Don't worry; I was perfectly safe.

"Papa, the talk is that la Torres is seeking a particular form of retribution. It seems that he doesn't seek your life as we expected. Instead, he wants to humiliate you, to cripple your abilities for all time."

Stephen frowned, not anticipating what his daughter was about to say.

"He wants to cut off your hand, Papa, your right hand, so that you will no longer be able to paint. He knows that painting is everything to you and he wants to destroy that. He thinks that if you lose your hand, you will take your own life in despair."

Stephen was shocked. He looked at the hand that had produced innumerable brilliant paintings for more than four hundred years. La

Torres was correct in his assumption: without his right hand, Stephen's life would not be worth living.

"Stephen," said Keung, "this whole situation is escalating. I can deal with la Torres in time but my resources aren't endless. Frankly, it would be easier if you and Lei-li went into China. There is a house where you will be safe. It is not the one where Mei-ling is buried, but one further up the coast, about a hundred miles from here. It is a remote spot, a walled compound in the country some distance from the nearest village. La Torres cannot possibly know about it."

Two evenings later, a group of six people dressed as Chinese servants slipped quietly from Stephen's house and made their way to the western end of the harbour. They were accompanied by Keung's guards until they had safely boarded two sampans. These were silently paddled out to a waiting sailing junk moored well round the point from the Green Island lighthouse, invisible in the moonless, cloud-covered night.

The six comprised Stephen, Lei-li, two guards and two servants. Stephen and Lei-li were shown to a cabin with two bunks, while the servants laid bedrolls outside the cabin door. The captain and his crew of five immediately set sail on an easterly course into Chinese waters.

As the sun rose over the South China Sea, they put into a small inlet on an uninhabited island some five miles offshore where the captain said they would spend the day out of sight.

Although it was only early April, the day was pleasantly warm and after a lunch of fish caught by one of the crew, Stephen decided to take a nap in the cabin. Lei-li said she wanted to make some sketches of the inlet from the bow.

As he opened the cabin door, Stephen turned to look at his daughter as she concentrated on her drawing. At twenty years old, she had grown into a beautiful young woman. Her long, jet black hair cascaded down her back from where it was caught at the nape of her elegant neck by a single clip, while her loose Chinese clothes hid her slender, lithe body. She glanced up at Stephen and waved, her pale grey eyes reminding him of the special bond that held them close, the bond about which she knew nothing.

Stephen awoke with a start to find a broad blade at his throat and a thin Chinese sailor squatting on the edge of his bunk, the man's gaunt face about three inches from his. From behind the sailor came a coarse voice.

"Be careful, you fool! If he makes a sudden move, you'll slit his throat and then I'll have to slit yours. We were told to bring him alive."

The thin sailor moved back, revealing a much older, fatter man sitting on the other bunk, smoking a pipe. His eyes were fixed on Stephen.

Stephen sat up with a start as he remembered where he was.

"Where's my daughter?" he yelled.

The older sailor studied Stephen's face impassively.

"Where is she?" repeated Stephen, beginning to panic.

"She's the wild one, is she? The young girl? I could see a bit of gwai lo in her."

He grinned lecherously. "She'll be fine." Then he added, raising his hands to mime a squeezing action, "In my hands."

Stephen made to jump up, but the thin sailor was on him and the blade back at his throat.

"Easy, gwai lo, at least she's alive."

"What do you mean?"

"You'll see. Come on, time to go."

The older sailor got up and pulled open the door. The thin man prodded Stephen with the knife and pushed him out of the cabin.

Once his eyes adjusted to the light, he was horrified to see ten Chinese sailors lounging on the deck, all cleaning large knives on some rags. Pools of deep red blood lay around them. The sailors ignored him, laughing and talking among themselves.

The thin sailor prodded Stephen in the back with his knife, forcing him to walk towards the port rail. Looking over, he saw a scene of pure horror. Floating in the blood-red water he quickly counted ten bodies – the captain and crew, the servants and the bodyguards.

His eyes wild with terror, his breathing laboured as his throat contracted involuntarily, he turned to the older sailor and tried to speak. "Where's my daughter?" he croaked.

The sailor grinned a toothless grin at him. "Gone," he said.

"Gone? Gone where?"

The sailor nodded in the direction of the mainland.

"Over there. Come on, it's time we went too."

He climbed over the starboard rail and down into a sampan. The thin sailor prodded Stephen to follow and then climbed down himself. He pushed the knife into his belt, took up the single long rear oar, and, standing on the stern of the small boat, rowed them out of the bay to a larger vessel anchored about a hundred yards from the island.

They sailed in the failing light to the shore of the mainland, anchoring outside a small cove. Stephen was again forced into a sampan and rowed ashore. As they came close to a rocky beach, two large men emerged from the darkening shadows. One of them pointed at Stephen. "Out!" he ordered.

They walked for about a mile inland through rough, uncultivated countryside strewn with rocks and boulders until they reached a small walled compound. Inside was a single storey stone building with smoke rising from a gap in its tiled roof. To one side were several empty animal sheds; Stephen was abruptly pushed towards the largest. One of the men slid out two wooden bars from the door, opened it and pushed Stephen inside. The door was slammed and barred behind him as he fell onto a pile of straw.

It was almost dark but from what he could see, there was no sign of any recent occupation.

"Lei-li," he whispered. Then he yelled at the top of his voice. "Lei-li! Lei-li!"

The night swallowed up his words.

"Lei-li," he cried more softly as he slumped to his knees on the straw. "Lei-li."

At first light, the two men brought him a jug of water and a bowl of rice, but said nothing. They came again at dusk.

The routine continued for a week, the men refusing to respond to any of his questions. On the sixth day, in the late morning, Stephen suddenly became aware of the rumble of a cart arriving. There were muted voices and then the sound of the cart leaving.

Half an hour later, the door bars were pulled away and the door flew open. The two guards walked in and stood to either side of the doorway. Stephen stood up warily and waited.

There was a shuffling from outside and a small man in peasant's clothing entered. His head was facing downwards, the wide basket hat on his head hiding his face.

The man stopped and looked up. Stephen gasped. It was Miguel la Torres.

"Surprised, Waters?" spat la Torres with a sneer as he tossed the hat to one side. "Did you really think you could trust that fool Kwok Fu-keung to help you escape? Well, your friend has let you down."

He let out a bark of derision.

"Oh don't look so distressed, Waters, he didn't betray you. He just didn't allow for my genius. I've had spies in his camp for years; I knew exactly what he was planning. That idiot of a junk captain wasn't difficult to follow and easy prey when he took his rest on the island."

"You bastard, la Torres. Where's my daughter?"

"Ah, your daughter. Pretty little thing. Quite a temper on her I'm told. I can't wait to tame her; I'm looking forward to that – she'll come in for some very special treatment. And once I've finished with her, when she's pleading for mercy, I've got friends with some very nasty habits. They specialise in breaking limbs. Snap. Snap." He laughed at Stephen's look of hatred, pulling aside his loose jacket to reveal a large knife attached to his belt. "In case you're thinking of trying anything, gwai lo, the three of us are well-armed."

"You don't think you'll get away with this, do you, la Torres? Kwok Fu-keung–"

"Is dead, gwai lo. By my own hand. You'll get no more help from him. And as for that harlot of his, I'm leaving that prize until I get back to Hong Kong, after I've dealt with you and had my fill of your daughter."

Stephen's mind suddenly filled with images of other times in his long life when he had come under threat. He thought of Johanne and Lars and how they had dealt with the louts on the dock in Genoa.

He looked at the two bodyguards and remembered Johanne's words. They were big, but they looked unfit, soft around the edges. They certainly weren't paying him much attention. He took a slight step forward to test their reactions. Nothing.

La Torres was still hurling abuse at him, waving his arms around and swaggering with his assumption of victory.

Stephen thought of Johanne's lessons and again of Lars on the dock, playing the scene in his mind. The trick was to apply enough momentum to the two men so their heads would crash together with sufficient force to stun them. To do that, he would need to catch them unawares and off balance.

He took a more deliberate step forward. La Torres noticed and yelled at his two bodyguards. "Wake up, you cretins, the gwai lo has ideas of escaping!"

The two men jumped to attention and reached out for Stephen, who took a sudden step backwards. As the men overreached, he ducked under their arms. Grabbing each man by the fastenings of his jacket, he pulled down with all his strength. They lurched sideways towards each other, their heads colliding with a heavy thud. Stephen pushed one of them hard in the direction of la Torres and stepped back to give himself room for the other. He delivered three lightning-fast punches – two to the body and the third a perfectly delivered upper cut to the chin. The man fell heavily, out cold before he hit the ground.

The second man now stumbled towards him, having been pushed away by la Torres who was screaming abuse and reaching for his knife. Stephen feinted in front of the large man then delivered the same two body blows to him. He was about to follow with an upper cut when he saw la Torres out of the corner of his eye. The small man was holding a dagger out in front of him and was starting to run at Stephen. Stephen pushed the doubled-up guard, sending him stumbling sideways straight into the knife. It entered his chest from the side, the sharp blade going deep and piercing the man's heart. He collapsed, the knife wrenched from la Torres' grasp.

La Torres turned and ran through the door and by the time Stephen emerged from the shed was about twenty feet away. He was surprisingly nimble.

Stephen set out after him, running at full pelt and slowly gaining on him. La Torres was still hurling abuse at him as he ran from the compound into the rough land beyond. The path was winding and he tried to shortcut it by jumping over the smaller boulders. He glanced behind him to check how close Stephen was and, as he did, he tripped on a hidden projection from one of the rocks, his speed carrying him over it as he fell. He tried to turn his body back, his arms flailing, but he wasn't in time to prevent his head crashing into a large jagged boulder ahead of him. He went down silently and lay motionless on the ground.

Stephen stopped short of him, wary, suspecting he would suddenly spring to life. But la Torres didn't move. Gingerly, Stephen approached him and nudged him with his foot. There was no response. He knelt down and put his hand on the man's neck, noticing the blood that was seeping from his head onto the stony ground. There was no pulse: la Torres was dead.

Stephen turned la Torres onto his back and searched him, hoping there might be some papers about his clothing that would indicate where he had sent Lei-li, but there was only another hidden dagger. Stephen took it and stood up. Then he remembered the first guard; he wouldn't remain unconscious for long.

He quickly retraced his steps towards the compound. He was close to the compound's gateway when he heard the whinny of a horse. He stopped, straining his ears to hear – the cart that had brought la Torres was returning. There was a stand of trees close to one wall of the compound and he quickly ran there for cover. Crouching down, he waited.

As the covered cart rounded the far corner of the compound, the guard Stephen had knocked out came staggering through the gateway, rubbing his chin and shaking his head.

"Ah Yu, what's happened?" shouted the driver . "Where is Tor-sang?"

The guard stopped and squinted at him.

"Tor-sang is not here, Ah Kong," he mumbled groggily. "The gwai lo jumped me and killed Ah Wong. They've both disappeared."

"Gods protect us! Have you looked in the house?"

The guard turned his head, still confused.

The cart driver drew a knife from his belt, leapt from his seat and ran to the house. He stopped a few feet short to listen, then ran through the open doorway. A moment later he was back out. "There's nobody," he shouted. "I'll search the land. Ah Yu, stay here and look after the honourable master."

He ran off in the direction of the coast, but not, Stephen could see, on a path that would take him close to la Torres' body. With luck the search would take some time.

He looked back at the guard. He had sat down on a large stone next to the cart with his back to Stephen, his head in his hands.

Stephen looked in the direction of the driver. He was now over three hundred yards away and disappearing from view as the land sloped downhill. He had not seen la Torres' body.

Silently, Stephen crept from the stand of trees, the small knife he'd taken from la Torres in his hand. He got within four feet of the guard when something snapped under his foot. The guard's head lifted, but he didn't turn. Stephen acted instinctively. He leapt forward and in one action threw his left arm around the man's neck, pulling him backwards, while with his right hand, he plunged the knife into the base of the man's ribcage in an upwards direction. The man slumped to the ground without a sound.

Stephen withdrew the knife and wiped it on the man's clothes, then he ran to the rear of the cart. As he yanked open the cloth covering, he saw a very old man sitting cross-legged on a cushion and facing him. He was holding a large revolver which was pointed straight at Stephen's head.

The old man was small and wizened, his eyes dark and malevolent, his hair worn in the traditional queue. There was something about his face that reminded Stephen of someone. Then he realised; it was the snarl. He had thought that it was la Torres' father who had been Portuguese and his mother Chinese, but it was the other way round; this man had to be his father.

"So you are Waters, the painter." The old man's growling voice interrupted Stephen's thoughts. "I came to watch my bastard son kill you, but perhaps I shall do it myself. I don't know why my son didn't snuff you out when he had the chance. He is a stupid fool."

He paused, his face contorted in anger.

"I should have killed him years ago, the worthless, arrogant dog," he continued. "I thought he had promise. I even offered him my name in spite of him being merely the son of my Portuguese concubine. I offered him the chance to be a Tong but he wanted to be a European. Pah! He has caused me so much trouble over the years. And so much trouble over you. You don't look like much to me. How could one insignificant gwai lo be such a problem?"

Ignoring the man, Stephen stared into his eyes. "Where have you taken my daughter? What have you done with her?"

The old man cackled a dry, derisive laugh. "The Eurasian slut? You will never find her, not that you will have the chance."

He raised the gun, the fingers of his other hand closing round the first to help him pull the trigger.

Suddenly there was a shout from where la Torre's body was lying. The driver had found him. The old man's head twitched sideways, his attention caught by the shout. In that moment, Stephen thought of Michel and the night Arlette died. Michel had killed one of the sailors threatening Henri by throwing a knife from the far side of the bar. He had practised it for hours. "It's easy, Papa, once you get the hang of it. You have to get the balance right by holding the tip of the blade just here."

Stephen acted instinctively. He turned the knife he was holding, clasped the tip of the blade between his thumb and index finger and flung it hard. It buried itself up to the hilt in the man's chest. With a look of complete surprise, the old man started to speak and then slumped onto the cushions. The gun fell from his hand.

Knowing he had only seconds before the driver returned, Stephen jumped into the cart, snatched up the gun and pulled the knife from the old man's chest. He jumped down and, keeping the cart between himself and the rocky land, ran to the corner of the compound wall and round the side.

He heard the driver reach the cart and the shout of surprise when he found the guard's body. This was quickly followed by another shout as he found the old man.

Stephen crept along the wall as far as a dense clump of bushes where he crouched down and waited. He saw the driver run round the wall and suddenly stop, his eyes darting around warily. Then he moved on slowly towards where Stephen was crouched. The man's eyes were still darting around when suddenly a thought seemed to cross his mind and a look of panic appeared on his face.

"The gun," he whispered, "the master's gun."

Stephen stood. "Yes," he said, "the master's gun."

"Don't move," shouted Stephen, emerging from the bushes and walking towards him, the gun pointing straight at him, "or you will be as dead as your master. Now sit down and place your hands on your head."

"NOW!" he barked as the man hesitated.

The man complied.

Stephen stood about six feet away from the man and kept the gun pointing at him.

"I need to know one thing from you, one thing only: where is my daughter?"

The man frowned, wondering what Stephen was talking about.

"My daughter. The Eurasian girl."

The light dawned in the man's eyes.

He hung his head. "A long way from here, master," he said. "Please don't kill me; I am no more than a worthless dog serving these men. I know nothing."

"The length of your life will depend on the information you give me."

The man's whole body sagged. If he told Stephen, he would be hunted down and slaughtered. If he didn't tell, he would be shot.

Stephen took a step forward and adjusted his aim. The man shrank back.

"There is a house, master, twenty miles from here. The other sons of the honourable master are keeping her there. It is a fearsome place, master, full of ghosts. Many people have died there. When the honourable master's sons hear of the death of their father and brother, their rage will know no bounds. They will inflict a terrible revenge on her. I hope she dies quickly, master, for her own sake. But even then they will continue to mutilate her body before they slice it up and feed it to the dogs."

Stephen clenched his teeth, trying to maintain control. "Where is this house?"

"Master, you would stand no chance if you went there. There are many guards. There will also be many guards scouring the countryside once the honourable master's body is found. You cannot hide from them, master. You are a gwai lo, even if you do speak our language."

"I'll take my chances," replied Stephen grimly.

The guard sighed. "You follow this path, master, through two villages and then you come to a third. There is a crossroads. You take the left road, which means you will be travelling west, for about ten miles. You will come to the house of the Tongs. But you will get no further, even if you get that far. They will discover you, take their pleasure by making you watch the abuse of your daughter, and then kill you in ways you can't imagine."

"Get up," snapped Stephen, "and walk to the cart. Keep your hands on your head."

The guard staggered to his feet and tripped his way to the cart. Stephen made him bind his own feet with a length of rope and then made him lie face down while he bound his hands. He checked the bindings on the feet and tied the two sets of bindings together, trussing him up like an animal for the market. Finally, he tied a gag round his mouth.

"If you are lucky, Ah Kong, your masters will spare you when they find you," he said and left the guard whimpering on the ground.

Two hours later, darkness was falling fast. Already disoriented from trying to follow the track from a distance, Stephen knew he had to find shelter for the night. He walked into some woods and found a spot under a fallen tree. He gathered some leaves, threw them over himself to cover his body as best he could and lay down. He hadn't realised how tired he was. He was instantly asleep.

He awoke with a start, his body stiff from the damp ground. It was daylight, but still early. He instinctively felt for the gun and the knife he'd put under the leaves he'd bunched for a pillow seconds before sleep had overtaken him. They were gone.

He sat up quickly. Seated about ten feet away on a log was a man dressed in a thick ground-length coat that was open, revealing normal baggy Chinese pantaloons and a shorter jacket. The man was smoking a long grey pipe and studying him. His face was relaxed, unthreatening.

"You have slept a long time, Waters Sin Saang; I trust you are refreshed."

Stephen stared at the man. "You know my name? How ... who are you?"

The man smiled. "My name is Lau Wong-shing. I trailed you in the night from the compound. You did well, Waters Sin Saang, dealing with all those people. I am impressed. But I am afraid to tell you that your luck will not hold out much longer if you keep roaming this countryside. There are eyes and ears everywhere; you will soon be spotted and reported."

"You … you trailed me? In the night?"

"It was not difficult. You left many signs. It is as well that no others were looking. However, they will be looking today. Once the old master Tong's body is discovered, there will be many, many people looking for you."

"Who are you, Lau Wong-shing?"

"I work for Kwok Fu-keung, or at least I did until that dog la Torres had him killed."

"He told me he killed him himself."

Lau laughed derisively. "He wouldn't have had the courage or opportunity. No, Ah Keung was killed by a traitor in his own camp, a traitor who has now been dealt with."

Lau sucked reflectively on his pipe and then continued. "Ah Keung was concerned that you might be intercepted, that he might have been betrayed. He has been suspicious for some time of la Torres' people in his own camp. So he sent me to keep watch. Unfortunately, I was travelling by land and I arrived too late to stop anything. I found the compound last night. The guard you spared took little persuasion to tell me what had happened and I followed your trail. It was well you spared him, but I am afraid I couldn't follow your example. He talked far too readily."

Stephen nodded absently. "Have you any word of my daughter? They took her from the boat while I was sleeping. They must have slaughtered the others in front of her. La Torres told me she was still alive."

"She will be at the house the guard told you about. But you cannot go there; it is far too dangerous. You must come with me now to the house you visited before, the house by the sea where your wife lies with her ancestors. You can remain there safely while I try to prevent the Tongs from hurting your daughter."

"I have to go with you, Lau Wong-shing."

"That is out of the question, Waters Sin Saang. It would take away any chance we have of success."

Taking a very circuitous route, it was three days before they reached the house. Lau was an expert tracker and equally expert at covering his own tracks. He laid many diversions as they went, concerned the enraged Tongs would be hunting them using dogs sniffing for Stephen's scent. They crossed many streams and changed clothes several times with clothing stolen from farms on the way. They threw the old clothes down steep ravines, hoping the dogs would waste time taking their masters on difficult and dangerous false trails. His efforts were successful: the pursuers lost all trace of them.

They arrived to find the household in mourning for Keung. Stephen remembered several of the older servants from his previous visit and together they shared their grief.

Stephen paced the house and gardens for ten long days, unable to concentrate on anything, hardly taking his food. He spent many hours at the gravesite talking to Mei-ling's headstone, trying to gain some solace. Every time he heard a cart or a horse arriving, he would rush to the courtyard, only to be disappointed as the head servant looked over at him and shook his head. Eventually, on the eleventh day, a maid rushed to him, bowing as she hurriedly delivered her message.

"Master, there are horses coming. Riding fast. Ah Mong thinks it is Ah Shing."

Stephen ran to the courtyard just as the riders were let in through the gates. The maid was right. A dusty Lau Wong-shing jumped from his horse and hurried over to Stephen. From the look on his face, Stephen knew instinctively that the news wasn't good.

Lau put his hand on his shoulder, guided him to a bench by a small fountain in one corner of the courtyard and sat him down.

"Waters Sin Saang, the news is not the best, but at least I can report to you with great confidence that Lei-li is alive and unharmed."

Stephen sat back, the tears welling up in his eyes.

"She is alive, and they have done nothing to her?"

"That much I know," nodded Lau.

"Then where is she? What has happened?"

"She managed to escape the clutches of the Tongs just in time.

There was a servant girl from the north in the household who herself had been abused one too many times by one Tong or another. She took pity on Lei-li and together they conspired to escape. The servant girl was very courageous and took huge risks, but it seems they got away. The details are sketchy and, as you can imagine, the Tongs are furious."

"Did you find out where they have gone?"

"All I know for certain is that they have gone to the north, a thousand miles away. I cannot imagine how she ended up in this region, but she did. I tracked them, as did my companions, for over a week, but for all of us the trails went cold. The servant girl is either very skilled herself or very lucky. However, the good news is that they have also evaded the Tongs, who have now all returned to curse their bad fortune. They have other problems on their hands – their criminal empire is in tatters, especially now you have killed their father and brother, and they will be plotting to re-establish themselves. Lei-li will no longer be of so much importance to them."

"Can we travel north, try to find Lei-li?"

Lau laid a hand on Stephen's arm. "Waters Sin Saang, this is China. It is a country in turmoil. Many things are happening all over the land. There is talk of revolution, of the Heavenly Throne being toppled. It is very hard to travel around, even for me. For you, a gwai lo whose name and features are well-known to his enemies, it would be impossible. You might speak Cantonese, but that would not help you in the north. And you could never pass for a Chinese."

He raised a hand as Stephen started to object.

"There is another thing. The Tongs may have given up their quest for Lei-li, but they will never give up their quest for you. As long as you remain in China, you will not be safe. It will only be a matter of time before someone betrays you. You have to leave. The same is true for Hong Kong; you would be no safer there. No, Waters Sin Saang, you have to leave China completely; go somewhere else. Back to your own country, perhaps."

"But I can't leave Lei-li, I can't!"

"You have no choice, Waters Sin Saang, no choice at all."

Lau Wong-shing arranged things quickly. He trusted no one and he knew that it would be impossible to keep Stephen's presence in the house a secret for long. The sooner he could spirit him out of China, the better. He understood Stephen's reluctance to leave and he promised he would continue the search for Lei-li. He explained with regret that he had very few contacts in the north, but he would use them all he could.

Not suspecting Stephen would be considering changing his identity, Lau suggested he do so and asked for a name he could use to pass on to a contact who would arrange a passage on a ship leaving Yokohama.

"Most of the ships my contact deals with are bound for America. I know you would prefer to head for England, but to arrange that would take longer, and the sooner you are on the high seas heading away from this continent, the better."

Stephen thought about a name and explained to Lau that he considered it would be better not to be English at all.

"I speak Italian, so I could become an Italian. That way it is unlikely that anyone would connect me with events in Hong Kong. I'll use the name Baldini. Stefano Baldini."

"That's an excellent idea, Waters Sin Saang. How come you speak Italian?"

"It's a long story, Lau Wong-shing."

As he walked with Lau Wong-shing to the cove where the sampan was waiting to take him to the ship, he took a letter for Fiona from his bag and handed it to him.

"I will deliver it personally, Waters Sin Saang. Don't worry, it will be in her hands within three days."

"Thank you, Lau Wong-shing. We have known each other for only a short time, but you have become a good friend. I don't know how I can repay you for your kindness."

"I am still Ah Keung's servant, Waters Sin Saang, and I act according to what I know his instructions would have been. But I thank you for your words. I also feel that we have formed a bond. I shall continue to search for your daughter."

He took a folded sheet of paper from his bag.

"This is the address of a trusted friend in Hong Kong. Send letters to me through her. Once you arrive in America, you should send me an address where I can send you any news I have."

Stephen stared back at the shore as the sampan took him out to the waiting ship. He waved to Lau, but in the darkness, he soon lost sight of him. He looked up at the sky. It was a clear, moonless night, full of stars. His eyes fell to the dark outlines of the cliffs and he thought of this vast land now receding from him that had swallowed up his daughter. He closed his eyes, trying to project his thoughts and his love to her, and saw her face turned towards him from where she had sat on the bow of the junk, smiling and waving to him.

# Chapter 23

## July 2009

Lawrence Forbes looked at the caller display on his mobile and pressed the green button.

"Cedric! Where are you?"

"I'm at Heathrow, Lawrence. I've just landed." Ced's voice was very flat.

"You don't sound on top form, old chap. How was the trip?"

"I suppose the words 'complete disaster' would about sum it up. They would sum up my future in this business, too."

"Oh dear, then you probably don't want to hear what I've been up to. I must admit I'm beginning to doubt my own judgement as well. My art world is falling apart."

"Tell me about it, Lawrence. No don't, not right now. Listen, are you free this morning? I'd like to drop by to show you what I've got before I head north and hand in my resignation. Is there still a Foreign Legion you can join?"

"I don't know, old chap, but if there is, I might join up with you. Yes, I'm completely free. We can cry on each other's shoulders, by the sound of it."

Slumped in the back of a taxi, Ced stared through the window as the vehicle made its way along a congested M4 motorway towards London. The events of the last few days were still spinning in his head, the inexplicable results from his program an ever-worsening nightmare.

The drive back from Arezzo to Rome in Verdi's Maserati had passed in almost total silence. Neither Ced nor Verdi was in the mood for talking, both of them too preoccupied with their own self-doubts. Arriving at Ced's hotel shortly after seven in the evening, Ced told Verdi he would get to work processing the images he'd taken of 'The Awakening' and the four paintings Giorgio Bonazzi had shown them. Unless there was some good news, Ced would meet Verdi at his office the following morning.

There was no good news. The comparisons of the images from 'The Awakening' confirmed Ced's thoughts from his visual examination that more than half of the work had been carried out by someone other than Piero della Francesca, the someone's hand being indistinguishable from Perini's, de la Place's, Lorenzini's and John Andrews'. Later in the evening, he would confirm Giovanni di Luca was also on the list.

The following morning, when Ced arrived at the Accademia, Verdi was already bent over a number of paintings laid out on his workbench. His black suit reflected his mood.

He looked up at Ced and shook his head. "There is nothing, Cedric, nothing at all that I can find in these paintings. It is driving me crazy. What do you have? Anything? Tell me you have something."

Ced shook his head. "When I get back to the UK and have access to the mainframe, I'm going to analyse the whole of 'The Awakening' to see exactly how much my program says Piero painted and how much our unknown artist painted."

"Yes, that is important, Cedric," agreed, Verdi, "but please keep this information to yourself. It must go no further, as we discussed yesterday."

"Don't worry, Corrado, my lips are sealed. It's our secret."

He stared distractedly at the paintings in front of Verdi on his bench.

"Corrado, I know this is a stupid question, but I have to ask it. 'The Awakening' has been dated, hasn't it? There's no possibility we are dealing with some huge fraud here?"

Verdi gave a resigned smile. "It's not a stupid question at all, my friend. But yes, it has. It was one of the first tests to be carried out. However, that doesn't stop me thinking as well that we are dealing with some sort of fraud, something so clever and so new that it has never been seen before. Something that is going to turn the art world on its head."

Ced nodded. "You know, Corrado, we've got to solve this thing; work out what the hell's going on. We can keep the whole thing under wraps for now, particularly the part about 'The Awakening'. But I'm not the only person working on a program to compare the world's art. It's only a matter of time, Corrado. Even if we keep this a secret for now, someone, somewhere is one day going to run the same comparisons and come up with the same conclusions. We have to find the answer."

"'Ere we are, sir. The National Gallery."

Ced continued staring through the window, oblivious to his surroundings.

"Sir, is everything OK? P'raps you didn't mean the National Gallery."

Ced came out of his trance.

"No, that's fine, thanks. I'll get out here."

Lawrence Forbes came down to meet him at the main entrance. As they climbed the stairs that led to the Gallery's administration wing, Ced outlined his findings from his time in Italy, leaving out any mention of 'The Awakening'.

"So let me get this straight, Cedric," said Forbes as he closed his office door. He held up a hand and counted off on his fingers as he spoke. "So far, you've got Moretti, de la Place, Lorenzini, Perini and now this di Luca fellow – who I must admit I've never heard of – and your program can't distinguish one from t'other."

"Yes," replied Ced, "but it's not only my program. I can't separate them on a visual examination, and what is more important, since he's the real expert, neither can Corrado. I've been thinking, this whole thing is getting more and more complicated and the ramifications are potentially enormous. The fewer people who know about it for the moment, the better. You haven't discussed it with anyone, have you?"

"Don't worry, Cedric, I haven't told a soul."

"Thanks, Lawrence," nodded Ced in appreciation. Then he slumped down into a chair as the frustration hit him again.

"On top of these several artists spanning some four centuries or so," he continued, staring into space, "we have the inexplicable link with John Andrews. He has to be some sort of master forger, Lawrence, but I can't see how he's managed to get access to such a wealth of work. Did your lab come up with anything on the Perini?"

"They're still working on it, but the preliminary results all indicate that it's genuine."

"God, I feel so stupid, Lawrence, so helpless."

"Me too, Cedric, and I'm afraid it gets worse."

"Worse?"

"Yes. I told you on the phone I've been following up on a few things. Obviously, with my expertise being the eighteenth and nineteenth centuries, I started digging around there. Following up on de la Place, I thought about a few other portraitists and landscape artists who painted in the same style from about 1750 until the late nineteen hundreds. Trouble is there were hundreds in the minor leagues."

"We're not dealing with the minor leagues, Lawrence," snapped Ced. "These guys were all bloody good. Top notch."

"I know they were, Cedric, but none of them achieved any major fame. Don't you think that's odd in itself? They were all brilliant but have remained largely unknown, and in the case of di Luca, for example, pretty much forgotten."

"I know!" replied Ced, raising his voice. "Since I came up with di Luca's name, I've dug a bit and seen half a dozen works. This guy was painting in Venice at the same time as Titian and he was every bit as good. And yet are his paintings priceless works of art on display in the world's major art museums? No! He's a virtual unknown outside academic art circles."

He paused. "Sorry, Lawrence, the whole thing's really getting to me. You were about to deliver some more bad news and I cut you off. What have you found?"

Forbes got up from his desk and walked over to a large display bench.

"Ever heard of Pierre Labreche?"

"Labreche. Mmm. Rings a vague bell. Worked in Paris? Couple of hundred years ago?"

"Yes, but before that he worked in Florence for many years. His

Paris phase was much shorter. He only ever undertook private commissions."

"Possibly why he remained in obscurity. It's becoming a familiar theme."

"Yes, well, I checked to see what we have here in the archives – there are none on display. I unearthed six Labreches. Come and have a look."

Ced unwound himself from his chair and walked over to where Forbes was standing, his whole bearing that of a defeated man. Forbes pointed to six canvasses.

"There they are."

Ced picked up one of the paintings and took it over to where Forbes had set up an illuminated magnifying lens. His examination didn't take long.

"Christ, Lawrence, here we go again. This looks very similar to the Andrews style. I'll need to spend a little longer and confirm it using the program." He flicked quickly through the others. "Yup, I'll need to check the lot in detail. Any others, before I shoot myself?"

"Only one, Cedric. It's over here," he said, pointing further along the display table. "Does the name Giovanni Bianchi mean anything to you?"

"No, I don't think so. Another Italian, eh? Strange; I should have heard of him."

"Don't think Italy or Renaissance, think London," suggested Forbes.

"London?" He sighed heavily. "Yes, perhaps it does ring a bell, but my head's too full and confused at the moment, Lawrence. Enlighten me."

"Well, I had to look him up as well. He was a young Italian who arrived on the London scene around 1820 or so. Just like all our other artists, there is no record of anything he did before that or even where he was from. He was successful for a while and then disappeared."

"You think he could be a contender for our ever-increasing Andrews group?" asked Ced.

"Possibly, yes, but I'd like your opinion."

Ced picked up the painting and examined it carefully. It was a portrait of a young woman in late Georgian fashions. Its quality and style were very similar to the Pierre Labreche portraits he had been looking at, and to the other artists on his list.

He nodded ruefully. "It's certainly a contender, Lawrence. I'll get out the camera and photograph it along with the Labreches."

"So where do we go from here, Cedric?"

It was two hours later and Ced had run all Forbes' paintings through his comparison program. The results were what he had anticipated, but being right gave him no pleasure.

"God knows!" replied Ced. "I'm going to go back home and I'm going to run everything through the program again. I'm also going to revisit all the algorithms I've written, check and double check all the assumptions I've made and examine the entire program. It'll all take time, maybe a couple of weeks, but it's got to be done. There has to be something, Lawrence; there has to be."

"I agree, Cedric, it's the only thing to do. I'll put my own eye to the visual examination that I should normally undertake, as I imagine Corrado Verdi is doing in Rome as we speak."

Ced checked the time. "Probably consoling himself with a siesta," he smiled.

"And what if, Cedric, what if none of us can come up with anything? What if after running all the checks you are still in the same position? What happens then?"

"I don't even want to go there, Lawrence, although I suppose I'm going to have to discuss it with the fraud squad. It'll be difficult to pin anything on Andrews if there's no evidence that he's been forging anything – no complaints and so on, nothing in his studio – but it can't just be left to rot. I'm sure the police will come up with some approach or other. Maybe a sting operation to try to trap him? But if he's as good as we think he is, he must have accomplices and an organisation behind him that's pretty sophisticated. If he gets wind of our suspicions, he'll disappear."

With nothing else to do in London, Ced caught a mid-afternoon train home. Sally was waiting on the platform for him. Her female antennae immediately sensed his depression and she folded her arms round him.

"Whatever's happened, hon? You look like you have the

problems of the planet on your shoulders."

He looked down into her eyes. "I think I have, Sal. I've never felt so totally defeated."

Back at the house, Sal snuggled up protectively to Ced on the sofa while he told her about his trip and the increasingly impossible situation that had arisen. True to his word to Verdi, he left any mention of 'The Awakening' out of his account, even though that problem played as heavily on his mind as any.

He looked across the room to where he'd put down his imaging equipment. "I know I should be setting up the files and starting on a schedule of checking and counterchecking, Sal, but my heart's not in it. I feel empty; beaten."

She hugged him tighter. "We'll sort it, hon. Did I tell you Claw's been in touch?"

"No, how is she?"

"She's good, but she's as frustrated as you are, in her way. She's convinced that there's something special about this Andrews bloke because of his DNA and she was desperate to conduct some more tests, but she'd run out of sample. Then she suddenly remembered something and she's got some."

"She hasn't been back to Andrews to ask for some more, has she?" said Ced with a start, the panic obvious.

"No," replied Sally, puzzled at the intensity of his reply, "she hasn't been anywhere near him. Don't worry."

"So where did she get the sample?"

She explained about the envelope. "And guess what?"

He waited.

"Well, come on, guess. What do you think?"

"I don't know Sal. I don't know anything anymore."

"She called yesterday morning. She used half the sample to run a whole load more systems – ten, in fact. And they're all new, Ced, all of them. This bloke Andrews has given a whole new meaning to the word 'unique'."

Ced nodded, not over-impressed. "But what does it mean? That he's got a whole bunch of rare alleles. So what? You say yourself they're on the junk DNA. I've seen him, Sal, Claw's seen him. He doesn't look any different from anyone else."

"Perhaps he doesn't, but she's not leaving it at that. She's contacted her old professor in London. He's an expert in gene analysis. She wants him to have a look at some of Andrews' genes to see if they're different."

"What's she expecting to find?"

"She doesn't know, hon. That's what pushing back the frontiers of science is all about: you don't know where it will lead you. But you have to admit it would be surprising if someone with all these rare alleles – no, not rare, unique as far as we know – if someone like that didn't also have something interesting in his gene make-up as well."

She sat up to look at him. "Christ, hon, you really are down. You'd normally be enthusiastic over something like this. Listen, I've got another idea too. I've been thinking about it ever since these problems with the paintings arose."

He waited.

"OK," she said, taking his hands and putting them in her lap as she held them. "I'm right, aren't I, that so far, all the comparisons and conclusions you've made about Andrews' work have been from the painting that Claw bought?"

"Yes," agreed Ced, "I've got very hi-res images of that painting, so the data's about as good as it could be."

"But it's only one painting."

"One painting's all it takes, Sal."

"Supposing there's something different about that portrait, something that doesn't normally occur in his other paintings."

"Such as?"

"I don't know, but say it's a variation in his technique."

"His technique is almost incidental, Sal. I've made comparisons directly between all the other paintings that his painting led me to and they all agree with each other, independently of his own work."

"I know that, but it all leads back to him, doesn't it? What I'm saying, hon, is don't you think it would help to have some more examples of Andrews' work so that you can have a better cross-section of his technique? Wouldn't it be better to have some more originals to work from?"

"What are you suggesting we do, break into his gallery and steal some?"

"Mmm, I hadn't thought of that, but it's possibly a bit risky. No, I was thinking of buying some."

"Buying some! They cost thousands of pounds."

"I know, I've been thinking about that. I've got some money in my savings account from when my gran died. We could use that."

"No, Sal, you can't do that. You can't go spending your nest egg on paintings; we're not quite at that stage of our lives yet."

"How else are we going to get the money?"

"Sal, that large landscape was marked up at seven and a half grand. That's a huge amount of money. Just suppose the guy turns out to be a master forger. It could be worthless overnight."

"Not necessarily. Collectors are perverse. If he gains notoriety, his work might shoot up in value."

"Well, I'm not about to let you risk finding out, Sal."

"It's my money, hon. Are you saying that if I take a trip to the Lakes and buy a painting, you wouldn't be interested in making a set of hi-res photos from it and using the data?"

"Sal, you mustn't! It could be pouring money down the drain."

"Listen Fisher, you're a scientist. Think like one. You know very well that one control isn't enough in an experiment. You need several. OK, we might have to make do with two or three, but it will be better than one."

"Sal–"

"Now are you going to let me go on my own to make the choice, or are you going to come too and advise me?"

# Chapter 24

## July 2009

The day after Ced's return from Rome, he and Sally drove north to the Lake District. Ced was distinctly uncomfortable with Sally's plan to use her savings to buy several John Andrews paintings and throughout the drive he continued to try to change her mind.

"Maybe I should lean on some of my art contacts and persuade them to set up a John Andrews exhibition. That way we could get a number of his paintings in one place and I could do the imaging when it was closed for the night."

"Hon, we really need answers now. It would take months to set up an exhibition like that, even if Andrews would agree to having one. And the chances are that he wouldn't if he's a master forger – he's not going to want to draw attention to himself."

"Well, he draws attention to himself by running a gallery and openly selling his work."

"Good point," said Sally. "If he were a master forger, he could command huge money for his work. Why would he need to run a gallery when it would be better to work quietly from an isolated house somewhere?"

Ced shrugged. "Perhaps he does it to throw off suspicion. A sort of double bluff."

"You've been watching too many spy movies."

"You know, Sal, I don't get it. Here we are, we're both fairly clever people; good at research; good at solving problems and as forensic scientists we're lateral thinkers. But neither of us can get our heads around this problem. Every avenue we go down, there are perfectly good and reasonable objections to continuing. There's simply no logic in any of it."

"There is," replied Sally, staring out of the passenger window at the motorway traffic, "it's just that we're missing it. But at least we're not the only ones confounded by this puzzle – Claw is tearing her hair out in frustration and from what you say, your two art experts Forbes and Verdi are doubting every opinion they've ever given."

"Yeah, it's baffling them and it's baffling my program. It's ridiculous. You can pick any number of artists and compare them with Andrews or Perini or the others – artists with the same sort of style, same period in history – and the program can make perfectly good and accurate observations about their work and distinguish them one from the other. But for a few artists scattered at random down the centuries, you can compare them until you are blue in the face and find there are no differences of any significance."

"Are they scattered at random? I mean, the ones you've identified were all Italian or French, weren't they?"

"Yes, but does that mean anything?"

"It might," persisted Sally. "There's something else – none of them overlaps, do they?"

"Hard to say since they all seem to appear at more or less the same stage in their lives with no known history, no mentors or references, no home town or rich fathers pouring money into their education. They're just there. But if you take the case of Giovanni di Luca –"

"The one in Venice in the early sixteenth century?"

"That's the one. Well, he beavered away for thirty years, but where he came from, no one knows, and then he suddenly upped sticks and sailed off into the sunset with his wife and family, never to be heard of again. But his life must have overlapped with Tommaso Perini since Tommaso was about thirty when he started working in Arezzo soon after di Luca disappeared. So he was around when di Luca was working."

"No, he wasn't around. He was alive, but not around."

"What's the difference?"

"The difference is that there's no record of their working lives overlapping."

"What does that mean?"

"I haven't got a clue," sighed Sally in exasperation.

They arrived in Grasmere at eleven thirty and spent a frustrating ten minutes searching for a parking place – it was a sunny Saturday in mid-July and the village was packed with tourists. Eventually Ced spotted someone leaving and squeezed the SUV into the vacant spot.

Sally turned to him. "We need a plan."

"A plan?"

"Yes, a plan. Of action. I mean you're not intending to go with me to Andrews' gallery, are you? You said you didn't part on the friendliest of terms last time, especially with your broadside about Moretti."

"No, I can't go back, but I'd like to have a look at some of the paintings before you lay out vast sums of money."

"OK, I'll do a recce. Perhaps he's out today producing a perfect copy of the Mona Lisa. Actually, do you think he'd recognise you? He must have hundreds of people passing through his gallery."

"If he's half the artist I think he is, yes. He'll have an excellent memory for faces."

"False moustache and glasses?"

"Go and do your recce," he said, kissing the top of her head and locking the car. "I'll sit on a bench on the village green and wait for you."

He paused. "No, I've got a better idea. There's a pub over the road and I'm starving. I'll go and look at the lunch menu while you browse. But don't buy anything!"

Sally walked along the street to Andrews' gallery. The large landscape and the smaller one with the country house were still there in the window. They were both now very familiar from the photographs Ced had taken. She was relieved to see that it was the larger painting that was marked up at seven and a half thousand pounds; the smaller one – the one she was interested in, given the subject matter was closer to a Moretti – was three thousand.

Taking a deep breath, she walked into the gallery. She looked around for any sign of John Andrews, but there was only a thirty-something dark-haired woman who was in the middle of a sales pitch with two customers. Sally walked over to the nearest display stand to take a closer look at the work of the man who was confounding her boyfriend's art world. A self-confessed philistine regarding art, even she couldn't help but be impressed by everything she saw. She moved around the displays of Lakeland views, and then on to the stands devoted to portraits.

"Are you looking for anything in particular?"

It was several minutes later and the crowd in the gallery had thinned.

Sally turned from where she had been studying a portrait of a young girl. She was a good six inches taller than the woman and she smiled as she looked down at her.

"I'm really interested in the views with the country houses over there, but I became quite entranced with these portraits. They are all so beautiful. This little girl is simply gorgeous."

"Thank you. She's my daughter, and a bit of a charmer."

"Are you the artist's wife?"

"Yes, I'm Lola. Lola Andrews," replied the woman offering her hand.

"Sally Moreton. Your husband really has the most remarkable talent."

"Thank you," smiled Lola.

Sally studied Lola's face and made a guess.

"Are you an artist too? Are any of these works yours?"

"Yes, I am, and no, they aren't," laughed Lola. "John is always telling me he wants to make space for my work here, but although I'm not bad, if I say so myself, I'm not in John's league. I sell my work through a friend's gallery in Ambleside. It sits much more comfortably against the other work on sale there."

"I'm sure it's far better than you're giving yourself credit for," replied Sally.

"No, really, I'm not being falsely modest. John is better than anyone else working in the Lakes today."

Sally picked up the portrait of Phoebe Andrews from the display stand and turned it over to see the price tag. Two thousand pounds. She gulped silently to herself.

"This is so beautiful; don't you just want to keep it for yourself?"

"It's not the first of her or her sister that John's painted, and it won't be the last. It was one of several he completed earlier this year. We've kept some, but there's only so much wall space in the house."

"Are her eyes really as pale grey as that?" asked Sally in what she hoped was an innocent tone. "They're very unusual."

"Yes, they are. Exactly like her father's."

"What's her name? I hope you don't mind my asking."

"Her name's Phoebe. It's on the back, but you were probably distracted by the price tag."

"What a lovely name," said Sally as she put the painting back on the display stand.

"Look, Ms Moreton," said Lola, "why don't I let you browse? Call out if you want to ask anything."

Lola walked to the counter where she made a pretence of busying herself with some papers, but, as she often did with customers, she kept a discreet eye on Sally. There was something about this tall, athletic-looking young woman that didn't add up. She didn't give the impression of someone who regularly visited galleries to pore over their contents.

She let Sally continue her viewing for a few more minutes and then walked over to her again.

"Seen anything you like?"

Sally shook her head. "I haven't seen anything I don't like," she sighed. "Every one of these paintings is a masterpiece."

Lola smiled at her enthusiasm.

"Does your husband often come to the gallery, or does he spend all his time in his studio producing these wonders?" asked Sally.

"Oh, he's normally here all the time. His studio is through there – that's where he produces all his work. But this morning he's in Keswick. There's an exhibition of local artists starting there next week and John has been persuaded to show some of his work."

"Persuaded? I should have thought an artist would always enjoy the possibility of an exhibition."

"You'd think so, wouldn't you? But not John; he hates exhibitions, says he can't stand the fuss. As far as he's concerned, the gallery is enough for showing his work. It drives me crazy: he's so good that he should be up there among the modern artistic elite, but he's simply not interested."

"How strange," said Sally quietly. "Tell me, when does the exhibition start?"

"There's a reception next Friday evening and then it's on for a month. The organisers want it to cover the really busy part of the summer season."

As they were talking, Sally had made her way indirectly to the rear of the gallery so she could get a view into the studio.

"What a lovely environment to work in," she said, nodding towards it.

Lola followed her gaze. "Yes, it is. It has very good light, even in the winter. Have a look if you want, John won't mind. Perhaps you'll find something he's working on irresistible and reserve it before he's even finished it."

Sally laughed. "Thanks, I'd love to. I'm fascinated to think that all this amazing work is down to the skill of the artist in transferring what he sees in real life into his brain and then through his arm and hand to his brush."

"That's very analytical."

"I'm a scientist," said Sally without thinking. "I like to know how things work."

"What sort of scientist?" asked Lola, snapping her response more forcefully than she intended, her suspicions aroused immediately.

Sally realised her blunder and thought fast. "I'm a sort of … physiologist," she replied.

"Physiologist?"

"Yes," said Sally thinking of the work one of her triathlete friends did. "I study motion, running, athletic performance. It's all linked with designing the best shoes, using the best materials, that sort of thing."

She watched for Lola's reaction, wondering if she had been convincing, but Lola had lost interest.

Sally checked her watch. "Look, I really must go. But thanks so much, especially for the peek at the studio. I'm very interested in buying something. Can I come back tomorrow? I'm staying up here overnight."

"Of course," said Lola. "John will be here. You can talk to him directly."

"Ced, it was absolutely amazing, even for an artistic no-man's land like me. I've never seen anything like it. You know how it is when you go to most galleries, you like one or two things but for the others, you wonder why the artist bothered? Well, in John Andrews' gallery, there was nothing, absolutely nothing that I didn't fall in love with. Even those landscapes with big houses, which I don't really go for, were incredible. I could have bought the lot."

"Just as well that I stole your credit card when you weren't looking," replied Ced as Sally paused for breath.

They were in the pub Ced had spotted earlier, his empty plate pushed to one side so he could reach Sally's chips.

Sally checked in her purse and found he was kidding. "I wonder what my credit limit is," she said, taking out her card and studying it.

Ced leaned across the table and kissed her.

"That's rather presumptuous, young man," said Sally, a mock look of shock on her face.

"I love you, Sal."

"Shut up and finish my chips. And close those big eyes before I drag you onto this table and ravage you."

He grinned and wolfed down the rest of the chips.

Sally sipped her fresh lemon soda. "You know, hon, the more I learn about John Andrews, the less inclined I am to think of him as a forger. I mean, his studio is there in the gallery, the door wide open. His wife let me go in and look around. There's nothing in there except his work, no old masters propped up in the corner that he's copying.

"Oh yes, there's an exhibition next weekend in Keswick, with some of his work in it."

"Really, that's great. I wonder if there's a catalogue."

"Dunno, but his wife said that he's incredibly reluctant to put stuff in exhibitions. Don't you think that's weird?"

"Not if he's a forger, no. But look, if there's an exhibition next weekend, there's no need for you to splash out on paintings. We can go there."

"And do what, hon? Andrews is hardly going to let you set up your cameras in front of his paintings, is he? And since you don't know the organisers, you're not going to be able to sneak in under cover of darkness. No, we've come here to buy, and buy we will!"

She looked at her watch. "OK, here's the plan. We'll find a nice romantic B&B to check into. Then we'll go for a run in the hills. This evening, once Mr A's gallery is closed and he's gone off home to his family and daughter with the pale grey eyes just like his–"

"Did you see her, the daughter?"

"No, I only saw the painting. I think it's the one that you showed an interest in and he wouldn't let you buy. It's back on sale."

"We must get that one; it will really define his style," enthused Ced.

"Put it on the list, hon, it's a mere two grand. OK, when the gallery's closed, you can put on your disguise and we'll saunter along the street like a couple of Russian secret agents to check the place out. You can see well into the gallery from the window so I can point out the paintings I think would be useful and you can say 'da' or 'nyet'."

"Sounds good. Then what?"

"Then I put on the fishnets and parade the streets of Grasmere to sell my body so I can pay for the paintings tomorrow."

Ced glanced at her sceptically. "The paintings cost more than a fiver, Sal. Ow!"

The following morning, after a hearty full English breakfast that Ced demolished while the landlady of the B&B looked on in rapture, they took a walk around the village to check if the gallery had opened. They were about a hundred yards away when they saw an ageing Volvo draw up outside the gallery. John Andrews got out of the passenger side, waved to Lola as she drove off and unlocked the gallery door.

"That was close," whispered Ced. "If we'd been a couple of minutes earlier, we'd have been right outside the gallery."

"I told you to wear the moustache and glasses, hon."

"Let's give it fifteen minutes. I could do with a decent cup of coffee; that B&B only had instant."

John Andrews lifted his eyes from the counter when he heard the doorbell ring and looked appreciatively at the tall and attractive short-haired blonde who had walked in.

Instead of heading to one of the displays, she walked straight to the counter.

"Hello," she said. "I was in here yesterday. I spoke to your wife."

"Ah, yes," smiled John, "she told me a physiologist had been studying my paintings."

He held out his hand. "John Andrews."

"Sally Moreton," she said taking his hand and laughing at his comment. "Pleased to meet you. I'm in awe of your work."

"Thank you very much. Now, Lola said you were interested in the landscapes. Is there any particular one you have in mind?"

"There are two, actually. And there's this." She pointed to the painting of Phoebe. "It's so beautiful, so delicate. I'd really like to put it on the list."

John smiled. "Yes, it's incredible how angelic they can look when they're not charging around."

"She's such a beautiful little girl," said Sally, picking up the painting again. "She's got your eyes. They're very unusual."

"Yes, I suppose they are," he shrugged.

They walked over to the landscapes. She'd agreed with Ced the previous evening that she would buy one with a country house set in parkland north of Windermere that reminded Ced strongly of a Moretti painting he knew. The other view she wanted was very different in style. It was a more abstract picture than most of Andrews' work, a view of Derwent Water in the northern Lakes, painted at sunset. Apart from loving it the moment she saw it, she astutely pointed out to Ced that given it was superficially very different in style, it would be a good test for his program.

"You're picking this up fast, Sal. You'll be programming next," Ced had commented.

"Well, that was easy," smiled John. "Any more?"

"I think three is more than enough. If I spend any more, I'll have my bank manager demanding I return my credit card before it melts."

"I think you deserve some sort of discount for three purchases.

Let's see, the overall tag price is, what, ten thousand. I think I could knock that down to, say, seven and a half?"

"Seven and a half?"

"OK, let's call it seven, shall we?"

"Oh, no, I wasn't trying to bargain. I was surprised at your generosity."

Andrews laughed. "Don't worry, seven thousand is fine. I hope my paintings will give you a great deal of pleasure."

"I'm sure they will," said Sally, suddenly feeling rather nervous about how much money she'd just agreed to spend.

"I'll go and wrap them up for you. Why don't you have another look around in case there's something else you like?"

"All of it?" she said, pulling a hopeless face.

John returned a few minutes later with the paintings wrapped. He had an envelope in his hand which he held up to her. Her eyes widened.

"I've put a description of the paintings in here for your reference, in case you ever want to sell them or insure them."

"I don't think I'll ever want to sell them," she said.

He held out the envelope. It was unsealed.

She stared at the flap. Lick the damn thing, she thought, willing him. Lick it!

But he continued to hold it out.

"Is there something wrong?" he asked, noticing her staring at the envelope.

"Er, no, that's fine, thanks," she said, taking it.

"I'm intrigued to know about your interest in the Windermere view, the one with Malton House in it," he said as they walked to the gallery door. "Is it somewhere you know well?"

"No, I don't know it at all."

"It seems a bit of an odd choice, that's all. I can understand the portrait and the Derwent Water view: one is modern and the other classical; they appeal to all ages. But the Windermere view, it's the sort of painting that tends to be bought by my older clients."

She smiled. She'd thought of an explanation.

"Am I that transparent?"

"Not at all. You're just young and there's a certain type of painting that young people buy."

"It's a present for my grandfather."

"Ah, that explains it."

"Yes, when I saw your work, I knew he'd like it. His father, my great grandfather, used to collect paintings and when he died, they were passed onto my granddad. He's got something of a collection now because he's added to it. Anyway, some of the ones he inherited were landscapes and views of big houses painted in England in the nineteen forties and fifties."

She paused, chewing her lip and hoping this fairy story was sounding plausible. She realised she should have stopped, not said so much, but she was committed now.

John said nothing.

"Well, when I saw your paintings, they reminded me of some of my granddad's paintings. The Windermere view is really quite like one he has, only I think yours is a lot better."

John smiled cautiously. "Who was the artist? Let me see. Philip Johnston? Bernard Collins? They are both quite well-known English landscape artists from that period who worked extensively around here."

"No, not the painting I have in mind. He's got one by Philip Johnston," she ad-libbed, "but it's quite different. I'm trying to think of the artist's name. It's not an English name."

She paused, pretending to think about it. "Oh, of course. It's quite like our family name; Granddad's commented on it before. He jokes that the artist must have been a foreign relative."

"I don't understand," said John, suddenly reminded of the various events of the past few weeks and no longer convinced by this girl in front of him stuttering her way through her story.

"Well, my surname's Moreton. So's my granddad's. He used to play around with the pronunciation. Say it as More-ret-on, with the emphasis on the RET. Then it became similar to the artist's name."

"Moretti?" said John, his voice cold.

"That's it, Mr Andrews. Moretti. Francesco Moretti."

She held out her hand. "Thanks so much. I'm thrilled with these paintings. I'll treasure them. And I know my granddad will be over the moon."

# Chapter 25

## 1905-1950s

John watched Sally turn on her toes and walk out of the gallery. Moretti again. Was it a coincidence or was Ms Moreton connected to the other young and awkwardly inquisitive visitors to the gallery?

Moretti. As he stood there watching her walk up the sunlit street, his thoughts tumbled back to 1940. Images of the Blitz in London streamed across his mind in rapid succession, images of searchlight beams exploring the skies; of the flashing of exploding bombs; of an artist's pad filling urgently with graphic scenes of destruction and death; of desperate hands with bleeding knuckles tearing at rubble. He put his hands to his ears to block out the memory of the hideous sounds of the booms and whooshes as the bombs exploded; of the droning of the engines of the bombers; of the gasps and screams of frightened and injured people. He turned to look at the landscapes in his gallery. Francesco Moretti. He thought of Catherine. He could see her beautiful, young face laughing at something he'd said and he thought of the time before Moretti, the time when he was Stefano Baldini.

As Stefano Baldini, living in Virginia in the United States, he had been frustrated and angered by the developments in Europe throughout the 1930s. The rise of fascism in Germany and Italy seemed to him far worse than any of the various extreme political movements that he had witnessed in Europe during the past five hundred years, although the desire to wield iron control over the population was nothing new. His fears had been brought to a head in September 1936 when his son Dominic, a headstrong and idealistic twenty-one-year-old, had decided to sail for Spain and fight as part of the International Brigade on the side of the Republicans. In his first battle, the defence of Madrid in November 1936, Dominic had been killed when a mortar bomb exploded near him.

Stefano and his wife, Catherine, whom he'd married in 1913, had been shattered. Dominic was their only child and the light of their lives.

Catherine came from old money in conservative Virginia, but to her father's constant frustration, she had displayed few of her family's republican ways as she was growing up. She was her own person, independently minded, and although inevitably moulded by the privileged upbringing her family's wealth had given her, she would not be dictated to about her future.

When she'd appeared at her family's palatial home in 1910 at the age of twenty with the youthful artist Stefano Baldini, her art tutor from the academy from which she'd recently graduated, the family was immediately suspicious. They had been pleased when Catherine wrote to say she wanted to bring home the tutor about whom they'd heard so much, but they were unprepared for the handsome young man who arrived with her, and to whom Catherine was clearly strongly attracted. A little delving turned her mother's suspicions into horror. The man was a total unknown, extremely vague about his background and origins and had no visible means of support besides selling his paintings and teaching art. At twenty-nine years of age, he was also rather older than most of the men Catherine's mother had in mind for her.

None of this mattered to Catherine. She was in love and although she hadn't even discussed it with Stefano, she was determined that he was the man she would marry.

They had met at the Eleanor Wray Academy for Young Ladies in Charlottesville, Virginia, where Catherine had been sent by her parents to finish her education. The two-year course at this academy for the daughters of the wealthy was aimed at fine-tuning them socially into interesting and informed hostesses, compliant and responsible wives and, eventually, good mothers.

Stefano had been the tutor for classes in art and art appreciation since he arrived from San Francisco in 1907 where he had spent two years teaching in a private art college. Those two years had been a time of frustration and worry while he waited in vain for news of Lei-li. He had kept in close contact with Fiona Trevelyan in Hong Kong, but neither she nor Lau Wing-shing in China discovered anything. Then, over a period of two months, Stefano's links with Hong Kong crumbled to dust. First he received a letter from Lau Wong-shing's contact that Lau had been killed somewhere in the north of China. The circumstances were vague, but it was possible the Tongs were involved. The second shattering blow was that the risks of dealing with legions of infectious patients in the hospitals that had now become her life had caught up with Fiona. She contracted cholera and despite the best efforts of her doctors, she died in early 1907.

On receiving this final blow, Stefano had to get away. He didn't feel much for San Francisco and there was no reason to stay. When his principal said she would give him a good reference for a post in Virginia she'd heard of, he thanked her profusely and headed east.

He had been teaching at the academy for a year when Catherine started her course in the autumn of 1908. They were attracted to each other immediately. Catherine reminded Stefano strongly of Beth, while for Catherine, Stefano was just completely different from any man she'd ever met. However, she understood that it would be unacceptable for her to have a relationship with a tutor; if anything were suspected, he would be sacked in disgrace, while she might be expelled. So she bided her time, getting to know him slowly, watching him carefully for signs that he might be attracted to her.

Once her two-year course was finished and she had graduated with honours, Catherine decided it was time to reel in her Mr Baldini. She'd noticed he often appeared distracted, his mind elsewhere, and, more worryingly, he often looked desperately sad. Whatever the cause, she wanted to share it; to help him with the grief that put the sadness in his eyes.

When her parents announced they were throwing a party in her honour to celebrate her graduation, Catherine made her move. She invited Stefano to the party and to stay on after as a house guest.

The party passed in a whirl of colour and sound. Stefano put aside his worries, revelling in the pleasure of sharing almost every dance with his enchanting ex-student, while for her part, Catherine watched him carefully, thrilled as she saw him relaxing more and more as the evening progressed, his eyes only for her.

Despite dancing into the night, the following morning they were up early to ride the estate and surrounding countryside on two of the family's stable of thoroughbreds. Catherine was surprised to find Stefano was an expert horseman and for two hours she put him through his paces, unable to shake him off as they galloped the hills and valleys of the Virginia countryside.

Breathless and exhilarated, they stopped by a stream to rest the horses, falling almost immediately into one another's arms and finally admitting their true feelings for each other.

"Well, Signor Baldini?" said Catherine. She had kicked off her riding boots and was splashing in the stream as he held her hand.

He pulled her round into his direction. "Well what, Miss Fletcher?"

"I want to know your story, mister."

"My story?"

"You have a past, a history, don't deny it. I want to hear it, to become part of it."

He smiled. "Then we'd better sit down; it takes a little telling."

She was shocked, totally unprepared, but the more he explained his art and the more details of his life he recounted, the more she was persuaded. The real turning point was the story of Lei-li. When later, at the house, he showed her the letter he'd received about Lau Wong-shing, she was convinced. Any final lingering doubts were dispelled completely when he showed her Fiona's letters.

Convincing Catherine's parents that marrying an unknown artist, the son of poor immigrants, was a different challenge.

"I'm not sure about your father, Catherine. I don't think I'm exactly the sort of upright establishment figure he had in mind for his beloved daughter. Not really from the right stock, you know," he added, mimicking her father's Virginian tones.

"Oh, under all that bluster, he's a pussy cat," she laughed. "I can get anything from him if I approach it properly. I have a plan to win them both over, before we announce anything about our relationship."

The plan was simple and foolproof. Stefano was commissioned to paint a series of family portraits. Catherine's father, Conrad Fletcher, declared them masterpieces, while her mother wept for joy. Catherine hung on to Stefano's arm ecstatically, overjoyed at the outcome of what she regarded as her coup.

They were married in the spring of 1913. They had hoped to go to Europe for their honeymoon – Stefano dearly wanted to show Catherine the various cities in Italy where he'd worked and some of the paintings he'd produced over the centuries. But the gathering war clouds in Europe prevented the trip and Catherine had to be content studying as many art books as she could get her hands on.

During their wedding ceremony, Catherine looked mischievously at Stefano and whispered in his ear. "Well, Mister di Stefano - Baldini - Crispi - whatever your name is, I can't wait to find out how the average four hundred and eighty-six-year-old performs. But does this young twenty-three-year-old maiden need to be very gentle with her old, old man?"

"You can be as rough as you like," he whispered back, pinching her discreetly. She squealed in delight.

Two years after they were married, Dominic was born. When he was killed, Catherine's only solace was that neither of her parents had lived to see it happen.

Dominic's death left both Stefano and Catherine devastated. They shut themselves away in their house and made it clear to friends that they wanted to see no one until they could come to terms with their grief. It was during this time that Catherine realised that it would not be long before Stefano would have to address the problem of his apparent age: with a few days' stubble on his face, the black of his beard was very strong, while his moustache and goatee, which he had worn for some years and had been reluctantly colouring, was white on the tips of its hairs but black below.

"If you let it go any longer, Steffi, the staff are going to notice," she smiled at him, rubbing his face with her hands.

"Cathy, I'm sorry. I've been so bound up in grief for the last few weeks that I entirely forgot to take care of myself."

"It's my fault, Steffi, I should have noticed."

Her face clouded. "But Steffi, what are we going to do? This problem isn't going to go away. The older you are supposed to be, the harder it's going to get to convince people that you are the age you say you are."

"Cathy, the reality is that I'm going to have to change fairly soon, sometime in the next two or three years. That will mean us having to go away and reinvent ourselves; to take on new identities. Or at least I will. And that will mean my suddenly becoming young again, back to twenty-something."

She nodded. "While I just get older. I knew this day was going to come; I guess I've been putting it off."

She thought for a moment. "You know, we never did make it to Europe. I really want to go to Madrid, for Dom, when it's safe there again."

Her face clouded momentarily at the thought of their son. Then she brightened.

"After Madrid, we can do a European tour. I can be the rich Yankee widow and you can be my gigolo. Carry my poodle around and entertain me whenever I have the need, which will be often, my young hunk." She prodded him playfully in the chest.

"I think I'd rather be your young protégé, the struggling artist you'd rescued from the obscurity of the gutter and given the opportunity to stun the world with his brilliance."

"No fear, mister! You'll be all dark and moody, full of tantrums and disappearing with your teenaged mistresses. It's poodles for you!"

"You know, Cathy, Europe's a good idea. I've been thinking about it for a while. The situation in Europe appalls me like it did for Dom. Right-wing thinking is one thing – there's more than enough of it here in the States – but these fascist bullies are totally unacceptable. They say that there's going to be a war in Europe, probably between the Brits and the Germans, a repeat of the Great War but with much greater firepower. And this time, it's the Germans who have the better resources. I can't imagine a Europe dominated by that madman Hitler; it's unthinkable. And to think that my homeland of Italy, unified nearly eighty years ago with all that promise, is now throwing in its lot with the Germans. That revolting little dictator Mussolini is evil; I simply cannot understand how anyone can take him seriously."

"He has the guns and the muscle, Steffi."

"The thing is, Cathy, I'm a European far more than I'm an American. I feel the need to return to help combat this evil."

"Oh God no, Steffi. We've already lost Dom. I simply couldn't bear losing you as well. It's too much to ask."

"I'm not talking about going alone, Cathy, nor going to the front line. We could go there together. I could be useful to them. After all, I speak a number of European languages and dialects, even if my vocabulary and phraseology are a little archaic at times."

"Steffi, can we think about it? I don't think I'm quite ready yet. Could you bear to keep on with the colouring of that beard? I'll help you like I always have. I'd like to hang on to my Stefano for a while longer."

They eventually decided to move to London in the spring of 1939. Their friends were appalled, given the deteriorating situation, and tried all manner of ruses for keeping them there, including flooding Stefano with orders enough to keep him busy for ten years. They finally convinced everyone that the trip wasn't going to be forever, but that they really wanted to be able to get into Spain – and more specifically to Madrid – to visit Dominic's grave as soon as it was safe to do so. On April 10, in New York, they made their way from the Waldorf-Astoria to their first class cabin on the Queen Mary and set sail for Southampton.

The magnificent liner fascinated Stefano. The last time he'd been to sea was when he crossed the Pacific from China to San Francisco in 1905. The Queen Mary was an altogether different experience. For the first-class passengers, she was a floating high-class hotel offering every luxury. Stefano watched from the railings in wonder as she cut her way powerfully through the Atlantic swell with grace and authority.

Although it was officially frowned upon, Stefano often made his way around the entire ship, partly to stretch his legs but mainly to escape the stuffy attitudes of many of the first-class passengers.

The second day out from New York had dawned with a wild, angry sky and an ocean spoiling for a fight. By midday, the storm was upon them, the ship's bow pounding into the sea and sending up walls of water onto the forward decks.

Stefano had been on the outside deck of the tourist-class area but on the insistence of the stewards, who were making sure everybody was safely inside, he was making his way towards a door on a slippery port side walkway. Above the noise of the waves, he heard a commotion from the bow. A violent struggle had broken out between two groups of drunken men the stewards had somehow overlooked. One man had drawn a knife.

Stefano looked on as a large man yelling in a strong Irish accent waded into the thick of the group, only to find that the much slighter and younger man holding the knife had lunged at him and buried the blade deep into his stomach. Screaming in pain and surprise, the Irishman grabbed the young man by the hair and flung him across the flooded deck, sending him skidding into the metal support of a side rail. As he hit the rail, a leather wallet slid out of the young man's jacket pocket and washed along the walkway towards Stefano, who automatically bent to pick it up.

Looking up, he was in time to see the youth regain his feet as the Irishman was again upon him. The smaller man ducked and the Irishman's momentum carried him onto the rail. As the ship's bow plunged from the highest point of its trajectory, the youth involuntarily stood up again and his head slammed hard into the larger man's bleeding stomach, propelling the man up and over the rail. One of the man's desperately flailing hands grasped at and held onto the youth's collar and the youth was lifted off his feet, disappearing with the Irishman into the foaming, crashing water.

Seeing their respective friends falling to what was a certain death had immediately rendered the rest of the two groups sober. Three of one group swayed and slipped in stunned slow motion to the rail. They were yelling a name impotently into the pounding waters and desperately searching for a sign of the body they knew in their hearts they would never see again.

"Francesco! Francesco!"

"Excuse me, sir, did you see what happened?" A steward was tapping Stefano on the shoulder and quietly guiding him back into the safety of the corridor.

Stefano turned to him, ashen-faced with shock. "Partly, yes."

He shook his head to gather his thoughts. "I don't think either of them had any intention of throwing the other overboard. It just happened."

The steward took Stefano's name and when he realised he was a first-class passenger, raised an eyebrow and pointed out that it would be far better if he remain in the first-class area – you never knew quite what was going to happen here amongst the tourist classes.

Stefano quickly made his way back to his cabin where he found Catherine reading, oblivious to the rough weather. He poured himself a whisky and sat down with a bump onto the bed.

Catherine took off her reading glasses and looked up. "Everything all right, Steffi darling? You look as if you've seen a ghost."

He told her what had happened and as he finished, he remembered the leather wallet he'd picked up on the deck. It turned out to be a document pouch containing not only the owner's American passport but also various other documents, including a British birth certificate. He showed them to Catherine.

"Francesco Moretti, twenty-eight years old, born in Manchester in 1911," she read. "Father seems to be Italian, from the name, but his mother's English — Maureen Jenkins. And there's a naturalisation paper - his father had British nationality. Look at the photograph in Francesco's passport, Steffi; he's not unlike you, allowing for your whiskers and glasses."

Stefano nodded. "I guess it's an ill wind, Cathy, I was going to try to get hold of whatever documents they are currently using in England. Now, I don't need to. It would appear that I've got my new identity."

Once they arrived in London, they rented an apartment in Wimbledon. Stefano cut his hair short and shaved off his moustache and beard, the transformation in his appearance dramatic. Two weeks later, reinvented as the twenty-eight-year-old Francesco

Moretti, he and his aunt Catherine moved into a more spacious apartment in St. John's Wood.

At the Home Office, Francesco was told that he would have to renounce his US citizenship in order to regain his British passport. This he did and by mid-August, two weeks before the outbreak of war, he had a genuine British passport and papers. Reporting to the nearest army recruitment post, he was disappointed to find that the current recruitment was for twenty to twenty-three-year-olds.

The outbreak of war came and went and life didn't really seem to change in London, apart from the need to be vigilant about blackouts and carry a gas mask. As autumn moved on into the winter of 1939 and then the spring of 1940, the mood of the population lifted as the threat of immediate invasion appeared to recede. They called it the 'Phoney War', and life returned almost to normal.

The reality of the war hit London and its population a hard and brutal blow with the outbreak of the Blitz on September 7, 1940. With no warning, the Luftwaffe began its long series of daytime and nighttime bombing raids, initially targeting the docks, with the single aim of bringing London, and therefore Britain, to its knees. Initially, the defensive systems were not ready for the onslaught, but within a few days, the number of anti-aircraft guns had been more than doubled, giving Londoners more reassurance that the enemy could be repulsed. Unexpectedly, the main effect was that some of the bombers were scared into dropping their bombs wide of their intended targets, resulting in more civilian casualties and damage to housing outside the docklands area.

On the afternoon of September 17, Francesco had been at an art supplies shop near Charing Cross Road in central London when the sirens sounded. Both he and the shop owner had little choice but to hurry to the nearest Tube station to take shelter.

Immediately after the all-clear, Francesco took a taxi back to St. John's Wood. As he approached his street, he saw a cloud of smoke rising from where only three hours earlier he had left his apartment block standing peacefully in the autumn sun. Catherine had stayed at home writing her regular letters to her brother and sister and their families back in Virginia, letters about her life in London with Stefano that had been increasingly straying into the realms of fiction.

When the fire was out later that night, it was too dark for the Fire Brigade to continue their search since the use of searchlights was forbidden in the blackout and during the inevitable raid that came as night fell. But Francesco continued manically to search all night, helped by the light of a moon just past full and flashes in the sky from the flares and searchlights hunting for enemy aircraft. He dug with his bare hands until they were raw and bleeding; until he could hardly see through the mist of sweat and tears; until he was pulled away by kind but insistent hands to the shelter of a mobile canteen and an ambulance.

Catherine's body was found in the late morning of the following day. In her right hand was a gold fountain pen that Francesco, as Stefano, had bought her for her fortieth birthday. The letters she had written were trapped under her.

"Was she a relative, sir?" A police constable had taken charge of the scene and was on constant guard against the looters that inevitably crept around, looking for the opportunity of anything they could take and sell.

"My wife," Francesco whispered through the grime on his face.

The constable looked puzzled. Even though her body was covered in dirt, Catherine's face was hardly marked and it was clear that she was a woman in her early fifties. "Your wife, sir?"

Through the haze of his mind, Francesco realised his mistake. He tried to speak but nothing came and his head starting spinning. The constable took his arm. "Take your time, sir. Why don't you sit down here for a minute?"

Francesco sat and stared at his torn hands. "My wife ... will be devastated. She and my ... my aunt were very close."

"Your wife wasn't here then?"

"No, she's in the States. She was coming over, but then the bombing started."

When a six-storey block collapses after a direct hit by a one-hundred-pound bomb, the contents can reduce to an unexpectedly low and dense pile of rubble. Several other bodies were eventually found, including one of a man who could not be identified. Among the papers found near Catherine was a passport belonging to a Stefano Baldini, aged fifty-nine. Francesco was asked if he knew him and he told the police that Stefano was his uncle, Catherine's husband. They had been expecting him for several days; he must have turned up that morning after Francesco had gone out. He was asked if he would go to the mortuary to formally identify both bodies. For Catherine, he stood for so long staring at her that the uncomfortable constable who had accompanied him had to cough loudly several times to bring him back from his thoughts. As for the other man, he was so badly disfigured that all Francesco could look at were his hands and two finger rings. The doctor had said the body was of a man in his late fifties and Francesco made a pretense of identifying the rings as Stefano Baldini's. He arranged for the bodies to be shipped back to the States for burial on the Fletcher estate, sending accompanying letters to Catherine's brother and sister explaining that he had been a neighbour and that he had got to know them both well during their few months in England. He expressed his sympathies, telling them that he felt their loss very acutely.

Francesco's first painting in what was to become a very extensive and famous series documenting the Blitz was of the bleak and ruined block in St. John's Wood. He had to work mainly from memory since the wreckers needed to make the ruins safe for neighbouring buildings. For the rest of the series, he was sketching frantically as the bombs were falling and the fires blazing, unconcerned for his own safety, not caring if he lived or died, risking his life countless times in the days, months and years following the bomb that had reduced their apartment building to rubble and taken his beloved Catherine. He would follow up the nights with days working in an almost manic determination, producing one painting after another of London's darkest hours.

His paintings were one of the reasons he still found it hard to join up to fight when the age limit was extended: the authorities considered he was doing a valuable job of documentation. He eventually got his wish in 1943 and Private Moretti later saw action in France as part of the D-day landings in June 1944. There he witnessed his fellow soldiers slaughtered all around him, but apart from a very minor flesh wound from a bullet that left a three-inch scar on his left shoulder, he emerged unscathed physically. However, the mental wounds were deeper perhaps than any he had suffered throughout his long life.

It took him many years to recover from his grief over Catherine's death. He blamed himself. If he had not insisted on their coming to England only months before the outbreak of war, Catherine would likely have lived comfortably into a ripe old age in rural Virginia. As it was, she had died needlessly and senselessly, a victim like so many others of the anonymous executioners raining their bombs on Britain during those dark war days.

Although relieved that the war was over, he found he was burned out, unable to paint any more and he withdrew from the more outgoing postwar artistic crowd. He moved to the country, eventually taking up his brushes and palette knives again to paint the country houses of the rich, although, despite being highly sought after, his output was far from prolific. Often several months would pass when he produced little; months when he preferred to lose himself walking the highways and byways of rural southern England. He was pleased to renew the strong attraction he'd developed more than a hundred years before for the English and their countryside: the neat fields and hedgerows and picturesque villages undisturbed by grandiose mountain ranges had a beauty all of their own. It was in exploring their nooks and crannies that he eventually found some sort of peace with himself, but the pain lingered for many years.

# PART II

## July 2009

# Chapter 26

There you are, Mr Fisher, three paintings that represent the bulk of my life savings. You damage them; you die!"

Ced tucked the package under one arm and put the other around her shoulder as they walked to his car.

"That's brilliant, Sal," he said, nuzzling the top of her head, "With these, I'm sure we'll resolve it. How did it go with Andrews? Do you still think he's squeaky clean?"

"I really don't know, hon. He's certainly enigmatic. And now I've seen him in the flesh, I can't believe how alike he is to the face in 'The Awakening'. It's uncanny. And those pale grey eyes are spooky."

"I got that feeling too; there's certainly a lot going on behind them."

They reached the car and Ced carefully stowed the package of paintings on a pile of blankets in the luggage area.

As they drove out of the village, Sally thought back to her conversation in the gallery.

"You know, he's such a nice guy, hon, really friendly, and then you say something and he seems to switch off and go somewhere else. I think he might be attention deficit."

"You think all men are attention deficit. What did you say to send him off?"

"I think it was the mention of Moretti's name."

"What!" Ced hit the brakes in shock as he turned to Sally, generating an angry blast from the car behind them. The car's tyres squealed as it roared past them, the driver gesticulating angrily.

Ced ignored him as he pulled up.

"You mentioned Moretti?"

Sally was puzzled by the strength of his reaction.

"Yes, but I did it carefully, gave him quite a clever story to lead into it. I was rather pleased with myself."

Ced was gripping the steering wheel, his eyes darting around.

"What is it, hon?" asked Sally, "Why is it such a problem?"

"We're worried that he's going to get spooked and disappear."

"Who's we?"

"Corrado and I. We're worried that Andrews will do a bunk if he suspects that anyone's onto him."

"Well, perhaps it would have been a good idea to include me in the loop."

"I didn't know you were going to start making up stories about Moretti."

"He asked why I was so interested in the painting with the country house. He obviously thought a young blonde like me was too Essex to appreciate it. I was put on the spot. Anyway, why do you think he'd suddenly run away? You mentioned Moretti to him."

"I know, but that was before."

"Before what?"

"Before I went to Italy."

"What happened in Italy?"

"I told you," he mumbled evasively. "Corrado showed me all these other paintings and they've turned out to be indistinguishable from Andrews' work."

"Oh, come on, hon! There's more to it than that. Why would you and Corrado suddenly be so worried? What else did you find out?"

Ced continued gripping the steering wheel, his jaw fixed.

"Ced?"

He sighed and turned his head to her. "You're right, Sal, something else did happen. But I promised Corrado that it would remain between us; that I wouldn't tell anyone else."

Sally's voiced hardened. "I'm not anyone else, Ced, I'm Sally, your girlfriend. I wash your smalls and we share intimate secrets. Remember?"

"I know, Sal, I know. But it's big. The implications are huge."

Sally said nothing, the anger written on her face. She waited.

"OK, Sal, but it really must go no further."

"Do I normally blab about things you tell me when they're confidential? All the cases that you're dealing with that are supposed to be just between you and the cops or some lawyer? Do I?"

"No, of course you don't."

"Well then, why should this be different?"

"It was a solemn agreement with Corrado. He's a very worried man."

"Ced. We're trying to work this thing out together. I think I've shown my commitment to it." She glanced pointedly to where the paintings were stowed in the rear. "We can't do it if we keep things from each other."

"I know, Sal, I'm sorry. It's really been bugging me."

She kissed him on the mouth.

"Right, so debug."

"It's 'The Awakening', Sal."

"'The Awakening'?"

"Yeah. As you know, the Italians have done extensive research into it to prove its authenticity. You don't often get a fifteenth century fresco by a famous artist appearing out of the blue. They've poured, and are still pouring, millions into it."

"And?"

"Well, when I was with Corrado, I took images of parts of it with the large format camera. With those and other hi-res images he has access to, I ran the painting against my program. The results I got then showed that only about forty per cent was actually produced by Piero."

"Who painted the rest?"

"I don't know. But whoever it was, his style can't be distinguished from all the others, you know, Perini, di Luca, de la Place. And John Andrews."

"Christ."

She was silent for a few seconds, then something else occurred to her.

"You said, 'the results you got then'. What did you mean? Are there more?"

"Yes. Since I've got back from Italy, I've been rerunning the images through the program, refining parameters, making the comparisons tighter."

"And what have you found?"

"The results I now have indicate that no more than twenty per cent of the picture was in Piero's hand. The rest was by one other person, just one, and he was deliberately trying to mimic Piero's hand. This is why the experts have been fooled in their visual examination: the differences are too subtle for the eye. But that's all assuming the program is worth anything, and if it can't differentiate all these other artists, then it's all meaningless."

"What does Corrado say about that?"

"I haven't dared tell him; I think he'd shoot himself. He's invested a lot of his professional stock in this painting."

"But you can't think that John Andrews had anything to do with it. I mean, it was discovered about twenty years ago. I know they dragged their feet over it once they realised there was something big underneath, but twenty years is twenty years. Are you trying to say that your master forger Andrews had access to some sort of partially completed Piero that no one knew anything about and he then completed it, while at the same time he did it in such a way that the whole art world was fooled into thinking it was a fifteenth century painting. Apart from the ridiculous logistics that would entail, no one is that good, and he would only have been about twenty years old."

"I hadn't thought about it like that."

"And the other question is: why would he do it? For fun? So that he can sit up here in the Lake District and laugh at the art world? There has to be a motive. And huge money would be involved."

Ced shook his head and banged his hands on the steering wheel.

"So we go round in the same circles again and come back to the same starting point. With all this, we're no closer to the truth."

"Let's get home, hon, get those paintings imaged and under the scrutiny of your program. They must hold the key."

Once home, Ced wasted no time in setting up his equipment to produce the images he needed for his comparisons. Downstairs in the sitting room, Sally studied each of her paintings. If nothing else, she was now the proud owner of three of the most beautiful paintings she'd ever seen.

She picked up a book. She wanted to leave Ced alone to run his program through its routines, even though she was desperate to see the results. But she couldn't relax. She marched up and down the room for a few minutes, then sat on the sofa and picked up the sunset view. It was almost abstract, the vibrant colours playing on the water in a symphony of light. To her eye, it was so completely different from the other two paintings that she couldn't imagine there would now be any confusion.

She made herself some tea, took some food from the freezer, looked at it blankly, turned up her nose and put it back. They would go out; they would be celebrating. A breakthrough. The cloud of confusion would be lifted. They would be able to relax again.

Three hours passed and still Ced was working in his study. Sally checked the time. Five o'clock. It was the first day for a long time that they hadn't gone for a run. She thought of going, but somehow the enthusiasm wasn't there. She realised that there was no noise coming from upstairs – no tapping on the keys, no chair moving around as Ced moved from the monitor to a screed of results and back. Silence.

Finally she could stand it no longer; she had to see how far he'd got. She walked up the stairs and into the study. The screens were blank, the printer idle. Ced was sitting in his chair staring out of the window.

"Hon?"

No answer.

"Ced, what's happened? Has the computer crashed?"

He swiveled the chair round and looked up at her. He chewed on his bottom lip and slowly shook his head.

"That's it, Sal. It's over. I can't do anything else. The program is a failure."

"Hon, what happened?" She dropped to her knees in front of him, taking his hands in hers.

"What happened is that I've run comparisons with your paintings and the others and it's no different from before. In fact, it's worse now I've got more than one Andrews sample."

"What about the sunset painting? It looks so different. Don't tell me the program says it's the same as all the others."

"The program tells us it's by the same artist as the others but that there are differences owing to a different style being used. It's designed to do just that and it has passed with flying colours. But then it's failed by not being able to separate these paintings from the other artists we've found. The only explanation is that they were all painted by the same person, which is, of course, complete nonsense."

"Unless all of them are products of some unimaginably complex forgery."

"Yes, but we've discussed that endlessly; it makes no sense. No, it must be in the assumptions made in the program. I'll check and check again, but frankly I doubt I'll ever be able to find it."

"Oh, hon, I can't believe it. I won't believe it. There must be some other explanation."

"I'm sorry, Sal, but I'm afraid you've wasted your money. I'll pay it back to you, but it'll have to be in instalments."

"The money's not important, hon, and anyway, I've got three amazing paintings. True masterpieces."

"Maybe I can sell them through one of my contacts in London. Although I think they are soon going to be my ex-contacts."

"Don't even think about it! I love all three of them and they are bound to appreciate. Maybe I should go and bump off Andrews. An artist's work is always worth more when he's dead."

"You know, the enormity of this thing is only now starting to hit me, Sal. I've given opinions based on this program. Legal opinions. There are people out there starting to structure insurance policies around it. I've got to stop everything. Forefront Forensics will sack me, or worse, sue me. They'll think I've done it on purpose for personal gain. I'm ruined. I'll never be able to hold my head up in the art world again."

Sally stood up, still holding Ced's hands. She pulled him gently to his feet and folded her arms around him, her head pressed against his chest.

"Ced, my dear, lovely, brilliant Ced, it can't come to that. We must be able to get help from someone else in the business. Who is there?"

"There are several people, Sal, but I doubt they can help. I don't want to sound bigheaded, but I'm the best. At least, I was. It's taught me a horribly painful lesson. I made the mistake of believing the preliminary results and charging ahead with the program without having completed the full validation of it."

"That's rubbish, Ced. I saw your protocol and you followed a stringent testing routine. You cannot be blamed for this. Your data and methods are impeccable. No one expects your testing to include every painting by every artist that's ever lived before you can release the results."

He squeezed her tight. "I don't know where I'd be without your support, Sal. You're brilliant, but I think we have to face facts."

"I'll only face them when I am absolutely certain that there are no alternatives. None."

He waved an arm at the hardware. "I've had it with this lot for today. Have we got any wine in the fridge? I think I need a drink."

"I put some there earlier. I think we might as well down a couple of bottles."

They walked downstairs, arms round each other. Sally went to the fridge while Ced walked over to the paintings. He picked them up in turn and studied them.

"Trouble is, Sal, they're brilliant. Amazing."

"Better put them somewhere safe, hon. If we both get as smashed as I intend us to be, they ought to be out of harm's way."

"I'll take them upstairs while you pour."

"Deal."

As she rummaged in a drawer for the corkscrew, the phone started to ring.

She stopped what she was doing and stared at it. Whoever it was, she was in no mood to talk; she wanted nothing more than to dispense some tlc to Ced. No interruptions. She let the phone go onto the answer message.

"Sal? Ced? It's Claw. Are you in? You must be, you always are at this time on a Sunday. Pick up if you're there, please, now, I really need to talk to you. We all really need to talk. It's very important Sal. It's about John Andrews. Please Sal, pick u–"

"Claw."

"Sal, you are in. Thanks heavens! Sal, something really strange has happened."

"Claw, strange and I are no longer friends. I've had strange up to the back teeth. I–"

"Sal, I should have phoned you earlier, but I didn't. I'm sorry."

"About what, Claw?" sighed Sally, resigned to the fact she'd have to hear her friend out. She recognised that breathless, earnest tone and knew there would be no resisting it.

"Well, that's it, I said I wouldn't tell, so I kept it under wraps."

"Claw, take a deep breath. You're not making any sense."

"Sal, I've been wanting to tell you all week, but I promised I wouldn't."

"God, not another one. I feel like a mother confessor today."

"What do you mean?"

"Just a little problem that Ced had in telling me something."

"What?"

Sally laughed. "Actually, Claw, I can't tell you."

"OK, I'm sure you have your reasons. But this thing, Sal, I should have told you, I wish I had earlier."

"Then make your wish come true by telling me now."


"Ced!"

"Coming Sal, I'm just making sure these beauties are safe. Have you got the wine poured?"

"No."

"Why not?"

"Because we're going to London."

"London?"

"Yes, London. Big city in the south-east of England; you must have heard of it."

Ced arrived at the bottom of the stairs.

"What are you on about, Sal? Have you started on the wine without me?"

"Ced, Claw called."

"I thought I heard the phone. How is she?"

"She's fine. Shut up and listen. She's been keeping secrets from me, just like you did."

"Secrets?"

"Ced!"

"Sorry."

"Last week, same day you went to Rome, I think, she went to London to see her old prof. You remember him, don't you? Frank Young?"

"No, I've never met him. Before my time."

"Oh yes, of course. Well, he's a professor of genetics specialising in immune systems. He and about a million others, but he's good, one of the best in his field. Claw took her sample–"

"Sample?"

"I told you, the one from the envelope flap that she's done extra tests on."

"Oh yes."

"She took the rest to Prof Young to ask if he would look at it to see if there is anything odd about it, immune-wise."

"Immune-wise? What does that mean?"

"It means whether Andrews' immune system is any different in any way as a result of his weird junk DNA."

"Interesting idea."

"Very, although it was a bit of a shot in the dark."

"What happened?"

"Well, the prof only did one test that runs the sample against ten diseases, that is, whether the sample has any raised or lowered immunity to them. Andrews' DNA showed raised immunity to all ten!"

"Wow! Wait a minute, aren't there rules about this sort of thing? Shouldn't the professor have sought Andrews' permission?"

"Yes, he should. But to keep Claw happy, he agreed to do one test on the condition that they get permission for any more they want to do."

"Fat chance."

"Exactly. Anyway, when the results for this test came out, the prof was prepared to throw caution to the wind and carry out more tests, although of course there's not much sample."

She paused and waved her arms in the air, fists clenched in frustration. "Why didn't Andrews lick that envelope today!"

She dropped her arms and continued. "He called Claw about two days ago to say that he'd completed another test and that it confirmed the first one. He told her that he'd do the rest next week. Then he phoned her this morning and said he hadn't been able to wait. He put the tests on yesterday and the results will be ready this evening. He wants her to go down to London to be there when the results come out."

"Bloody hell – a Sunday evening? What sort of time does he think they'll be ready?"

"Around eleven, I think."

"He obviously thinks he's onto something. Wonder what it is?"

"I'm not sure. I think Claw has some idea, but she's not committing herself. The thing is, she wants us to go too."

"Why?"

"Well, I think, hon, she reckons the answer to all these problems might lie in these results."

"I can't see why this bloke's DNA is going to explain the problems with my program, can you?"

"Off the top of my head, no. But Claw's no dummy when it comes to genetics and if she thinks it's important, then I think we should go with it."

"And you've already said yes."

"I have. We're driving down to her place and she'll take us from there."

"OK," sighed Ced. "This is turning into quite a day. Look, I want one guarantee."

"Which is?"

"This isn't the first time that we've forged ahead, Sal, convinced that this time we'll have the answer to the problem, only to end up even more frustrated. If tonight it all goes wrong, stuff the white wine, I want to head into oblivion with a good malt. I don't care that I don't normally touch spirits or that tomorrow's a working day: I'll call in sick."

"From what I've heard about the professor, that shouldn't be a problem. I'm sure he'll join you either to celebrate or commiserate with a bottle from his extensive collection."

When Frank Young met them at the laboratory's reception, Claudia knew from his face that something strange had happened. He was so distracted he was hardly able to go through the courtesies of being introduced to Ced and Sally and he was silent in the lift as they went up to the laboratory.

"What is it, Prof?" asked Claudia cautiously, hoping he wasn't angry with her for bringing Ced and Sally, although she'd called ahead to explain.

Young walked them over to a computer monitor.

"About ten minutes ago, the computer stopped processing the numbers for the third test I told you about. The results are on the screen here. I think you should be able to interpret them, Claudia."

Claudia sat down in front of the screen and worked her way through the data. She looked puzzled, turned to speak, changed her mind, and read the data again. Sally looked over her shoulder. She was less familiar with the process but she understood enough to raise her eyebrows at the numbers.

Claudia turned to Young.

"What does this mean?" she asked.

"I think we should wait for the results of the final test before we try to interpret what it means," he replied.

"Have you ever seen anything like this before?" said Claudia.

"Never."

"Would you mind telling me what it is that's baffling you all?" cut in Ced, "I've no idea what any of these data mean. Could you give me a layman's guide?"

"As I said to Claudia, Mr Fisher, I really think we should wait for the results of the final test before we start to digest what this means and what the implications are."

"Implications?"

"Please, Mr Fisher, it will only be about fifteen minutes."

Exactly seventeen long minutes later, a table of data appeared on an adjacent monitor. Young, Claudia and Sally turned their attention to it.

"Well?" asked Ced, exasperated by their continuing silence.

Claudia turned to him. "The third test the prof ran followed on from the first two tests. It went much further than they did and it indicated very strongly what this fourth test has confirmed."

"Which is...?"

"Which is," said Young, "that this man appears to be immune from disease of any kind."

"When you say disease, you mean he can't catch things like a cold, or measles, or tuberculosis?" asked Ced.

"Precisely," answered Young. "He'd be totally resistant to them. But there's more than that. His body would also be completely resistant to conditions arising from mutations or regenerative problems, such as cancer. Nor would it be susceptible to other diseases that you might regard as degenerative."

"So he could live a long time if there's no disease out there to get him?"

"It depends what you mean by a long time," replied Young. "It will need confirmation and much more work, but so far, all the results would appear to indicate that barring accidents or life-threatening attacks on the man – such as somebody shooting him – there is no reason for him to die."

Ced frowned, trying to take in what this information meant. "But wouldn't he end up looking horribly old, like one of those characters in a movie who's a hundred and twenty? You know, all wizened and gaunt."

The professor smiled. "No, that's exactly the point. If you regard ageing as a type of disease where the body's ability to maintain itself becomes increasingly compromised, if you overcome that disease, it would be possible to remain in a state of equilibrium for, well, I don't know how long. If this man's immune system has the properties I think it has, he could be hundreds of years old and still look like a man in his prime."

Ced sat down hard in a chair as the truth hit him.

"Christ! This means that his paintings are indistinguishable from Moretti's, or de la Place's, or Perini's or di Luca's because he painted them. He was all of those people. The person depicted in 'The Awakening' doesn't just look like him, it is him!"

He turned to Claudia and Sally. "Girls, he knew Piero della Francesca. Knew him! He worked with him! John Andrews worked with Piero della Francesca!"

Sally threw her arms around him. "Ced, Ced, you know what this means?"

He frowned, still overwhelmed by the unbelievable words he'd just uttered.

"Ced, it means your program was right all along. There's nothing wrong with it at all. It's brilliant, Ced, completely mindblowingly brilliant!"

# Chapter 27

In the cold light of the following morning, Ced's euphoria had been replaced by an aching sense of anguish. The impact the professor's discovery would have on his program had hit him as he awoke, groggy from too many glasses of single malt.

They had spent the night in an apartment that was part of the laboratory.

"There's plenty of room," Young told them, "three bedrooms, each en suite. We included it in the design because it's so often necessary to work late. I sleep many a night here rather than trudge all the way back to the nether end of Kent in the wee small hours."

And it had been the wee small hours before they had even thought about sleep. Following the result of the fourth test, they discussed the implications endlessly, as well as checking and rechecking the data to ensure it wasn't flawed.

As a leader in his field, it was the professor who had the clearest grasp of their staggering discovery.

"It makes perfect sense, really," he told them casually, as if such findings were everyday events. "Our bodies work away from the moment of conception, building and building, following the predetermined pattern of our own genetic code. We go through various stages as we grow and develop into fully mature people. This process goes on longer than most people realise: we are not fully mature with everything at its peak until sometime in our early thirties.

"Now, as we grow, things can and do go wrong. Mutations can

occur; illnesses develop. But the big one is once we have stopped maturing. I suppose there might be a period where we are in balance, but pretty soon, having spent so long climbing to the dizzy heights of our maturity, we start to slide down the slippery slope of decay. The ageing process starts to take over as the myriad processes going on in our bodies begin either to fail or to become less efficient. It's hardly noticeable at first - lines form on the face, hair might change colour, muscle tone cannot be maintained at its all-time peak. If all this can be stopped, if the processes keeping us in our prime at an age of, let me see, I think it would be early to mid-thirties – it will vary from one person to another – if these processes can be maintained, then there would be no degeneration."

"Do you think he's a one-off" asked Claudia.

Young shook his head. "Well, we don't know. It could be that all the necessary factors have come together just once in this man; that he's unique. But given that he must have inherited these alleles and passed them on to his children, there must be a chance that there are others like him. We simply don't know enough about it yet."

"And," said Sally ruefully, "he's likely to be completely resistant to providing any more material for further research."

Ced shrugged his shoulders. "I can understand why he's resistant, he must have spent his whole life trying to hide the fact that he's not ageing. Imagine it. We know he is old enough to have been alive in the fifteenth century; he might be even older. But think about the problems. He'd have lived in a world where life was cheap – widespread infant mortality; diseases that we now shrug off with a quick dose of antibiotics would often have been fatal; epidemics of one thing; plagues of another. He would have remained untouched by it all, never even catching a cold. And then there would have been the realisation that he wasn't getting older. First not looking any older and then nothing seizing up, his physical condition remaining the same. If he was religious – and he lived in early Renaissance Italy so he probably was – he would probably have thought he was possessed by the Devil. Even if he didn't think that, others would have, and they were pretty full on with burning heretics and witches. He must have been constantly looking over his shoulder."

"There are also families," added Claudia. "He's married with kids now; presumably he's been married many times before. He could have had legions of kids. I wonder if those rather strange pale grey eyes are any indication of his situation. If they are, then his little daughter could be the same."

"This is absolutely fascinating from so many points of view," said the professor. "But one thing's for certain: he must have developed quite a few coping skills – stories he tells, answers to questions, maybe ageing himself artificially when it's necessary. After all, if he has had wives and children, he can't just abandon them after a few years when he should be showing signs of ageing."

"I wonder what he does about his identity," said Sally,

"Good point," replied Ced. "We know he's had a number of identities. How and when does he choose them? Does he steal them? Make them up? It was probably easier a few hundred years ago, but these days it would be harder. I wonder if he stole the name John Andrews from someone."

"You know, Mr Fisher," said Young, nodding his head as an idea occurred to him, "you could get quite a few answers about his history from your program, especially now you have total confidence in it."

"How do you mean?"

"Well, it might take a bit of processing time, but couldn't you run your John Andrews data against every artist you have access to? That would give you a list of artists who John Andrews has been in the past. It could also tell you who he was first because before he was born, no artists would match him."

"Unless he's thousands of years old," replied Ced. "I don't have exemplars from Roman or Greek times. It's a good idea, though, but it will take some time."


As the conversation drifted on with each of them raising ideas and questions, they moved to the apartment where Young opened some red wine for the girls and produced a selection of single malts for Ced and himself. Ced wanted to try them all, but their sublime spell overtook him and he was soon sound asleep on the couch where he sat.

He awoke with a start four hours later as a shaft of sunlight broke through some patchy morning cloud and burned straight into his eyes. Completely disoriented and wondering why his tongue no longer fitted inside his mouth, he staggered to the kitchen and drank several glasses of cold water.

The events of the night before flooded into his consciousness in waves. It was then that the logical consequences of his program being so good hit him like a speeding train. He slumped onto a kitchen stool, his head in his hands. He was still in the same position when, half an hour later, Sally shuffled into the kitchen, also looking for water.

"God, hon, what a night! Do you think all moments of eureka-type discovery are celebrated with a hangover? You should see yourself; I've seen better-looking cadavers." She gulped down a glass of water and turned to him again. "You know, for a potential Nobel Prize winner, you look awfully glum."

Ced didn't move.

"Hon, come on, you've produced something utterly amazing and you look like your pet goldfish just died. You left the doubts about your program behind last night. Remember? Come on, superstar!"

Ced shook his head and turned to her.

"It's not as easy as that, Sal. There's a problem."

"How can there be a problem? Your program can reliably, accurately and with one hundred per cent confidence differentiate every artist under the sun."

"No, Sal, it can't."

"Come on Ced – you've just woken up from a bad dream. Your program is brilliant."

"I know it is, Sal."

"I think you should go back to sleep, hon; you're making no sense and this chain saw in my head is getting louder."

"Sal, the problem with the program is that it can't differentiate, say, Andrews from Tommaso Perini."

Sally was incredulous. "That's because they're the same person, hon. Are you suffering from short-term memory loss? That problem was solved last night."

Ced screwed his eyes up against the sunlight. "Sal, think about it. If my program is used by anyone else – and there are people emailing me daily about it – sooner or later one of them is going to compare two or more of the artists that John Andrews has been. They're not going to be able to differentiate them because they can't be differentiated."

"Why is that a problem?"

"Because they will think the program is faulty and come back to me with tons of questions. Questions I won't be able to answer because, Sal, no one knows about John Andrews and it's going to have to remain that way. Just because we've discovered his secret doesn't mean we can tell the world. That would be totally irresponsible and potentially very dangerous for him. We might no longer live in the fifteenth century, but there are still plenty of prejudices out there. There is no way that his secret can become public knowledge."

"You know, the same thoughts occurred to me, Mr Fisher." Frank Young had walked into the kitchen and heard the end of their conversation. Ced glanced across at him, noting with irritation how perfectly fresh he looked.

"It's a dilemma. You can't release the program in case its apparent shortcomings are spotted, and yet if you don't, someone else somewhere will write a very similar program eventually, and they will have the same problems."

"That's true," said Sally, "but they will be working without the knowledge of Andrews' DNA results. They will think, like Ced did, that there's a problem in the code."

"And never be able to resolve it," added Ced.

"Surely," suggested Sally, "it will be a long time before anyone starts comparing a minor fifteenth-century artist with a minor nineteenth century one, say."

"You'd think so," replied Ced, "but with all the hi-res images available, they are going to do exactly what the prof suggested last night and run everything against everything else, simply because they can. And then the apparent paradox will surface."

"Then," smiled the professor, "for any one else who decides to write their own program, it will just have to remain a paradox. But for yours, Mr Fisher, I should have thought it would be possible for you to hide some code in it that makes it give a false result whenever any of the different John Andrews personas are compared. That way it would never match an Andrews with a Perini or anyone else."

Ced rubbed his chin thoughtfully. "It would be totally dishonest," he said.

Then he nodded slowly as his mind started working on the problem.

"It would have to be very well hidden – the program is going to be scrutinised very thoroughly."

He paused and then grinned. "But I think it's do-able. And it will solve things with Corrado and Lawrence. I'll just tell them I've cracked the problem."

# Chapter 28

Lily Saunders looked at her watch for the hundredth time in three hours as she absently drummed her fingers on the table in front of her seat. Was the train running late? Trains were never early.

She was worried that if she arrived late in Penrith, the man delivering her rental car wouldn't wait. A ticket inspector walked past and she hailed him. "Excuse me, sir, are we going to be on time in Penrith?"

The inspector smiled to himself. American tourists! You'd never get an English woman calling you 'sir'.

"We're due into Penrith at eight minutes past the hour, madam; we shouldn't be more than a couple of minutes late."

The train was on time and as it pulled out of the station near the northern end of the Lake District, it left Lily standing on the platform. She eyed her two huge suitcases and cursed her stupidity in bringing so much with her. She was unused to travelling and she didn't know how long she would be staying. As a result, more than a few extra jackets, trousers, skirts, tops and pairs of shoes had found their way into her luggage. At least both the suitcases were on wheels. She hefted her large handbag and her portfolio case over her shoulder and, taking a suitcase handle in each hand, set off down the platform.

The twenty-year-old agent from Lakeland Car Rentals was lounging against the car in the station car park, smoking a cigarette. He saw the woman struggling through the station foyer, stubbed out his cigarette and sauntered over to her, his eyes roving over her trim figure. She was younger than he'd imagined, and probably quite a looker under those huge sunglasses.

"Ms Saunders?"

"Gee, yes, that's me," said Lily in relief. "Lily Saunders. I hope I haven't kept you waiting."

"No, luv, train were on time, weren't it. Coupla bits a paper to sign an' we'll have you on yer way."

Lily looked at the car in amazement. It was tiny! She was used to the new compacts in the States; this thing looked as if it would fit inside one.

"It is an automatic, isn't it?" she asked the young man, wondering if it was really big enough to have a gearbox.

"Yeah, luv, these'uns are all automatic."

"Thank God for that," she smiled, "I couldn't have managed with a stick shift."

The agent tried and failed to get both suitcases into the car's tiny boot.

"One o'these'll have to go on back seat, luv," he panted, wrestling with the second case. "That OK?"

"No problem, so as long as the car can handle all the weight."

He laughed as he stowed the second case and sat in the front passenger seat to explain how to operate the SatNav. He asked her where she was going and set it to Keswick for her.

"OK, luv, just the paperwork. Can I see your licence?"

She handed him her New York Drivers License and he copied down the details. He looked up, puzzled. "Says 'ere you was born in 1960. That a mistake?"

"No, that's correct," she lied.

He shook his head. Yanks! She must be all plastic; she didn't look a day over thirty. Christ! He'd considered chatting her up but she'd turned out to be older than his mother!

For the next terrifying ten minutes, Lily attempted to guide the car along the left side of the road in the direction the disembodied male voice of Jason from the SatNav was leading her. Along the A66 to Keswick, she saw a sign for emergency parking by the roadside. She decided her situation qualified and pulled in.

She took a deep breath, opened her large map of the Lake District and located roughly where she was. She'd come all this way; she couldn't give up now. Hell, there was hardly any traffic and she was used to driving around New York City! Then a little voice reminded her that in New York City they drove on the right side of the road.

She pulled a map and some printouts from her handbag. Among the printouts was a photograph of a painting a girlfriend had bought in England a few weeks before while on a European trip. As soon as she'd returned, she had brought it over to show Lily.

"Take a look at this, Lil," Jenny Talberg had yelled as she burst through the door of Lily's studio in the Upper West Side. "Don't you think it's just darling?"

Jenny was a large woman in every way: large frame, large hair and large personality. At six foot one she towered over the slightly built, five foot four Lily.

Lily had taken the painting and studied it, her eyes widening in disbelief. It was of a young girl of about five or six. She immediately noticed the sparkling, mischievous eyes looking straight back at her and an impish smile that was about to burst into peals of laughter. She caught her breath, the excitement of what she was holding welling up inside her. She had seen similar portraits before, portraits of herself that her father had painted. She held the painting close and studied the brushwork. The style was so familiar – she had watched her father applying that delicate brushwork on so many occasions as she grew. Later, when she was old enough, he had taught her how to paint like that. She still did, and now, finally, after many difficult years, her skills were recognised and her work sought after.

She realised her hands were shaking. "Jenny, Jenny, oh dear wonderful Jenny! Wherever did you get this?" Her voice was a hoarse whisper; she was still shocked at seeing the painting and at the realisation that perhaps her father was alive.

"It was in the cutest little English village you could imagine, Lil," enthused Jenny, "in an area they call the Lakes. It's a spectacular part of the country."

"What was the name of the village?"

"Er, Grass Moor, I think, or something cutesy British like that."

"Grass Moor," said Lily, "I'll have to look it up. Did you meet the artist?"

"Sure did, Lil!" Lily hated being called Lil and Jenny was the only person allowed to use the diminutive, simply because she was Jenny and always had. "He's quite a looker; you'd like him. Wife's a bit pushy though. He's the sort of reserved English-gentleman type: very polite, well spoken. And boy, what an artist! He does these fabulous portraits, kids like this one, adults, older people, and then he does landscapes of the Lakes area. Jeez, Lil, you'd kill for them."

Lily looked up at Jenny and their eyes met. Jenny gasped. "Oh my God, Lil, I forgot. The eyes. D'you see the eyes on this little girl – it's his daughter – they're just like yours. And his eyes. Lil, this is incredible–"

"They're just like mine too?" said Lily.

"Yeah, kid, they are. Isn't that amazing?"

Yes, thought Lily, really amazing.


The first time she'd had any notion that her father might still be alive had been in the nineteen fifties when she's seen some paintings by Stefano Baldini. By then, she knew she was very different from other women. She had never been ill in her life and now, in her late sixties, she was as young-looking and beautiful as she had been at thirty, her silky jet-black hair as thick and lush as it had ever been, her figure trim and firm. And unlike any other woman of her age, the previous year she had given birth to a son.

She'd seen the Baldini paintings by chance at an exhibition in Chicago, where her husband, Brad, worked at the time – as far as Brad knew, she was twenty-five and she wasn't about to enlighten him further. There were three: a portrait of a beautiful young woman with a look of confidence and contentment about her that reminded her of Fiona Trevelyan, and two landscapes of the Virginia hills – haunting autumnal views that made your heart ache to be there.

No one at the exhibition knew much about Stefano Baldini, but she'd later found out he'd been killed in the Blitz in London.

The news had been a desperate blow, especially when she realised they had both been in the States at the same time in the thirties, although still separated by three thousand miles.

Then in 2001, when the Internet was growing fast, she'd been researching some British artists online and she'd come across one with an Italian name: Francesco Moretti. The site only had low resolution images of some bucolic English landscapes but they were familiar enough to set her thinking. When she discovered there were three Morettis in the Metropolitan Museum of Art in New York where she now lived, she went to see them immediately. By now her circumstances had changed. Brad had died of old age and her children, the son born in 1951 and a daughter born in 1960, also called Lily, had both died tragically and young. It was her daughter's identity papers and passport that she currently used.

Seeing the Morettis in the Met convinced her that she was again looking at work by her father. But like Baldini, Moretti was also dead, drowned in the Adriatic in the early seventies. Two dead artists, both of whom were her father. She wondered. Clearly Baldini hadn't died as reported; perhaps Moretti hadn't either. But until Jenny burst through the door with the portrait of Phoebe Andrews in her hands, Lily had learned nothing more to indicate her father was living, or where he might be.

She had immediately set about planning a trip. It was only in recent years she'd had enough money to even consider a trip to Europe, and somehow it had always been put on the back burner. Now there was no stopping her.

She put away her printouts and leaving the map open on the passenger seat – she wasn't totally confident in Jason – she pulled out of the lay-by and headed gingerly on her way.

The first few miles of the road were dual carriageway, which helped her confidence a little, but then the road became two-way again and she slowed to about twenty miles an hour. Ahead on both sides of the road she could see the rugged hills of the Lake District appearing before her, golden and dramatic in the late afternoon sun. She began to relax, but every time a car passed in the opposite direction, she found herself gripping the steering wheel in panic.

Arriving in Keswick, she pulled into the first car park she saw. She checked her map, located the Keswick Galleries and headed towards them.

They were housed in an old building that had once been a church hall. There was a large banner over the door: Lakeland. An Exhibition of Twenty Local Artists. Open 10-7 Daily.

She stopped and looked up at the banner, her heart pounding.

Was this really happening, after all these years? She smoothed her clothes and touched her hair. What was she going to say to him? What if his wife was there? Would he recognise her? Her hair wasn't in the same style, but facially she didn't really look very different from the last time he had seen her. The memory of that day on the sailing junk in the South China Sea flashed across her mind. She had been perched on a railing at the bow of the boat, sketching. She'd waved at him as he turned and smiled at her before heading to their cabin. The memory of the tranquil moment of happiness was etched into her mind. It had been her last with him before the nightmare of the attack by the pirates and the silent slaughter that followed. She had never understood why she'd been spared; why she'd been whisked away, tied up, bundled into a cart under a pile of blankets and transported miles across the country. No one had ever told her anything.

"John was here," said the girl selling brochures at a desk by the door. "I saw him about an hour ago; he's around somewhere. His work's over there on the right."

Lily walked through the hall to where John Andrews' paintings were displayed, half expecting that at any moment she would see her father appear and walk past her. She looked around the immediate area, but there was no one who seemed to be connected to the paintings.

She approached the display stand and studied the paintings. She smiled to herself; she was convinced she was right.

"I'm afraid they've all been sold, if you were thinking of buying one," said a softly spoken male voice from behind her. She spun round, her heart in her mouth, only to find the owner of the voice was a balding man with horn-rimmed glasses perched on the end of his pointed nose.

She smiled, trying to speak as she swallowed her disappointment.

"I, er, I hadn't really thought about buying one, I was just looking at them. They're so beautiful."

"Well, when you've finished admiring these, you might like to see some of the other work here. Mine's over there," he said with a tone of self-importance.

"Thanks, I'll come along in a moment."

She turned away, aware that his eyes were roving unashamedly over her body, and continued to look at the paintings. She moved along the display stand and then turned again, almost bumping into the man. He had followed her.

"Excuse me," she said. "Er, do you know if John Andrews is here, I was really hoping to speak with him."

"You'll have to join the queue, Miss… er?"

Lily paused and smiled to herself. "Saunders," she said, "and it's Mrs."

"Oh," replied the artist looking beyond her around the hall. "Hubby around, is he?"

"No, he's up in the hills training some Special Forces troops in advanced unarmed combat."

The man's face paled.

"What did you mean, that I'll have to 'join the queue'?" she asked.

"Oh," gulped the man, trying now to sound casual, "there have been people buzzing around his paintings all day. And then about an hour ago, there was a monied-looking chap, you know, dressed casually but expensively. Full of praise and interest in John's paintings. Bought the remaining four, just like that. Chatted to John for a while, and then they both left. John didn't say where he was going or how long he'd be but they were probably going back to his gallery. He's sold all these in the last twenty-four hours and now he'll be selling more. Lucky bugger."

"Is it far to his gallery?" asked Lily.

"No, not far. Have you got a car?"

"Yes," replied Lily.

"It's in Grasmere, about thirteen miles from here. Should take you about twenty-five minutes. Once you get there, look for the Green Man pub. It's just beyond that. Not that you'd miss the gallery," he added wistfully. "It's probably thronging with buyers."

"Thanks," said Lily, "I think I'll go along there now. I'd like to catch him before he goes home."

The artist looked disappointed. "Don't you want to look at some of the other work in the exhibition?" he asked, pointing toward his own display stands.

"I'd love to," said Lily smiling at him and walking away, "I'm here all weekend. I'll call in again tomorrow."

"Good. See you then," replied the artist. "Bring your husband," he added rather flatly.

She saw the gallery immediately she entered the village, but the street was packed with cars so she followed the signs to a pay-and-display car park, parked her car and walked back. It had been a hot day for the Lakes and many people were relaxing on the green as the late afternoon sun cooled. The village pubs were doing a roaring trade.

She crossed the road from the green and walked up to the gallery window. She sighed happily as she saw the display – the more Andrews paintings she saw, the more she was convinced.

This time, she thought, this time he'll be here.

She looked past the paintings in the gallery window and into the gallery itself. The only people she could see were a middle-aged couple, large and blond, moving among the displays, and a woman standing by a counter looking anxiously at her watch. There was no sign of John Andrews, but then she noticed a doorway at the rear of the gallery that led into another room. A studio? Perhaps he was in there.

She saw the middle-aged couple turn and say something to the woman at the counter, who smiled distractedly. The couple walked towards the gallery door and opened it. Lily waited for them to pass and then started to walk into the gallery. But the woman from the counter had followed the couple and was now blocking the way, still looking at her watch.

"I'm sorry," she said, "but we're closing."

Lily stared at her in dismay – the notice on the door said the gallery was open until seven thirty; it was now shortly after six.

"But–" she began.

"I know it's early, but I have to get away. Sorry," said Lola.

"That's very disappointing after coming all this way," said Lily, "I was really hoping to talk with Mr John Andrews."

"I'd like to talk to him myself," replied Lola tersely. "I've got to pick up my girls and he's supposed to be here. I don't know where he's gone."

"Have you tried calling him?" suggested Lily.

"What? Yes, of course I have. But John's hopeless with phones.

He forgets to turn his on half the time, or leaves it in the car. There was no answer."

"Well, at least that means it's on," said Lily helpfully.

"I suppose it does. Did you say you've come a long way?"

"From New York City."

"New York? To see John? Why?"

"A friend of mine bought one of his paintings recently, a painting of a little girl. It's wonderful. I was over here in England, so I thought I'd check out the gallery."

"We've sold a couple of those lately. Is your friend English?" she asked, remembering the one John had sold the previous weekend to Sally Moreton.

"No," laughed Lily, "Jenny's American. Very. You'd remember her if you'd seen her. She's very tall, lots of hair."

"Oh, yes," smiled Lola, "I do remember her. A few weeks ago. She was very gushy about the portrait. In fact, about everything."

"Sounds like Jenny," laughed Lily. "You must be John's wife."

"Yes, I'm Lola, Lola Andrews."

"Lily," replied Lily, taking Lola's outstretched hand, "Lily Saunders."

"Are you around for long, Ms Saunders? Only it's all rather difficult at the moment. If you can come back tomorrow, I'm sure John will be here."

"Please, call me Lily. Yes, I am here tomorrow," she said as she looked wistfully past Lola at the displays in the gallery.

Lola noticed and said, "Look, you've come a long way. Why don't you have a look around for a few minutes while I make some more phone calls to see if I can locate John."

"Gee, Lola – may I call you Lola?"

Lola nodded, smiling.

"Lola, thanks, that'd be great. I love his work. I was at the exhibition just now."

"Oh, really? Well, that answers one question. I was going to call someone there to see if he knows where John's gone. The artist exhibiting next to him."

"Bald guy with specs? Roving eyes?"

Lola laughed. "Yes, that's the one. Roland McIntyre. Thinks he's God's gift."

"How delusional can you get?" said Lily.

"Yeah, when he looks in the mirror, he sees a movie star," said Lola, shaking her head.

"Well," replied Lily, "the Hollywood wannabe told me John had left about an hour ago – that'll be more than an hour and a half by now. Apparently, he was deep in conversation with a man who'd bought four of his paintings and then they left together. He'd assumed they'd come here."

"Well, they didn't," said Lola thoughtfully. "That's very strange. I wonder who it was. Did Roland say what he was like?"

"Said he was expensively but casually dressed, that's all."

"OK, let me call Roland. A description might give me a clue." She waved a hand at the gallery. "Help yourself."

Lily rubbed her hands together in glee and walked into the gallery. She couldn't believe her eyes. For the first time in over a hundred years she was surrounded by her father's work. It was like being back in the studio in Hong Kong. Even the subject matter was similar: portraits and landscapes. The only difference was the dress of the subjects in the portraits, and the scenery in the landscapes, the resting-dragon-shaped hillsides of Hong Kong having been replaced with the wild rugged beauty of England's Lake District.

She was engrossed in a portrait of a young woman when Lola came back over to her. "Roland said the man was in his fifties, bit shorter than John, greying hair and, as you said, expensively dressed. Gushing and pushy, according to Roland. From what he heard of their conversation, he said the man was well-spoken, with a Yorkshire accent. Said John looked pretty pleased with himself as they left. I've no idea who he might be."

"What happens now?" asked Lily.

Lola sighed in frustration. "I don't know. John's got the car and I'm stuck without it. I'll have to phone the mother of the friends my girls are playing with and tell her I'll be a bit late."

"Does John know you're picking up your daughters?"

"Damn right he does. What the hell does he think he's playing at? He knew I was on a tight deadline. God, he really does live in a world of his own at times!"

"We can take my car, if you like," said Lily.

"What? No, I couldn't. I don't even know you. Look, that's very kind but–"

"Think nothing of it. I'm staying up here in a B&B and I've got nothing else to do. I'd be pleased to help out."

Lola thought about it. "Well, if you really don't mind, that would certainly get me out of a spot."

"I'm afraid there's one problem," said Lily. "My luggage is a bit on the large side. Is there somewhere we can stow it for a while to make room for your daughters?"

"We can put it in here in the gallery. Where's your car?"

"In a car park beyond the village green."

"Why don't you run and get the car? I'd better stay here in case John rings. Are you sure this is OK?"

"Really, it's no problem."

Ten minutes later, Lily pulled up outside the gallery. Lola was pacing up and down outside.

"Sorry," said Lily, "it was a bit further than I thought."

She dragged her two suitcases onto the pavement.

"How many months have you come for?" said Lola as she helped Lily wheel the suitcases into the gallery.

She locked up the gallery and climbed into the passenger seat.

"This is cozy," she said. "I've wondered what these are like inside."

She watched in growing frustration as Lily edged away from the kerb and headed back through the village at about ten miles an hour.

After a couple of minutes she said, "Lily, I don't know if you're confused with our speed limits or worried about brawny cops flagging you down, but it is acceptable to go a little bit faster."

"Sorry, Lola, I have no problem whizzing about New York City, but I can't seem to get used to driving on this side of the road."

"Would you like me to drive? We might get there today."

"Sure. But is it OK with the insurance?"

"I doubt it, but we're not going far and I'll try not to prang it."

They swapped seats and Lola roared off.

"Gee, I didn't know it went this fast," said Lily, impressed. "It'll teach me a lot, just watching you."

"I think that's the first time anyone has ever said anything complimentary about my driving," laughed Lola. "It was complimentary, wasn't it?"

"Sure, this is fun," said Lily as they overtook a stream of slow-moving traffic. "It's like being back home."

As they sped along the main road to Ambleside, Lola asked Lily, "Where's your B&B?"

"I'm not sure; I haven't checked in yet. It's called Grasmere View Cottage."

"Madge Cooper's place. It's very nice; you'll like it. It's on the Thirlmere road, towards where we live."

They pulled up outside a house on the outskirts of Ambleside. As Lola got out, the girls saw her and ran to the car.

"Mummy, have you bought a new car?" said the excited Phoebe.

"It's cool," added Sophie.

"No, I'm afraid I haven't," said Lola. "It belongs to my friend, Lily. Daddy's gone somewhere in our car. Come and say hello."

Lily got out of the car and bent over to the girls, holding out her hand.

"Hi, you must be Sophie," she said, making sure she addressed the elder one first, "and you must be Phoebe. Your mummy told me all about you on the way over here."

She looked through her sunglasses into Phoebe's pale grey eyes and wanted to hug her.

"Why are you driving, Mummy?" asked Sophie.

"It was quicker because I know the way, sweetheart," said Lola. "Come on girls, pile in."

They said their goodbyes to their friends and drove off.

Phoebe was studying Lily from the back seat.

"You speak funny like that big lady who buyed a picture from Daddy," she said.

"Phoebe!" said Lola.

Lily laughed. "I guess that big lady is my friend Jenny. Yes, Phoebe, you're right. That's very clever. My friend bought a picture that's of you and she showed it to me. So when I met you just now, it was like I already knew you."

"Did she buyed one of Sofe as well?" asked Phoebe.

"No, she didn't. But she wants to next time, when she comes back."

"P'raps you could buy one and take it to her."

"Phoebe!" said Lola again. "Lily might not want to buy any paintings."

"Oh, I do. If I could, I'd buy the lot," laughed Lily. "I must say I'm impressed with your little sales agent here."

"Start 'em young," smiled Lola.

As they headed back towards Grasmere, Lola realised they had a problem. "Lily, look, I hope you don't mind, but I really need to get the girls back home. Would you mind very much if we dropped them off first and then got your bags? We don't live far away. There's a neighbour who can keep an eye on the girls while we go back to the gallery."

"No problem. I'm having fun," said Lily.

"Thanks, that's brilliant," said Lola, pulling her phone out of her bag and hitting the speed dial number for John. "I'll just try John again and see if he's turned up."

There was no answer and Lola threw the phone back into her bag in annoyance. "Where the hell is he?"

They followed the main road that by-passed Grasmere in the direction of Thirlmere where John and Lola had a cottage at the far end of the lake. Lola roared up the main road like a rally driver, cresting the brow of a hill and racing down the other side.

"This thing handles well, Lily, I'm impressed. It's nice to drive a car that was made this century for a change, instead of one of Mr Volvo's original designs."

They turned left off the main road and headed down a tree-lined track towards the lake, stopping by a group of cottages about a hundred yards from the shore.

"Here we are, home sweet home," announced Lola. "Come on, girls, out you get, Lily's got to get to her B&B."

"Can't she stay here, Mummy? I want to show her my rabbits," said Phoebe.

"Lily will be far more comfortable at the B&B, Phoebe, but..." She looked at Lily. "Rabbits?"

"I'd love to see your rabbits, Phoebe," enthused Lily. "Have you got some too, Sophie?"

"Sophie's got two boys and I've got two girls," said Phoebe. "They're all brothers and sisters, but Mummy says we can't put them together or there'll be lots more."

"That's rabbits for you," laughed Lily as Phoebe took her hand and guided her over to a shed next to their cottage.

She looked around at Lola who was following them. "It's so beautiful here, Lola, divine. I can't believe that only two days ago I was in New York."

"Yes, it's lovely, especially in the summer," said Lola, "but the winters can be a bit chilly."

"I'd forgotten all about English understatement," smiled Lily wistfully.

After Lily had been introduced to the rabbits, they went into the cottage where both girls began to retrieve their mountain of dolls to show their new friend.

Lola saw Lily biting her lip as the little girls chattered away to her. "Are you OK, Lily?" she asked.

"Yes, fine," said Lily, taking a tissue from her bag and blowing her nose. "They just remind me … of someone …" She smiled, but Lola could sense that she was struggling with some memories.

"OK, girls, that's enough. Lily's come a long way and she's very tired. I've got to take her to the B&B. We'll see her tomorrow. I'll get Kitty to keep an eye on you."

"Oh!" the girls moaned in unison.

Phoebe put down the doll she was carrying and came over to stand next to where Lily was sitting.

"Lily?" she asked.

"What is it, Phoebe?" she smiled.

"Can I try on your sunglasses?"

"Phoebe!" said Lola, exasperated. "She's got this thing about sunglasses. She's always asking people in the gallery if she can try theirs on. I think the customers reckon she's trying to nick all their designer gear for me."

"That's OK," laughed Lily. "She can try them on."

She took off her sunglasses and held them out to Phoebe. The little girl took them and looked up at her. She froze, staring at Lily's eyes.

Lola immediately noticed the strange look on Phoebe's face.

"Phoebe, what is it?"

Lily dropped her head.

"Oh," she said, "I forgot." She turned to look at Lola.

Lola had noticed that Lily had Asian features, despite the large sunglasses, but she'd thought no more of it. Lots of Americans were of Asian origin. Now that she saw her eyes, everything suddenly became clear. She knew who Lily was. But for the moment, she had to make light of it, for the girls' sake.

"Wow, Lily," she said brightly, "how amazing. Your eyes are like Phoebe's, the same pale grey colour. That's pretty unusual. Look Phoebe, Lily's got the same colour eyes as you and Daddy. Special friend, huh!"

Phoebe said nothing as she stood there clutching Lily's sunglasses.

Lily smiled at her. "Aren't you going to try them on?" she said.

Phoebe looked down at the glasses. "It's OK," she said, handing them back to Lily.

"Right, girls, Lily and I have to go," said Lola.

Lily got up and walked to the door. She turned. "Bye girls."

"Bye," they said together.

"Will you come back tomorrow?" asked Phoebe.

"Would you like me to?"

Phoebe nodded slowly and picked up one of her dolls to give it a cuddle.

They got in the car and Lola drove away from the house, but shortly before the main road, she stopped. She turned in her seat to look at Lily.

"Lily," she said.

"Lola, I…"

Lola smiled. "I wasn't asking you anything, I was just saying the name. Lily. But it's not Lily, is it?" She paused. "It's Lei-li."

"You know?" gasped Lily.

Lola nodded slowly. "I never really believed John when he told me. I thought he was making up some daft story for reasons I didn't understand. But recently one or two things have happened that have made me realise it's true. And this confirms it."

Lily nodded, the emotion welling up in her.

"I'm his daughter, Lola. John's daughter," she said, unable to hold back the tears. "I'm a hundred and twenty-four years old, and I'm his daughter."

Lola put her arms round her and let her cry.

# Chapter 29

For Lily, the walls of the dam containing more than a hundred years of secrets, hopes and fears breached as she cried into Lola's shoulder. She finally knew for certain that her father was alive, but she was now even more desperate to see him.

Lola sat back and took Lily's face in her hands, her eyes taking in every detail.

"Lily," she said, "it's still so unbelievable. Look at your skin, your hair! Everything about you is younger than me!" She shook her head and smiled. "I should be very jealous. I can see time passing every time I look in the mirror these days, but for you, that's a totally unknown experience!"

Lily laughed as she wiped her eyes with a tissue. "In the early days, before I understood what was going on – not that I understand it now, but at least I've accepted it – I spent hours scrutinising my face and my body. I was desperate for wrinkles, for a grey hair! Can you imagine?"

"Bizarre. But you can perhaps understand why I was so sceptical when John told me his story. It's too crazy for words. I mean, for you to be a hundred and twenty-four is one thing, for John–"

She caught the question in Lily's eyes as she spoke.

"Oh my God, you don't know how old he is, do you?"

"How could I? When Papa and I were separated in 1905, he had told me nothing. I don't think he ever even told my mother."

Lola stared at her, her normal flippancy gone. "It's sounds so strange to hear you call him 'Papa'."

"I've never thought of him otherwise. That's what he is: my papa."

Lola smiled at the thought. "Your mother. What was she like?" she said quietly.

"I was only nine when she died, but my memory of her is that she was lovely. A typical Cantonese mother in many ways – fussy, bossy, quite strict. But very loving, and she adored Papa."

Lola smiled wistfully. "Of course, he wasn't John then, was he?"

"No, he was Stephen Waters. My original name was Waters Lei-li, or in Cantonese, Shui Lei-li."

"That's beautiful. What was he like?"

"A lovely, gentle man. I remember him mostly dressed in a sort of Westernised adaptation of Chinese clothing, but also in the rather stuffy fashions of the British colonial 1890s."

"How amazing!"

"But you were right just now, Lola. I don't even know how old he is. I assume you do."

"From what he's told me, yes, and now I've no reason to think it isn't true. Let me see, I'm useless with numbers. He said he was born – this still sounds so ridiculous – in 1427. So that makes him–"

"Five hundred and eighty-two!" gasped Lily. "My God, am I going to live that long?"

"Barring accidents, why not?"

"What do you mean?"

"Well, John has always taken great pains to explain to me that he's not immortal, that he can be killed like anyone else. In fact, he had two sons who were like him and like you, but they were both killed."

"When?"

"Long before you were born, Lily. One of them in the French Revolution. I can't remember about the other one, except that he was murdered."

"Oh, Lola, that's terrible. They were my brothers. Do you know if there are any others, others like me?"

"John thinks that Phoebe is – he says it's because of her health and her eyes, which I find all rather disturbing. I mean, you expect – want – your children to outlive you, but to think that one of them might live for hundreds of years, perhaps even more, it's too much to take in."

She paused, distracted.

"I think there was only one other, a daughter, hundreds of years ago. John never met her and he's not even definitely sure she was like you. But the thought of her still worries him if he dwells on it. Do you have a good memory, Lily?"

"Yes, I do, incredibly good. I can remember things from throughout the whole of my life as if they happened yesterday. In great detail."

"John's the same. I think he very often goes back to the past in his mind; the memories are so strong. I sometimes nag him when he's clearly somewhere else. I shouldn't really, poor man, his head must be so full of history."

"But," she said, snapping out of her nostalgia, "his memory isn't brilliant today. Where the hell is he? He's never this unreliable. What a day to choose – the day when his long-lost daughter turns up!"

She picked up her phone and tried her husband's number again. No answer.

She started the engine. "We'd better get back to the gallery; there might be a message from him there and we have to get your stuff."

As they walked through the gallery door minutes later, Lola saw the red message light blinking on the phone. She hit the play button.

'Lola? Are you there? It's Jennifer. Can you pick up? Or if not, call me as soon as you get this? It may be nothing but I saw your car by the road on Back Lane. In the middle of nowhere. The door was unlocked but there was no one around. Is everything OK?'

Lola checked the time of the call. Six twenty-six. Only a few minutes after they'd dumped Lily's luggage and she'd locked up the gallery. It was now seven thirty.

Lily stopped what she was doing with her luggage and hurried over to Lola.

"Who was that?"

"Jennifer Craington. She's an artist friend. Lives up in the hills above Derwent Water. Fairly potty. I'd be surprised if she could recognise her own car if she drove past it, let alone ours. I'll call her now."

As she turned, the phone rang again. Lola checked the number and hit the handsfree button.

"Jennifer! Sorry, I was literally picking up the phone to call you. I've only just got your message."

"Sorry, Lola, I'm sure it's nothing. But when I saw it, I was worried. I thought perhaps you'd broken down."

"You're sure it was our car?"

"Yes, I recognised the damaged bumper from when John had that fight outside the Green Man."

"It wasn't a fight, but it sounds like our car. Where exactly was it?"

"On Back Lane, about halfway along, where the road rises. There's a gated lane on the right going up to the old quarry. Your car was there, just off the road."

"I know where you mean. You say the door was unlocked?"

"Yes, and the keys were still in the ignition. Do you want me to go back, or to fetch you?"

"Thanks, Jennifer, that's very kind, but I've got a friend with me who's got a car. We'll go straight over there now."

"OK, Lola. I hope everything's all right."


"Back Lane?" said Lily, as Lola rang off.

"It's a minor road near our cottage. I often use it as a short cut to avoid Keswick if I'm going to Penrith."

"Oh," said Lily, none the wiser. "Well, we'd better get straight over there."

"Yes," replied Lola distantly.

"You look worried, Lola. Do you think there's a problem?"

"I don't know. John is very fastidious about locking the car. He would never, ever, walk away from it with the keys in the ignition and the doors unlocked."

She looked over at Lily's luggage.

"We'd better sling your stuff back in your car, anyway," she said, without any enthusiasm. "The B&B's in the same direction."

"Forget my stuff; we'll get it later," said Lily. "We need to get over to the car. And this time, I'll drive; I think I've got the idea now."

She had. They jumped into the car and raced out of the village back in the direction they'd just come from. Shortly before the turning they'd taken earlier to the Andrews' cottage, Lola pointed out a fork to the right.

"That's Back Lane," she said.

Lily braked hard and swung the car across the road.

"You certainly are getting the hang of it, Lily," said Lola, hanging on tightly to her seat. "I imagine driving around New York with you is quite an experience."

Lily laughed. "Speedy Saunders, they call me!"

Two miles along the road, they saw the Volvo. Lily pulled up a little way back from it and they got out. Lola marched off in the direction of the car, but Lily called out for her to stop.

"We should check around the car, not disturb anything."

"Why?" frowned Lola. "What do you think's happened?"

"I don't know, but I think we should be careful."

"Well, Jennifer was here before us so it's already disturbed," pointed out Lola.

"Even so," cautioned Lily.

A padlocked metal gate barred the track leading off the uphill side of the road. There was a 'No Access' sign to one side. The fence that ran along that side of the road was overgrown with brambles, while behind and below them, running along the downhill side of the road, was a stream: St. John's Beck.

Lola peered through the car's passenger window.

"Jennifer was right," she said. "I can see the keys. And there's John's phone! It's sitting in the well between the seats. No wonder there's been no answer."

"Look at this, Lola," called Lily from beyond the front of the car. Lola walked along to where she was standing.

"Look! See those tyre prints in the soft ground? They're from big tyres, must have been a sizeable vehicle, like an SUV – an Explorer or something."

"Right little Sherlock Holmes, aren't you?"

Lily nodded absently as her eyes continued to scan around the area. "I never was much of a scientist, but I love all those crime scene shows on the TV."

"They leave me cold, I'm afraid," said Lola, puckering her lips.

"What does it mean?"

"Well, the tyre prints are fresh. Could Papa have driven here and then gone off in another car?"

"Why would he do that?"

"I've no idea. Lola, do you think we should call the police?"

"The police?"

"Yes. Something's not right here. I mean, think about it. We have Papa disappearing from the exhibition with some stranger but then instead of going on to the gallery, they've driven here where your car's been abandoned with the keys and Papa's phone left in it. And there are definite signs of another car, a big one."

Lily saw the look of fear in Lola's eyes and realised she'd made her point rather forcefully. "Look," she said, putting a hand on Lola's arm, "that sounded a bit alarmist. There's probably some perfectly rational explanation."

"No," said Lola, shaking her head. "You're absolutely right. We should call the police. God, you don't think John's been kidnapped, do you?"

"Kidnapped! Why?"

"I don't know. A lot of strange things have been happening lately."

"What sort of things?"

"Odd people turning up at the gallery, asking questions about John. Wanting samples from him. Asking difficult questions about his work, linking it with some of his earlier work from years ago."

"You mean like I did in the States? From before he was John Andrews?"

"Yes. It worried John because, unlike you, they weren't people who should know."

Lola took out her phone. "What am I going to say?"

"Tell them your husband's gone missing and you're worried. Tell them that you've found his car abandoned."

Lola sighed. "I know the police. They'll be all condescending and tell me not to worry while thinking he's gone off with his girlfriend."

"Call them, Lola."

Lola looked at the phone. "I can't just call 999. They'll think it's a prank."

"If that's like our 911, then, yes, you can. Here, let me do it." She held out her hand for the phone, but Lola kept hold of it, shrugged her shoulders and punched the numbers.

"Hello, er, police please. Yes. I want to … what? My name? Er, it's Lola Andrews. Mrs. Yes. It's about my husband. What? Um, Thirlmere View Cottage, Pott's Lane, near Legburthwaite. What? What's happened to him? I'm trying to tell you! Look, I know this sounds crazy, but I think he's been kidnapped. Yes, kidnapped. Where? I'm on Back Lane, er, the B5322, north of Thirlmere. His car's here, abandoned, and the keys are in it. I'm really worried. Can you send someone? OK, yes, I'll wait here. No, I won't touch anything. Yes. Thank you."

She rang off.

"Why do they make you feel like a criminal?"

"Shall we sit in my car while we wait?" suggested Lily.

Lola nodded and they walked back to the car. Lily opened the passenger door for her and Lola slumped into the seat.

"What did you mean by 'samples' just now?" asked Lily as she sat in the driver's seat.

"Samples? Oh, yes. There was a young woman who turned up at the gallery pretending to be interested in John's paintings, but then she said she wanted a sample for DNA testing."

"For DNA testing? What, out of the blue, she turned up and asked him for a sample?"

"No, not out of the blue. She'd tracked him down. John'd had to give a sample to the police. Somebody had driven into him in the car park outside a pub near the gallery and there'd been an argument. But the police officer who turned up decided it was a fight and he arrested John and the other bloke. They both had to give samples for DNA testing."

"Wow! I'd heard the laws in your country were pretty strict, but I didn't know they could do that."

"Yeah, bloody police state."

"So who was this girl?"

"She was the scientist who tested his DNA. She said it was pretty unusual and she wanted to do some more tests."

"They give out your names as well?"

"No, they certainly don't. She was way out of line and John told her so. Sent her packing. But she bought a painting, one of John's old lady ones. Then, coincidence again, a chap turned up a few days later saying he was an expert in forgery and asking John all sorts of questions about copying paintings. He spotted the similarity between John's work and Moretti's and commented on it to John."

Lily stared at the car in front of them.

"Do you think all this might be connected?"

"It could be, but I don't see how."

"No, nor do I. You know, I don't think we can tell the police much of this. They'd want to know what was so special about Papa, and we certainly can't tell them that. They'd think we were crazy."

"Yeah, probably suggest he'd been kidnapped by little green aliens."

"You know," she added, "the other thing that's odd. John was in Keswick and apparently heading for the gallery. He wouldn't come this way. And even if he did, the car's facing in the wrong direction. It doesn't make any sense."

They both started as they heard a siren getting louder as a police car raced down the lane from behind them.

They got out of the car and waited while PC Jeff Roberts put on his cap and got out of the patrol car.

"I can see they're really taking this seriously," said Lola quietly to Lily, "sending the village bobby."

"Mrs Lola Andrews?" asked Roberts, looking at a form on a clipboard as he walked towards them.

"Yes," said Lola.

"And?" he said, looking at Lily, his eyes wandering over her figure.

"Lily Saunders. Mrs."

"So, what's all this about a kidnapping, Mrs Andrews?"

He paused. "Andrews? What's your husband's first name?"

"John."

"Artist? Likes his drink?"

Lola sighed, "You're not going to tell me you were the one who arrested him in Grasmere a few weeks ago, are you?"

"That's confidential information, madam, I can't answer that."

"I think you just have," she said.

Once they had shown Roberts the unlocked car, taking great

pains to explain how careful they had been not to touch anything, he started to take their worries seriously. He asked Lola if she had a spare key. She found it in her bag and gave it to him. He carefully opened the boot, sighing quietly in relief when he saw there was no body in it. He called in to his control and was given his orders: touch nothing and wait for CID.

The duty CID inspector from Keswick arrived within twenty minutes along with a female sergeant. They were sympathetic but doubtful about the possibility of a kidnap. Knowing about the fight, they asked about John's drinking habits but Lola explained that he hardly drank at all. Nevertheless, PC Roberts was despatched to check the muddy lane beyond the gate and to walk down to the river. He returned saying there were no fresh footprints and no sign of anyone.

After much questioning and form filling, they began to wind up.

"A lot of people go missing, Mrs Andrews, for all sorts of reasons. We normally don't do anything for at least twenty-four hours, unless there's good reason to."

"Such as?" asked Lola.

"Well, if it was a kidnapping, the kidnappers would likely be in touch fairly quickly about a ransom."

"A ransom? We don't have any money."

"So you've said, Mrs Andrews. And you can't think of any other reason why your husband would be kidnapped?"

"None at all."

"Your husband does know your mobile number, doesn't he, madam?"

"Of course he does."

"It's just that with speed dialing and phone memories, a lot of people don't know numbers you'd think they would know. I can never remember my wife's phone number."

"He knows it, I'm sure."

"Well, in case they phone your house, assuming that you're right and this is a kidnapping, I suggest you return home and wait. I can arrange for your gallery phone to be diverted to your home as well, if you like. Then all calls can come to one place."

"I can do that myself, inspector, I'll only need to call into the gallery on the way home and press a couple of buttons."

"If you do hear anything, Mrs Andrews, please let us know immediately. And if your husband calls from anywhere …"

"I understand what you're saying, inspector, but I know he hasn't run off with his fancy woman. Trust me."

"I'm sure you're right, madam," he said, without conviction.

He gave her a card. "Meanwhile, I'm afraid you can't have your car until the SOCOs have had a look at it. That won't happen until tomorrow. If I could borrow your spare key, I can lock the car, so it should be safe enough. I'll get PC Roberts to photograph those tyre prints so we can find out what sort of car left them."

It was after ten thirty and the long summer evening's light had almost gone. As Lily drove Lola back to the gallery to set the telephone and to collect her luggage, she noticed Lola was wringing her hands with worry.

"That was some ordeal, Lola. I think we both need a drink. Look, it'll be OK, you know."

"I don't know; the more I think about it, the more I worry."

Lily thought back through their conversation of earlier.

"These people you mentioned, the young woman who turned up asking about DNA, and the forgery expert who noticed the similarity between Papa's paintings and the Morettis, d'you know if they left their names or contact numbers?"

"No, I don't. If they left business cards, John will probably have chucked them where he chucks all cards – in a big box in the counter drawer. It's his filing system."

Lily smiled. "I think we should take a look. If there are numbers, one or both of them might well be worth talking to."

When they arrived back at the gallery, Lola checked the telephone for messages, but there were none. She pressed a few buttons to divert calls to her home.

"Where's this box of calling cards?" asked Lily.

"I'll fetch it, and I'll get John's address book as well. Sometimes he writes phones numbers in it in his elegant copperplate."

Lily laughed. "Just like mine, by the sounds of it. He taught me!"

"Listen," said Lola. "Let's take the box and the address book back home. I really need a drink and there's nothing here."

She laid a hand on Lily's arm. "Lily, I'm feeling really twitched by all this. Would you mind staying the night at our place? There's plenty of room and I'd really like to have someone there."

"Of course," said Lily. "But I doubt I'll sleep much. What with jetlag and all that'd happened, I'm running on pure adrenaline, but some red wine would help."

Lola smiled. "Thanks. I'll call Madge Cooper and explain."

Arriving back at the cottage, there was a note from Kitty to say the girls were sleeping at her house.

"That's good," said Lola, checking her watch. "I won't disturb her now; she goes to bed quite early."

They suddenly realised they were both starving, so while Lola put together some bread, pickles and cheese, Lily went where she was directed to fetch a bottle of wine and poured them both a glass.

They settled on a large soft sofa in the living room. Lily put down her glass and pulled over the box of name cards. There were dozens. She took out a handful and flicked through some.

"Pass me some," said Lola, holding out a hand. She studied the names. "I don't know why John keeps these things; they must go back years. He never does anything with them."

"Well, let's hope his hoarding comes up trumps," replied Lily, tossing the ones she'd read into the upturned lid.

After a few minutes, Lily found what she was looking for. "This could be one of them," she said, holding up the card. "Does the name 'Claudia Reid' ring a bell?"

"Yes, I think that was her," said Lola, looking up.

Lily read from the card. "'Claudia Reid, B.Sc.; Ph.D. Senior Biochemist, Forensic Science Service, West Midlands.' Is that far away, Lola?"

"About three hours' drive, at a guess. Two, the way you drive. Are there any phone numbers?"

"Yes, there're a couple of office numbers with extensions, but there's no cell number."

She turned the card over. "Oh wait, there's another number handwritten on the back. Is that a cell phone number? – I don't understand the system in your country." She handed the card to

Lola.

"Yes, it is," said Lola. "P'raps she fancied John and gave him her personal number."

"Perhaps she thought he might change his mind and offer a sample, and she wouldn't necessarily want to take that call at work," suggested Lily. "Hand me your phone, Lola, I'll try calling this number. We can see what this Dr Reid has to say for herself."

Lola checked the time. "It's nearly midnight, Lily."

"Look, Lola, if she's involved in all this, she hardly going to be tucked up in bed; she's going to be talking to Papa about whatever it is she wants."

"In which case, she's hardly going to answer the phone."

"Won't know till we try. But my thought process is that if she's not involved, unless she's out partying, she might be in bed asleep. If it seems that we've woken her up, that would kind of indicate she's not involved."

Lily punched in the number into Lola's cordless house phone. After six rings, a sleepy voice answered. "Hello?"

Lily smiled at Lola, putting her hands together by her head to mime someone sleeping.

"Am I speaking with Dr Reid?" she said.

"Yes," came the cautious reply.

"Dr Claudia Reid?"

"Yes. Who's calling?"

"I'm a friend of John Andrews."

"John Andrews?" The tone was guarded.

"Yes, John Andrews. The artist. I believe you've had some dealings with him."

"Well, I bought a painting from him. When I was in the Lakes." The voice was more alert now. "I bought a painting at his gallery. It was a portrait that reminded me of my grandmother."

Too much information, thought Lily. This girl's worried.

"You didn't only buy a painting from him, Dr Reid, did you? You took some photographs of other paintings in his gallery. His daughter saw you."

"Yes, I did. So what? That's hardly a reason to call me up in the middle of the night."

"You're a DNA specialist aren't you, Dr Reid?"

Silence.

"Dr Reid?"

"Yes."

"What's your main area of interest in that field – research?"

"Yes and no. I mean, I do some research, but my main work is DNA Profiling. Look, what's this all about? Who are you?"

"Have you tested John Andrews' DNA, Dr Reid?"

"I, er, no. I mean, I don't know. I have no way of telling. The samples we test aren't identifiable to an individual. It's all part of the confidentiality of the system."

"So you're saying that when you, as a DNA specialist, turned up at John Andrews' gallery to buy a painting and photograph others, that was all a coincidence, was it?"

"Yes, it was. Why shouldn't it be? I have an ordinary life outside the laboratory just like other people. Why shouldn't I go to an art gallery and buy a painting?"

"Why would John have your business card?"

"I often leave my business card when I do business with people."

"And scribble your private number on the back?"

"Yes. I don't like using my work phone for personal calls."

"You were expecting a personal call from John?" Lily looked across at Lola as she said this. Lola raised her eyebrows.

"No, I–"

"Dr Reid, I don't believe you. I think you tested John's DNA, and you found it to be odd, unusual, different in some way. You then used your connections to find out who he was and contacted him. Isn't that illegal, Dr Reid?"

There was no answer.

"Dr Reid. Would you answer me, please?"

"Look, who are you? Will you please explain why you are making this call in the middle of the night?"

"John Andrews has gone missing, Dr Reid."

"Missing?"

"Yes, it looks like he might have been kidnapped. So I think you have some explaining to do."

"Kidnapped!" She sounded genuinely shocked to Lily's ear. "What do you mean, 'explaining'?" She was indignant now. "I don't know anything about any kidnapping. When did this happen?"

Lily could hear the worried tone in Claudia's voice through the protests.

"It happened earlier on this evening. The police are involved. He was taken from his car and they are searching for fingerprints as we speak. We're seeing the police first thing in the morning to tell them all we know about his recent dealings – customers and so on. And we'll certainly be mentioning your name."

More silence. "Look, I told you, I know nothing about any kidnapping and I'd really rather you didn't mention my name to the police, at least until we've had a chance to talk some more."

"Why are you so worried about the police being told your name, Dr Reid?"

"I think you know very well," muttered Claudia, guiltily. "Listen, where are you?"

"I'm at his cottage with his wife. More to the point, where are you?" said Lily.

"I live in Warwickshire. If I leave now, I could be with you in about three and a half hours, especially at this time of night."

"You're coming straight away?" asked Lily, surprised.

"If you think John Andrews has been kidnapped, then you don't want to waste time. I'll be there. How do I get to the cottage?"

"I'll pass the phone to John's wife to give you directions," said Lily.

# Chapter 30

Claudia stared at her phone in shock and disbelief. "Shit!" she yelled in frustration. "Shit! Shit! Shit!"

What the hell had happened? She'd told no one about the results from the previous Sunday night and she was convinced neither Sally nor Ced would have said anything. As for the prof, he had been adamant that they keep it to themselves; he had been the first to realise the implications for John Andrews. He wouldn't go back on his word now. Would he?

They had all agreed they needed time to absorb the implications of the findings. The prof wanted to pore over the data line by line, check all the procedures, reassess everything manually. Claudia and Sally had taken printouts of the data home with them to do the same. Claudia looked at the large pile of papers by the bed. She'd scrutinised them for hour upon hour but had found nothing wrong.

Ced had wanted to run a huge set of comparisons of John Andrews' work against as many fine art images from the fifteenth century onwards as he could lay his hands on. He wanted to find out how many artists through the centuries fell into the 'John Andrews group'. But it would take time; he certainly wouldn't have finished yet. They'd all agreed to contact each other once they'd finished and then discuss the way forward.

She shook her head in disbelief. How could Andrews have been kidnapped?

She looked at the phone still in her hand and decided she had to call Sal. She checked the time. Midnight. She hit the first number of the speed dial and then remembered. It was Saturday night and both

Sally and Ced had a mini-triathlon early Sunday morning in the depths of Cheshire. They would have been in bed hours ago. She couldn't possibly disturb them, especially since Ced had been moaning about his training having gone down the tubes along with the professor's whisky.

Who was the woman? She'd sounded American and she'd been as aggressive as a cop from some detective series.

She went to the bathroom and splashed water onto her face. She stared into the mirror. Had all this happened because she'd bent the rules and tracked down John Andrews? Was she to blame if he'd now been kidnapped? Were they going to tell the police about what she'd done? She had to get up to the Lakes as fast as possible.

She threw on some jeans, a T-shirt and a thin cotton jacket, pulled a brush through her hair, grabbed her keys, purse and mobile phone and ran out to her car.

Lola was dozing fitfully in the armchair when she saw the car headlights. She looked over at the clock: three fifteen. If that was the Reid girl, she'd made good time.

She opened the front door to the cottage. The outside light had come on, bathing Claudia's car in a fierce white light as it drew up near to where Lily had left her rental. Lola watched her get out and recognised the small, slightly built young woman from when she had seen her in the gallery a few weeks before. She seemed flustered as she juggled with her things, dropping her purse as her fingers sought out the key fob to lock the door.

"There's no need to lock it; it's pretty quiet around here," called Lola quietly, not having to raise her voice in the silence of the night.

"Oh, OK," said Claudia, picking up her purse. She walked over to where Lola was standing.

"I'm Claudia Reid," she said, her eyes wary as she tried to see Lola's face in the glare of the light shining straight at her.

"We've met," replied Lola, an edge to her voice.

"Yes," said Claudia, with a weak smile, "at the gallery. You came in with your children."

"You'd better come in," said Lola, turning and walking into the house. She headed for the kitchen. "You made good time. Would you like some coffee? I'm making some for myself."

"Thanks, I'd love some. The motorways were quiet and your directions were perfect. I was worried I'd get lost on all these dark roads, but I found you straight away."

Lola nodded as she spooned the coffee into the plunger pot. Spilling some of the ground coffee, she angrily grabbed a cloth to wipe it up. She wanted to shout at this naïve-looking young woman, scream at her, ask her what the hell she thought she was doing. She grasped the counter top with both hands, trying to calm down.

"Can I help?" asked Claudia.

"No!" snapped Lola. "I'm perfectly capable of making coffee."

Claudia took a step back.

"Is there … is there any news? About your husband?"

"No, nothing."

Claudia heard a movement behind her and turned to see a yawning Lily coming through the door from the living room.

"You must be Dr Reid," said Lily, rubbing her eyes. "I'm Lily Saunders. We spoke on the phone."

"Hello," said Claudia, hesitantly holding out her hand. "Please call me ... Claudia." The last word was almost lost as she noticed Lily's eyes.

Lily saw the question on Claudia's face but said nothing. She turned to Lola. "Is there enough in the pot for me, Lola?"

"Plenty," said Lola, still trying to control her emotions.

Sensitive to Lola's mood, Lily took three mugs from a rack and placed them on a tray. "Do you take milk? Sugar?" she asked Claudia.

"No, neither, thanks," replied Claudia almost inaudibly.

Lily put the coffee pot on the tray and picked it up. "OK, let's go through," she said with a nod towards the living room door.

They sat – Lily and Lola on the long sofa, Claudia in the armchair. Claudia took her coffee and sipped at it, feeling the instant buzz of the caffeine.

"OK, Claudia," said Lily, sitting back and taking charge, "time to spill the beans. What's going on?"

Claudia took a deep breath. "I told you on the phone that I know nothing about any kidnapping. I've been racking my brains all the way up here trying to make sense of it. Honestly, it was a total shock."

"It may have been," said Lily evenly, "but it's too much of a coincidence that soon after you came up here asking about DNA samples, someone else turned up claiming to be a forgery expert–"

"Ced," interrupted Claudia.

"What?"

"Ced. Cedric Fisher. He's called Ced."

"You know him?"

"Yes, I do."

"I thought so. Right, Dr Claudia Reid, senior biochemist, from the beginning, please."

Claudia looked cautiously at the two women. Lola's face was dark and brooding, her eyes staring piercingly at her; Lily was serious, business-like.

She began by telling them about her results and how strange they were. She tried to explain about DNA profiling, about junk DNA and her research, but it came out rather garbled – the intensity of their stares was making her nervous.

"So let me get this clear, Claudia," said Lily. "You're saying that when you got these results, they were so strange that you felt you couldn't ignore them. You had to follow them up."

"That's right."

"So why didn't you go through formal channels? Why did you resort to seeking out John yourself? Were you worried that someone else would steal the limelight? That this 'discovery' of yours would be claimed by one of your colleagues?"

"No, that's not it at all," replied Claudia indignantly. "Well, not really. It's simply that there are no formal channels; these findings are unprecedented. But I was concerned that even with these results, my research interests wouldn't be taken seriously so I decided to make my own enquiries while I conducted some more tests. The problem was that the personal information was totally confidential. It's a very sensitive matter. I couldn't just press a key on the computer and look up the name and address."

"So you broke all the rules by finding out where it came from."

"I knew that it was from Cumbria, because that information is in the ledger, as was the name of the submitting police officer."

"So you called him up and he told you John's name?" said Lola incredulously, her eyes flashing. "So much for confidentiality!"

"No, it wasn't like that. Sally recognised his name."

"Sally?" asked Lily.

"She's a friend, also a biochemist, who works in a forensic lab; a different one from mine. She's Ced's girlfriend."

"This gets cosier and cosier," said Lola sarcastically.

Claudia paused to glance at her and then continued. "She knew the police officer, PC Roberts. She'd, well–"

"Roberts?" frowned Lily, turning to Lola. "Wasn't that the name of the Romeo we met earlier? The one who was undressing us with his eyes?"

"That sounds like him," said Claudia.

"So your friend Sally put in a good word for you and he told you what you wanted to know," said Lola. "Well, his days with the police are numbered."

"No, he didn't tell me. Sally called him – she was worried he'd arrest me, report me, that I'd lose my job."

"I'd still be worried if I were you," growled Lola.

Claudia recoiled slightly, the remark striking home.

"Sally persuaded him that I was well-intentioned and he agreed to give me a hard time and send me packing. But something I said about DNA and research set him thinking. He's got a son with a genetic abnormality, apparently. He still didn't give me the name, but he told me enough for me to narrow it down to your husband."

"But he wasn't interested," said Lily.

"No, definitely not. He gave me a hard time too. Threatened to report me, but then said he was willing to forget it if I stopped there and went no further. He was about to boot me out of the gallery when you turned up." She looked at Lola. "That's when I bought the painting."

"Why did you do that?" said Lola.

"No reason other than I loved it. I don't know anything about art but I could see that it was very special. I'd never seen anything like it. I couldn't really afford it but I bought it anyway."

"And you snapped away at others in the gallery," said Lola accusingly.

"Yes, I did. I don't really know why. I wouldn't normally do that sort of thing. But I was so impressed by the paintings, and I was fairly overwrought – it had been a tense day with a shredding by PC

Roberts and then one by your husband. I just did it. It was for positive reasons. I thought Ced would be interested."

"Sounds like you and this Ced person have quite a thing going," muttered Lola.

"What? No, not at all. He's Sally's boyfriend; they're crazy about each other. I love him dearly, but not like that. Sally's my best and oldest friend."

"OK," smiled Lola thinly, "you've convinced me. What did your Ced think of the painting?"

"He loved it. Borrowed it immediately to get a set of hi-res images for his program."

"Program?"

"He's a forensic art expert. He's brilliant. He's written a program that analyses paintings and compares them with artists. It's incredible."

"He's the one who turned up later at the gallery and spoke to John?" said Lola.

"Yes. But that was after I saw John's face in a painting."

"What?"

"Well, when Ced saw the painting I'd bought, he explained to me all about the technique, how like the old masters it was. He thought it was quite exceptional. He dug out this book to show me with a lot of paintings by a Renaissance artist, um, Piero della Francesca, and in one of them, it's called 'The Awakening', I saw that one of the faces of the figures in it looked exactly like your husband's."

"And what did your friend Ced think of that?" asked Lily.

"He wanted to see John for himself. He was astounded by the likeness. So he came up here, to the gallery. That's where he saw the other paintings."

"What other paintings?" said Lola.

"The landscapes, the ones in the window. He said they reminded him of another artist's work. So he talked to your husband about technique. You see, Ced's field is art forgery, he–"

"He thinks John is a forger?" yelled Lola.

Claudia began to feel that everything she said was digging a bigger hole.

"He wanted to make hi-res images of his other paintings, to test his program, because John's technique was so like the old masters.

But John wouldn't let him; he got quite angry. He wouldn't even sell him a painting."

"I remember," said Lola. "I was cross with John."

She snapped her fingers as something fell into place. "But Ced did get hold of it, didn't he, that and some others. That young woman who bought the portrait of Phoebe along with the landscape and the sunset, she was Sally wasn't she? This Ced Fisher person sent her here to buy them. Am I right?"

Claudia nodded.

"Why? Why was he so keen to buy them?"

"He'd used his program to compare my painting with the pictures I took of the landscapes, and with the other artist whose works he thought they were similar to, and he couldn't tell them apart. His program couldn't distinguish John's work from this other artist."

"Who was…?" asked Lola, although she knew the answer.

"Er, Moretti, Francesco Moretti?"

Lola nodded in understanding. "And then?" she said.

"Well, then he found some other paintings by other artists that he also couldn't tell apart from your husband's work."

"Other artists?"

"Yes, he was in the middle of a forgery case in his lab, and because he was getting strange results with the Moretti, he put the images of the genuine paintings he was using as controls from the case into the comparison routine. More to test it than anything. And he found another he couldn't distinguish."

"Strange," said Lola rather dismissively.

"Yes," replied Claudia, "and since then he's found some more. It's been very upsetting."

"Upsetting! Poor thing! My husband's been kidnapped and your Ced is upset because his bloody program doesn't work. Perhaps his program's no good."

"No," said Claudia quietly, "his program's fine."

"Then explain it," snapped Lola.

"I can't."

"Can't or won't," said Lily quietly.

"What do you mean?" said Claudia, unable to keep the guilt out of her face.

368

"Claudia; your emotions are written all over your face. And what I'm reading right now is that you are not telling us everything."

"I have!" protested Claudia. "I've been very honest with you."

"So far, perhaps, but there's more, isn't there? More than just you got inquisitive over a result and you broke the law to track down the reluctant donor of the sample that gave the result, and more than that your best friend's boyfriend's written a computer program that should be good but is now baffling him. None of that leads us further down the road to discover what's happened to John, why he's been kidnapped. There's still a huge gap in the middle of this story. Tell us what else has happened, Claudia. You're a scientist who wanted to know all about John's DNA. What have you found out?"

Claudia's shoulders sagged.

"There have been some more tests done, on another sample of John's DNA," she said meekly.

"Where did you get that from?" demanded Lola angrily.

"From an envelope."

"You stole John's mail?"

"No! He gave me a sealed envelope with the description of the painting I bought. He licked the flap to seal it. I'd used all the original sample from the police in the profiling. Then I remembered the envelope."

"And what did your new tests tell you?"

Claudia paused. "Look, I … I promised I wouldn't tell."

"For God's sake!" yelled Lola. "My husband's been kidnapped, his life might be in danger and you may be responsible, directly or indirectly. And you're telling us that there's something you've found out that you don't want to tell us? This is serious, Dr Reid! So either you tell us or I get on the phone right now to the police and tell them about you. I've no doubt they will be able to get the truth out of you soon enough, before they send you off to prison for breach of the Official Secrets Act, or whatever law protects your database!"

Lily saw the tremor on Claudia's lower lip. She leaned forward and laid a hand on her arm.

"Claudia, you've come a long way in a hurry tonight because you're worried about John and because you think you might be responsible in some way for what's happened to him. You've been very forthcoming so far with your account. There are no secrets now, Claudia. You have to finish it off."

Claudia retrieved a tissue from her jeans pocket, wiped her eyes and blew her nose.

"I'm sorry," she said. "It's all so difficult and confusing." She turned to Lola.

"Lola, how much do you know about your husband?"

"Whatever do you mean?" frowned Lola.

"I mean, where he comes from, what his background is."

"That's none of your business," said Lola defensively.

"It's just that ... well ... let me put it this way. I took the DNA sample from the envelope to my old professor in London. He's an expert in immune systems, in the genetics of immunity. I told him about what I'd found. He was initially very reluctant to carry out any tests. He has to be very careful over privacy and permissions. He realised that I'd ... bent the rules," – Lola shifted on the sofa and gave a snort – "but finally he agreed to do one screening test. I mean, it was a bit of a shot in the dark whether the unusual structures in John's DNA would have any connection to immunity. We agreed that if there was anything, we'd have to go to John to explain things and try to get some more sample. In the interests of genetics research."

"I can imagine what John's answer would have been if you'd tried that," said Lola.

"Exactly what I said," agreed Claudia. "Well, the results were very interesting. It was a screen to indicate enhanced or reduced immunity to ten different diseases. John's DNA showed total immunity for all ten. I mean total. Off the scale. For that to happen for one of the conditions is almost unprecedented; for ten, it's unimaginable."

"So I'll bet your professor got all excited with that and wanted to do more," said Lola, unable to keep the sarcasm out of her voice.

"Um, yes," nodded Claudia, chewing her lip.

"I really feel as if I'm betraying a confidence here," she added, but noticing the cold glare on Lola's face, she continued.

"Well, you realise, even from that one test, what it might mean," she said, but neither Lily nor Lola said anything or showed any change of expression.

"It means," she continued, "that John must be remarkably healthy. Is that correct, Lola, that he's never ill? Has he, in fact, ever been ill?"

Lola stared at her for what seemed like an age. "Never," she replied at last.

Claudia nodded. "That's what I thought."

"So the professor threw caution and the law to the wind and conducted more tests. Is that right?" said Lily.

"Y-Yes," said Claudia reluctantly, "you could put it like that. There was enough material to carry out three more tests."

"And?"

"Well, that's why I asked you, Lola, about John's background, how much you really know about him."

Lola's face was now set, showing no hint of what she was thinking.

"The thing is, the results indicated something really crazy, I mean, unbelievable. Something so bizarre that you'll think I'm nuts to even voice it."

She took a deep breath. "You see, the results show that John's immune system is perfect. Absolute. This means that he would never, ever be ill. He can't catch any disease. But it means more than that. It means the cells in his body remain in pristine condition; they never mutate or deteriorate. I mean, they get replaced like everyone's, but the replacements are always perfect, never changing. The most profound outcome of this is to do with ageing. John won't age. He will stay young."

She stopped. She had expected them to be surprised, but all she could see were guarded frowns on their faces.

Claudia closed her eyes and sat back in her chair. She shook her head slowly in realisation. "Oh my God!" she said, her voice scarcely more than a whisper, "You know, don't you? You know John's secret!"

She felt the tension drain away. "This means we are correct in our interpretation. Our conclusions are right, aren't they? John really is hundreds of years old!"

Lola finally reacted. She leaned forward and reached out to take Claudia's hand. "Yes, your conclusions are correct. What I, we, really need to know is how many people you have told. Who knows about this, Claudia?"

"Only the four of us. The prof, Sally, Ced and me. No one else. We agreed absolutely that we should tell no one. There are a couple of other people, art experts, who know about Ced's problems with his program. But they have no inkling of why it's giving the unaccountable results for certain artists – that John is, in fact, all these other artists."

"You worked that out, then," said Lola.

"It's the only plausible explanation. Ced's program proved to be truly brilliant after all. It was just that the only explanation for the results was so far off the wall that none of us even considered it."

Her eyes were sparkling now, the enthusiasm of having their conclusions confirmed temporarily eclipsing thoughts of John's kidnapping. She turned her attention from Lola to Lily, realising that Lily had said nothing. She saw a far away look in her eyes. Those eyes. Suddenly everything clarified in her mind.

"Lily?" she said hesitantly.

Lily smiled gently at her, seeing in her eyes that she understood.

"Lily, who exactly are you? You didn't really introduce yourself, apart from your name."

"Who do you think I am?" said Lily, the smile becoming enigmatic.

"It's the eyes. I think so, anyway," said Claudia, now a little flustered. "You're like John, aren't you? You're a relative."

"Yes," laughed Lily, "I'm a relative. But which relative, Claudia? Can you guess?"

"Well, um, you're Asian. No, not completely. Part Asian. Yes. John doesn't appear to be Asian in any way, so you could be his daughter if your mother was Asian."

Lily nodded and then laughed. "Or maybe John has lost his Asian looks through several generations. Perhaps I'm his grandmother, or great grandmother!"

Claudia looked stunned. "Really? Yes, I suppose–"

Lily clapped her hands together, still laughing. "Claudia, it's not too difficult to throw you into confusion is it? You were right first time. I'm John's daughter."

"Then how ol–?"

"How old am I? I shan't ask you to guess this one; it's too difficult. I was born in Hong Kong in 1885. I am like John – who, of course, wasn't John then – in that I am never sick. Your explanation about immune systems, although rather beyond my nonscientific mind, answers many questions."

Claudia gazed at her in wonder. "I don't know what to say. Yes, I do! What about John? How old is he?"

"How's your maths?" said Lola. "Oh, of course, you're a scientist."

"Actually my maths is rubbish; I can't do anything without a calculator," said Claudia.

"Try this one. 1427."

Claudia stared at her as she worked it out. Her eyes widened. "Piero della Francesca?" she asked.

"Mentor and close friend."

"Wow!" gasped Claudia. "Ced will be so thrilled. The first thing he said was that John could have known Piero."

"Lola?" she continued. "Your daughter, the one Sal bought a painting of. Her eyes. Is she…?"

"John thinks so," nodded Lola. "She's never had a day's illness in her life. And believe me, I've given her every opportunity: measles parties, mumps exposure. Sophie's had the lot, but Phoebe – nothing. Not a sniffle, except when she bawls, which she can be very good at."

She paused. "Claudia, I know this is all a bit gobsmacking; it has been for me, too. Lily and I only met yesterday afternoon and John has no idea she's even here. But we really have got to concentrate on what might have happened to John."

"John doesn't know you're here?"

"No," said Lily. "It's a long story, Claudia, one we must leave until later. I last saw my father in 1905, when I was twenty years old."

"Oh my God!"

"Yes, which is why I'm so anxious to get to the bottom of this and find him. As is Lola."

"Yes, of course, but I–"

"Claudia," said Lola matter-of-factly, "I'm now perfectly willing to accept that you know nothing about any kidnapping so there's no need to continue being defensive. What we've got to do is work out why John might have been kidnapped."

"What we need to know," added Lily, "is what could be gained by kidnapping him. What would the discovery of my father's DNA, and mine, mean in terms of genetic research, genetic engineering? Although I don't really understand what that term means."

Claudia leaned forward to explain.

"Working out how your DNA gives you your perfect immune system could have unbelievably profound implications for all sorts of medical research. It could provide a way of treating many diseases, not necessarily with a view to giving people eternal youth or extended lives, although inevitably you'd expect that people would live longer, but–"

She broke off and gasped, her hand flying to her mouth.

"Oh my God, do you think that someone has found out about John and kidnapped him to be some sort of guinea pig, someone they can study further?"

"I think we have to assume that, Claudia."

Claudia shook her head.

"But there's no need to do that! All they would need is a larger sample from John. Some more blood would be ideal. But not much – a hundred millilitres would be more than enough for endless research."

Lily smiled. "You're thinking like an honest scientist. But don't you see, every researcher in this field in the world would want to get his hands on John's blood, and mine, come to think of it, if they knew about me. The outcome of the sort of research you mentioned would be worth untold millions to whoever got there first – drug companies for instance, not a few of whom are more than willing to resort to underhand practices to improve their profit line. Worse, there could be rich individuals who want to keep the knowledge to themselves. Think of the power they could wield."

"You mean they'd be thinking of it as a sort of elixir of eternal youth?" said Claudia. "Yes, that would be worth a lot, although you can't just change someone's DNA. You're making it sound like some sort of James Bond movie, with an evil baddie trying to become immortal and rule the world forever."

"A bit melodramatic, put like that," said Lily, "but yes, it's possible."

"So," said Lola, "if we assume for a moment that someone has found out about your results, who could that be and how have they found out?"

Claudia frowned. "As I said earlier, there's just the four of us. I know that I haven't told a soul, and I'm convinced that neither Sally nor Ced would either. But equally, I'm also convinced that the prof wouldn't. I mean, he's a bit eccentric, but he's totally honest."

"Tell me about where he works. What's the security like?" said Lola.

Claudia thought about it. "The security is very tight indeed. Actually, it's a slightly odd set-up. It's affiliated to Kings, but that's only for the secondment of research students. The lab is privately funded, I'm not sure by whom, and it operates quite independently of the college. But the prof is happy because he's free to devote himself to his research full-time."

"But presumably he's accountable to someone," said Lola. "He must have to deliver something."

"Yes, of course," replied Claudia, "but there are breakthroughs all the time in his field. Most of them are minor in the scheme of things, but they would be enough to keep his sponsors happy."

"I think it could be worthwhile speaking with your professor, don't you?" said Lily. "He might have got overexcited and talked to someone; someone who has bigger and grander ideas."

Claudia shrugged. "I suppose it's possible. But I know Frank Young; I really don't think he would be involved in anything criminal."

"Maybe not intentionally, but brilliant academics can sometimes be a tad naïve when it comes to dealing with the real world," added Lola, looking pointedly at Claudia.

Claudia blushed.

"So what's our plan of action?" asked Lily. "It's four fifteen in the morning now and I think we all have to get some rest, especially if we've got a lot of driving to do. Will your professor be beavering away later on today? It is Sunday."

"He's probably in the lab now – he often works late and stays overnight," said Claudia. "I'm pretty sure he'll be there – I'll check first thing in the morning."

"Then I suggest we drive down to London and pay him a visit. What do you think, Lola?"

Lola was unsure. "I'm supposed to be seeing the police. And there's also the possibility that John will call, either the gallery or here. And then there are the girls. I don't know what to do."

"I suggest you sleep on it, but it sounds like it would be better if you stayed here. We can keep in touch by phone," said Lily. "One thing occurs to me, Claudia. Has the professor ever seen Papa?"

"Papa? Oh, sorry, I forgot. No, I don't think he has."

"In that case, he won't make any connection between Papa and me, from the eyes, I mean. I'd rather keep him in the dark over that one; the fewer people who know, the better."

"Yes, I agree," said Claudia. "Although it might be better if you didn't meet him for the moment. We'd have to explain why you'd suddenly been brought into the loop, and if by some remote chance he is involved in John's kidnapping, that could be very dangerous for you. But there's no reason why you shouldn't come. After all, we're trying to find out where John might be and if we do I'm sure you'll want to be involved with trying to rescue him."

"Damn right I will. What about your friends, Ced and Sally. Do you think they should be in on the visit? Where do they live?"

"They live in Knutsford. It's on the way, not far off the M6. And yes, I think they must be involved. But one problem is that they're taking part in a mini-triathlon first thing in the morning."

"What time will they be finished?"

"It's summer, so it'll start early. I should think it'll be over by 10.30 or 11. They should be home by 11.30. I'll call them before they start to make sure they are."

"OK," said Lola, standing up and stretching. "I'm dead beat, as I'm sure you both are. I'll sort out the beds for you. Lily, I suggest you sleep in the girls' room, but be prepared to be bounced on when they come charging back in the morning. Claudia, I'll put you in the guest room."

As Lily walked to the door to get one of her bags from the car, Lola put a hand on her arm.

"Lily," she said. "He will be all right, won't he?"

Lily put an arm round her.

"He'll be fine, Lola. Don't worry; we'll have him back in no time. He and I have a lot of catching up to do."

She tried to sound calm and reassuring, but after the conversation with Claudia, she felt sick with worry.

# Chapter 31

John was very happy with the way the art exhibition was going - two paintings sold at the Friday evening reception and four more the following morning, the first day of public viewing. At this rate, he might not have to remain at the Keswick Galleries for much longer. He hated exhibitions.

It was now Saturday afternoon and the hall was starting to fill again after the lunch break. Returning from the coffee bar a few steps along the road, John saw a tall, well-groomed man in his early fifties studying the largest of his four unsold landscapes. He put down the paper coffee cup and walked over to the man.

"Hello, I'm John Andrews. Can I help in any way?"

The man straightened and turned, a look of pleasure on his face.

"You're the artist who has produced these masterpieces?" replied the man, holding out his hand and shaking John's firmly. "I'm delighted to meet you. The name's Hastings. Christopher Hastings."

He turned to the display.

"They are truly remarkable, Mr Andrews, I don't think I have ever seen the Lakes reproduced on canvas with such skill. I'm in awe."

"Thank you, Mr Hastings, you are very kind."

"Kindness has nothing to do with it; these are the work of a master. Now, I take it these wretched little stickers indicate that six of these paintings have already been sold?"

"They do, but there are still four remaining."

"Damn, I thought that was the case. I should have come earlier if I'd known." He paused, reflecting on one of the reserved paintings for a moment. "God, I really love that one of Windermere."

He shook his head, accepting the loss.

"Never mind, the unsold ones are equally as brilliant. I especially like this sunset view of Ullswater. One of my favourite lakes, you know. Would you object if I bought all four?"

"Object?" said John, trying to disguise his delight. "Certainly not, Mr Hastings. It's a free world and you are welcome to buy as many as you wish. There is only one constraint that the organisers of the exhibition have imposed, which is that all the paintings remain here on display until the exhibition is over. After that, they can be dispatched by courier to wherever you choose."

"Not a problem, dear fellow. But I wouldn't trust them to a courier; I'll send one of my chaps up with a car to fetch them."

John picked up his order book. "What sort of deposit would you like to leave? Most people seem content to leave about a quarter of the price."

"If you're happy to take a cheque, I'll pay in full right now," smiled Hastings. "I want to make sure of my purchase. And can we put one of those little stickers on each of them? I don't want to raise someone else's hopes by making them think they're still available."

John removed the sheet of stickers from the back of the order book and placed one next to each of the four paintings.

"There we are. Each one is now secure. Might I ask for a contact address in case there's any delay?"

"Yes," replied Hastings. "But let me write your cheque first."

"Thanks," said John as he glanced at the sum on the cheque. He smiled to himself. A very successful day. Perhaps exhibitions weren't so bad, after all.

He opened his order book, his pen poised. "Address?" he asked.

"Oh, yes," replied Hastings, "I'll give you a card." He put his hand to his trouser pocket but stopped as he turned to the paintings again. "The information leaflet says you have a gallery in Grasmere. I assume you have more of your masterpieces on display there?"

John laughed. "There are many paintings there, Mr Hastings, yes."

"Are they all landscapes like these?"

"No, there are also many portraits."

Hastings' eyes danced with joy. "Portraits! My other weakness."

He clasped his hands in front of him. "Mr Andrews. Would it be possible to visit your gallery? I'd really like to see more of your work. As well as buying works for my personal collection, I also want to adorn the reception areas of my company with something special instead of the bland derivative stuff that the so-called interior designers foist on us. I could be in the market to buy quite a few." He nodded encouragingly at John.

John shrugged, smiling as he did. "No time like the present, Mr Hastings. If you like, we could go there now; it's not too far. I've certainly finished here for the day, thanks to you."

Hastings beamed at John like an excited child. "Could we really? That would be wonderful. I was hoping you would agree since I have very limited time. I have to get back to London tonight. We can go in my car, if you like. My driver is waiting along the road."

"Thanks," said John, "but I need to get my car back to my wife for shortly after five. She has to collect our daughters from a friend in Ambleside."

"Ah, the responsibilities of family life. I remember it well, and yet it's over all too soon. Before you know it, your daughters will be borrowing the car rather than asking for a lift."

"Fortunately I have a few years before that happens," smiled John.

He gathered his things and headed for the door with Hastings, waving merrily to Roland McIntyre as he passed him. He couldn't fail to notice the envy on McIntyre's face, but he kept his smile fixed.

"Where's your car, Mr Andrews?" asked Hastings as they walked down the steps to the street. "Jeffrey, my driver, will pick me up here as soon as I call him."

"It's parked right behind the hall. I'll pull out into this road from that turning down there." He pointed along the street.

John left Hastings calling his driver and walked buoyantly to his car, taking out his phone to call Lola as he did. He paused, looked at the keypad and changed his mind. He wanted to see the delight on her face when he told her how successful the day had been.

As he pulled out on to the main road, he saw Hastings standing by the rear door of a black Porsche Cayenne. Hastings waved, indicating that John should pull in front to lead the way, and then jumped into his car.

John took the A591 that led out of the town in the direction of Thirlmere and Grasmere while the Porsche followed close behind. Looking in the rearview mirror, he realised he could see nothing of the car's occupants, its dark glass windows and the angle of the windscreen rendering the view opaque.

Shortly after they passed the right turn that led to John and Lola's cottage, there were signs indicating a left turn onto a minor road that led to Threlkeld. As they drew level with the junction, John noticed the Porsche's headlights suddenly flashing a few times. It slowed, pulling onto the tarmac surface of the corner a few yards beyond the junction. John slowed and pulled to a halt about twenty yards beyond, wondering what the problem was.

He saw the rear nearside door of the Porsche open and Hastings stagger out clutching his mouth and his stomach as he ran towards the wooden fence that bordered the road. John jumped out of the Volvo and ran back to where Hastings was now almost kneeling and apparently vomiting. Out of the corner of his eye, he saw the driver's door open and the driver start to climb out.

"Mr Hastings, whatever's wrong?" called John, putting a hand on his shoulder and bending over him.

Hastings waved an arm behind him, as if to indicate that John should keep clear while he continued to retch into the grass.

"Mr, um, Hastings?" It was the driver who had walked up behind John.

Suddenly Hastings stood up and turned round, all the earlier geniality gone from his face. He pulled a handkerchief from his trouser pocket and wiped his mouth.

"Actually, Mr Andrews, I'm perfectly well. I decided that here was far enough."

"Far enough?" said John, puzzled. "Far enough for what? I don't understand."

"Yes, Mr Andrews, far enough. You see, I don't really have any interest in going to your gallery, despite the attraction of viewing your work."

John took a step back and frowned. "Then what are we doing here? What's going on?"

"Quite simple, Mr Andrews. I came to see you today because I need you to come with me." He glanced around to check that they were sufficiently hidden from any passing traffic by the large body of the Porsche and the open door.

"Go with you? What do you mean? Why should I want to go with you?"

"I'll explain it all in due course, Mr Andrews, but for the moment, I'd appreciate it if you would get into the car."

"I most certainly won't! I have no inten–" John felt a prod in the small of his back and spun round. The driver, who had been joined by a second man who must have been in the front passenger seat of the car, was pointing a gun at him.

John involuntarily lifted his hands away from his body while turning his head back to Hastings. "Have you gone mad? I think you've made a big mistake. Who do you think I am?"

"No mistake, Mr Andrews, I know exactly who you are," replied Hastings calmly. "Now, please, get into the car. We don't want any unpleasantness."

"Unpleasantness? Are you intending to shoot me if I refuse? They'll hear the gunshot echoing around the valleys all the way to Ambleside. You'd never get away with it!"

"Look at the gun, Mr Andrews. It's silenced. If Jeffrey were to fire it, there would only be the slightest of pops," said Hastings curtly. "So, in the car please, before I'm forced to ask Jeffrey to shoot away one of your kneecaps. A very painful injury, I can assure you. It would certainly make your journey most uncomfortable."

His eyes blazed with the look of a man clearly used to getting his own way and to having his orders followed immediately.

"So I suggest you get in. Now!"

"Martin," he called to the second man from the car. "It would be better if Mr Andrews' car weren't quite so prominent. Follow us in it for a couple of miles until there's a suitably quiet spot."

The man called Jeffrey waved the gun at John while standing sufficiently out of reach to prevent John even thinking of trying to knock the gun from his hand. John still didn't move. An increasingly exasperated Hastings took a step towards him and looked him coldly in the eye. "Mr Andrews, if the threat of injury doesn't worry you, before I instruct Jeffrey to go through with it, perhaps the threat of injury to your wife and family will change your mind. I can easily send Martin here over to Grasmere to pay your wife a visit."

John took a step towards Hastings. "You hurt my family, Hastings and I'll–" He stopped as the gun was again prodded firmly into his back.

"Really, Mr Andrews," growled Hastings, "you're in no position to start threatening me. Now get into the car; we're wasting time!"

John reluctantly climbed into the car, taking the seat behind the driver. Hastings took the gun from Jeffrey and climbed into the front passenger seat. As Jeffrey closed the driver's door, John heard the locks click. He was trapped.

Both cars swung in tight U-turns and headed off along the minor road to Threlkeld. About halfway along the four-mile stretch of road, Jeffrey pulled the Porsche over to the right by a metal gate. Martin pulled up behind and got out. Jeffrey opened his door and looked back.

"Boss says that'll do, Mart, we don't want that heap o'junk slowin' us down. Get in the back here with Andrews."

Martin slammed the Volvo's door and hurried over to the Porsche.

John eyed him warily as he settled onto the seat beside him. He was a big man in his early thirties who looked as if he spent many hours working weights. John could see that he was in no position to throw a damaging punch in the restricted space of the rear of the car, so he slid against the door, keeping his distance.

"Where the hell are we going, Hastings? When are you going to tell me what's going on?" said John as the car sped off.

Hastings pulled down his sun visor and looked at John in its mirror.

"I told you, Mr Andrews, all in good time."

"Look," said John, "my wife's expecting me back at the gallery. She needs the car." As he said the words, John realised how irrelevant they sounded, but he was clutching at straws.

"Yes, she'll probably be calling you quite soon. I think perhaps you'd better give me your mobile phone. Martin, take Mr Andrews' phone, would you?"

John patted his pocket and remembered he'd left the phone in his car.

He raised his arms and let Martin search for it.

"Doesn't seem to be here, boss," said Martin.

"What have you done with your phone, Mr Andrews?" said Hastings, turning round to look directly at John.

"I left it in my car," he said.

"Oh, well, no harm done," replied Hastings, smiling. "Your wife will just have to fume at you for not turning up and not answering your phone. She'll think you've gone off for the afternoon with your girlfriend."

John glared at him disdainfully.

They drove on in silence. After about half an hour, Hasting's phone rang.

"Peterson. Yes, successful." He glanced at his watch. "By about eleven, I should think, depending on the traffic. Yes, certainly we'll begin right away; there are several confirmatory tests I want you to run immediately."

He ended the call and stared through the window.

"I thought you said your name was Hastings," said John.

"I'm a bit like you, Mr Andrews," came the reply, "not quite what I seem."

"What's that supposed to mean?" said John.

"I think you know very well, Mr Andrews, but we can discuss all that later. As far as Christopher Hastings is concerned, he's someone I pull out of the cupboard when I want to throw up a bit of a smoke screen. Someone in the exhibition hall might have overheard our conversation, you see, and heard my name."

"So your purchase of the paintings was all a charade. Hastings doesn't exist and the cheque's a fake."

"I needed to get your attention and win your confidence, Mr Andrews. What better way to do that than to flatter you by pretending to buy some of your work?"

"So who are you?"

"Wallingford Neville Peterson, Mr Andrews. Wally to my friends."

"I'll stick to Peterson," snarled John. "When are you going to tell me where we are going and what's going on?"

"As I keep telling you, Mr Andrews, all in good time. You're perfectly capable of reading the road signs, so you'll know where we are. It's quite a long journey; I suggest you sit back and relax."

By ten in the evening, they were on the M25 going around London. At the Leatherhead exit they headed south in the direction of Horsham. About two miles north of Horsham, they turned right, now heading west on a series of country lanes.

What concerned John more than the calm self-assuredness of his captor was that apart from the initial play-acting as Hastings, he'd made no attempt to hide his own identity and nor did he seem concerned that John could work out exactly where he was. It could only mean that Peterson had no intention of letting him go.

They entered an area of dense woodland and soon the headlights picked out a brick wall running along the left side of the road. At least nine feet high, it was topped with several rows of razor wire with signs informing anyone crazy enough to try to climb over that it was electrified. There were security cameras every fifty yards. After half a mile, the wall curved back from the road to reveal a large gateway with a guardhouse and metal sliding gates. A sign to the left of the gateway announced that the premises behind all the security was the home of Peterson Biotech.

The driver lowered his window as a guard walked over to them. "Everything quiet, Sims?" called Peterson across the driver.

"All fine, sir," replied the guard. He turned and waved to another guard in the guardhouse and the gate slid silently open.

They drove down a long, curving tree-lined avenue. In the distance, John could make out a low-rise steel and glass building. Softly lit with a dull purple glow, it appeared to be hovering in the air against the darkness of the countryside. About two hundred yards from the building, the car turned right down a narrower avenue and they entered the gravelled forecourt of a large Victorian house.

The exterior of the house and the edges of the forecourt were lit by a series of soft yellow lights. As the car came close to the house, two powerful spotlights were triggered, flooding the area around the car to an almost daylight brightness.

The driver popped the locks and both he and Martin jumped out of the car. Martin opened Peterson's door while Jeffrey opened John's.

"Here we are at last, Mr Andrews," said Peterson, walking round the car and handing the gun to Jeffrey. "Home, sweet home. Let's go inside, shall we?"

John got out slowly, stiff from the journey.

Martin walked ahead up a short flight of steps that led to the main door while Peterson nodded to indicate that John should follow. Jeffrey brought up the rear, the gun still clasped in his hand. As Martin reached the door, it was opened from the inside by another man of similar bouncer build, his face expressionless as he stood aside to let them in.

They entered a large circular hall with a flight of stairs curving up from the left to the upper floor. There was a pair of wooden doors opposite the entrance, while other doors led off the hall to both left and right.

"Mr Andrews," said Peterson genially, "I imagine you would like to use the facilities before we have our little chat. Martin, show our guest the way, would you?"

Martin turned to John and tossed his head in the direction of a door under the stairs. He walked ahead and opened it to let John in. John noticed that inside the small washroom there were no windows, nor was there a lock on the door.

He stared into the mirror above the washbasin, frowning darkly at his reflection as he splashed water onto his face. He had not spoken a word since they'd left the Lakes, but his mind had been racing throughout the journey, trying to decide exactly what this Peterson person might know and how he might have found out. He had a strong feeling that his abduction was connected to Claudia Reid and Ced Fisher, a feeling reinforced by his arrival at a biotech company. They must have worked out something about his DNA, but exactly what he'd no idea.

A banging on the door interrupted his thoughts.

"Wait a moment!" he shouted. He used the toilet, washed his hands and opened the door, almost bumping into Martin as he did. He glanced around the hall. Peterson had disappeared, but Jeffery, who was still holding the gun, was standing a few feet away, while the third guard was by the main door.

"This way," said Martin, nodding towards the double doors. He opened one and indicated that John should walk in ahead of him. He and Jeffrey followed him into the room.

The door opened onto a large sitting room and library stretching over forty feet to double glass doors at the far end. An ornate fireplace was the centrepiece of one long wall, with three cream leather sofas in front of it arranged around a glass coffee table. Bookshelves covered most of the opposite wall and a huge wooden desk occupied the space in front of them. On either side of the fireplace more double doors led onto a softly lit terrace. A lawn stretched away into the night beyond it.

As they walked into the room, John saw Peterson standing behind the desk next to a dark-haired woman of about forty. She was dressed in a black, knee-length skirt, black tights, black court shoes and a mid-blue silk blouse. With her hair pulled back into a large jewelled clip, she looked like a lawyer, but then John noticed a white laboratory coat thrown casually over the back of a chair next to her. She was looking over Peterson's shoulder at a sheaf of papers he was reading. Peterson looked up.

"Ah, Mr Andrews, please come in. Let me introduce you to a lady you'll be having quite a few dealings with : Dr Hannah Frobisher."

The woman walked towards John, a wide smile on her face.

"Mr Andrews, I can't tell you how delighted I am to meet you." She held out her hand as her eyes roamed over John's face. "Remarkable," she said, "quite remarkable. We have so much to talk about."

John ignored her outstretched hand. "I can assure you, Miss Frobisher, that the feeling is anything but mutual. As far as I'm concerned, we have nothing to talk about."

He turned towards Peterson. "Well, Peterson, we're here, so where's the explanation you promised me?"

"Indulge me a few moments more, Mr Andrews. You must be parched after that long drive. What can I get you to drink?" He held up his own glass, into which he'd already poured a generous measure of whisky. "Whisky? Brandy?"

John realised that he was very thirsty, but the last thing he wanted was alcohol.

"A soda water," he said.

"Certainly," smiled Peterson. He bent to a small refrigerator under a side table and retrieved a can of soda. Picking up a cut-glass tumbler from the side table, he emptied the can into it. He glanced up at the two guards. "You two can take your places on the terrace."

Martin moved to the French windows to the left of the fireplace, opened one and walked outside, closing the door behind him. Jeffrey did the same to the door at the far end of the room. They both stood facing into the room, their hands clasped in front of them and their legs apart.

Peterson walked over to John to hand him his drink.

"There, Mr Andrews, my two guard dogs are safely ensconced outside where they can see everything you do, but, thanks to the double glazing, they will not be able to hear a word of our conversation. I'm afraid I thought it necessary to post them there in case you got any silly ideas into your head while we are talking."

He turned and pointed to the sofas. "Please, make yourself comfortable; we have much to discuss."

"We certainly do," said John, taking the drink but otherwise not moving. "I demand to know what's going on. Why have I been kidnapped and brought to this house?"

"Oh, Mr Andrews, kidnapping is such a strong word," smiled Peterson.

"What else would you call it? I've been threatened and brought here against my will. I demand an explanation."

"Please, Mr Andrews, let's sit and discuss this, shall we? It's been a long journey."

John glanced at the guards staring at him from the terrace and suddenly felt very tired. He walked to the nearest sofa and sat down. Hannah Frobisher followed him and sat on the sofa at right angles to his, gazing at him with a look of wonder. As her eyes darted from his face to his hands and his hair and back again, he felt like a specimen under a microscope.

Peterson smiled, pleased with the small victory, and sat on the sofa opposite John. He leaned forward, took a sip of his whisky, and placed the glass on the table.

"Now, Mr Andrews, let me answer some of your questions. I have brought you here because you are a very unusual man. You have very rare traits. I want us to work together to learn about those traits for our own mutual benefit and I am sure for the benefit of mankind."

John stared at him in stunned amazement. "Look, Peterson, or whatever your name is, I have absolutely no idea what you're talking about. I'm an artist, not a businessman. I don't see how my paintings are going to save the world."

Peterson smiled condescendingly. "Mr Andrews, I didn't say anything about your paintings. You really are being far too modest, and if I may say so, rather coy. We all know your traits include far more than your painting, skilled though it is. You're a very special person, perhaps even a one-off. Isn't that correct, Mr Andrews?"

"Whatever makes you think that? Apart from a certain ability to paint, there's nothing special about me at all, I can assure you."

"Mr Andrews. Your constant denial of what we both know to be true is becoming tiresome. Now, you have something I want and I'm willing to pay you handsomely for it. Very handsomely, indeed. Enough to keep you in the lap of luxury for the rest of your life."

He paused and laughed. "Of course, that's a rather bold promise."

"You're mad," said John as he made to stand up. Peterson raised a hand to stop him.

"Please, Mr Andrews. I'm anything but mad. But I am getting a little bored with your attitude. I can only assume that it comes from so many years of having to keep things to yourself. How many years is it, Mr Andrews? I'm intrigued to know."

At this question, Hannah Frobisher leaned forward expectantly.

John kept his face as deadpan as he could and said nothing. Exactly how much did the man know?

Peterson sighed in exasperation. "OK, Mr Andrews, I'll lay my cards on the table. I know that you are not what you seem to the rest of the world. I'm aware – although I found it hard to believe at first and I must admit that now I come to say the words out loud, they sound absurd – but I'm aware that you have what is sometimes dramatically referred to as the secret of eternal youth."

He paused to watch John's reaction, but there was nothing.

"Isn't that correct, Mr Andrews?" There was now an edge to his voice. "You don't age, do you? You are never ill? Come on, Mr Andrews, there's no point in continuing to deny it."

John's face remained impassive, although his mind was anything but still. How could this man have possibly found out his secret?

When John continued to say nothing, Peterson drained his glass of whisky and stood. "You know, you're really playing very hard to get."

He walked over to the side table to pour another whisky from a crystal decanter. "Are you sure you won't have something stronger than soda water? It might help you find your voice."

When he sat down again, he looked at John expectantly.

"Well, Mr Andrews, do you have anything to say? Or are you going to maintain this ridiculous silence?"

John sighed, held his arms out to either side and shrugged his shoulders.

"I don't know what to say. I feel as if I've become part of a second-rate movie. I've been kidnapped by you and two heavies straight out of central casting and brought here to this house that seems to be attached to some sort of laboratory. You then come up with some crazy story that I've got ... what did you call it? ... eternal youth? You should be certified, Peterson. You're insane!"

As he was talking, he was watching Peterson's eyes boring into him. They were cold and ruthless.

Peterson took another sip of his whisky, sat back and nodded.

"You're good, Mr Andrews, very good. Then again, I can imagine you've had a lot of practice. But I have more to tell you. Explanations. Perhaps once you've heard them, you'll drop this pathetic charade."

He leaned forward. "The reason I'm so confident, Mr Andrews, is that there have been some tests carried out on your DNA, tests that have yielded remarkable results, possibly the most profound results in the history of science. They explain why you are never ill and why you do not age. But what's really exciting are the opportunities that this knowledge gives us."

He smiled. "It occurs to me that you must have absolutely no idea of why you have these profound characteristics. After all, you probably come from a time when science was hardly sophisticated. But you must have wondered over the years, surely? Well, Mr Andrews, I feel very honoured and privileged to be the one to explain it to you.

"Actually," he continued grandly, "it's very fitting that I should be the one. After all, it was my organisation, my money and my flair that have brought together some of the world's greatest scientific minds and given them unrestrained opportunities to test their ideas and theories. It was my vision, Mr Andrews, that has resulted in the breathtaking discovery of the significance of your DNA."

He took another sip of whisky, giving John time to absorb his dramatic words of self-importance.

"The answer, Mr Andrews," he continued after a few moments, "is simply this. You have what appears to be the perfect immune system. You understand what that means, I assume?"

"I know what an immune system is," said John dismissively.

"Of course you do, but a perfect immune system? Do you understand the implications of that?" He held up a hand and smiled. "I'm not testing you, Mr Andrews, I don't expect you to answer. Let me explain. A perfect immune system is one that can fight any disease. It explains why you have never been ill. Nothing on the bacteria or virus level can touch you. Your body can see off any and all invaders. But that's just the beginning. Your body, because of your immune system, has conquered the deterioration of cellular material that results in ageing. Your system is capable of repairing any damage to your cells, or perhaps even preventing that damage in the first place. Think of the implications that this could have. A whole new avenue is now available for fighting disease, and for combatting ageing. You are living testimony to that, Mr Andrews; living testimony! The time has now come for the rest of the human race to reap the benefits as well."

John was stunned. After nearly six hundred years, he finally had an answer. Over the last thirty years, as the understanding of DNA had deepened and more and more articles and TV documentaries had improved public awareness, he had increasingly suspected that his genetic make-up was at the heart of his 'condition'. But as a non-scientist, his overall understanding was hazy. Suddenly, this scheming man sitting opposite him had explained it all. His mind was racing, trying to absorb what Peterson had told him, but also trying to think of a way of convincing Peterson that he had seized the wrong person.

"And you say," he interrupted, "that you got all of this absurd-sounding information from my blood sample? I'm sorry to disappoint you but I haven't given a blood sample to anyone, so I suspect that no matter how profound you think your results are, I'm not the person you are looking for. It's a case of mistaken identity."

"I didn't say blood sample, Mr Andrews," replied Peterson, trying to sound patient. "I said we tested your DNA. Cast your mind back a few weeks. You gave a buccal swab sample. I don't know why; you must have been arrested for something. But the important thing is that you gave a sample that the police automatically sent for profiling. The results of that profiling were very profound, totally different from anything seen previously, and they inspired the scientist who carried out the tests to seek you out. That scientist knew the findings were important, but didn't know why."

"I admit that I did give a sample to the police some weeks ago following a minor, ridiculous incident," agreed John reluctantly. "I think this is where the confusion must come from. My sample must have been mixed up with another person's. This DNA you're talking about isn't mine; it's someone else's. Somehow my name has got on the sample."

Peterson nodded. "I agree that mix-ups can happen, but not in this case. You see, we tested another sample from you. There is no doubt you are the source of the DNA material."

John shook his head. "The swab that idiot police officer took is the only sample I've given to anyone. So these results you're talking about can't be from me."

Peterson smiled patronizingly. "You really don't understand much about DNA, do you? The second sample was from an envelope. Your saliva was on the seal where you licked it."

"What envelope? How did you get hold of it?"

"How we got hold of it, Mr Andrews, doesn't matter," said Peterson dismissively. "The fact is that it indisputably came from you and your DNA, which matched the original police sample, was on it."

Peterson raised his glass and emptied the rest of the whisky. "So now, Mr Andrews, I think you must agree that all your protestations have been answered. There is no mix-up, no mistake. You are the source of the DNA I've been describing and you are exactly as I have described – you are never ill and you are far older than one would infer from your looks, perhaps immensely older."

A rustle from the direction of Hannah Frobisher caught John's attention and he glanced at her. Her eyes were now even wider at the mention that John might be 'immensely' old.

John refused to give Peterson the satisfaction of agreeing that he was right. He shrugged wearily. "So what do you want from me,

Peterson? Why have you kidnapped me?"

"Mr Andrews, it's very late and you've had a tiring time of it this evening. I can understand why you've been reluctant to discuss your particular characteristics with me; you're used to hiding the way you are from others. That's perfectly understandable. This is why I resorted to the measures I took this afternoon: I knew you would never have come with me willingly. But now your secret is known – now there is an explanation – you must realise you are suddenly a very valuable commodity. I couldn't have you disappearing, which is one reason I decided it was necessary to ensure you are protected."

"Protected! This isn't protection. It's imprisonment!"

"It's for your own safety, Mr Andrews. Imagine the problems you would have if your special characteristics became common knowledge."

"How I deal with my problems is my business and I hardly think your motives are as unselfish as you would have me believe. If you were concerned about my welfare, you wouldn't have resorted to kidnap and threats. There's also my wife. She's going to be beside herself with worry by now. I insist that you let me call her. If my car has been found, she will have called the police."

Peterson waved a dismissive arm. "The police won't help her. Their only understanding of what you call kidnapping is that it is invariably followed by a demand for money. That's not going to happen, Mr Andrews. After all, you have very little money. All your worth is in your DNA. So you see, once there is no ransom demand, the police will very quickly lose interest. Despite all your wife's protestations, they will think you've run away with some lover. I don't know if your wife knows about your special characteristics or not. If she does, she's hardly going to tell the police – they'd think she's completely crazy. And if she doesn't know, well, she can't offer that as an explanation.

"So the short answer to your request is 'no'. There will be no contacting your wife, either tonight or in the future."

John stared at Peterson, trying to gather his thoughts and think of a way he could deal with his predicament. He looked around the room and through the windows in the direction of the large building he had seen when they arrived.

"What exactly is this place, Peterson? You've talked about biochemistry and genetics; is it some sort of secret laboratory?"

Peterson laughed. "There is nothing secret about it, Mr Andrews. Well, most of it, anyway. Peterson Biotech is a world leader in research into genetic-based diseases and in developing probes for that research. Our turnover is measured in billions of pounds.

"I was even knighted for my contribution in keeping British genetics research at the cutting edge," he added, feigning modesty.

"And all that happens here?" asked John incredulously.

"Oh heavens, no. Our production facilities are positioned at various locations around the country and our research teams similarly spread among the leading universities. What goes on here is rather special. Here we have a small cadre of dedicated scientists working on groundbreaking genetic research into a number of areas. Naturally, their work is secret; that is the nature of such research. But at the centre of that group we have Dr Frobisher's team who, er, seek out particular avenues of interest that are emerging and direct their progress to ensure that opportunities are not lost."

"You mean you steal other people's ideas and claim them as your own."

Peterson laughed coldly. "You really are a very cynical man, Mr Andrews."

"So what exactly is it that you want with me?" said John. "How do I fit in with your machinations?"

Peterson pointed towards the sheaf of papers on the desk.

"The results contained in those papers are what has got us so excited about you, Mr Andrews. We need to verify them, but that will only be the beginning. We want to know the limits of your condition: exactly how immune you are to a wide spectrum of conditions. Not only bacterial infections and viruses, but other factors too. Those that attack the body by altering its DNA – cancers, exposure to radiation, that sort of thing."

He smiled. "There are so many ways you can help us directly to come to a better understanding of how it all works. And Dr Frobisher here can't wait to begin. To that end, she has put together a panel of preliminary tests she wishes to conduct tonight before we move onto some more profound considerations tomorrow."

John looked down, weighing the glass he still had in his hand. He shook his head. "No, Peterson, you won't be doing any tests on me, not tonight or at any time."

With one fluid movement, as fast as when he had thrown a knife in the past, he flung the glass directly at Peterson's head, taking him completely by surprise. The heavy crystal glass caught him squarely on the bridge of his nose and right eye, shattering with the impact and cutting deeply into the skin. Blood flowed immediately from the wounds and Peterson yelled in pain. As his hand instinctively shot up to his face, the shards of broken glass lacerated his fingers, adding to his pain. Hannah Frobisher screamed in shock.

John didn't wait to see any of this. As the glass left his hand, he leaped to his feet and ran to the hall doors. He flung them open, running from the room before either of the two guards waiting on the terrace had time to react.

At the sound of the commotion in the room, the third guard in the hall leapt to his feet. John knew he was there and he skidded to a halt in front of him, raising his fists defensively. The man smiled derisively and lunged at John. John swayed and landed three hard punches on the man's face, knocking him off his feet. As John darted past him and grabbed the handle of the main door, a shot rang out and a bullet whistled passed his ear, splintering the doorframe.

"Stop there, Andrews!" a voice commanded, but John ignored it and pulled open the door.

Outside, unexpectedly, was Martin who, as soon as he'd heard Peterson yell, had run round the outside of the house from the terrace. John hardly had time to register the large man's presence when he found himself lifted off his feet by a powerful punch to the stomach. Completely winded, he collapsed to the ground. Martin turned him onto his face, grabbed his wrists and handcuffed him in one well-practised movement.

Gasping for breath, John found himself being hauled to his feet and half carried back into the hallway. Jeffrey had arrived at the door and he pointed the gun threateningly at John's head, while the third man, whose nose was bleeding heavily, looked about to take a swing.

"Enough!" Peterson boomed from the sitting room door, his voice muffled by a large, heavily bloodstained handkerchief he was clasping to his face. "Bring him back in here! Hannah, go and get the wheelchair!"

Still wheezing from the punch to his stomach, John was dragged back into the room.

"That was very stupid, Mr Andrews, very stupid indeed!" yelled Peterson angrily. "Your rashness has succeeded only in defining exactly how we shall deal with you from now on. Martin, secure him to that!" He pointed to the wheelchair Hannah Frobisher had retrieved from a nearby room.

Martin spun John round and undid the handcuffs, grabbing an arm firmly and twisting it down, forcing him to sit heavily in the chair. Before he had time to react, both John's wrists were cuffed to the chair's arms, his legs tied together and fixed to the foot supports. A belt was then threaded round his chest, under his armpits, and secured at the back. He couldn't move.

He looked up at the confusion around him and smiled grimly to himself. Peterson was bleeding heavily and would require several stitches to his nose and eyebrow, while the guard from the hallway's right eye was bruised and half-closed, his nose bleeding.

"Jeffrey!" commanded Peterson. "Go with Martin and Dr Frobisher to the laboratory. Hannah, you can take your samples whenever you're ready; you will find your subject in no position to resist. But just to be sure, I suggest some sedation would be prudent."

John found himself being spun round towards the door and wheeled through the hallway to another door that led down a long corridor. Hannah Frobisher hurried on ahead and opened a door that led into a small laboratory. She instructed Martin to position John against a wall while she went to a bench where there were some surgical instruments, packets of syringes and vials of injection solutions. She picked up a syringe and assembled it, pushing the needle into one of the vials. As she slightly pressed the plunger to ensure there was no air in the solution, she called over to the two bodyguards.

"Thanks, both of you. You can wait outside. Mr Andrews is in no position to do anything, so I shall be quite safe."

Jeffrey looked hesitant.

"If you're concerned, Jeffrey," added Frobisher irritably, "you can watch through the windows from the laboratory next door."

Once they'd left, she turned to John.

"As you've probably realised, Mr Andrews, Jeffrey and his colleagues are not privy to what we have found out about you. There is a need for total confidentiality."

"Then they must be wondering what the hell you are up to," grunted John.

She laughed. "Not at all. They think you are some sort of industrial spy; that you have stolen secrets from the company. Nothing more. There is no way they could even comprehend the truth."

She paused and John watched her hovering with the syringe, still staring at his face.

"What is it you find so fascinating about my face?" he snarled. "You've been staring at me like I'm some sort of freak all evening."

"Mr Andrews," she said softly, "I'm aware that you are very old, possibly several hundred years old, in fact. Having seen the results of your DNA profiling and the genetic tests, I understand why it is that you haven't aged, but seeing you in the flesh is still a shock. I suppose I'm searching for signs of ageing that aren't there, simply because, despite understanding the science, it's all so incredibly hard to believe."

John's face remained expressionless. He refused to give her the satisfaction of admitting what they'd discovered about him was true and, given their intention of subjecting him to a battery of tests that he suspected could kill him, he was certainly not going to engage in any cozy conversation about himself.

Unaware of the thoughts going through John's mind, Hannah Frobisher continued.

"That was quite a performance back there in the study, for anyone, let alone someone who is hundreds of years old. You've obviously picked up a few survival tricks over the years. Tell me – I'd love to know – what is your age?"

John fixed his eyes onto hers. "As I told Peterson earlier, whatever these results are you've got from someone's DNA, they are nothing to do with me. There has been a mistake; you've got the wrong person. There is nothing special about me apart from an ability to paint. You've got yourself mixed up in something very sinister, Miss Frobisher, and if you persist in this nonsense, you could end up in a lot of trouble. You are breaking the law and you'll end up in prison. I suggest you exercise some damage limitation and let me go now. Maybe the detailed scrutiny you've been directing to my face should tell you the obvious: I look like a man of forty because I am a man of forty."

Hannah Frobisher shrugged. "As you wish, Mr Andrews."

She pulled up his sleeve, found a vein in his arm and inserted the needle.

John glanced up at her one last time as the room started to spin and then went black.

# Chapter 32

"Sal, it's Claw."

"Wow! You're up early for a Sunday morning. What's happened?"

"Look, I know you've got your triathlon this morning–"

"Yeah, you only just caught us. We're about to leave."

"Sal, something's happened. What time do you think you'll be home? I need to call in and see you."

"Sounds serious, Claw. Tell me all. Do you want us to cancel?"

"Yes, it is serious, but no, I certainly don't want you to cancel. You've been training hard for this. Anyway, I've got to try to snatch some more sleep and then it will take me about a couple of hours to get to you, by which time you'll be almost finished."

"Are you at home?"

"Um, no, I'm in the Lakes. Look Sal, it's a long story and there's not time to go into it now. I'm sure that Ced is champing at the bit to leave. I just wanted to know that you were going to be home straight after the race. Enjoy your event and don't worry."

"Yeah, right! Like close your eyes and don't think of a white horse. OK, Claw, we'll be finished by ten and we'll get home as quickly as we can. It should be by about a quarter to eleven."

"OK, I'll be waiting. And good luck!"

Claudia and Lily pulled up outside Sally and Ced's house shortly after ten-thirty. Claudia sat back and stretched.

"You must be exhausted, Claudia," said Lily. "You should have let me do some of the driving."

Claudia smiled appreciatively. "Thanks, I'll be fine. But almost no sleep, two long drives and all this tension, it's catching up on me."

They had decided to leave Lily's rental car at Lola's in case the police didn't release the Volvo, leaving at 8.30 after several cups of strong coffee. Claudia had set the alarm on her phone for 6.00 to catch Sally at home, but she'd managed to get back to sleep again. Lily's short night had ended when Sophie and Phoebe returned to the house at 7.30, running straight to their room and squealing with delight at finding her there. Despite her tiredness, she pulled them both into bed and hugged them. Her two adorable half-sisters. There was only one piece missing now to complete the picture.

There was a toot and Ced's SUV pulled up behind them.

"I'll stay here while you explain about Papa," said Lily to Claudia. "Then we'll do the introductions."

Claudia opened her door and climbed out of her car as Ced unwound his long limbs from his. He was mud-splattered but looked pleased with himself. He ambled up to Claudia.

"Hi, Claw," he said, bending over to kiss her cheek. "Sal's only just told me you were popping in. What's up?"

"I'll tell you in a mo. How did you get on?"

He grinned like a child at Christmas. "Third place, Claw. And a great time, despite being poisoned last weekend."

"Self-inflicted, Ced," said Claudia, shaking her finger at him reproachfully. Then she smiled. "Congratulations, that's brilliant. How about you, Sal?"

"Not bad, Claw, thanks," said Sally as she walked up to the car. "Twelfth overall and second in the cycling leg. Could have been better, but I'm pleased enough. Now, no more mystery, Claw, what's happened?"

"John Andrews appears to have been kidnapped."

"Kidnapped!" echoed Sally in alarm. "When? How?"

She recounted the events of the previous afternoon.

"It has to be connected to everything we've found out," she said, "which means that the prof must have told someone, since none of us has."

"Certainly not," said Sally. "It's what we all agreed. But I can't believe that Young would have broken his word."

Claudia nodded. "I know, but I can't think of any other explanation. I think we need to see him asap. I've called him to ask if he's in the lab today and he is, so I think we should go down there. Do you agree?"

"Absolutely," replied Ced. "How did he sound?"

"Actually," said Claudia, "he sounded perfectly normal. Said he'd be delighted to see me and discuss the results some more. Certainly didn't sound like he was hiding anything. I didn't mention that you'd be coming."

"Claw, who's that in your car?" asked Sally.

"Oh, heavens," said Claudia, "I'd forgotten about Lily. I'll introduce you. You're going to find this totally unbelievable. Are you ready for a shock?"

"You mean a bigger shock than hearing that John Andrews has been kidnapped?" asked Sally, raising her eyebrows.

"Bigger," replied Claudia. "Much bigger." She called to Lily.

Lily got out and turned towards them, smiling. Ced and Sally's mouths dropped open as they noticed her eyes.

Lily walked round the car and held out her hand. "Hi, I'm Lily Saunders."

Sally looked from Lily to Claudia and back again, registering the amusement on Claudia's face, despite the seriousness of the reason for their visit. She took Lily's hand. "Sally," she said, "Sally Moreton. I don't wish to be rude, but your eyes. This isn't just a coincidence, is it?" She turned again to Claudia.

"It's not only the eyes," said Ced as he studied Lily's face. "It's the whole shape of your face. You must be related to John Andrews. Oh, sorry, I'm Ced Fisher."

"Delighted to meet you, both of you," laughed Lily. She looked up at Ced. "You're very observant, Ced, but from what I've heard about your work with art analysis, I'm not surprised."

"Let's go inside," said Claudia, "We've had almost no sleep and we're desperate for some more coffee. I'll make a huge pot while you two get the grime off yourselves. Then all will be explained."

Twenty minutes later in the sitting room, Lily had told them who she was.

"I knew it!" exclaimed Sally. "I told Ced when we were showering. I was convinced you had to be John Andrews' daughter."

She jumped up and took Lily's hands in hers. "God, this is so exciting. Lily, I need to give you a hug." She pulled Lily to her feet and threw her arms around her.

Lily laughed. "I seem to be drawn to tall people. My girlfriend Jenny in New York, who started this whole thing off for me when she bought a picture from Papa, she's about your height!"

Sally held her out at arm's length, the excitement lighting up her face. "It's incredible," she enthused. "Lily, are you an artist like John?"

"Yes, I am. He taught me most of my skills when I was growing up. He's a brilliant teacher."

"That was in Hong Kong?" said Ced. "What was he called then?"

"Stephen Waters."

"Stephen Waters. Mysterious colonial artist. I should have made the connection, but I was only thinking in terms of Europe. He disappeared suddenly, fell out of the pages of history like so many of John Andrews' personas."

"Disappeared is right. Like I did. I was kidnapped, then I escaped to northern China, only to find myself trapped into years of servitude. I had no idea what happened to Papa. I still have no idea, except that I now know he went to the States as Stefano Baldini before he came to England as Francesco Moretti."

"Yes," nodded Ced. "We've made the connection with those two. There must also have been someone else between Moretti and Andrews, but I haven't tracked him down yet."

"Matthew Allen," said Lily, "Lola told me."

"Matthew Allen," repeated Ced. "Very obscure, though I've heard of him. Worked in the West Country. Devon. I don't know much about his work."

"Wow, Ced, you're good!" said Lily in admiration. "You really know your stuff."

"It's what I do, Lily," he replied, reddening slightly in embarrassment at her praise. He tapped his lip with the knuckle of his index finger. "I don't think Matthew Allen will be too easy to find, but I'm sure I can rustle up some Stephen Waters. Let me get my computer."

He loped from the room, returning a moment later clutching his laptop. Opening it up, he tapped on the keys, his eyes flashing over the screen.

"There, two images. Both from the Hong Kong Museum of Art. There's a landscape of what I assume is Hong Kong harbour and a portrait of a Chinese child. No, wait a minute, she's Eurasian." He looked at Lily in amusement and turned the screen towards her. "Does she look familiar?"

Lily glanced at the picture and leaned her chin onto her clasped hands. "It's me at the age of eight!" she exclaimed in delight. "It was painted not many months before my mother died. She loved that painting. Gosh, it's so exciting to know it still exists and that it's safe in a museum."

She took the computer and studied the image in detail. "How wonderful, after all this time."

Claudia decided it was time to get them back on track.

"Listen guys, it's brilliant that we've made this connection but I really think we should be getting on to London; it's quite a long drive."

"Yes," agreed Ced, "and from the dark shadows under your eyes, not one you should be making. We'll go in my car. It's bigger and you can both doze on the way."

"And you're not tired, I suppose," countered Claudia. "After all, you've only just run a triathlon!"

"It was a mini, Claw. I just need some grub before we leave and I'll be fine."

"Actually," said Sally, "is it wise that Lily meets the prof? Since she's the same as John, she's as vulnerable as he is. I think you should stay here, Lily."

"No way, Sally," said Lily, "although I hear what you say – Claudia and I have already talked about it. We agree that it wouldn't be a good idea for Young to know about me for now. But we have to consider the possibility that he is innocent as well – there could be some other explanation as to why whoever's kidnapped Papa found out about him. I can stay in the car while you three talk to Young and decide whether you think he's a bad guy or not."

403

"OK," replied Sally, "a fair compromise. Do you have a mobile, Lily?"

"Yes, but it's for the States. I haven't tried it here yet."

"Right. In case it's a problem, I've got a spare which I'll program to speed dial mine, Ced's and Claw's so that we can all stay in touch."

Twenty minutes later, once Ced and Sally had wolfed down some bacon and eggs, they were on their way. Within five minutes, both Lily and Claudia were sound asleep in the back of the car. Sally turned to look at them.

"Ced," she said quietly, "I can't believe it. That beautiful Chinese woman with a flawless complexion sitting in the back of our car is a hundred and twenty-four years old. Isn't that incredible?"

"I'll go carefully over any bumps," he replied, accelerating onto the motorway.

"Idiot!" she said, thumping him playfully on the arm.


Three and a half hours later as they crossed Vauxhall Bridge in London, Sally nudged them both awake.

Lily looked out at the view. "So this is the famous River Thames," she said. "Where's Tower Bridge?"

"It's a bit further along the river from here," laughed Sally, "but you'll see the Houses of Parliament and Big Ben across the river once we're over the bridge. Listen, I've been thinking; rather than stay in the car in some car park, I think it would be better if you went somewhere public to sit while we talk to the prof. There's a nice cafe at the Royal Festival Hall where you can sit and take in the sights. We'll park the car and install you there. And you must promise not to go anywhere. OK?"

"Sounds good to me," replied Lily.


They found her a seat in the cafe and she repeated her promise not to move. Still Sally hovered.

"Sally," said Lily, "stop worrying, I'll be perfectly fine. Apart from you three, Lola is the only other person in England who knows about me. I'm not about to be accosted here. And if I am, I can scream very loudly, I can assure you."

"OK," nodded Sally, "but if you're in any way worried, hit the speed dials on your phone. Both Ced and I can run very fast; we'll be here within minutes."

"Thank you Sally, you're an angel."

As they walked towards Frank Young's laboratory, Claudia phoned him again to say she was two minutes away. He told her he'd meet her in the lobby. They arrived moments later and told the bored security guard that they had an appointment. Almost immediately, they heard the ping of a lift and the professor appeared.

"Sally! Ced!" cried the professor with a welcoming smile. "How good to see you. Claudia didn't say she had you in tow. What a pleasant surprise. I should have thought you'd have better things to do on a fine Sunday afternoon than drive all the way down here. Come, I've just put some coffee on, let's go up to the lab."

As the professor was chatting away lightly to Claudia in the lift, Ced caught Sally's eye and raised his eyebrows. She squeezed his hand and shrugged. The professor was hardly acting like a guilty man.

He buzzed them through the security system and took them to his office. "So, what's prompted your visit?" he said, busying himself with making coffee. "Have you dug out anything from the data? I've been over it a dozen times and I'm as convinced as I was the first time I saw it that we've got it right. I took a break yesterday, at my wife's insistence, but it's such an important discovery that I couldn't stay away for two days running. I've been poring over the data printouts again since you rang this morning, Claudia."

"Prof," said Claudia hesitantly, "something serious has happened and it has to be connected to our findings."

He frowned, appearing genuinely puzzled.

"What is it, Claudia? You certainly all look very serious."

"John Andrews has been kidnapped."

"What! When? Are you sure?"

"Quite sure, Prof," replied Claudia, and she told him what she knew of events of the previous afternoon.

As usual, the professor was ahead of them. "And you're thinking, presumably, that since we are the only people to know about John

Andrews, that I must have told someone, since none of you has. Am I right?" he said as Claudia finished.

Claudia looked down, embarrassed.

"That was the only conclusion we could make," said Sally quietly. "We're not accusing you of anything. We were, well, wondering if you've had any conversations with anybody, or if anyone could have seen the results."

He smiled kindly. "You're right, of course. It was the only conclusion you could draw under the circumstances. However, I haven't told a soul and no one has seen these results." He pointed to the pile of papers spread around his desk. "The papers have stayed with me. I've taken them home every night, locked in my briefcase."

"Can anyone else access your computer?" asked Ced.

"Absolutely not! Everything is passworded and the original files are several layers of security into my system. The firewall is one of the most advanced of its kind."

"Have you made any notes that indicate what the results are all about, anything that gives names? John Andrews, for instance?" asked Ced.

The professor nodded. "Yes, actually, I have. After our conversation of last weekend, it was such an exciting discovery, especially when allied to all the art findings that you've made, Ced, that I made notes on it all. I may be knowledgeable in the field of genetics, but the art information was new to me and I didn't want to forget any of it. But the notes are only on the computer; I haven't even printed them out."

"May I have a look?" asked Ced.

"Certainly. I'll turn on the computer. I haven't even done that today because I've been working from the printouts."

Once the system had loaded, he entered a master password and then several more to access his own files. He paused and checked the screen, frowning as he did. He typed a few more keys, hit the return and stared at the screen.

Ced was watching his face. It had gone as white as a sheet. "I don't understand it," he whispered, his words almost inaudible.

"What?" asked Ced, leaning forward in his chair.

"They're gone."

"What have gone?"

"All the raw data from our tests on Andrews' DNA and all the results. They're not here. Even the notes I made have gone. That's impossible."

He tapped in some more instructions. "Everything else is in place as usual. But anything connected to Andrews is no longer here. Nothing. It's like it never existed."

"When was the last time you called up the data on the computer, professor?" asked Ced.

"Friday morning. It was all here on Friday morning."

"Did you add to your notes at all after you made them?"

"No, as I said, they were an aide memoire. I completed them the day after our discovery."

"Mind if I have a look?" asked Ced.

"Go ahead," said the professor, vacating his seat. "But I doubt you'll be able to get into the system; the security, as I said, is cutting edge."

"We'll see," replied Ced as his fingers flew across the keyboard. The screen went blank for a moment and then lines of code appeared. He scrolled through them rapidly, searching for something. After scanning through the data for several minutes, he typed in some more instructions and the data on the screen changed again, although it still consisted of lines of seemingly incomprehensible code.

He sat back. "I thought so," he said, rubbing his chin.

"What is it, Ced?" asked the professor, amazed that Ced had cut straight into his system.

"Well," replied Ced, nodding to himself as he scanned the lines. "The system is good, but it's not that good. There are certainly several layers of security and flags that would ping if someone was trying to hack in, as you would expect. But the worrying thing is that there seems to be an external link."

"What do you mean?" said Young, frowning.

"As far as I can see at the moment," replied Ced as he tapped some more keys, "it looks as if your computer is linked to another one at a remote location outside of the system in the laboratory. What that means is that as long as a person at the remote location knows your passwords – and they can easily get those by monitoring your keystrokes when you log in – everything on this computer is mirrored at their location. Your files can be searched and read. All of them. And they can be deleted. Who set this up?"

Young sat down in an adjacent chair. "You mean someone has been spying on me?"

"Yes, that's exactly what I mean," said Ced as he turned to the prof. "Is whoever set this up connected with your source of funding?"

Young gulped as his mind raced to make sense of the situation. He nodded slowly. "My funding comes from a company called Peterson BioTech. You've probably heard of them. Claudia and Sally certainly will have." He glanced at the girls.

"Yes," said Sally, "they're a British company and one of the biggest worldwide suppliers of biochemical and genetic markers for testing."

"Exactly," said Young. "I have close contact with many of the scientists working directly for the company. It's a highly respected outfit that has been hugely successful. They're channelling millions back into research every year, much of it into universities or satellite laboratories, such as this one. It sounds generous, which it is, but it pays dividends as Peterson gets first crack at many of the big breakthroughs that are happening. But it's all very carefully controlled and monitored. They are absolute sticklers for transparency and openness. I can't believe the company would be responsible for what's happened here."

"Maybe they've got a rogue employee," suggested Ced, "perhaps a plant from a competitor who's monitoring results as they appear and, if something is thought to be big enough, simply stealing it. After all, who's to say that other companies aren't running similar research to yours? Who's your contact there? Maybe we should speak with him."

"My contact is the visionary who started the company and who controls all the research. You've probably heard of him: Sir Wallingford Peterson."

Ced nodded. "Bright boy, tons of honours in biotech and genetics at Cambridge when he was young. Entrepreneurial type who capitalised on his brains and business skills big time. A real rags-to-riches story, as I recall."

"Yes," said the professor, "he came from a very humble background in Yorkshire, but he's now a billionaire."

"Well, he obviously didn't install this system by himself, so who did?" asked Claudia.

"You're right," said the professor, "but he was very involved. His people – actually it was only one person – set up everything."

As he was talking, Ced was still attacking the keyboard. "I keep hitting the same barriers, but that might be because I'm doing it from your system. Let's try another way."

He pulled his laptop out of his bag and fired it up. He connected it to the Internet via a plug-in modem to keep it isolated from the laboratory system and started to enter instructions.

"I'm going through a few proxies so the remote system can't detect where I am," he explained as his fingers flashed over the keys in a blur. "There, I thought we'd get further that way." He typed something and hit the return button. For a moment a logo for Peterson BioTech appeared, but the image quickly decayed.

"Gotcha!" he said. "You all saw that, didn't you? I won't be able to repeat it. Their system has automatically closed that door and will now be slamming a few others."

Young stood and paced the room, his hands behind his back and his head down.

He stopped and turned to Claudia. "You said that Andrews was at his exhibition and a man came to buy his paintings and they left together. Did anyone give a description of the man?"

"Yes," replied Claudia. "He was in his early fifties, distinguished looking, self-assured. Wavy grey hair, elegantly cut, swept back. He was casually but expensively dressed. Beige designer slacks–"

"And a blue and white checked shirt," said Young, finishing off her sentence. "That's Peterson himself. He must be directly involved, the bastard!"

He banged his fist hard on a bench, startling the others. "What a fool I've been! Lured by the offer of his money to a life of full-time, no-strings research. Except that he was watching my every move, reading every result as it appeared. He must have someone monitoring me all the time, and, I assume, others like me. That would explain a few things that have happened. Twice now I've come up with something pretty profound, only to be preempted by a call from Peterson sounding very excited, telling me that his scientists down at their specialist research laboratories near Horsham had come up with identical findings. When I've said I was about to break the same news to him, he would suggest that I move onto a slightly different line since his people had it all in hand."

"But you've never had results simply disappear," said Sally.

"No," he replied, "but I've never had anything remotely as important as what we've discovered."

His eyes suddenly darted around the room. He went to his desk and opened a drawer, peering into it carefully. Then he opened another and did the same.

"Interesting," he said. "Someone's been in here."

"How do you know?" asked Claudia

"I'm a little paranoid about internal security. It may be difficult to get into the laboratory from the outside, but once you're in, most places can be accessed. So I leave a few things in very precise positions. Inside these drawers, for example, there are pens and other things I never touch. And they've moved. Someone has been looking for something."

"They must have been looking for any printouts of the data and results," said Ced. "With those as well, you'd have no record of anything. And if they have Andrews, you'd have no further access to any DNA. I suggest you make a number of copies of everything and store them in a very safe place, like a safety deposit box in a bank. If they think you're carrying them around in your briefcase, they might well be snatched as you're walking along the street."

"Of course," added Young, "they would have no idea about the copies that Claudia and Sally have. Although if they realised their involvement, they might assume they have copies and start looking for them."

"You mean burgle our houses?" said Claudia, horrified at the thought.

"I think you have to consider that possibility, yes," replied Young.

"Did you mention them, the girls I mean, in your notes?" asked Ced.

"No, not by name I didn't. Only you, Ced."

"What exactly did you put in those notes?" asked Ced.

"I described how we'd found that Andrews must be very old;

how, from your work, we knew he was the same person as Moretti, Bianchi and others. I also mentioned that the second round of immunity tests was done on a sample from an envelope, but I didn't describe how it was obtained. And I summarised the conclusions we'd made regarding Andrews' immunity and the reasons why he doesn't age."

"So they've got some of the story but not all of it," said Claudia.

"If someone from Peterson BioTech read that on Monday soon after the prof wrote it, they could have alerted Peterson," said Sally. "With John's name, he would have quickly found out where he lived and he would probably have picked up the information about the exhibition. Perfect timing for them, really."

"What worries me," added Ced, "apart from the kidnap, of course, is that without the source material to repeat the tests, our raw data, results and interpretation are pretty much worthless. We could have fabricated the whole thing."

"Yes," agreed Young, "I have been having the same thoughts. And if they now have Andrews, they could work away using DNA from his blood for as long as it takes to come up with the huge breakthroughs in gene therapy that would inevitably result."

"Or they could do something altogether more sinister," mused Ced, "like work out how to change people's genetic structure to include the appropriate arrangement to give them enhanced or total immunity. They could then sell that to a select set of people for a huge price."

"Mmm, that really is a bit Hollywood-esque," smiled Young, "but ultimately, I suppose, not totally beyond the bounds of possibility."

"Excuse me," said Sally suddenly, "I need to make a call." She walked out of the office while Young's eyes followed her suspiciously.

"Don't worry," laughed Ced, noting the prof's reaction, "we know what it's about; she's not tipping off Peterson."

Sally pressed the speed dial for the phone she'd lent Lily.

"Hi, Lily, everything OK?"

"Fine thanks, Sally, although I'm getting a bit awash with coffee. How's it going?"

"The prof is as innocent as we are. But we've found that his computer system was secretly linked to another and everything he puts on it is read. He's been spied on big time."

"Wow, that's bad news. But at least the prof's in the clear, so it should be safe for me to meet him."

"Actually, Lily, I still don't think it's a good idea. I suspect the prof's going to confront the person he thinks is responsible. Supposing that person kidnaps him and makes him tell him everything? If he doesn't know about you, then he can't tell."

"Good point, Sally. I'll sit tight and wait for you."

As Sally went back into the room, she overheard Ced suggesting the professor should visit Peterson immediately, just as she'd predicted.

"Where does he live?" Ced was asking.

"He lives in a big old Victorian house at the Horsham site of the company's research arm."

"How unusual would it be for you to visit on a Sunday evening?"

"A bit unusual, certainly, but then again, with something of the importance of the results we have, he wouldn't expect me to wait. And if I turn up there full of excitement about the significance of the findings, he can't let on that he already knows; he'll have to hear me out. I could tell a lot from how he reacts."

"How good is the security there?" asked Ced.

"It's tight, at least on the perimeter. No one gets in without an appointment, even me. But one call to Peterson would solve that. If I call and say I have a breakthrough of profound importance, he's going to want me there as quickly as possible. But I'd have to go alone; none of you would be allowed in."

"Do they search cars when they arrive?" asked Ced.

"No, well, certainly mine has never been searched."

"What sort of car do you have?"

"A Passat hatchback."

"Good. Plenty of room in the boot under the parcel shelf."

"Ced!" cried Sally. "What are you thinking of doing?"

"Simple," replied Ced. "The prof drives up to the gates, having phoned ahead – I think you should delay that call, professor, until you're only a few minutes away so that Peterson doesn't have any time to do anything about Andrews, assuming that he's got him there. You can say that you were so excited that you jumped into the car and forgot to phone. I can hunker down in the boot. When we get there, once you've gone in and it's all quiet, I'll slip out and do a recce of the place; see if I can find anywhere that they might be holding John Andrews."

"No, Ced," said Sally emphatically, "that's far too dangerous. The grounds might be crawling with security guards. If they catch you, the least they will do is hand you over to the police as a trespasser. But more likely, they'll lock you up with John Andrews and I'll never see you again."

"Are the grounds crawling with guards, prof?" asked Ced.

"As far as I'm aware," replied Young, looking sheepishly at Sally, "there will be two or three of Peterson's personal security guards in the house. The assumption is that the perimeter security is excellent – they have a very effective CCTV monitoring system around the entire perimeter, which is several miles, and a high wall that is very difficult to scale. So the grounds near the house, which have a good cover of bushes, should be safe enough to check out the house from."

"There we are!" smiled Ced, clapping his hands together. "That settles it. There's very little risk. The prof and I can keep our phones on vibrate only and text each other with info."

"I'm still not happy with it, Ced," said Sally angrily.

"Look, Sal," said Ced. "If you think it through, we are all responsible for getting John Andrews into this situation. We have an equal responsibility to get him out of it."

"In that case," chimed in Claudia, "I go in with you. It's more my fault than anyone's that he's in this predicament."

"Claw," sighed Ced, "that can't happen. With all due respect, if the chips are down, I can run bloody fast. I've also done a bit of martial arts stuff – a long time ago now it's true, but it's in there somewhere. You might be little and easier to hide than me but, frankly, that's the only plus you have going for you. I don't want to have to keep looking out for you when I should be concentrating on Andrews and watching my own back, as well as perhaps the prof's. Sorry."

"Ced," said Sally, her tone showing that she was resigned to the fact that he was going ahead with his plan, "if you get any indication that Andrews is there, any at all, you mustn't try to rescue him. He's bound to have guards with him. No heroic gestures, OK? Just leave with the prof. We'll call the police and insist they go in, despite whatever protests Peterson puts up."

Ced caught the professor's eye. They both knew this was an unlikely scenario.

"Sure, Sal, I won't take any unnecessary risks," replied Ced, trying to inject some confidence into his smile.

"Well, whatever happens," said Claudia, "we'll follow you down to Horsham in your car and wait a mile or two up the road for you. You never know; we might be needed."


As Sally and Claudia walked back to the cafe at the Royal Festival Hall to fetch Lily, Sally repeated her misgivings over the whole scheme.

"I really don't like this, Claw. Suppose they've got guns. We're not the Famous Five; this is real life and in real life, people don't do this sort of thing. Criminals aren't all stupid, you know; they sometimes get the upper hand."

"I know, Sal, but Ced's set on it and I really can't think of another option. If the police were told now, they'd call Peterson and he'd soft-soap them. He's an important man; they'd always believe him over us."

"Oh my God!" cried Sally as they walked into the restaurant. "She's not there! Claw, Lily's gone!"

They rushed up to the table where they'd left Lily. It had been cleared and there was no sign of her.

"I knew I should have phoned again," said Sally, her eyes searching the tables. "I was so preoccupied by this scheme of Ced's that it went out of my head."

"Perhaps she's gone for a stroll down by the river," said Claudia.

"No, she wouldn't do that. She swore she would stay put. Christ, Claw, this just gets worse."

She retrieved her phone from her bag and punched the speed dial for Lily's phone.

"Lily! Where are you?"

"Right behind you, honey!"

"What!" Sally spun round to see Lily standing there looking bemused.

"Lily!" cried Sally, throwing her arms around her. "Where were you? You nearly gave me a heart attack."

"Sorry," said Lily, "but it's been a while and with all that coffee, I simply couldn't wait any longer. I had to find a bathroom."

# Chapter 33

John Andrews opened his eyes to find himself floating on his back on the ocean. Tiny waves lapped at the board he was strapped to, but they didn't disturb it. There was no wind and the sun was fierce, the sky a blinding white.

He knew this sea and recognised the smells from the land that he couldn't see but instinctively knew was nearby. He couldn't remember why he was there but he knew he'd been floating for a long time; waiting for someone. He tried to move his arms but they were firmly tied to the board; the only thing he could move was his head. As he turned it to one side, the water lapped onto his cheek. It was warm, soothing. He noticed a movement out of the corner of his eye and strained his head to see what it was. As he did this, the board turned, as if controlled by his head. He saw the movement again. It was a sailing junk. Of course! He was in the South China Sea. But why was he strapped to the board and not on the junk?

He strained his head again and the board seemed to be propelled closer to the junk. Now he could see a figure sitting on the bow. It was Lei-li. She was sketching something. He called out but she couldn't hear him. He yelled as loudly as he could but it made no difference; she didn't look up.

His eyes moved along the boat and he could make out another figure. It was a woman in a very old-fashioned dress. She was smiling and waving at him. Beth! It was Beth! She called out to him as she waved, but he couldn't hear her. He cried out her name, but she didn't respond. Suddenly another figure appeared carrying several mugs of beer. She had the headscarf on she always wore in the tavern. Arlette! She walked up to Beth, put down the beer and turned to wave at him.

Suddenly the wind got up and the sail of the junk filled. The boat moved towards him. He saw that the sail had a huge picture painted on it. Why hadn't he seen it before? It was the Madonna del Parto and the face was Maria's. But instead of that serene look of impending motherhood, her face was turned towards him and he could see her mouthing a word. What was it? What was she saying? It was his name! She was saying it slowly, over and over. Luca! Luca!

As the junk approached, he glanced back at Beth and Arlette and saw that climbing the sides of the boat were dozens of pirates. Now they were on the deck, creeping slowly towards the unsuspecting women, who were still smiling and waving at him. He realised there were now four of them – Millie and Catherine had joined them. They were dressed in riding clothes. All four were waving and smiling at him but he still couldn't hear them. He yelled out to warn them, but they took no notice. In the bow he saw a pirate raise his sword above his head, about to strike Lei-li. But she held up a hand to stop him and started sketching furiously. Now he could see who it was she was sketching – it was Mei-ling, her head turned towards him, ignoring the pirate and smiling that quiet, knowing smile of hers.

He looked back to the pirates and saw that they weren't pirates at all; they were his children. There was Niccolò, Piero, Sofia and Gianna, all waving at him and laughing. Behind them were Henri and Michel. And Tella and Fausto. They were all talking to someone. It was Dominic! Then Lola appeared and walked over to where Lei-li was still sketching furiously. Sophie and Phoebe were with her, dancing round her and turning to wave to him. There was someone else with them, a woman. But she had her back to him. He could only see her long black hair, not her face. She was talking to Lei-li who was smiling back at her.

The wind got stronger and the junk started to circle round him, getting closer and closer as it did. The circling got faster and faster as the roar of the wind increased. He lost sight of everyone on the deck as the movement became a blur, the light getting brighter and brighter as the screaming wind became deafening. His head thrashed from side to side as the intensity of the light and noise overwhelmed him and pushed him down into the water. The sea flowed over his head and, as he went deeper and deeper, silence and darkness replaced the noise and light.

His eyes snapped open. He was sweating. He couldn't move his arms or legs, but he could lift his head. He was strapped to what seemed to be a hospital trolley. He turned his head as much as he could to try to see where he was. The room was quite small, about ten feet by eight, with a door in the short wall ahead of him. Apart from a bench running the length of the wall beside him, there appeared to be no furniture in the room.

As he moved his head, his temples pounded. He felt nauseous and his throat was parched. Then he remembered the injection that Hannah Frobisher had given him. Fragments of their conversation and the earlier one with Peterson drifted back into his mind.

So the young woman, Claudia Reid, who had come to his gallery and bought a painting, had been in league with these people. She must have shown them the results of his DNA profile. When they wanted more sample, she had used the flap of an envelope he had obligingly licked for her when he sealed it. She probably hadn't believed her luck when he did that. Whatever tests they'd done must have been very comprehensive for them to work out the facts about his condition. And now they wanted to test him to breaking point.

The door ahead of him opened and Hannah Frobisher walked in. She smiled down at him. "Ah, Mr Andrews, you're awake. How are you feeling?"

He tried to speak but his throat was too dry.

"I'll get you some water," she said, walking behind him. He heard a tap running and she pressed a plastic beaker to his lips with one hand, holding his head up with the other.

"Whatever did you inject me with?" he gasped hoarsely.

"Only a mild sedative; nothing too strong. I needed to make sure you were fully relaxed. You might have noticed your arm is a little sore. While you were sleeping, I withdrew about a litre of blood from you for my research. You might be feeling a little weak, but that will soon pass. It was important to take the blood now before there's anything else circulating in your body. A litre will give me enough to work on for years, you'll be pleased to hear."

"How wonderful," he growled. "How long have I been asleep?"

"Let me see," she said, looking at her watch, "it's now three in the afternoon, so you've been out for about fourteen hours."

"I thought you said it was a mild sedative."

"Well, relatively mild," she said, shrugging. "I thought that after all the excitement of last night, it would be better if you were kept out of things. You caused a lot of trouble, you know, Wally was wild with anger. I had to patch him up and send him to bed with a sedative as well. I put seven stitches in his head and five in his hand; he is not a happy man. In fact, he's still very angry with you. And Henry has been given the day off; he needed stitches too, four of them. He's been complaining of headaches after you hit him. Still, I'm sure a few hours rest upstairs with his favourite malt will calm him down."

John stretched on the trolley, moving as much as he could.

"Is it really necessary to keep me so tightly bound? It's extremely uncomfortable and I could really do with using the bathroom. Surely with all Peterson's resources he can afford to have a few of his musclemen guard me instead of leaving me trussed up like a turkey."

"You're not really in a position to make demands, Mr Andrews. Wally is unlikely to be receptive to them."

"It's not a demand; it's a request."

She put her head on one side coquettishly and appeared to be thinking about what he'd said.

"OK," she said lightly, "I'll pop along and ask him."

Fifteen minutes later, she returned followed by Jeffrey and Martin.

"Wally took some persuading but he's agreed that you can be strapped to a chair. But if there's even a hint of any further resistance or an attempt to escape," she said, wagging her finger at him, "you will be strapped tightly to that trolley day and night."

She looked down at him and smiled sweetly. "Now, there's a bathroom through the door behind you. The boys will accompany you while you freshen up."

Resisting the temptation to react to the guards' deliberate rough handling of him as they unstrapped him and took him into the small bathroom, John ignored them as best he could and concentrated on stretching his limbs and aching neck. As he rolled up his sleeves to wash at the basin, he was surprised to see a plaster covering the crook of his left arm where Hannah Frobisher had drawn his blood. A large bruise spread beyond it.

When he had finished, the guards took him back to a metal chair that Frobisher had fetched, and they strapped him to it.

"Thank you, boys," said Frobisher to the two guards. "I don't think it will be necessary to stand guard. Your room is just down the hall and I'm sure you'll hear me if I scream."

The guards grunted sullenly and left the room.

"So what happens now?" asked John.

"Well, we're waiting for some results from a DNA profiling we've carried out on your blood. Wally said it was important to be absolutely certain we are dealing with the right man – I think all your protestations must have worried him, although personally, I have no doubt at all. After that, because we're in the fortunate position to have all the results from Professor Young, we can skip the next step."

"Who's Professor Young, another one of your conspirators?"

She laughed, looking at him coyly. "You're making it all sound very sinister, you know, Mr Andrews. He's an eminent geneticist who works in a laboratory funded by Wally's money. He's quite brilliant, if a little naïve. We keep tabs on his work so that if he comes up with anything interesting, we know about it almost before he does."

"So when Peterson claimed last night that all this work had been carried out here, he was lying. You spied on this Professor Young and stole his results."

"His research is entirely funded by us so I don't think 'stole' is very appropriate. We have every right to see all his results."

"Yet you still find it necessary to spy on him. You must feel very insecure about the people you fund."

Hannah Frobisher tossed her head petulantly at the remark and shrugged.

"Hardly your concern, Mr Andrews."

"You were in the process of answering my question," continued John. "What happens now?"

"Ah, yes. Well, since we don't feel it's necessary to repeat all the tests that demonstrated your immunity, we can forge ahead with a more interesting battery of tests that will tell us precisely how effective your immune system really is. We want to pit it against some of the big guns. Wally's idea is to do this slowly, since we don't want to overwhelm your system. We'll start with some strong forms of a few common diseases to see how your body copes, and if all goes as I think it will, we'll start to increase the virulence. It will all take time, several weeks probably, but assuming that Professor Young's interpretation is correct, you should suffer no discomfort at all." She smiled sweetly.

"So you intend to expose me to a whole range of deadly diseases?"

"Oh, they're not deadly to you, Mr Andrews, so you have nothing to worry about."

"You're insane. You obviously intend to carry on subjecting me to more and more danger until you eventually kill me."

"That would be a very disappointing outcome and one I really don't think we need consider," she said archly. "You don't seem to appreciate the very special nature of your immune system, Mr Andrews."

"And when do you intend to start this madness?"

"The profiling of your DNA will take a little while longer, so I intend to start tomorrow."

She looked at her watch. "Mmm, unless the results are ready sooner than I thought. I'll pop along to the lab and check on progress."

John sighed. He felt as if he was in a bad dream. This time yesterday he had been quietly selling his paintings at the art exhibition in Keswick and now he was being held by lunatics.


About an hour later, Hannah Frobisher returned carrying a metal dish.

"Good news, Mr Andrews! The DNA profiling has finished and the results confirm you are the person from the original profiling. So you can stop all this pretence and mystery and tell me about yourself. Tell me about your lives, your loves, your work over the centuries, Mr Andrews. How many people have you been? Were all of them famous artists? I'm fascinated to know."

She put down the metal dish and stroked one of his hands. "Just think how old these hands are! And yet they appear as young and fresh as mine. Younger. How many wonderful masterpieces have they created?" She smiled warmly at him. "What an enigma you are, Mr Andrews."

John glared at her. "My life is none of your business and I'm certainly not going to dignify your criminal activities by engaging you in a little heart-to-heart chat. As far as I am concerned, you can go to hell!"

"Then we're in the same position as we were last night," she replied petulantly. "I'll just have to get on with my work if you're going to be so stubborn."

She picked up a syringe and vial from the tray and pushed the syringe needle through the vial's septum, pulling back the plunger to fill the barrel.

"Wally has agreed there's no reason why I can't start my immunity experiments immediately, so I'm going to administer the first of a number of cocktails I've prepared now. This one is a simple mixture of four viruses and three bacteria that have very short incubation periods. In other words, we'll be able to see very quickly how your body is coping with them."

She pulled up the sleeve of his shirt and plunged the needle into his shoulder.

"There," she said, removing the needle and wiping the puncture site with a swab. "That was easy, wasn't it? I'll just attach these temperature and blood pressure probes to you and we're finished."

# Chapter 34

The girls were still some distance short of Horsham when Sally's phone rang. It was Ced.

"Hi, Sal, we're a couple of miles from the estate. Peterson was quite shocked when the professor called him just now, but he's agreed to see him. So I'm about to get into the back. Sal, are you there? Say something."

"I can hear you, Ced, I just can't get as excited about it as you."

"For heaven's sake, Sal, there's no need to sound so mournful; I'm not about to be executed. Look, I've been checking out the house on the Peterson estate using Google Earth on my phone and it's easy. The grounds around the house are full of trees and bushes. There's loads of cover. All I've got to do is slip out of the car into the bushes, move around the side of the house for a look-see, text the prof, get back in the car and we're out of there. It'll be a piece of cake."

"Unless they've dug up all the bushes since the photos were taken," protested Sally. "I still think it's a hell of a risk, Ced."

"Nonsense, Sal! I'll be very careful, I promise."

"No heroics, OK?"

"Look, Sal, I'd better go; we can't be far from the gate. Love you, hon."

"You too, marathon man. And for God's sake, be careful!"

"Here's the wall of the estate now," said the professor as Ced pocketed his phone. "I'll pull up and you can clamber into the back."

"Couple of things before I do that," said Ced, pressing a few buttons on his phone. "First, your phone is definitely on vibrate only?"

The professor pulled out his phone and adjusted it.

"It is now."

"Good. Mine too. I won't text you until I'm ready to leave."

He reached up to the car's interior light. "I'll switch off this light so that when I get out, it doesn't go on. You need to lock the car when you get out, so that none of the guards can snoop inside it. I can get out from the inside – you don't have child locks activated, do you?"

The professor's eyes crinkled in mild amusement and appreciation of Ced's attention to detail. "No Ced, I don't. Not for many years now. You'll be able to get out."

"Good, that's it then. Good luck with Peterson. I'll fold myself up in the boot – oh, yes, I'd better release the button on the rear seat so I can push it down."

"Good luck, Ced, and take care."

Ced climbed into the luggage area of the hatchback and Young shut the tailgate. Running his hands through his hair for the umpteenth time, he drove on up to the main gate, stopping in front of the guardhouse. He lowered his window and turned his head to show his face to the guard.

"Hallo, Eddie, Sir Wally's expecting me."

"Yes, sir, he called just now. You're working late on a Sunday, sir."

"No peace for the wicked, Eddie."

The gate slid open to let him in and then closed again immediately.

"OK, Ced, we're in," he called.

"Magic," came the muffled reply.

He followed the roads to the house and parked near the bushes Ced had seen on Google Earth. Looking up, Young saw the guard, Jeffrey, walking over to meet him. He grabbed his briefcase and got out quickly, shutting the door behind him and beeping it locked.

"Not too much danger of it being nicked from here, professor," said Jeffrey, casting an inquisitive glance at the car, his face unsmiling, as always.

"Force of habit, Jeffrey," laughed Young, pocketing the keys.

They walked into the main entrance hall and Jeffrey escorted Young into the sitting room where Peterson was seated behind his desk absorbed in some papers. He looked up as the door opened, stood and walked over to Young. He offered his left hand since the right one was bandaged.

"Well, Frank, this is a surprise on a Sunday evening. Don't you ever stop?"

"Good heavens, Wally," cried Young, looking at the plasters and bruises on Peterson's face. "Whatever happened? Are you OK?"

"A bit sore, to tell you the truth, Frank," replied Peterson, his face not completely hiding the lingering anger he still felt about the incident of the previous night. "The whole thing was a silly accident, and entirely my own fault. Took a spin around the estate in one of the old Land Rovers. Brakes aren't too good and I was going a bit fast. I had to swerve out of the way for a deer that appeared out of nowhere and I drove into a tree. Stupidly, I wasn't wearing a seat belt so I got what I deserved."

Young ran his hands through his unruly hair and shook his head.

"Sounds like you were jolly lucky to get away with a few cuts and bruises, Wally. You should take more care of yourself; you're an important man."

Peterson shrugged. "Drink, Frank? I feel as if I could do with one."

"I'll wait until I've run through these papers with you, if that's OK," said Young. "I need to keep a clear head. But I think you'll want to celebrate after I've told you what it's all about."

"As you wish," said Peterson, pouring himself a scotch. "Take a seat and you can explain to me what all the excitement is about."

"Sorry for the short notice, Wally," said Young. "I've been going over these results all week and today I finally decided that I wasn't delusional or even stark staring mad. Having formed that opinion, I couldn't wait to pass on the information to you."

"Certainly sounds exciting," said Peterson, trying hard to inject some enthusiasm into his voice.

Young took a deep breath and started, intending to make the story long and slow to give Ced plenty of time, knowing full well that Peterson had already seen the information. Nevertheless, Peterson knew only part of the story and Young wanted to keep it that way. He also intended to obscure some of the facts relating to Claudia and Sally, neither of whom he'd named in his notes.

He took the sheaf of papers from his briefcase and placed them on the table.

"Before I get to these, some background. One of my ex-Ph.D. students came to me a couple of weeks ago with a very strange tale. He works–"

"He?" interrupted Peterson, his strong tone clearly expecting Young to give a name.

"Yes, he," said the professor, surprised at how forceful Peterson's question had been. "His name's, er, Barry Bassett," he said, improvising and surprised at the name that had popped into his head. Barry Bassett was one of his wife's three dogs. "He works for a Forensic Laboratory near Birmingham that carries out DNA profiling of buccal swabs taken by the police. He's interested in rare alleles and he's convinced that junk DNA has a function."

"Not that old chestnut," scoffed Peterson, rather unconvincingly.

"You may laugh, Wally, but it seems he's come up trumps."

He paused, watching Peterson sipping his drink.

"Well?" said Peterson, when the pause didn't end.

"Actually, Wally, I should say that in telling you all this tonight, I'm breaking a confidence. But what's contained in these papers is so profound that I felt obliged to tell you, regardless. After all, with all the funding you provide to my lab, I effectively work for you."

Peterson nodded in approval but said nothing.

"Thanks to Barry," continued Young, "I have made probably the most significant discovery since the elucidation of the double helix. It's going to transform genetic research and the treatment of many diseases. Not immediately, but in the medium-to-long term. I'm talking about using genetics to combat and resist disease in a way that's never before even been dreamed of. And not only that, Wally, but also to resist ageing."

Peterson did a reasonable job of feigning surprise.

"That's quite a claim, Frank. I think you'd better explain."

Young told him about Claudia's results and how she had tracked down John Andrews, referring to her all the time as 'Barry Bassett'. He explained that quite by chance, the Andrews' paintings had led her down a different track with her friend Ced Fisher. He took Peterson through Ced's frustrations with his program and the final realisation that his program was correct.

Having reached this point, he returned to the potential commercial implications and how he thought it only reasonable that Peterson BioTech should benefit. He explained that he thought that 'Barry' would agree and that there should be a place on a research team for him, given how he was instrumental in the discovery.

Peterson nodded absently, not in the least bit interested in Barry Bassett. "So you say that this man's DNA structure not only gives him absolute immunity to all disease, but it has also arrested his ageing?"

"Exactly, except I don't think arrested is the right word. Having reached maturity, I don't think he's capable of ageing further at all."

"Remarkable. It would need to be demonstrated, of course. I mean, it's all very well to come up with this theory from your tests, but the proof of the pudding and all that."

"Quite," said Young. "We'll need to genetically modify some lab animals to give them the same properties. With rats, we'd soon know whether they are ageing or not. And in vitro studies of Andrews' blood would help, if he can be persuaded. As I've told you, he's so far been very resistant to any involvement."

He noticed the hint of a smile flash across Peterson's face.

"But this is your area, Wally," he continued. "You're the public relations man and you certainly have the resources to persuade Andrews to come to the party."

Peterson took another sip of his drink. "You know, Frank, all this testing is going to take some time – several years, probably. I think, given the nature of this discovery, we need to be sure of the immunity situation as quickly as possible. I wonder if Andrews could be brought on board and persuaded to be subjected to a few immunity tests – using innocuous viruses and bacteria, of course – ones that would do him no harm if we've got it wrong, but which would quickly confirm his immunity if your theory is correct."

Young was genuinely shocked. "You can't be serious, Wally! You can't go conducting basic research of this nature on a person! It's ... it's against every code of ethics that was ever written. Supposing his immunity is selective in some way we don't understand; we could end up killing him. Heavens, man, we can't bulldoze our way through the research; we have to be patient and methodical. There must be no room for doubt."

Peterson smiled condescendingly – this narrow-minded scientist could hardly be expected to appreciate the bigger picture.

"I hear you, Frank, but you have to consider a few things here. Not so much with the immunity per se, but its relation to ageing. From what you are saying, it seems to me that it might be possible through the development of gene manipulation to extend people's lifespans. You and I aren't getting any younger, Frank, and I can't think of two more worthy recipients of such treatment than us. Why shouldn't we benefit from this discovery? But, in order to do that, we can't have the research taking years. The matter has to be expedited."

Young sat back and ran his hands through his hair once again. "My God, Wally, I think you're serious. You of all people should know that the business of gene therapy, gene manipulation and so on, is still very much in its infancy. There's a long way to go from here to extending someone's life. We're probably far too old; the sort of research I'm anticipating could take decades."

"Supposing we channelled everything in that specific direction?" countered Peterson.

"It won't be some magic potion that gives you immortality, Wally. Stop dreaming of eternal youth and get real."

"I disagree," said Peterson smoothly. "If Andrews' genetic code gives him immunity from disease and ageing, why shouldn't that code be deciphered and given to others? My resources are profound, you know, Frank; I could mobilise an army of researchers for this."

"You know, Wally," smiled Young, "we need to go through the data together. You're a biochemist and geneticist; it's very important that you are in total agreement with my interpretation and don't just accept everything I've said without question."

Peterson suppressed a groan. He'd already been there but he couldn't admit it to Young. He would have to humour him until he'd made a decision over what he was going to do with him.

Ced checked the time on his watch. It had been twenty minutes since Young had walked into the house with Jeffrey. There had been no text. It was time to move.

He slowly pushed the backrest forward and uncurled his body to crawl into the rear passenger space. Once there, he raised his head to look around, again keeping the movement slow. There was no one outside the house. He gently unlocked the door and opened it. He waited, but, again, all remained quiet. He carefully slid from the car to the gravel and gently pushed the door closed. There was the slightest of clicks but it alerted no one. Keeping crouched down and with the car between him and the house, he moved quickly into the nearby bushes.

The shrubbery was denser than he had anticipated and it was with some difficulty that he made his way through it and round to the side of the house. Here he found that Sally had been correct: the layout of the garden had changed since the Google Earth photo had been taken. Instead of a large area of bushes and shrubbery, a dense hedge about eight feet tall ran down the side of the house, a gravel path separating the two, but on the outside of the hedge, a lawn had been planted that extended to a wooded area some hundred feet away. Although he was effectively screened from view from the house, anyone walking onto the lawn or on the edge of the woods would see him. He would have to be very careful.

Keeping close to the hedge on the lawn side, Ced moved slowly along it, trying to work out the house's layout. The part he could see was relatively new, a two-storey extension to the rear of the house stretching some eighty feet. At the point where the original house met the extension, he could see a room with a light on, but a window blind prevented him from seeing into it. A door next to the window led onto the gravel. Beyond that, several larger windows looked onto the gravel path from rooms in the extension. Some had lights burning in them, the July evening light blocked by the nearby hedge.

Ced was about to weave his way through the bushes for a closer look when he heard a door open a few feet from him. Two guards came out and lit cigarettes. He shrank down and remained motionless. He was relieved to see that rather than starting a patrol, the guards appeared to be having a break.

One of the guards leaned back again the wall and took a deep pull on his cigarette. He was only about six feet from Ced, but, with no thought that there might be somebody beyond the bushes, his eyes didn't focus in that direction.

"Been up to see Henry this afternoon, Jeff?" said the guard.

"Couple of hours ago, Mart. He looks pretty good to me; I think he's milking his bruises for all he's got. It's unlike the boss to give time off like that and Henry's taking full advantage of it. Bloody skiver."

"I can't believe how that Andrews bloke got the drop on him like that. Really caught him napping. Andrews is lucky it weren't me that he hit. Peterson wouldn't have been able to stop me. I'd have decked him and beaten him to a pulp."

"S'pose it ain't too surprising that Andrews can look after himself. If he's a spy for one of these other companies like the boss says he is, then he'd expect trouble occasionally. He'd need to know how to throw a few punches."

"I reckon he got lucky. But it's all very well for Henry slowly working his way through his scotch upstairs; it just leaves the two of us to look after the house. It's OK today, I s'pose – it's Sunday – but he'd better be back to normal tomorrow."

Martin sniggered. "You know, Jeff, I thought you'd blown his brains out when I heard you fire that shot."

"A warning shot, Mart. I could have dropped him if I wanted, but the boss said he wasn't to be hurt. Mind you, he felt that pile driver of yours into his guts all right!"

"You betcha," grinned Martin. "He didn't see that one coming!"

"Right," said Jeffrey. "Well, we've got him all trussed up like a hog now; he ain't going nowhere. All he's got to look forward to are a few sessions with that vicious Frobisher bitch. Once she's stuck a few needles into him, he'll be as quiet as a mouse, and probably stay that way forever. I've seen the results of her work before." He shook his head. "Not pretty, I can tell you."

"Yeah," nodded Martin. "Rumour has it that there's one or two of her experiments buried on the estate. If this bloke really is a spy, he won't be getting out of here, that's for sure. By the way, who was that other geezer who arrived just now?"

"That's the professor. He's one of the boss's paid monkeys who do all his research for him. Lives in his own world, that one. The boss pats him on the head, pays him some money for his research and he's happy. He must have hit the jackpot to come down here on a Sunday night; he certainly looked pretty pleased with himself. He and the boss are heads together in the sitting room right now."

He took a last pull on his cigarette and stubbed it out on the sole of his shoe. Martin followed and closed the door behind him.

Ced listened carefully, but he couldn't hear the sound of a lock turning or bolts being thrown. He waited a few minutes in case there was any further activity, but the light went out and all was quiet. He walked slowly along the outside of the hedge, peering through it when he came to windows where there were lights burning. The rooms appeared to be laboratories. There were arrays of analytical instruments on the benches, each with numerous illuminated displays, switches and computer monitors, while biohazard handling cabinets lined the walls.

Through the second window, he could make out a figure in a white laboratory coat walking around. He decided to risk going closer, hoping the increasing gloom outside contrasting with the light in the laboratory would prevent him from being seen. He pushed carefully through the hedge and moved gently to the gravel path, easing his weight down slowly to minimise the telltale crunch that could give him away. He could see that the figure was a woman who was moving from one instrument to another, checking readouts and writing notes on a clipboard. He wondered if she was the 'vicious Frobisher bitch' the guards had referred to. She certainly had a grim purposeful look on her plain-featured face. He watched as she went to one of the large fridges, removed a vial and then left the room.

Ced crept slowly up to the window and tried it, but it was locked. Walking very gingerly on the gravel, he continued towards the rear of the house, coming eventually to another door. It was also locked. Looking along the remaining length of wall, he could see that the other rooms were in darkness and beyond them, a large open area of gardens.

He retraced his steps along the gravel path until he reached the door that led into the guards' room, noticing on the way that the white-coated woman had returned to the laboratory. He tried the door handle and found it to be unlocked. Opening the door, he slipped quickly into the room, closing the door quietly behind him. In the semi-darkness inside the room, he could make out two other doors, one of them slightly ajar. He peered through the crack and saw the large entrance hall. The two guards were standing by the main door, engrossed in quiet conversation.

He stepped back and gently turned the handle of the other door. It opened into a brightly lit corridor. To his left was another door that must open into the main entrance hall; to the right the corridor led away towards the rear of the house. Along the corridor, there were doors leading off both sides, the ones to the right clearly opening into the various laboratories he had seen from the outside. He estimated the door to the laboratory where he had seen the woman working was about thirty feet along the corridor.

Trying the first door on the right, he opened it to see a small unlit laboratory, an internal glass partition looking onto the adjacent room, also unlit. Through a similar glass partition in the second room, he could see into the laboratory where the woman was working, writing notes on her clipboard from a display on a monitor. He was relieved that she had her back to him: if she had been looking his way, there was a good chance she might have seen him.

Back in the corridor, he moved to the left side. The first door he tried was locked, but the second opened. The light was on. Tensing, he peered into the room. To his amazement, he found himself looking at John Andrews, who was strapped to a metal chair by his arms, legs and body, his face a mask of simmering anger as he glowered at Ced.

John opened his mouth to speak, but Ced brought his finger up to his lips as he quietly closed the door. He was relieved to see the room had no half-glass partitions.

He moved closer to John. "Are you OK?" he whispered.

"So far," muttered John. He frowned at Ced accusingly. "I know you, don't I?"

"Ced Fisher. I came to your gallery a few weeks ago."

"Of course. What the hell are you doing here? I assume you're in this thing along with these other lunatics?"

Ced shook his head. "On the contrary, I'm here to help you escape. I feel very responsible for your predicament. So does Claudia."

"Is she here too?" said John.

"No, she's waiting in the car outside the estate, along with Sally, my girlfriend, the one who–"

"I know, bought several paintings from me. You've got some explaining to do."

"Yes, I know, but it's a long story which will have to wait," replied Ced. "Have they hurt you?"

"No, not yet, but they have every intention of trying. So far they've taken a litre of my blood, sedated me for hours on end and that female ghoul of a scientist who wants to carry out experiments on me has injected me with what she called a cocktail of bacteria and viruses. She said they were basically harmless, that she's testing my response. From what they've told me about myself, and from what I know already, I don't think there will be any reaction. But you wouldn't understand that."

"Actually, Mr Andrews, I understand perfectly well," said Ced. "I know all about you and I'm in awe. I know about your age and that you knew Piero della Francesca. And I know about your remarkable immune system. Believe me, I'm determined to get you out of all this."

John was shocked. "It seems as if suddenly the whole world knows about me," he said bitterly.

"No, Mr Andrews, only a very few people do. Unfortunately, some of them aren't very nice people, so the sooner we get you away from here, the better."

"Well, you could start by undoing these straps," said John.

Ced walked round behind him and bent to release the straps securing his legs. As he did, John whispered urgently to him. "Wait! I can hear her coming back; her heels are quite noisy. Leave that strap in place so that it looks OK and get into the bathroom; it's through that door." He nodded towards a door at the far end of the room.

Ced adjusted the strap and slipped quickly into the bathroom, closing the door just as the door from the corridor opened. Hannah Frobisher came in carrying another metal dish containing a vial and a syringe. John saw that this time she was wearing disposable rubber gloves.

"How are you feeling, Mr Andrews?" she said, her smile lacking any warmth.

"Not good," he lied, his eyes fixed on the new vial and syringe. "I think I'm running a temperature."

"What! Let me see!" She quickly put down the dish on the side bench and bent to look at the readouts displayed on the monitors for his temperature and blood pressure.

She looked up and smiled at him coolly. "Very funny, Mr Andrews. You're either trying to wind me up or you're having a psychosomatic reaction to the first injection. Not to worry – everything's normal. You're absolutely fine. Which, frankly, is what I should expect."

She smiled evilly at him, her eyes sparkling. "Now, I've a little surprise for you. I've been reconsidering the immunity-testing programme that I've set up for you and, given that I'm totally convinced of your ability to see off all comers in the disease world, I can see no reason why we shouldn't accelerate it. I know that Wally is very keen to get the results from all the obvious disease candidates out of the way and then move on to more esoteric studies on you. Neither of us can wait to see how your system handles exposure to various levels of radiation. If your body can resist that, it would be truly remarkable.

"But we have to get the ordinary diseases out of the way first. So, I've decided to take the bull by the horns and pump a few more little beasties into you. I do this in the full confidence that they are going to have no effect on you at all. As far as I'm concerned, it's a totally no-risk situation. About the only thing you'll feel is the prick of the needle as it punctures your skin."

"What?" shouted John. "You really are stark staring mad, aren't you? You've only just pumped the first lot of your rubbish into me and now you want to pump in more without waiting for the results? What kind of scientist do you call yourself? Have you no patience at all?"

She laughed. "Very good, Mr Andrews, quite a performance, but I'm afraid you really don't know what you're talking about. You see, the trick of being a pioneering scientist is knowing precisely when and how you can cut corners. And I am completely confident that what I'm about to add to the earlier cocktail that's already being neutralised by your body will do you no harm at all. You see, there's simply no point in waiting."

She raised her shoulders and put her hands together in front of her face. "This is so exciting! Wally's going to be so pleased," she exclaimed gleefully. "Let's get going, shall we?"

She turned to the bench, put on a facemask that she pulled from her pocket and picked up the vial from the dish.

"What have you got in there?" said John angrily.

"It's an interesting little cocktail, one that I have to be quite careful about handling myself since I don't have the advantage of your immunity. I'm not going to tell you what's in it; I don't want to get your blood pressure up," she sniggered. "But I will say that it's far less friendly than the first one I injected."

She paused, her head on one side as she acted out thinking about something. "Actually," she smiled conspiratorially, "I will tell you one of the components. It's rabies. Imagine that, Mr Andrews, you'll be injected with a full, powerful dose of rabies, and nothing will happen!"

She pushed the syringe needle into the vial and withdrew the yellow liquid. Very carefully squeezing the plunger to remove the air, she put down the vial and turned to walk towards John, holding the syringe out in front of her in both her hands, her eyes focused on the needle.

"Here we are," she said excitedly.

John wasn't listening – he was also concentrating on the syringe. As she came within range, he suddenly kicked out hard at her with his right leg, his foot connecting sharply with her hands.

Frobisher squealed in surprise as her hands jerked back hard towards her upper body, turning as they did. Her head snapped back and the syringe needle buried itself deep in her neck. Instinctively grasping the syringe tighter, the palm of one hand caught the plunger and pushed it down the barrel, discharging about half its contents into her body. She stood there grasping the syringe, her face a picture of horror, knowing only too well the consequences of the injection she had given herself.

Not waiting for any reaction from her, John lashed out again, his foot thumping hard into her abdomen and sending her tumbling backwards. Her hands were still grasping the syringe and she made no attempt to break her fall. She sat down hard on the floor, her head cracking into the wall. Stunned by the blow, her whole body sagged and her hands dropped to her sides, the syringe remaining firmly embedded in her neck.

"Fisher!" cried out John in a loud whisper. "In here, quickly!"

Ced rushed in from the bathroom, stopping in surprise to see the semiconscious woman on the floor.

"Christ!" he exclaimed quietly.

"Undo these straps quickly, and don't touch her!" commanded John.

Free of the constraints, he pulled off the probes, stood up and pointed to the bathroom door.

"Stand in that corner there!" he said. "You mustn't go anywhere near her; I don't want there to be any risk of that stuff coming into contact with you."

He bent over and took Frobisher's hands, hauling her to her feet and swinging her round to sit in the chair. Grabbing a towel from the bench, he tied it as a gag and then secured her hands, feet and body to the chair with the straps.

Her eyes flickered as she came round. John stood up straight and looked down at her without any pity. "Rabies, Dr Frobisher? That will be a pretty painful death, I understand. I wonder what else was in that injection?"

He saw the horror in her eyes as she struggled against the constraints.

He turned to Ced, who was still standing in the corner, looking pale.

"Did you hear our conversation?" asked John.

Ced nodded, his eyes still on Frobisher. "I was about to rush in, but you beat me to it," he said.

John smiled grimly. "I think you arrived just in time; releasing my legs was all that was needed."

Coming to his senses, Ced walked around the still struggling Hannah Frobisher. "We'd better get out of here," he said.

John nodded. "Yes, but before we do that, there's one thing that I must do first. They took a litre of my blood. If we leave now, they'll still have it to work on. I want to find it and flush it down the drain."

"It'll be in one of the fridges in the lab," said Ced. "I saw her working in there through the windows from outside in the grounds. It's along the corridor."

Ced opened the door quietly and peered up and down the corridor. They had made very little noise and Hannah Frobisher's single squeal had not been loud. No one had been alerted.

Ced opened the door to Frobisher's laboratory and looked around. "It'll be in one of those fridges," he said, pointing "You start looking while I text the prof."

"The prof?" asked John.

"I didn't get in here all by myself. Professor Frank Young, who was Claudia's supervisor for her research and who worked out all the stuff about you, is with me. All his results and notes were stolen from him by the owner of this place–"

"Peterson," said John.

"Yes," replied Ced. "The prof engineered getting in here and he's currently with Peterson distracting him while I look for you. I've got to tell him it's time to go."

# Chapter 35

Frank Young was in full flood. He had spread his papers across the coffee table and was systematically explaining the minutiae of the data to Peterson, taking care not to overlook the smallest detail. For his part, although he was well qualified as a geneticist, Peterson had ceased to follow the arcane reasoning several minutes earlier. His eyes had glazed over and his mind was elsewhere, sorting through a number of options for silencing the professor for good.

Young felt the phone vibrate in his pocket. Continuing his account, he pulled it out and glanced at it. There was one word on the screen: Go!

He deleted the message and made a play of looking at his watch. He looked up nervously at Peterson. "Good heavens, I had no idea it was getting so late. That was a text from Janet; she's wondering where I am. I forgot to call her in my enthusiasm to get down here. She's obviously tried the lab; I'd better call her."

He looked back at the phone and was about to press some keys when Peterson's hand closed over his. "Before you do that, Frank, there's someone I'd like you to meet. Two people, in fact. One is Dr Hannah Frobisher. You haven't met her, have you?"

Young shook his head. "No, is she new? She must be very keen, Wally, working on a Sunday evening."

Peterson smiled, but as Young caught his eyes, he saw they were glacial.

"Oh, she is. Very keen. And very talented. She's been working for me for quite a while now, but on certain very special projects; ones that I have to keep under wraps."

I'll bet she does! thought Young. Ones that you steal straight from the computers of suckers like me.

Peterson maintained his false geniality. "You'll be very impressed with her, Frank. She's got tremendous insight into cutting-edge genetics, and her laboratory work is inspirational. You'll have tons to talk about; you have so much in common."

He stood and held out an arm towards the hall door. "I think it would be better to talk to her first and then call Janet once you know how long you are going to be."

"Who's the other?" replied Young as he stood up, not liking the turn this meeting was taking. If Peterson was about to introduce him to Andrews, he clearly had no intention of letting him go.

"Ah," smiled Peterson, "that's my little surprise. Let's take a walk, shall we?"

He ushered Young into the hall. The two guards broke off their conversation and turned towards him.

"Everything all right, lads?" asked Peterson.

"All quiet, sir," replied Jeffrey.

"We're going to the laboratory," said Peterson. He glanced at his watch. "It's almost time for your rounds; you might as well come with us."

He opened the door to the corridor that led to the laboratories, leading the way while the two guards stayed close to Young's heels. Stopping outside the door to the room where Andrews had been held, he turned to Young, smiling. "First, Frank, my little surprise, although Dr Frobisher might well be in here too. Let me check."

He walked in to find Hannah Frobisher as John Andrews and Ced had left her a few minutes before: bound to a chair and gagged, with the syringe containing the remains of its lethal load still stuck in her neck.

"What the hell...!" he yelled.

Jeffrey and Martin responded immediately. Jeffrey moved quickly between the professor and the door, blocking his way, while Martin laid a restraining hand on the professor's arm. Jeffrey glanced into the room and was shocked to see the dishevelled Frobisher, tears streaming down her face as Peterson bent over her.

"Hannah, what's happened?" said Peterson. "Where's Andrews? What the devil is this syringe doing in your neck?" He reached out and pulled gently on the syringe. As he did, Frobisher shook her head vigorously, trying to stop him. Already loosened from when her hand had grabbed at it, the barrel separated from the needle and the contents oozed onto Peterson's bandaged right hand.

"Blast!" he yelled, throwing the barrel onto the bench top as Frobisher continued to shake her head furiously, her eyes wide with horror.

Peterson released the gag and, as Frobisher coughed and spluttered, he undid her wrists and legs.

"Wally!" screamed Frobisher. "Wipe your hand on that towel! Now! Before it soaks into your wounds."

Peterson frowned at her and picked up the towel. "Before what soaks into my wounds? Where's Andrews?" he yelled again.

"He might still be in the lab; I think that's where they went. Wally, you have to do something! I'm going to die, Wally. You must help me!"

Peterson saw the fear in her eyes and looked down at his hand.

"What was in that syringe, Hannah?" he said, his voice menacing.

"I was about to inject Andrews with another cocktail. I wanted to accelerate the procedure. I decided there was no point in waiting since he was obviously not going to be affected by any of the bacteria and viruses. I thought you'd be pleased to move onto the next phase as soon as possible. But his legs had been freed and he kicked out at me. The syringe needle went straight into my neck."

"What was in it, you stupid bitch?"

She shrank back as he raised his undamaged hand to strike her.

"Rabies," she whispered. "And a very virulent form of hepatitis."

"Christ!" yelled Peterson, diving for the tap and ripping the bandage from his right hand. "And I've squirted the damn stuff into an open wound!"

He turned on the tap and soaked his hand, looking down in horror at the still unhealed lacerations from where he'd grabbed at the breaking glass when it smashed into his head the previous night.

He rubbed frantically at his hand under the running water and it started bleeding again.

"Jesus!" he yelped, the wounds stinging. He grabbed at a paper towel and wrapped it round his hand.

He turned angrily to Frobisher, who was still cringing in the chair.

"You stupid, stupid bitch!"

"Wally, you've got to do something," she wailed.

"What do you suggest? Take you to the nearest A&E? All I can do for you is lock you in a soundproofed room so no one can hear your screams as you die. And pray that your cocktail hasn't got into my system as well!"

He slapped her viciously with the back of his left hand, a large signet ring cracking into her upper jaw. She sagged into unconsciousness.

"Idiot!" he growled through clenched teeth.

He turned and saw Jeffrey, who was watching but not fully understanding the implications of what he'd seen and heard.

"Don't stand there gawping, you halfwit!" yelled Peterson. "Follow me! Andrews is probably still in the building. And bring Young with you!"

He pushed past the guards and ran along the corridor to Frobisher's laboratory. He flung open the door in time to see John on the far side of the room flushing the last remnants from the container of blood down a sink. Ced was standing next to him.

"Grab them!" ordered Peterson to the guards, who were following, half dragging the bewildered professor with them.

At the sound of the door and Peterson's voice, John spun round. He dropped the blood container into the sink and looked round quickly for something that he might use as a weapon. He picked up a glass reagent bottle and hurled it at Peterson, following it almost immediately with a second. Peterson saw the first one coming and ducked to avoid it, but the second caught him a glancing blow on the ear.

John charged after his missiles and as Peterson reeled from the impact with the bottle, John punched him squarely in the face with a left. Peterson's head snapped back and he fell into the path of Jeffrey, who had let go of Young and was running to his boss's aid.

As Jeffrey pushed Peterson to one side, Martin, the other guard, flung Young into a corner and raced after his colleague. John squared up to them, noticing out of the corner of his eye that Ced was still by his side, crouched in a martial arts pose. The guards skidded to a halt and Martin, who was opposite Ced, crouched into a similar stance, his mouth a sneer.

He weaved his arms in the air, moving slowly closer to Ced. "What are you waiting for, sunshine?" he snarled.

As he began to leap at Ced, he was stopped in his tracks by the metal base of an apparatus stand crashing hard onto his head. The professor had been quick to regain his balance after stumbling into the corner of the laboratory and had immediately picked up the heaviest thing he could find. Coming up on the guards from behind, he had brought the metal base down on the head of the one closer to him.

Not waiting to see the effect of the professor's blow, Ced delivered two crushing blows of his own to Martin's torso and throat. The guard collapsed unconscious. Distracted by the unexpected movement, Jeffrey glanced sideways towards Martin, giving John the opportunity to deliver three Johanne specials to his head. Jeffrey's knees buckled and he fell to the ground with a grunt.

The blow to Peterson had been less powerful and he was starting to stagger to his feet. Ced was the first to notice and, having taken two steps in his direction, kicked out hard to Peterson's head, sending him sprawling once again.

Ced turned to John, the tension in his face relaxing into a smile of satisfaction. "I knew that stuff would come in useful one day."

But John wasn't ready to relax.

"We need to tie these three up so we can get out of here before they raise the alarm," he said, pulling open the drawers closest to him. Finding some cord and a roll of tape, he bound the guards hand and foot and gagged them. He then completed the job with Peterson.

"I won't gag him," he said looking up at Ced. "His mouth is bleeding from where you kicked him. I don't want him to choke on his own blood. He seems to be out cold, so I don't think he'll be a problem."

Standing up, John saw the professor leaning heavily against the wall, the tension of the moment having caught up with him.

"You must be the professor that Ced mentioned," said John, walking up to him. "Are you OK?"

"Fine," nodded Young, his hands weaving their usual path through his hair.

"That was a very well-timed diversion," smiled John. "Your intervention gave us the edge we needed. Thank you very much."

"Glad to be of assistance," replied Young, looking into John's eyes. "I'm delighted to meet you at last, Mr Andrews."

The usual humour in his eyes then dissolved as he looked down at Peterson. "You scheming bastard," he snarled. He walked across the laboratory and opened the door of one of the freezers. He pulled on a protective glove and reached in, retrieving a vial to read its label, and then several others.

"God Almighty!" he exclaimed, shaking his head in amazement. "There's enough viral and bacterial material in here to wipe out most of Europe!"

His eye caught a tray of syringes and he picked one up. "I've a good mind to give Peterson a dose of his own medicine. Literally."

John held up a hand. "I can understand how you must feel, professor," he said, shaking his head, "but what has happened so far is all justifiable; it was self-defence. If you inject this maniac with that stuff, you could be on a murder charge."

Young stood still, his hand grasping the open freezer door. Then he slowly replaced the vial he was holding and closed the door.

"You're right. We'll let the law deal with him. Despite his wealth, title and connections, he'll have a job worming his way out of all this."

Ced, who had been checking the guards' bindings, stood and said, "I really think we should leave. I know there's another guard upstairs who's off duty. He doesn't appear to have heard anything or he would have been charging through that door by now. But I think we should go. We can decide what to do once we're away from here."

"You're right," agreed Young. "It's possible there are other guards around the grounds as well. I'll call the gate from Peterson's sitting room."

"We'd better check that Frobisher is still secure," added John as they left the laboratory and ran up the corridor. He opened the door to the room where he'd been held and was surprised to see the unconscious Hannah Frobisher slouched in the chair, a large red weal across her face.

"She's no longer bound, but I think she'll be out for a while. Peterson must have found out what she was up to and lost the rag," he said to the others as he caught up with them in the corridor.

They ran through the hall into the sitting room. Young went to the desk and ran his finger down the list of internal numbers next to the phone. He picked up the handset and punched a number.

Putting his hand over his mouth, he barked an instruction, mimicking very accurately Peterson's mild but noticeable Yorkshire accent.

"Peterson. My guest is leaving. Open the gate for him, would you?"

He put down the phone and they ran to his car. As they approached it, he saw Ced pulling out his mobile.

"No time for that, Ced. Call once we're through the gate. Get down as low as you can in the back, both of you. I intend to drive through the gate too fast for them to get a look inside."

It was now fully dark and the professor switched the headlights to main beam as they approached the gate, making it impossible for the gate guards to see into the car. He heaved a sigh of relief as he saw the gate slide open. Hardly braking, he passed the guard at about thirty miles per hour, giving a toot on the horn and a wave as he did.

As he accelerated up the road, he called out. "OK, we're all clear. You can make that call now Ced."

Ced was immediately upright and punching the speed dial buttons for Sally's phone. "Sal!"

"Ced! Are you OK? Tell me you're fine!"

"All fine, Sal."

"Thank heavens for that. Listen, we've found a rear gate in the fence–"

"Sal!"

"–We can pull it down with a rope I found in the car. It's all quiet here so I don't think–"

"Sal!"

"–anyone has seen us. I'm sure it'll be–"

"Sal! Listen! We're out! There's no need to pull down any gate or fence. Just drive away and we'll meet you on the main road."

"You're out? Ced, that's brilliant!"

Ced continued listening to her as he looked towards John.

"Yes, he's here with us, Sal, and he's fine. We'll be with the three of you in a few minutes."

He turned to John and grinned mysteriously. John frowned at him, puzzled by his look. He was about to ask him to explain when Ced turned to the professor.

"The girls will meet us at the junction up here, Prof, where the side road goes off around the estate."

Young nodded and then caught Ced's eye in the mirror.

"Did you say 'the three of you' just now when you were talking to Sally, Ced? Are there three of them now? Who's the third?"

"Yes, Ced," added John. "Who is the third? You only mentioned two when you were explaining things to me back there."

Ced pursed his lips. "Mr Andrews... Actually, after what we've been through together in there, would it be OK if I called you John?"

John laughed. "Certainly, if you tell me what all your amusement is about. I suspect it's more than a feeling of relief to be out of that very dangerous situation."

Ced's enigmatic smile broadened into a grin. He took a deep breath. "Well, John, your interesting day is about to get even more interesting, but this time in a very positive way."

He turned his head to look up the road and nodded towards a pair of headlights that had appeared down a side road.

"Look, there are the girls now."

# Chapter 36

Frank Young pulled his car onto the grass verge beyond the junction with the lane that ran around the Peterson Biotech estate. Ced jumped out almost before the car had come to a halt. Moments later his SUV turned onto the main road and stopped a few yards in front of the professor's car.

Sally threw open the driver's door and ran to Ced, launching herself into his arms and bursting into tears.

"Ced! Hon! Are you OK? Every minute has seemed like an hour. What happened in there? Have you really got John Andrews out in one piece?" All of this was broken up with a flurry of kisses, hugs and sniffs.

Ced laughed. "Yup. One piece and very much alive and kicking. He's a useful chap to have around when things get tight."

He felt Sally tense at his words.

"Not, of course, that they did. Not really," he added.

"And you're OK, Ced?" she gasped, leaning back to scrutinise him as she frantically wiped her eyes.

"Yes, Sal, I'm fine. Look – two arms, two legs, a head; all in the right places. No problems."

"God, I was getting really panicky, hon," said Sally. "You were gone for ages."

"It wasn't really that long, was it, Sal?"

"It was pushing two hours, Ced. An eternity when you're waiting out here imagining what that nutcase and his henchmen might be doing to you."

"Two hours? It seemed like a few minutes."

"Yeah, well, I was all for hitching up the car to that gate, ripping it off and charging into the place blowing a bugle. The others had to hold me down to stop me."

"Christ, I'm glad you didn't do that, Sal, it could have ruined everything."

"That's what they said as they sat on my head."

"It all went perfectly, hon," whispered Ced as he held her tightly to him. "Bit of an adrenaline rush, though; more than running a marathon. But I think I'll stick to those in future, even so."

As he held the sobbing, laughing Sally, he saw the front passenger door of his car open and Claudia get out. She smiled at him, the relief etched into her face. She walked slowly over to the professor, who had also climbed out of his car, and fell into his arms as he opened them to her diminutive form.

"Oh, Prof, is it really all over? I can't believe that all this has happened. You're not hurt in any way, are you?"

"I'm absolutely fine, Claudia. Really. There's no need to be concerned about me." He looked over to where Ced and Sally were standing and then back towards his car as he heard John Andrews get out.

"It was the most remarkable piece of teamwork. It couldn't have worked out better if we'd rehearsed it a hundred times."

He saw that John was smiling at his words and he nodded back to him.

"Now tell me, Claudia," he added, holding her away from him to look her in the eye. "Ced tells us there are three of you. How has that happened? Who's the third?"

Claudia bit her lip in excitement as she glanced at John Andrews, knowing he had overheard the professor's question. She looked back at Ced's SUV and saw the rear passenger door open. She let go of the professor and reached out for John's hand.

"Mr Andrews. John," she said. "I can't tell you how relieved I am to see that you're not hurt, that these wonderful men have helped to resolve this awful situation that I think was all my fault. I want to explain it all to you and to say how sorry I am that it happened. But there's time for that later. Right now, there's someone here who's been waiting to meet you, to see you again after a very long time."

She turned, and still holding his hand, led him towards the other car where Lily was now standing. The headlights of the professor's car were shining on her, but she was shielding her face with her arm, trying to keep her composure.

Puzzled, John looked across at the figure, then back to Claudia. She smiled up at him.

"This is Lily," she said softly.

He turned his head towards Lily as she dropped her arm and looked up, the headlights now showing her face in stark detail. She smiled at him and it was the smile that had stayed with him for more than a hundred years, the smile he had last seen when she sat at the bow of a sailing junk in the South China Sea.

"Lei-li," he whispered.

"Papa!"


Frank Young looked on in bemusement at the scene playing out in front of him. Sally's sobbing had turned into floods of tears as she'd watched John and Lily fall into each other's arms, while Ced had buried his face into Sally's hair. Claudia had moved to the rear of the SUV where she was leaning against it for support as her body shook with emotion.

Not understanding the significance of the moment, the professor coughed loudly. "Look," he said, "I really think we should go. It won't be long before some sort of alarm is raised. Worse still is the thought that Peterson and his guards might, as we speak, be regaining their equilibrium and deciding to come looking for us. We need to get right out of the area."

Nobody moved, so he coughed again. "Ced, are you going to be OK to drive your car?"

Ced nodded, his head still buried.

"Good," said the professor, matter-of-factly. "I suggest that you and Sally take John and, er …"

"Lily," said Claudia quietly.

"Yes, Lily. While you, Claudia, can come with me. And while we are driving, perhaps you can tell me what this latest surprise is all about."

John and Lily weren't really listening, so Claudia ushered them into Ced's SUV, after which she guided Ced and Sally in the same direction.

"Where are we going?" asked Ced.

"I suggest we go to my house," replied the professor. "It's a couple of hours from here, down near Tenterden, in Kent. I very much doubt Peterson has a clue where I live; I've certainly never discussed it with him."

They set off, with the professor's car leading the way.

"OK, Claudia, tell me all. Who is Lily? If I remember rightly, you said John's wife was called Lola, not Lily, and anyway, from that little speech you made to him, you clearly weren't referring to his wife."

"I take it, Prof, that you didn't get a chance to see her eyes."

"Her eyes? No, I didn't."

He paused as the significance of Claudia's remark hit him. "You mean they are the same as John Andrews' eyes? Is she the same as him?"

"She's his daughter, Prof, born over a hundred years ago."

"Well I never. So there are others. Claudia, that is the most fascinating piece of information. Tell me more!"

Claudia told him all she knew about Lily. As she did, she realised she knew almost nothing about her apart from a brief outline of her time in Hong Kong as a child and young woman, and of her quest to find her father in the past few weeks. But the professor soaked it up, nodding at all she told him.

"I can't wait to talk to her in more detail. I hope she's willing to let me test her DNA. It will be fascinating to compare it with John Andrews'; it will add a whole new perspective to the research on Andrews' genes. Gosh, Claudia, this is really exciting. And I can quite understand why you kept her secret from me earlier. I presume she was waiting for you somewhere when the rest of you came to my laboratory."

"Yes," replied Claudia rather guiltily. "As always, you've anticipated what I was going to say. As we explained earlier, we were worried that you were in cahoots with Peterson. If that had been the case, then obviously you shouldn't find out about Lily, and nor should Peterson. We resolved that one earlier, but then we thought it would still be better if you didn't know in case Peterson kidnapped you as well as John Andrews, and then tortured you."

Young laughed. "Torture is perhaps a little melodramatic, but he certainly had every intention of holding me there. You were very wise, Claudia, all of you, not to tell me. What I didn't know, I couldn't have told anyone. Protecting the truth about Lily was of paramount importance, as it still will be once we get beyond whatever is going to happen now."

"What do you think is going to happen now, Prof?"

"Hard to say, Claudia. It all depends on how Peterson reacts and whether he throws in the towel. He must know that he's got very little chance of getting what he wants now. One thing I would say is that I think you should give up that job of yours and get back to frontline research with me."

Claudia laughed. "Prof, you've just been through the most incredible ordeal and you're still thinking about your research!"

Young shook his head. "My ordeal was nothing compared to John Andrews'. That madman Peterson and his equally deranged assistant Hannah Frobisher had every intention of subjecting him to a horrific barrage of tests in order to find the limits of his immunity. They had no scruples whatsoever. Peterson even had a crazy dream of some sort of eternal youth for himself. It's that sort of thinking that emphasises the need for total anonymity for Andrews, and now for Lily as well. It's essential that their secret is known to as few people as possible."

"Do you think that Peterson and his assistant knowing will complicate things?" asked Claudia.

"It doesn't help. However, he's broken the law in kidnapping John Andrews, so we should have a bargaining tool."

"I'm not so sure," said Claudia. "He sounds like a clever man. It won't take him long to realise that he needs to clean up any trace of John ever having been there. If he manages that, it's your word against his."

She turned to look back beyond Ced's car. "Is there a chance that he's following even now?"

"I doubt it," smiled Young grimly. "We left him securely tied up and he's been knocked around a bit in the last twenty-four hours, mainly by John. You know, that man really knows how to look after himself. He has lightning reactions and his aim with a bottle is excellent."

"With a bottle? Sounds like there was a bit of a struggle," said Claudia, raising her eyebrows in interest.

"Well, he had his two heavies, as I think they'd be called. But between them, Ced – who, I should add, is no slouch either when it comes to self-defence and martial arts – and Andrews pretty effectively sorted all three of them out."

Very modestly, Young neglected to tell Claudia of his own part in overcoming the guards.


In the following car, Sally finally took her eyes off Ced for a moment and turned to John.

"You really should call your wife, John; she'll be at her wits' end. I think the last time Lily called her was about three hours ago when we were driving down here."

John turned to Lily in surprise. "You've spoken to Lola?"

"Oh yes, Papa. I've been keeping her informed of progress. We're the best of friends, you know. I really couldn't ask for a sweeter stepmother."

He shook his head and laughed. "I can't believe how much has happened in the last two days. May I use your phone?"

"Use this British one that Sally lent me," said Lily.

John punched his home number and Lola answered almost immediately.

"John! Where are you? Are you all right? Is Lily with you? Oh, God, I've been out of my mind. They haven't hurt you, have they?"

He spent several minutes reassuring Lola that he was fine, glossing over most of the details. "I'll tell you all about it when I get home, sweetheart, but that's not going to be until tomorrow, I think. We're now heading for the professor's house in Kent to get a good night's sleep. I suspect that after what's happened, the police are going to be involved, but we all need to sit down and talk about it."

Once she was calmer, Lola asked to speak to Lily.

"Hey, Lola. Yes, we're all fine." She turned her head to look at John as she was speaking. "Yes, really, he's OK. As chipper as the last time I saw him! What? Yes, that was a while ago. No, honestly, he's in one piece. We haven't heard the full story yet, but apart from his having had a gruelling experience, I'm sure he's fine, so don't worry. We're all together now and that's how it's going to stay. Yes, OK, I'll pass you back. We'll see you very soon, Lola, big hugs and kisses for my little sisters."

She passed the phone back to her father and hung onto his arm as he spent the next few minutes continuing to reassure Lola.

When he shut off the phone, he turned to Lily and smiled warmly.

"Little sisters. What a lovely thought. I'm not quite sure how we're going to explain you to them."

She laughed. "Lola and I have already talked about that. I'm going to be a long lost cousin."

"You two certainly seem to have everything sorted out," he replied, shaking his head.

"It's lovely having two sisters, Papa, even if they are quite a bit younger. Have there been any others?"

"Others?"

"Between Sophie, Phoebe and me?"

A look of sadness clouded John's face. "One, Lei-li, only one. A brother. My son, Dominic. He was killed in the Spanish Civil War."

She rested her head on his shoulder. "Oh, Papa, I'm so sorry. I didn't think of bad things. I didn't mean to bring up unhappy memories."

He smiled and kissed her hair. "We have a lot of catching up to do, Lei-li."


They made good time driving to the professor's house. He had called ahead to his wife, Janet, to explain that he was bringing five guests for the night but that he wasn't able to tell her all the details. Janet was used to his enigmatic ways, knowing that some of his work was classified, so she greeted them with a welcoming tray of sandwiches and drinks, made sure they were comfortable and then discreetly disappeared to bed, claiming she had a busy day ahead of her.

As Janet left the room, Sally turned to the professor. "Your wife's an angel, Prof. If Ced came home with five strangers who looked like they'd been through some awful experience, I'd be beating his head to find out what was going on. She's taken in all in her stride."

Young laughed. "You might think I'm an eccentric old fool, Sally, but I've had a few interesting jobs over the years that Janet has learned not to ask about. And because of those jobs, I've made a few contacts that I think are going to be useful to us."

He sat down on a sofa near John and Lily.

"John, we're going to have to decide what happens from here on. The decision's yours, of course, but I think you are still in a difficult position. There are going to be many questions about what happened tonight and they are not going to be easy to answer. Your secret, if I may call it that, is still known to very few people. It should remain that way. Unfortunately, among the people who do know are Peterson and Frobisher."

John shook his head. "You can discount Frobisher," he said and explained how she had come to inject herself.

"After that," he added, "I was determined to destroy the blood she'd taken from me. We were doing that when Peterson and his guards found us in the laboratory."

Young nodded. "Peterson found Frobisher in the room where you left her. The guards prevented me from seeing what was going on in there, but there was a lot of shouting and when Peterson ran from the room to the laboratory, he no longer had the bandage on his hand. He was rubbing it with paper towels. Something must have happened in there to make him rip his bandages off."

"Now I think about it," said John, "when we left Frobisher tied up, the whole syringe was still in her neck. But when I checked on her as we left, she was unconscious in the chair but no longer tied up, and I'm pretty sure the syringe wasn't there. In her neck, I mean. Maybe Peterson pulled it out and spilled some of the contents on his hand."

Young nodded thoughtfully. "If he spilled the mixture you described onto an open wound, he'd be in trouble. Perhaps that's what all the shouting was about. Certainly when he ran from the room, there was more than anger on his face: there was fear as well."

"So perhaps they are both going to die," said Claudia.

"Was Ced in the room when this stuff was flying around?" said Sally, panic in her voice.

"Shortly after, yes," replied Ced. "John ordered me to the corner of the room while he tied up Frobisher. I touched nothing and nothing spilled on me. Don't worry!"

"So," said the professor, "while Dr Frobisher is not likely to be a problem, we don't know about Peterson. If he washed his wounds well, he might be lucky."

"I've been thinking about what I overheard the guards saying," added Ced. "They'd been told that John was some sort of industrial spy. They mentioned something about Peterson eliminating spies in the past and Frobisher helping bury bodies. If that's the case, then Peterson is hardly going to make a fuss to the police. I mean, what's he going to say? He's not going to tell them about John; they'll think he's mad. And now there's a possibility there are bodies buried in the grounds. I think he's on thin ice."

Young got up and paced the room for a few minutes before returning to sit with them.

"I've known Peterson for quite a few years, and I can assure you that he's completely ruthless. If he thinks there's a chance of getting his hands on John again, he'll try. We can't possibly handle this ourselves; he's far too dangerous. We were lucky this time because he didn't suspect we knew about him. We wouldn't be so lucky the next time; he would take every precaution, I can assure you."

"You're sure he doesn't know where you live?" asked Sally.

"Fairly sure. And given the state he's in, I don't think he's likely to come bursting through the door. Equally, I don't think he's going to go charging up north looking for John – not yet anyway. But we are going to have to start taking some precautions tomorrow."

Janet interrupted him, calling from the hallway. "Frank. Sorry to butt in, but there's something that I think you ought to see."

"Come in, darling," called Young. "What is it?"

Janet came into the room wearing a dressing gown and carrying a mug of tea.

"Sorry," she said again. "I don't know if it's got anything to do with whatever you're talking about, but I couldn't sleep so I switched on the television to Sky News. I was starting to doze when a news flash came on the screen. It was the name that caught my attention since I know that you've had a lot of dealings with them."

"What name do you mean, Janet?" asked Young.

"Peterson Biotech."

"What about them?"

"Well, the news was reporting that there's been a major fire at their research headquarters in West Sussex. Somewhere near Horsham, I think they said. It sounded quite serious and I thought you'd want to know."

"My God!" exclaimed Young.

He looked around. "Where's the remote control? Here." He switched on a television in the corner of the room and pressed the channel button for Sky News. A ticker-tape news flash was running across the bottom of the screen with the information about the fire. They watched while the newsreader finished the lighthearted report he'd been reading. He then paused as he listened to a message in his earpiece, switched his smile into a look of concern and continued.

"More on the fire in West Sussex at the research headquarters of the major British biochemical company Peterson Biotech. Our reporter has now arrived at the scene and it would appear that the fire is not in the main research building as originally thought, but in a large house on the grounds of the estate. The house is thought to be the home of the founder and chairman of Peterson Biotech, Sir Wallingford Peterson. Firefighters are attempting to tackle the blaze, but the fire officer in charge has expressed his surprise at the intensity of the fire, given that, and I quote, 'It's a domestic premises, albeit a large one.' Firefighters are said to be concentrating their efforts on preventing the fire from reaching the main research buildings. At present, it is not known if Sir Wallingford or any of his staff were in the house when the fire started. We'll be updating this bulletin as soon as we have more."

Young switched off the television. The six of them sat in silence, not believing what they'd heard.

Ced was the first to speak. "What on earth's happened? The place was perfectly fine when we left it."

"I imagine we'll find out soon enough," said Young. "But for now, I think we can stop worrying about Peterson or his people searching for any of us."

# Chapter 37

As Hannah Frobisher slowly drifted back into consciousness, she was aware of a painful throbbing in her jaw and her left ear, while her head was pounding with a fearful headache more powerful than any migraine she had ever experienced. Her eyes slowly focused and she realised she was half lying in a chair. Her mouth felt desert dry.

She slowly moved her right leg, but her awkward position was unstable and her leg slipped. The chair lurched sideways and she fell to the floor, banging her throbbing head against a cupboard door and sending a bolt of searing pain through her jaw. She lay there for a few more minutes before she tried moving again.

With some difficulty, she hauled herself into an upright position, sitting with her back against the cupboards and her legs stretched out in front of her. The events of an hour earlier replayed themselves through the spinning confusion in her mind. As the image of John Andrews kicking out at her blended with one of the enraged Peterson hitting her with his full force, another more fearful image took their place: a vial in a deep freeze. It was labelled 'Rabies'. The awful realisation of what had happened hit her: she had been injected with the rabies virus. Then the image of another vial appeared. Hepatitis. One of the rare, highly virulent forms. That had been in the injection as well. She lurched sideways and vomited on the floor.

As she tried to open her mouth to expel the vomit, the pain in her jaw became excruciating. She found her mouth would only partly open and she was almost choking on the liquid-solid mix pumping up from her stomach. Finally, after much effort, she spat it out and collapsed panting against the cupboard door.

She found she was sweating profusely. She thought again of the vials. How had she been injected? Her hand drifted up to her throat and she found the syringe needle still stuck firmly into her neck. Angrily, she pulled it out, causing her to yelp, but again her jaw resisted and the pain screamed at her. She felt around her jawbone and realised it was dislocated – Peterson's violent blow.

Her eyes narrowed in anger. How could he have done this to her after all she had done for him? How could he betray her, dump her like so much rubbish? She had undertaken his secret research, put her own life in danger with the potential exposure to so many organisms. She had willingly experimented on those fools who thought they could steal his work, and then helped him dispose of their bodies in the grounds.

And now she was going to die, alone and in terrible pain. She knew that the deadly organisms would already be attacking her immune system, that they would even now be feeding on her, multiplying to such immense numbers that her defences would be swept away.

She thought back to when Peterson had found her, had released her, had been concerned about her before he knew of her folly. He had pulled the syringe barrel from her neck. She had tried to warn him, but the gag on her mouth prevented her. Shaking her head had only made it worse. The barrel had separated from the needle and the remains of its contents had soaked into Peterson's bandaged hand, into his wounds. Would he be infected as well? She hoped so. He deserved no better. He had betrayed her.

Her eyes focused on the door. Where was Peterson now? He must be looking for Andrews and the other man who had appeared from nowhere. What had the guards been doing? They were supposed to prevent this sort of thing. The building was very quiet. Why was there no activity? They must have caught them by now. Where had they taken them?

Water. She needed water. Slowly, she pulled her feet under her and hauled herself to a kneeling position by the cupboard. One more effort and she was standing, leaning onto the bench. She shuffled along the cupboards to the sink and ran the tap. She filled a paper cup and tried to drink, but her jaw made it difficult. Most of the water spilled down her, but she eventually managed to swallow enough to feel slightly better.

Holding onto the bench, she dragged herself to the door and opened it. Still that eerie silence from the building. She remembered Andrews saying something about destroying his blood, the blood she had taken from him. She had to stop him. Keeping a hand on the wall, she made her way slowly down the corridor to the main laboratory. Her laboratory. The door was open. She stood at the doorway, holding the frame, shocked by what she saw. There were the two guards, Jeffrey and Martin, unconscious on the floor, both of them tightly bound. Beyond them, closer to the freezers, was Peterson, also bound, also unconscious.

How could this have happened? These two guards, who prided themselves on their physical prowess, had been overcome by Andrews and the other man? Andrews, who must have been in a weakened state. How was this possible? The incompetent fools. They were paid to protect the laboratory, paid to protect Peterson. They had failed.

She stumbled over to where Peterson lay face-up on the floor. She thought again of his betrayal. Then the memory of the inevitability of her imminent death washed over her like a tidal wave, carrying her rationality away with it and scattering it irretrievably. Her wild eyes darted around the laboratory. Her laboratory. Her work. All wasted. All for nothing. Years of sacrifice, years of empty promises from Peterson, the man she had loved but who had never once reciprocated that love. All wasted. Her head dropped and she regarded the unconscious form at her feet, her mouth distorting in a hideous snarl. Grasping a nearby bench for support, she kicked him as hard as she could in the ribs. Kicked him again and again. Kicked him in the head, in the mouth until it was oozing blood. She slumped back against the bench, her head tossing wildly, the tears streaming.

She worked her way back to the guards and knelt down, feeling into their jackets. Where were their guns? They were supposed to carry guns. Another failure.

Fighting the nausea that was threatening to overwhelm her, she staggered back to the corridor and slowly made her way to the guards' room at the far end near the hallway. She pulled open the drawers of a desk standing on one side of the room. There was a gun in the lower one. Picking it up, she dragged herself back to the laboratory where she saw Peterson stirring. She ignored him. She rather hoped he would witness what she was about to do. Then she remembered the third guard, Henry, who had been injured by Andrews. Where was he? Of course, he was upstairs in his quarters, probably passed out with whisky by now. Better not take any chances. She looked around and her eyes fell on a large roll of absorbent paper. Would that act as a silencer? Better than nothing. She picked it up and placed one open end against Jeffrey's head. She leaned on the other end with one hand and pushed the gun into the hole. But she was unbalanced and the roll of paper slipped. She fell to the ground like a drunk, giggling at her stupidity and feeling lightheaded.

She got to her knees and placed the roll of paper once again, taking care this time that it didn't slip. She pushed the gun as far as she could into the other end and fired. Jeffrey's body jerked and blood oozed from an exit wound on the far side of his head, the pool gradually growing larger.

She heard a grunt from behind her. Martin was coming round. Not even trying to stand, she shuffled on her knees to where he was lying, placed the roll against his head, inserted the gun, and pulled the trigger. He twitched abruptly, and then lay still.

"You maniac! What the hell are you doing?"

The scream made Hannah jump in fright and she dropped the gun. The first shot had brought Peterson round and, as he raised his head, he had seen Hannah shoot Martin.

She picked up the gun, got to her feet and staggered over to him, taking care not to get too close.

"Put that thing down now! You stupid bitch, you've ruined everything!"

He tried to turn so that he could haul himself up. Hannah watched his struggle with vague interest as she raised the roll of paper, pushed the gun into it and fired at his chest. Peterson collapsed on his back, his eyes now rolling in fear.

"Hannah!" he gasped as the bloodstain from the wound spread across his shirt. "It doesn't have to be like this. We can work something out. We're a team, Hannah, we–"

The shot to his head silenced him. She was not interested in his proposal.

She stood up straight and stared at him dispassionately. "Barthtard!" she spluttered through her damaged jaw.

She looked around the laboratory. Her laboratory. She was in command of it and she would decide when it would end. And it would end now.

Along the far wall were several large metal cupboards for storing solvents, all of them highly flammable liquids. She opened all the doors and surveyed the contents. She thought for a moment. She looked up at the ceiling to the sprinklers and smiled. She had designed this laboratory; she knew how it functioned and how it could be stopped. The hydrant room was next door, the source of all water for the laboratory, including the sprinklers. On the far wall of the hydrant room were all the valves for controlling the water. They were large and she wasn't feeling very strong. But slowly she closed each one. There would be no water.

The foam extinguishers were all in portable units arrayed along one wall of the laboratory. They would discharge eventually in the heat of the fire, but it would take a while. She left them alone.

Returning to the solvent cupboards, she picked up a five-litre bottle of light petroleum and staggered off with it to the sitting room. She put it on the desk while she pulled a large number of books from the library shelves and threw them around the floor. Satisfied with her pyre, she poured the contents of the bottle over the scattered books, the sofas and the carpet. Tossing the bottle aside, she returned to the laboratory to retrieve another bottle of solvent. Using this and several others, she spent the next fifteen minutes spreading their contents throughout the remaining rooms on the ground floor, most of which were parts of the laboratory complex.

Almost overcome by the spreading fumes, she returned one final time to the main laboratory and liberally doused the three bodies with solvent, making sure Peterson was particularly well soaked.

She surveyed her handiwork, making sure she had covered all the essential areas. Finally she bent over Jeffrey's body and searched in his jacket pocket. She knew he smoked and there was his lighter.

She returned to the sitting room, taking the roll of absorbent paper with her. She tore off a length and lit it. When it was burning well, she tossed it onto the solvent-soaked carpet. It ignited with a whoosh. Almost immediately, the whole room seemed to be ablaze. With great effort now – she was exhausted and her head was pounding – she went from room to room, igniting the vapours in each with a paper taper as she went until she was back in the main laboratory. Her laboratory.

She made her way to the far corner, next to the freezers where she hadn't poured any solvent. She sat on the floor, tore off a final length of paper and screwed it into a ball. She held the lighter to it until it was burning well and then threw it the length of the room where it landed next to the bodies of the guards. The room burst into flame.

As the fire rushed towards her, she retrieved the gun from her pocket, took a last look at her laboratory and smiled. Then she put the gun to her temple and squeezed the trigger.

# Chapter 38

Frank Young ran his hands through his hair.

"You realise that this fire changes everything."

They all turned to him, waiting for him to explain.

"You see, if the house has burned down, and the fire is as severe as the news report indicated, then even if Peterson, Frobisher and the guards have escaped, there will be nothing to show that John or Ced were ever there. They can deny all knowledge of the place. Anyway, it's unlikely that Peterson is going to start pointing fingers at them; it would be too risky for him."

"Wouldn't the guards at the gate have seen John in Peterson's car when they arrived?" asked Sally.

"I doubt it," replied John. "The rear windows of his car are tinted, and the guard didn't look in the back."

"Exactly," continued the professor. "No, as far as the gatehouse guards are concerned, I was the only extra person there. They have a record of me arriving and leaving. And my departure was preceded by what they think was a call from Peterson."

He paused, seeing the puzzled look on the girls' faces.

"I called the gatehouse and gave what I think was a passable impression of his voice," he smiled.

"Brilliant!" exclaimed Claudia.

Young continued. "Any evidence of John or Ced having been there will have been destroyed in the fire. I can say, hand on heart, that I went there to discuss a matter of great scientific interest with Peterson. When I arrived, I found he had been in some sort of accident and that he really wasn't up to listening to what I had to say.

After a while he tired, at which point I agreed to go back the next day when he was rested. That I left some considerable time before the fire started will be corroborated by the guards at the gate."

"So that's what you'll tell the police?" asked Lily. "I assume they will come calling."

"Yes, but probably not until some time later today."

He glanced at a clock and stifled a yawn. "You know, I think it would be better if none of you was here when the police come. Let's try to get a few hours sleep and then you should be on your way."

Four hours later, at eight in the morning, Lily was the first to emerge into the Youngs' kitchen. Still jet-lagged, she had tossed around fitfully in the bed the professor's wife had directed her to, ecstatic to have been finally reunited with her father, but with her head buzzing from the events of the past few hours.

She was pouring some coffee when John walked into the kitchen. She put down her cup and hugged him.

"Papa, I can't believe I'm standing here with you. I keep pinching myself in case it's all a dream."

He smiled and kissed her.

"I'm speechless, Lei-li. To have you here, it's, well, it's what I've dreamed of for so long."

"You must be shattered, Papa, after all they put you through."

"Actually, I've probably had more sleep than the rest of you, even if it was drug-induced. Frobisher knocked me out for over half a day after I tried to escape."

"But you're not feeling any effects of that other horrible injection she gave you?"

"Nothing," he said reflectively. "It would appear that their predictions about my immunity, and presumably yours, are all true. I feel fine."

"Thank heavens; I don't want to lose you now, not after so long."

He wrinkled his nose. "That coffee smells good. Got any to spare?"

"I'll pour you one," she said.

"Can you make that two?" said Claudia, walking into the room.

"Hey, Claudia," said Lily, "did you manage to get any sleep?"

"A little. But my head was spinning with everything. And I

thought every little noise I heard was the police knocking on the door."

They laughed.

"I've got a bit paranoid about the police lately," she added ruefully.

"I'm not surprised," said John, an amused twinkle in his eye. "You have bent a few rules, after all."

"I know. I'm so sorry. I'm amazed you're even talking to me. I've caused you so much trouble."

"I suppose," said John thoughtfully, "when I consider it objectively, something had to happen sooner or later. With modern technology, it was only a matter of time before something was found out about me. About us, I should say," he added, touching Lily's arm.

"It was different a hundred years ago," he said. "Communication was far more limited and papers had almost no security. It was much easier for you to simply disappear and re-emerge somewhere else as someone else. Not so easy now. I hope the professor might have some ideas on where we go from here."

"I think he will," said Claudia, sipping her coffee. "He seems to have contacts in all sorts of places."

At that moment, Janet Young bustled into the kitchen declaring they must all be starving. She set about preparing a huge breakfast of eggs, bacon, sausages and fried tomatoes, with piles of toast and homemade jam.

"Wow, that smells amazing," cried Ced as he bounded into the room several minutes later, Sally still clutching his arm. "I don't think I've ever felt so hungry."

They were all tucking in enthusiastically when the professor joined them. "I've been looking at the news reports," he informed them. "The fire is out and it would appear that the damage is very extensive. The house is more or less gutted, although they did manage to prevent the fire from spreading to the main research laboratory buildings."

"Any news of Peterson or the others?" asked Claudia.

"Nothing yet, but I think the scene is still too hot for them to go in and search."

"Do you really think they might have been in there?"

"It's a possibility, Claudia, some of them, at least. We'll have to wait and see. I'll let you know as soon as I hear anything." He pushed a hand through his ever-unruly hair.

Revitalised by Janet Young's breakfast and several cups of coffee, the five of them set off shortly after nine. Once they were on their way, John called Lola and they agreed they would all meet up at Sally and Ced's.

Lola's timing was perfect. With the aid of a Satnav she'd borrowed from her neighbour, she found her way faultlessly to Ced and Sally's house, arriving a minute after Ced's SUV pulled into the driveway. Sophie and Phoebe bounded out of the car and raced up to Lily.

"Lily! Lily! Are you really our cousin?" they both squealed as she bent to hug them.

"I am, my darlings, I am!" she laughed tearfully, hugging them tightly.

Lola folded herself into John's outstretched arms, her hands stroking his face and hair while her eyes searched into his.

"John! I–"

"It's OK, sweetheart," he said, hugging her. "It's all over."

They stood there for a few minutes saying nothing. Then he stood back, smiling at her. "I can't believe that Lei-li turned up, almost as I disappeared, and that the two of you seem to have become instant friends."

"More than friends, John. Lily's family. She needs us John; she needs you especially. It's fantastic that she's here." Her eyes danced in delight. John thought he had never seen her so happy.

"A dream come true, believe me," he said softly.

They all moved inside, the two little girls swinging happily on Lily's arms, firing questions at her, wanting her to tell them all about New York. Sally made tea and coffee, filled a large plate with biscuits, smacking Ced's hand as it instantly moved towards them. "There's homemade elderflower cordial for the girls, Lola. Do you think they'd like it? My mum made it a few weeks ago."

"They'll love it, Sally, it's their favourite," called Lola as her eyes roamed over a pile of art books scattered around the living room. "So this is the nerve centre for all the art history research. The rumbling of John Andrews."

"More like the desperate frustrations of Ced Fisher," laughed Sally, walking into the room carrying a tray. "It's just as well Ced doesn't have long hair, there would be handfuls of it all over the floor from where he'd been tearing at it. He was beside himself with confusion over why his program didn't seem to work."

"When all the time it was working brilliantly," added John, picking up one of the books. He smiled as it opened to a portrait by Tommaso Perini.

"Well, that one takes me back," he said, scrutinising the detail. "I'd love to see it again. Where is it?" He read through the text under the picture. "The Met in New York. A well-travelled painting."

"You can see it when you visit me," said Lily, "which according to the girls, will be tomorrow, if not sooner!"

"The last time I was in New York, I stayed at the Waldorf-Astoria," said John, a faraway look in his eyes.

"You didn't tell us you'd been to New York, Daddy," cried Sophie. "When did you go?"

"Many years ago, sweetheart, long before you were born."

"Did Mummy go with you?" asked Sophie.

"No, sweetheart, she didn't."

"Did you seed Lily there?" followed Phoebe.

"No, she didn't live there then."

"This is surreal," commented Ced, offering John a biscuit. "You know, John, I'd love to show you my program, but I realise that now is not the time. I hope we can get together soon on it."

"Without doubt, Ced. I'm fascinated by it and I really want to try to understand how it works, even though I'm a caveman when it comes to computers. I want to see if I can fool it."

"Challenge accepted!" beamed Ced.

"Actually," he added, "joking aside, that's exactly what you need to do: find a new style that the program won't connect with your present one. That won't be easy. In fact, I wonder if it's possible."

"Fun to find out," smiled John, picking up Sophie to give her another hug.

"Ced!" called Sally. "Your phone's ringing. It's by the front door."

Ced walked through to the hallway and found his phone. The caller was Frank Young.

"Prof. Hi. We've just got back. How are you?"

"Good, Ced, thank you. I thought I'd let you know that the police have been to see me. They left a few minutes ago."

"Everything OK?"

"Yes, I think so. They seemed to accept my explanation. They told me the fire investigation will take a few days, but in their preliminary sweep through the site, they found five bodies."

"Five!" exclaimed Ced, shocked that what they had all thought a possibility had been confirmed.

"Yes, five. Four in the laboratory and a fifth in the hallway, but he seems to have fallen from the floor above when the ceiling collapsed."

"The other guard?"

"It would appear so. Now the interesting thing is, apart from that guard, who was probably overcome by smoke while he was sleeping, the four in the laboratory all appear to have been shot in the head."

"Shot? All of them? But who–?"

"Yes, shot, and one of them, who was female, was apart from the other three and she had a gun in her hand. They are treating the whole thing as a probable murder/suicide. They need to wait for the post mortem to identify the bodies properly, but they are fairly sure that one of the three men is Peterson – there's a ring on the remains of a finger that I confirmed I'd seen him wearing – while they think the other two are the guards. They were well built, they said. They know from the guardhouse at the gate that Hannah Frobisher was on-site and although the female body is very badly burnt, they're working on the assumption that it's her. The gatehouse guards appear to have had their ears to the ground and the gossip is that there was a lot of tension between Peterson and Frobisher. Apparently, she carried a torch for him, but he ignored her unsubtle advances. They think there might have been a huge row. Frobisher was known to have been a difficult, highly strung and demanding woman."

"Did the fact that the three men in the laboratory were all tied up concern them at all?" asked Ced.

"They found it a bit strange, but I think they are working on developing a story that will include it. They are satisfied with what they've got and in the absence of anything really compelling to the contrary, if I know the police, they will accept the story and close the case. Of course, the post mortem will support the initial indications over the identities and since the bodies are so badly burnt, any evidence of Frobisher having been injected with anything will have been destroyed in the fire."

"If Peterson really is dead, what will happen to your research?" asked Ced.

"I don't know; I'll need to talk to the Peterson Board about my general research. However, now I know about John, I want to continue the work on his DNA and I don't think that can be carried out under the umbrella of a commercial company. It's too delicate. Listen, Ced, is John still there? I'd like a quick word if I may."

"He's here, Prof. I'll get him for you."

In the hall, John listened while Young told him about the police and the findings at the scene of the fire.

"I don't think there is any further cause for worry about Peterson and his henchmen, John," said Young as he finished. "Any potential threat to you or your family has now gone away completely."

"But I've been thinking beyond that potential problem to another one that I don't think will go away. That is, the ongoing predicament for both you and Lily of identity. You must already realise that changing identities as you have in the past is becoming increasingly difficult, and it's only going to get harder as time goes on."

"You're right, professor. It's a serious problem. I honestly don't know what to do about it in the future."

"Well, my thoughts on the matter, for what they're worth, are as follows. Peterson's maniacal moves aside, you must realise that both you and Lily would be of immense interest scientifically for legitimate research, albeit, highly confidential, research that won't mean taking litres of blood from either of you or pumping anything into your bodies. Not only that, there is another sort of research, which would also need to be highly confidential, but which would be invaluable. Both of you are in a position to give an unprecedented insight into the minutiae of everyday life over a huge tract of time – particularly you, John, since you are so much older. You are living resources of priceless value for a great variety of academics: general historians, art historians, social scientists, linguists; the list will be a long one. My point, John, is that you have a lot to offer, and, in return, it should be possible to solve your problems, if the whole thing is set up with the right people."

"The right people?"

"I've taken the liberty of calling a person I've worked with on classified projects on a number of occasions. He works for the government, obviously. Like many of these people, you never really find out what they do and to whom they answer, but they have all sorts of contacts and inside information that very few people are privy to. I've given this person the vaguest outline of a hypothetical situation, not mentioning either art or absolute ages, no more really than the suggestion that there could be people who are very much older than they seem and how there could be a situation of mutual benefit both to them and to the government. He has said he will get back to me. When he does, John, I can guarantee from my own dealings with him that whatever transpires will be completely legitimate and will be handled with the utmost secrecy and delicacy."

He paused, waiting for a response, but John was silent.

"John," continued Young, "think about it and talk it over with Lily. I know over the past forty-eight hours you've had a horrific experience with exactly the wrong sort of person. This would not happen with the people I have in mind; I'd stake my reputation on it. It could be the answer to your problems."

"OK," said John, at last, "Lily and I will discuss it. Thank you, Frank, I'm very grateful for your concern and your desire to help us."

"You're very welcome, John. Of course, I have a vested interest," he added lightly. "Research into your immune system will more than fill the rest of my working days."

"Didn't they give Watson and Crick Nobel prizes?" said John.

"You know more about science than you pretend," laughed the professor, "but let's not get ahead of ourselves."

# Chapter 39

During the two weeks following John's rescue and the subsequent fire at Peterson's house, Lily and John spent many hours catching up with the past. Lola ran the gallery, leaving her husband and newly-acquired stepdaughter, who was some eighty-six years her senior, ensconced in the studio, the door closed. The long summer evenings were spent relaxing, with all the family taking walks along the shores of Thirlmere near the Andrews' cottage, the young girls seeking out new and secret spots for the adults to sit and take in the dramatic sunsets over a glass of wine. The weather was kind and they all retreated into an idyllic period of contentment.

John was anxious to know the details of Lily's abduction in 1905, of her many years as an unwilling servant in northern China, her escape and her years since in America.

He shook his head guiltily. "Lei-li, I was on the same continent in the 1930s and by then living a very comfortable life with Catherine and Dom. If I'd had any hint of the fact that you were living in San Francisco, I should have been there like a shot."

"I know, Papa, but how could you possibly have known?"

She smiled, her eyes twinkling. "You should have known from your own life that both of us have an enduring ability to overcome hardship, to wriggle our way out of difficult and threatening situations."

"I never gave up hope, Lei-li. Just as I have never completely given up hope about Paola, the daughter I have never even met. You know, I feel sure she's alive somewhere."

Lily sat back and stared into the middle distance.

"What is it, Lei-li? Where have your thoughts suddenly taken you?"

She sighed and her eyes focused back onto him.

"It's probably nothing, but mentioning Paola again and now knowing more about us has jogged a memory. You remember I told you about seeing the paintings by Stefano Baldini back in 1952, the ones I was convinced had been painted by you? Well, not long after I saw those paintings, I remember seeing an article in one of the glossies – it might have been *Life* or *New Yorker*, or something similar. They ran features on artists of various sorts, sometimes well-established figures and sometimes up-and-coming hopefuls. It made a huge difference to a young artist if their work could be reviewed in a prestigious magazine. The article took my attention for two reasons. First, it was about a young female sculptor who had an unusual name: Mali Whittaker. I'd never heard the name before; it's kind of unusual even these days, which is probably why I remembered it."

"It's a very pretty name."

"Yes. It's Thai. It means jasmine, or beautiful flower. Lovely, huh?"

"Yes, charming. But there's more to this than a name. What was the other reason the artist took your attention?"

"Well, in the 1950s, most of the photos in the magazines were in black and white, as I'm sure you'll remember. But in this article, the photo of the artist and her work were in colour. And what struck me about her was her eyes. They were exactly like mine.

"By then, I had long known there was something unusual about me – I was over sixty years old and looked in my late twenties. I'd even had a baby the year before. Of course, I'd met other people with eyes like mine, not exactly the same shade but pretty similar. But this woman's seemed somehow especially similar."

"Did you follow it up?"

"No, I didn't. I had no reason to. I was living in Chicago at the time. I think this Mali Whittaker was living somewhere on the West Coast, but I don't remember where. Interesting though, don't you think? Strong artistic ability and the same eyes?"

"And a trail that's almost sixty years cold," sighed John. "But yes,

I do. I wonder if copies of the magazine are still available. Perhaps you can see them on the Internet these days."

"I'll check it out."

"Imagine, Lei-li, wouldn't it be incredible if we could find Paola?"

"I shouldn't get your hopes up, Papa. It could be nothing. As I said, eyes like ours are not unique to us."

"I'd like to see her photograph, nevertheless. If it was Paola, there would have to be a family resemblance. I can still remember her mother, Francesca, as much as I should prefer to forget her."

She laughed. "Was she that bad?"

"She was a demon! After nearly five hundred years, I still have nightmares about her."

Lola put her head around the door.

"John, sorry to butt in; Frank Young's on the phone."

"Thanks, sweetheart, I'll take it in here."

He reached out for the receiver of the extension.

"Hello, Frank."

"Sorry to interrupt you, John, I know how much you are enjoying catching up with your daughter. Gosh, you know, it seems so strange to be saying that, knowing what I do about your ages. It's such an exciting prospect."

"No problem, Frank," said John, smiling to himself at the professor's enthusiasm. "What can I do for you?"

"Well, actually, it's more what I think I can do for you. The person I told you about has called back. He said my information was greeted by what he called 'strong interest'. These people aren't exactly known for being demonstrative, so 'strong interest' indicates they are beside themselves with excitement. He arranged for someone to visit me and this man will be coming to see you very soon. I was asked to sign all sorts of official documents, as I'm sure all of you will be too. As a result, I can't discuss with you what we said, except to say that I apprised him of your condition, and the scientific reasons behind it. I must say, John, he seemed remarkably unsurprised by the whole thing, but maybe that's the way he's trained to respond to bizarre situations. If you and Lily are in agreement about this, I'm to call him and he will make contact with you. His name is Digby Smith. He will say that he is an old friend of 'the prof'. He won't use my name."

"It all sounds very cloak and dagger, but, yes, we're certainly in agreement. I'll wait for his call."

"Obviously I don't need to remind you of the need to keep this all confidential."

"I'm used to keeping my own secret, Frank."

"Yes, of course you are. How naïve of me."

About two hours later, Lola looked round the studio door again. "Sorry, you two. John, I think the man the professor called about is on the phone. Polite, but insistent that he talk to you."

John lifted the phone. "John Andrews."

"Mr Andrews. My name is Digby Smith. I'm an old friend of the prof. I was wondering if I could arrange to visit you and Ms Saunders for a little chat."

"Certainly, Mr Smith. When would you like to come?"

"Would tomorrow morning be convenient? Say, around ten o'clock?"

"That would be fine. I'll expect you tomorrow."

"Thank you, Mr Andrews. Thank you very much."

The following morning at precisely ten, the door to the gallery opened and a slim man in his late thirties wearing a well-cut dark grey business suit with a plain, dark grey tie over a white shirt walked in. He was carrying a sleek, black leather briefcase. He glanced around the gallery and seemed to relax when he saw there were no customers. He walked up to where John, Lola and Lily were standing by the studio door.

"Mr Andrews?"

"Yes, I'm John Andrews."

"Digby Smith," smiled the man, his bright blue eyes fixed straight onto John's. "We spoke yesterday. Thank you very much for agreeing to see me so quickly."

He glanced expectantly at Lily and Lola, and John picked up the hint.

"This is my wife, Lola," he said. "And this is Lily."

Smith shook Lola's hand and then Lily's, his eyes lingering on hers.

"Lily Saunders," said Lily. "Pleased to meet you, Mr Smith."

"The pleasure's all mine. I'm delighted to meet you all."

He turned back to John. "Is there somewhere private we can all talk?"

"Am I included in this little heart-to-heart?" asked Lola.

Smith smiled. "If you would be so kind, Mrs Andrews; to start with, at least. There are one or two formalities that we have to go through and I'm afraid you are part of them. After that, it's up to you."

"Come through to the studio," said John, showing him the way.

Smith cast a professional eye around the studio and declared it perfect for their purposes.

"I'm afraid," said Smith, opening his briefcase as he sat in one of the armchairs, "that before we start, I'm going to have to ask you all to sign copies of the Official Secrets Act."

"This is the law that says we'll be locked up in the dungeons of the Tower of London if we breathe a word of anything that's said, isn't it?" said Lola, smiling to herself as she caught the look of horror in Lily's eyes.

"Something like that," responded Smith, "only these days we have far less comfortable places for incarceration."

"Touché, Mr Smith," said Lola. "I can see that we're going to be friends."

"Please read through the covering document while I briefly explain what it is I'm asking you to sign," he said, passing them each a sheaf of papers.

Five minutes later, he collected the documents and put them back in his briefcase. "OK, that's the formalities out of the way," he said, his eyes looking slowly from one of them to the other as he sat back in the armchair.

"I feel like Mata Hari," said Lola.

"It does all seem a bit formal, I agree," said Smith. "But it's as much to protect all of your interests as it is the Government's.

"Let me start by explaining myself. I work, as I think you realise, for the British Government. The actual ministry and department don't really matter. Suffice it to say that knowing what I already know from the professor about you, Mr Andrews, and you, Ms Saunders, I can assure you that what passes between us will be

474

treated with the utmost secrecy. In order to ensure that, I can tell you that the number of people on my side who will know about you directly, that is, your names and whereabouts, will be limited to me alone. All dealings with you will be conducted through me and all records of our interviews will be produced by me, not a secretary, and they will be securely locked away in a vault. Anticipating the question I can see on your lips, Mrs Andrews, in case anything untoward happens to me, if I'm run over by a bus, for example, I have colleagues, one of whom would take my place and who then, and only then, would take over access to the records. That access cannot happen without my knowing while I'm alive. I can't go into the details of how that works; I'm afraid you'll simply have to take my word for it."

"You must be answerable to someone," said Lola.

"Obviously. But my senior officers will know of you only by code names. That is how we shall discuss you. They have no need to know your real names or any others you adopt. And to emphasise how secret we regard this matter, I can tell you that knowledge of it does not go outside the department. For example, the PM doesn't know and neither does Her Majesty."

"Presumably these records are stored on a computer," said Lily. "Computers can be hacked. How secure are yours?"

"A good point, Ms Saunders," said Smith, his face remaining serious. "We accept that computers can be hacked into and for this very reason, absolutely nothing from the records about you or from the interviews will ever go on any computer. When I type up the notes, it's on an old-fashioned typewriter. Everything is paper records only and they are stored in part of a fireproof vault to which only I have access."

"Wow!" nodded Lily, impressed. "So the old methods are the best."

"OK," said John, "tell us how we can help you and what we can expect in return."

"What you can expect in return for what you give us, Mr Andrews, can be summed up as 'peace of mind'. I know that as a result of your age being far greater than it would appear, you and Ms Saunders have a problem with identity. The professor has already explained that to me. What we can offer you is a guarantee of new identities as and when they are required. New names, new papers and new locations. In perpetuity. Not only you, but your family as well. Obviously you won't always be dealing with me because I will get older and one day retire. But there is a continuity plan."

He paused to see if they were following him.

"This will presumably apply to Phoebe as well?" asked Lola.

"Phoebe?"

"Our younger daughter. It would appear that she is the same as John and Lily."

"I didn't realise that; I'll make a note of it. But yes, there is no question: of course it will apply to her. Now, as to what you can give us, I only know the bare bones of the situation. That is, I only know, as I have said, that you are both quite old, and that you, Ms Saunders, are Mr Andrews' daughter. What I would ask now is that you give me some more details so that we can decide on how we can structure a programme of research."

"Well, let me start, then," said John. He told Smith his age and paused, waiting for a reaction.

Smith nodded slowly, taking it in. He looked around the studio. "And you are an artist?"

"Yes. I have always been an artist – that's how I've made my living, using various names through the ages. I was trained by Piero della Francesca."

Smith sat forward in his chair, registering a reaction for the first time. "Fascinating. Absolutely fascinating. Professor Young made no mention of your always having been an artist," he said, rubbing his hands together.

"Mr Smith?" said Lola. "May I ask a question?"

"Certainly."

"You say you have colleagues. At your level, I think you described it. If you are the only one dealing with John and Lily, what do the others do?"

Smith looked hesitant for the first time since he'd arrived. "They are there for back-up, as I've explained. This isn't my only task. I have other responsibilities, as do they."

"It's just that you didn't seem very surprised by what John told you about his age. Tell me, if you can, are there others?"

"Others?"

"Yes, like John and Lily, and, of course, Phoebe. Are there others like them on your books?"

Smith sat back and considered his response. As he did, both John and Lily leaned forward in anticipation. This insight from Lola, which they had missed, had them thinking once again about Paola.

Smith exhaled slowly and stared out of the window. "This is my judgement call," he said. He paused, debating in his mind exactly what he should say. Finally he turned to them.

"I think you have a right to know. It's hardly others. There is one, to my knowledge. He is handled by one of my colleagues. Obviously I know nothing about him, absolutely nothing at all."

"Him. It's a he?" said John and Lily together.

"Yes, that much I do know," replied Smith, puzzled by their response. Then he realised. "Were you expecting it to be a woman?" he asked.

"Hoping is perhaps a better word, Mr Smith," said John. "Let me continue with my story. Aren't you going to take notes?"

"If I may, yes. They will be destroyed once I have typed everything up."

"OK," smiled John. "This could take a while. Would you like some coffee?"

Two hours later, John had led Smith through an outline of his life and identities. He had included mention of Lily, although he was leaving details of her life to her. Smith made copious notes throughout, sometimes interrupting for more detail, but mainly listening attentively and in increasing awe as the story unfolded. Lola had excused herself from the proceedings early on, saying she had to mind the gallery.

John concluded his outline with a summary of recent events to explain how they had reached their present position. When he finished, Smith stopped writing and looked up.

"Yes, the professor gave me Dr Reid's name as well as Mr Fisher's and Dr Moreton's. I shall be visiting them to get them onside, so to speak. It's remarkable, given what happened to you, that the number of people who are aware of your situation, if I may call it that, is limited to so few."

"I assume Frank Young told you what happened regarding my kidnapping?"

"He was actually quite vague about it. He said that he thought it should come from you."

"Did he? Well, if I tell you, I hope it's not going to backfire on me and change the way the police are looking at it," said John defensively.

"How could it, Mr Andrews? What we are discussing here is in total confidence. It is, in every sense of the word, a secret of the highest level. In that respect, I am like a priest. You can confess to whatever you like and there will be no repercussions on you."

John laughed and described the events at Peterson BioTech.

As John finished, Smith looked up from his notes and nodded. "You had a fortunate escape, thanks, I should say, to the professor and Mr Fisher. Now, let me explain how I perceive we shall proceed. As I mentioned earlier, I intend to be the conduit through which all discussions with you are made. What I have in mind is that both of you would be in a position to provide invaluable insight into everyday life throughout the span of your lives. Living witnesses, if you will. I am in touch with professors of various relevant disciplines at a number of our better universities whom I intend to apprise of certain facts. I shall ask them to provide detailed questions relevant to their subject that I can pose to you and I shall take the answers back to them. That way your identities remain protected. Now obviously, they can't publish the findings. But they would gradually, over a period of years, include carefully worded details from your accounts into texts, papers, etc., that, given their prestige, would slowly become accepted as facts by a sort of process of diffusion. That way, the details you provide would be taken, eventually, as read, and if it's done properly, the source material can be blurred enough not to matter. It's a very subtle process."

"It all sounds a little dishonest," said John.

"It's not dishonest, in that they would be facts. But the provenance of those facts would have to be carefully controlled.

"Regarding Professor Young," he continued, "I can tell you he is going to be given the resources to undertake extensive research into the genetic side of the matter. He will require some samples from you both but he assures me that is all he will require of you."

Smith closed his notebook. "That all seems very satisfactory. For you, Mr Andrews, I can see that the whole process of interviews is going to take some considerable time. It could stretch into years. What I suggest, if you are agreeable, is that I pay you a visit once a month and we can sit here for a few hours and talk over whatever set of questions I have in hand. Would you be willing to give up that amount of time?"

"If that's what it takes to ensure that I never again have to forge or steal an identity, or run away in the depths of the night, it's a small price to pay. I'd be happy to oblige. But that raises a question about Lily. You've been including her in all the points we've discussed, but as I'm sure you realise, she's an American citizen. Not only that, she has a flourishing business in New York that she shortly has to return to. Is that going to complicate matters?"

Smith steepled his hands together onto his mouth and pursed his lips. "In theory, it could, but it rather depends on you, Ms Saunders. The British Government is not prepared to discuss any of this with your government or any other government. Ever. I doubt you would contemplate making your own advances to your government; you would probably be rebuffed as a crank. And now you've signed the Official Secrets Act, you would not be able to tell them anything about what has gone on today, nor indeed anything about your father, not if you want to return to this country at any time. So I confess I've led you into something of a dilemma quite deliberately. What I'm proposing is that you remain an American citizen with your present identity for as long as is convenient to you. As and when you wish to move on, we can arrange for you to disappear, or for your supposed death if you wish, and you would re-emerge in a new identity as a British citizen. How do you react to that?"

Lily laughed. "Apart from the fact that you've given me very little choice, I am perfectly happy with it. Having been born in Hong Kong when it was a Crown Colony. I shall be very pleased to reclaim my British identity in due course."

Smith smiled. "Good. That's settled then. As far as interviews with you are concerned, I presume that now you have re-established contacts with your family, you intend to be spending some time here in the UK every so often. We shall be more than pleased to provide you with tickets to do that whenever you wish. That goes without saying. If you would agree to a series of interviews every time you are here, that would be splendid."

Lily beamed, suddenly excited at the prospect of frequent visits she hadn't anticipated. "It would indeed be splendid, Mr Smith."

Smith stood up. "Before I go, perhaps we can call Mrs Andrews in for a final word."

"Of course," said John. "I'll fetch her."

"Are you leaving us, Mr Smith?" asked Lola as she came back into the room with John.

"For today, Mrs Andrews, yes. I shall need some time to digest all I have heard. But I intend to become a regular and frequent visitor, if that's not too inconvenient to you."

"If you intend to be getting under our feet for the foreseeable future, Mr Smith, it will only be convenient if you take off your Ministry coat and cut some of the formality. First names is the norm around here. Can we agree to that ... Digby?"

"Absolutely, Mrs, er, Lola. First names are so much better. Perhaps I can finish the formal side once and for all with one last little speech that I am obliged to make. It is simply this: I have to emphasise once again the need for absolute secrecy on all the matters we have discussed. As you now realise, it's not only for John and Lily's sake – and indeed Phoebe's too – although the importance to them is paramount. There are others to consider as well. For so many reasons, the privileged circle who share this secret of yours must remain as small as possible."

"I think we all understand that well enough." smiled Lola.

"I know you do. But I should emphasise that my organisation is here to help you in every way possible. It might happen in future that someone inadvertently gets wind of something unusual about you and starts perhaps to put pressure on you. If anything like that happens, no matter how trivial it seems, you should contact me immediately so that it can be addressed."

"Does that mean that every time John gets arrested for fighting in pub car parks, you can make it go away?" asked Lola, raising her eyebrows innocently.

Smith laughed. "Something like that, although I don't recommend making a habit of it."

# Epilogue

## September-October 2009

Claudia Reid stepped lightly across the village green and stopped outside John Andrews' gallery. It was Saturday morning and the town was busy with late season tourists. She looked through the window at the various paintings displayed there, a confident smile spreading slowly across her face. She caught her reflection in the glass and adjusted her broad-brimmed straw hat. Still smiling to herself, she pushed open the gallery door. How different she felt from the first time she had walked through that door over three months earlier. She'd been a bag of nerves then, expecting to be arrested at any moment.

Lola looked up as she heard the door open.

"Claudia! How lovely! What a surprise! How are you? It's been ages."

She walked over to Claudia and hugged her. "Love the dress!"

"Thanks, I only bought it yesterday. I got it in an end-of-season sale. Isn't this weather amazing? I can't believe it's late September and the drive up here was fantastic. Gosh, Lola, it's so lovely to see you. How is everyone?"

"All fine, Claudia," said Lola, amused at Claudia's typically breathless delivery. "John's finally picked up his paintbrush again, after much nagging from me. He and Lily have been out and about trying to outdo each other with the excellence of their lake views. She's got a great talent and she'll have some wonderful work to take back to New York with her. Tell me, have you given up your job yet?"

"I finished yesterday. I'm taking a few days off and then I start work in the prof's lab. I'm very excited about it."

"Have you had many visits from our Man from the Ministry?"

Claudia laughed. "The inscrutable Mr Digby Smith? No, not too many, although something strange happened after the first visit."

Lola raised her eyebrows in question.

"Well, I told him all about my results from John's buccal swabs and how I'd bent the rules by seeking John out, as well as by sitting on the results – I still hadn't told my bosses when Smith talked to me – I kept putting it off. I explained that I was rather worried about how my bosses were going to react when I sprung the file on them and what they might do with the information. He just nodded quietly and told me to hang fire; that he'd look into it."

"And? What happened?"

"That conversation was on a Friday. When I went into the lab the following Monday morning, I looked for the file and it was missing. So I checked the computer system and all record of it had disappeared. There was nothing. It was like the swabs and results had never existed. So officially, John's DNA was never profiled!"

"Wow! Our Digby's reach is a long one. Didn't anyone at the lab say anything?"

"That was equally strange. Nothing at all was said, but I did get a few accusatory glances from the principal manager – he had this sort of wounded look on his face for days. Anyway, apart from that, Digby's obviously just got me programmed into his calendar to contact every now and then. He calls for what he terms 'a little chat' to check I'm OK, which is very sweet. Bit of a cold fish, though."

"You're telling me! I've tried to break through that starchy Whitehall exterior but it's not easy. Getting onto first-name terms was something of a coup – I reckon that lot are all cast in a mould and programmed from birth. You know, once he's gone, I can never really remember what he looks like. It's as if they're chosen to be anonymous. And he never loses that formal edge; I reckon he probably sleeps in his tie."

Claudia laughed. "I know what you mean. He's sort of, well, grey."

"That's it. He should be Digby Grey, not Digby Smith."

"It must be quite a job, transcribing all that stuff before he hands it over to the academics."

"Yes, but he's relaxed a bit on that. He's now recording the conversations to make his life easier and to ensure accuracy. Some of the recordings are for language experts. He's had John speaking in his original Tuscan dialect from San Sepolcro, the Naples one he learned when he went there, and several others. John's very meticulous about it, wanting to be sure that what he says is correct. I know a bit of Italian, but when he goes back there, I can't follow a word. Apparently the linguist Digby is passing the stuff on to says some days it's like having Dante making recordings for him, others it's like listening to a fifteenth century villager. He's ecstatic, but also frustrated because he can't publish it."

She looked round as she heard the gallery door. "I'll just see who that–"

Sophie and Phoebe charged into the room, interrupting her. "Mummy! Mummy! Look what Lily bought us–"

They skidded to a halt when they saw Claudia.

"Do you remember Claudia, girls?" asked Lola.

They scrutinised her unsubtly. "You're the lady who taked photos on your phone," said Phoebe, somewhat accusingly.

"You're quite right, Phoebe, I did," laughed Claudia. "And I came to your house. Do you remember that? Do you know what? I'm so glad I took those photos because it helped me look at so much more of your daddy's work. He's the best artist in the world, you know; you're such lucky girls to have him as your daddy."

"That's very kind of you, Claudia," said John, walking into the studio with Lily. "Something of an exaggeration, though," he laughed.

"Not at all, John," said Claudia, getting up to give him a hug. "You're a real live Old Master working here in the twenty-first century. What could be better than that?"

As she turned to Lily to greet her, she heard Phoebe mutter quietly to Lola. "Daddy's not old, Mummy."

Over lunch, Claudia asked Lily about New York City. She'd been there once and wanted to know where her studio was.

"Upper West Side, just off Broadway. Quite a smart address. I was left the place … by a relative of my late husband." She whispered the last part behind her hand to prevent Sophie and Phoebe from hearing.

"That's near Central Park, isn't it?"

"A stone's throw. I go jogging there every morning, along with an army of other New Yorkers. It'll be strange going back. I love New York City, but my heart has now moved across the Atlantic."

"When will you be back?"

"As often as possible, and certainly for Christmas. The girls and I have already been making plans."

"We'll have to have a big party. And we can celebrate Sal and Ced's engagement too."

"Yeah, I heard about that. Wonderful news. When did he pop the question?"

"It's more how he popped the question," laughed Claudia. "Typical Ced. He and Sal were out on their mountain bikes, up to their ears in mud. They were jogging through a particularly muddy field carrying their bikes, when Ced suddenly sank to his knees. Sal thought he was injured. He fished around in his cycling top and pulled out a box with the ring in it. He said something like, 'Sal, I wanted to find somewhere special to us. This is it, a muddy field in the pouring rain and feeling knackered. I want to do this forever, Sal. With you. Will you marry me?' Then he held up the ring."

"What did she say?"

"She said, 'Fisher, you're the most romantic man who ever lived. I'll love you always.' She let him slide on the ring on her finger, then she pushed him over headfirst in the mud and jumped on him."

"Well, it's certainly different from candlelight and soft music," laughed Lily.

Three weeks later, Lily had finally returned to New York. John was working in his studio when he heard the gallery phone ring. A moment later Lola leaned into the room.

"John, there's someone on the line called Adam Fowler. Says he wants to talk to you."

"I don't recognise the name. Did he say what he wanted?"

"No, he just said he would very much appreciate talking to you.

He was very polite. I thought he was one of Digby's crowd, but he has a slight foreign accent, and that would never do with them!"

"OK," said John, putting down his brush, "I'll take it on the extension in here."

He walked over and lifted the receiver.

"John Andrews."

"Hello, Mr Andrews, my name's Adam Fowler."

The voice was rich and deep, and somehow familiar.

"Yes, Mr Fowler, what can I do for you?" replied John, searching his memory to identify the voice.

"I was rather hoping I could arrange to come and visit you."

There was the tone again, familiar and yet not.

"Are you interested in my work?" asked John.

"I am very interested in it. I had the good fortune to see a matching pair of your portraits recently. I believe you sold them to a friend of one of my friends."

"Really?" John tensed. He'd sold quite a lot of work recently, but the man on the other end of the phone was very specific. A matching pair. He'd only sold one matching pair of portraits recently.

"Who was this friend, Mr Fowler?"

"His name is Smith. Digby Smith."

John caught his breath. No one outside their tight-knit group should know of Digby Smith's name, and no one should be able to connect John to him. He should ring off and call Digby Smith immediately. Checking the caller display, he saw that the number was withheld. However, he felt sure that with Smith's resources, his technical people would have no trouble tracing any phone that called him, number withheld or not.

"Mr Fowler, I'm sorry, I'm really busy at the moment. I've a gallery full of impatient-looking clients and my wife's had to step out. Could I call you back? If you could give me your number..."

There was a deep laugh from the other end of the line.

"Ah, mon ami, as cautious as ever. Do you think the authorities are still after you for sticking your sword in that scum Louis Brochard in the backstreets of Marseille?"

"What...?"

The voice at the other end of the line switched from English to a broad Marseille accent of the seventeenth century.

"Didn't you recognise my voice, Philippe? Even after all these years – and it's been a few, heh – I knew yours instantly, even speaking that barbaric language."

"Jacques? Jacques Bognard? How can... Jacques is it really you? Are you–"

"The same as you, Philippe? Yes, I am. We're part of a very select group, the two of us."

"Jacques. I didn't know. Back then. I had no idea."

Almost without thinking, John had slipped into the same Old French that Jacques was using.

"And I wasn't sure about you," said Jacques. "I was suspicious, but not sure enough. As you know, it doesn't pay to advertise our particular characteristics."

"But your eyes, Jacques, they're not like mine."

There was another deep laugh.

"It's not a prerequisite to have pale grey eyes like yours, remarkable though they are."

"It isn't? I've never met anyone like us who didn't have them."

"Your sons, Henri and Michel, they had them. They are the same as us, huh?"

"Yes, they ... were," said John hesitantly.

"Were?"

"Yes, Jacques. They are both long dead. Henri murdered."

"Gisèle?"

"Yes, effectively."

"And Michel?"

"Executed. In the French Revolution."

"A noble cause. I nearly suffered the same fate myself. I'm sorry, Philippe. It brings home our mortality, despite whatever it is that keeps us alive."

"It was a long time ago, Jacques."

"Time. A strange thing. So many memories, but somehow they all seem like yesterday."

"For me too. An acute memory seems to go with the territory. Jacques, where are you? You said your name is Adam Fowler now. Are you in England?"

"Yes, I live in London. Quite a successful businessman."

"I'm not in the least surprised. In fact, I'd only be surprised if you told me you weren't successful. How did you find out about me?"

"Through Digby Smith."

"But I thought he only dealt with me. That's what he said."

Another deep laugh.

"What does he look like, your Digby Smith?"

"Er, he's about my height, slim, sandy coloured hair. Late thirties."

"Not short, overweight, balding and about fifty?"

"Definitely not."

"Well, my Digby Smith is."

"I don't understand."

"Philippe, it seems to be a little quirk of this secret crowd. They like to keep themselves anonymous, so they're all called Digby Smith!"

"How bizarre."

"That's the English for you."

"I knew there was another like us, like me, I mean. After some persuasion, my Digby Smith agreed to tell me, although he said he was unaware of anything to do with the other person. He said a colleague dealt with him. The only thing he let slip was that the person was a man. It was supposed to be all part of the secrecy."

"I understand from my Mr Smith that they've been having a huge internal debate over whether we should be introduced. It suddenly occurred to them that we might know each other, or might have known each other some time in the past. They discussed it for weeks and they finally gave my Mr Smith a description of you that he was authorised to pass on to me. No name, just a description, but I knew you at once from that alone. When they said you were an artist, that confirmed it. They were amazed. However, once I knew it was you, I insisted that I should make contact. They agreed, knowing it was safe to do so, since obviously security is as important to me as it is to you. I wasn't about to announce it to the newspapers."

"Jacques, this is absolutely wonderful. Unbelievable. When can we meet?"

"That's why I called, mon ami. I want to visit you as soon as possible."

"That would be wonderful. But I can come to you. Why don't I come to London?"

"No, I'd like a trip to the Lake District. I haven't been there for, well, for a long, long time. May I come tomorrow?"

"Jacques, you don't have to ask."

"Then, mon ami, I look forward to seeing you tomorrow. Oh, what's the address?"

As he put down the receiver, John was in a daze. He turned to see Lola standing in the doorway looking very surprised.

"Whatever language was that, John? It sounded like some gutter form of French. Is our Digby conducting his interviews on the phone now?"

His eyes slowly focused on her as her words filtered through the thousand thoughts and memories flooding through his mind. He walked over and took her in his arms. His eyes were alive with excitement. "Lola, you'll never believe who that was."

The following morning, John was too excited to settle to his work. He paced around the gallery, stopping constantly by the window to peer up and down the street. It was a grey, wet morning: a typical Lakeland autumn finally asserting its authority after a lingering and blissful extended summer.

"John!" cried an exasperated Lola. "For goodness sake, wearing out the floor won't bring your friend here any quicker! If any customers come in, they'll think you've gone potty. You'll put them off. Go into the studio and do something!"

"I can't think about painting, Lola. Don't you realise how I feel? It's been more than three hundred and thirty years since I've seen this man."

"Then another half an hour won't make any difference. Now shoo! You're getting under my feet!"

He reluctantly did what he was told, but not before instructing Lola to call him the moment Jacques arrived.

"You can't mistake him. He's a bear of a man, as tall as Ced but bigger built."

Close to one o'clock, the gallery door opened so quietly that Lola hardly heard it. She looked up to see the doorframe filled with a large, smartly dressed and powerfully built man who appeared to be

488

in his mid-thirties. He dropped an umbrella in the stand and looked over to Lola.

"Shh!" he hissed softly as she turned to call John. She looked back to see the man had lifted his index finger to his lips, while his eyes wrinkled in amusement.

He tiptoed over to her and held out his hand.

"Adam Fowler," he whispered. "You are Philippe's wife?"

"Philippe? Er, yes, well, I'm John's wife, actually," she replied, echoing his whispers and rather awed by his huge presence.

"Of course. I apologise. Is he through there?" He nodded towards the studio. "I looked through the window but couldn't see him, so I assumed he was working somewhere."

"I don't think he's doing much work, but he is through there, yes."

Suddenly, as if by magic, Fowler produced a large bunch of flowers from under his coat.

"These are for you, Madame. I thought the colours would remind you of the summer that has now decided to desert us. I don't think I'll ever get used to this climate."

Lola tilted her head and smiled coyly, impressed by his Gallic charm.

"Thank you, Mr Fowler, how very kind."

"It is nothing, a mere token. Now, may I go through and disturb your husband?"

"Please, be my guest. I'll find a vase to put these in. They are absolutely gorgeous."


Adam Fowler stepped softly over to the studio door and gently pushed it open. He looked in and stood quite still, absorbing the moment as his eyes fell on the friend he hadn't seen for so long.

John had finally picked up his paintbrush. When the voice with the strong Marseille accent rang out, he was momentarily startled.

"That is exactly how I have pictured you in my mind all these years, mon ami: working at your easel."

John spun round and there was Jacques, the ever-reliable sea captain who had saved his life. He tossed the brush onto a small table next to his easel and strode over to his friend.

He stopped short about three feet from him and stared into his eyes, his head shaking with emotion.

"Jacques! I can't believe it! Is it really you? You look thirty years younger than the last time I saw you!"

Jacques threw back his head and laughed loudly. "As do you, Philippe. The years have been good to us, heh!"

They hugged fiercely, Jacques lifting John off his feet and spinning him round as they continued to laugh in the sheer pleasure of the moment.

"Lola!" called John.

"I'm here, John," she said from the doorway, regarding the two men before her rather as a proud mother would her sons.

"This is Jacques – my old and dear friend Jacques. Jacques Bognard."

"I know, John. Jacques, Adam – oh, so many names! He has given me the most wonderful bunch of flowers."

"Ever the Frenchman, Jacques," laughed John.

"Well, I've been a Frenchman far more than I've been an Englishman, that's for sure, and the French ways are not so bad; they rub off on you after a while."

"You must be tired after your journey, Jacques," said Lola. "What can I get you to drink?"

"I am fine for the moment, thank you, Lola. But we must celebrate; I have something in the car."

"You drove all the way up here this morning?" said John, surprised.

"Yes, it is rather further than I anticipated. I apologise for being later than I intended."

"You must be tired. Come, sit down."

"Oh, I dozed most of the way, so I feel very fresh, and certainly invigorated to see you both."

"You dozed…?" said John.

"I told you, Philippe, I have become quite a successful businessman; successful enough to enjoy the services of a driver to take me around. I've never been able to get to grips with motorcars. And these days, all this traffic. It's a total nightmare. Give me a horse anytime!"

Lola made some coffee and they sat in the studio swapping stories, wanting to know everything about each other's lives since Marseille. After ten minutes, Lola jumped up. "I'm going to close the gallery. I shan't be able to concentrate on any customers. Let me go and lock the door."

"Before you do that, let me get my bottles," said Jacques, taking out his phone and calling his driver.

Five minutes later, they heard the gallery door open. "That'll be Crawshaw," said Jacques, standing and walking to the studio door. He half turned back to them and spoke behind his hand. "He knows me as Mr Fowler, by the way."

"Thanks, Crawshaw," they heard him say. "Did you succeed in booking a hotel?"

"Ja…. Er, Adam," called John. "You must stay with us. As long as you can put up with the girls."

"That would be wonderful, thank you," Jacques called back. "I'd be delighted to make their acquaintance. Crawshaw, just sort out somewhere for yourself, old chap."

Jacques opened the basket to reveal several bottles of champagne and some glasses. He filled three of them and raised his in a toast.

"To old friends and old friendships. May they endure forever."

They chinked their glasses and sat back, silent for a moment.

John took a sip and looked affectionately at his friend.

"I went back to Marseille, Jacques, about a hundred years after you spirited us away on your ship. I went to the churchyard and saw the graves. What you did for Arlette, Georges and Mathilde was quite incredible. The graves were perfectly kept."

"They still are, Philippe. They must be the best-kept graves in France," laughed Jacques.

They talked through the afternoon until it was time for Lola to fetch the girls from school.

"Oh dear," she said, blinking at the effects of the champagne. "I don't think I should be driving after all this bubbly."

"Easily solved," said Jacques, taking out his phone once again. "Crawshaw will take you."

Lola giggled as she got up. "The girls will be impressed. I hope they don't think it'll happen every day."

About half an hour later, she returned with the girls and introduced them to Jacques. He instantly won them over by sitting on the floor to talk to them as they stood next to him, their eye levels now about equal. As with the flowers, he produced two beautifully wrapped presents from nowhere and handed them over. They unwrapped them gleefully to find two large, exquisitely dressed dolls.

"I hope they are not too old for dolls," said Jacques to Lola. "I don't like all these modern electronic things."

"Too old?" laughed Lola. "Look at them!"

The girls were examining the dolls' clothes and stroking their hair. Phoebe was talking to hers as if she had known her all her life.

"I'm going to leave you two to talk while I take these girls home for tea," declared Lola. "Come up to the house when you are ready."

Jacques smiled. "Use Crawshaw, Lola, he likes to be busy. I'll call him to fetch us later. D'accord, mon ami?" he said to John.

Phoebe and Sophie glanced up, not understanding. But they said nothing.

Once Lola and the girls had left, Jacques opened another bottle and the pair continued with their reminiscences. The stories arose in no particular order, centring more on where they had both been at various times during the past three hundred years. They found that they had been living quite close to each other on more than one occasion.

"It's amazing we didn't bump into each other before," said John.

"Think how our lives might have changed if we had," mused Jacques. "We probably wouldn't be sitting here in the Lake District of England, although we might still be sipping champagne."

John looked into his friend's eyes.

"You know, for some reason, I've been assuming all along that because we first knew each other over three hundred years ago, that we are contemporaries. Yet why should we be? We have only talked of our time together in Marseille and our lives since then. What about before? I certainly wasn't a young man when I first met you, as I suspect you weren't. In fact, when I first met you, I was over two hundred years old; I am now not far short of six hundred. What about you, Jacques, how old are you?"

Jacques took a sip of his champagne and leaned forward. He raised his glass and touched it against John's. Looking over the top of it, he sighed a world-weary sigh. "Philippe, my dear friend, to tell you the truth, I cannot say precisely how long I've been around. I only know it's in the region of two and a half thousand years."

# Afterword

On 5th September, 2012, the many scientists working on the Encode Project (The Encyclopedia of DNA Elements) published papers in various scientific journals explaining that noncoding DNA, or junk DNA as it is more widely known, is anything but junk. Their work has now shown that junk DNA has a profound significance in the myriad processes controlling the way our bodies work. The next few years will doubtless bring many new insights into this hitherto little-understood part of our genetic code.

Yes, Claudia was right!

But whether the triggers that junk DNA operates to switch on and off various bodily processes include those that cause ageing and, if they do, they can be controlled, remains to be seen...


David George Clarke
October 2012

# Acknowledgements

Writing a novel is a solitary process but nevertheless one that requires the author to ask much of many people.

I could not have indulged in the journey without the constant support and encouragement of my wife, Gail. From day one, she has been there as a sounding board for ideas, a reviewer of drafts and an enthusiastic supporter of the project. The book is dedicated to her, with love.

I am also eternally grateful to many others who have helped me on my way. In the early days, my old friend and colleague, Dr Bob Bramley CBE, former Chief Scientist of the UK Forensic Science Service and the first Custodian of the UK National DNA Database, helped me to get my head round DNA and legal procedures. Then, much later, he read through the entire book and provided me not only with very positive feedback on the story, but also put me straight on many DNA-related matters. I am indebted to him, but I will say at this point that I didn't always take his advice and therefore any deviations in the story from what might happen in the real world are entirely my responsibility.

Once the first draft was finished, I prevailed upon my good friends Anne Mensini Foster and Sanford Foster who diligently dissected the grammar and spelling on every page and gave me huge and wonderful feedback. Anne also put me straight on a number of art-related matters. They both worked tirelessly, devoting many hours to the task. Simple words cannot express my gratitude to them.

Thanks for editing, and for very positive comments, are also due to my son-in-law, Simon O'Reilly – the fastest copy editor in the East!

The first few chapters were read in a draft form by Carol Jessop in Mtwapa, Mombasa, and Cedric Harben in Città di Castello, Italy. Thanks to both for encouragement at an early stage, and thanks also to Cedric for the loan of James R. Banker's fascinating book: *The Culture of San Sepolcro during the Youth of Piero Della Francesca,* Pub: University of Michigan Press.

Several others have kindly read through the book in draft form and all were very positive in their comments. Thanks go to Sian Bramley; my sister, Jill Pemberton; Sarah Barnes; my daughter, Lea Woodward; son-in-law, Jonathan Woodward; and Jill Harrison. Jill Harrison also wore her Art History academic's hat as she read it. Thanks, Jill, for our discussions and your input.

My daughter, Lea, and my son, Daniel, have both drawn on their considerable business and marketing expertise to help me get the book out there, and thanks to Lea's computing skills and her husband Jonathan's design talents, I also now have a great website. It was also through Lea that I was introduced to Joanna Penn of www.thecreativepenn.com. After an hour's very fruitful consultation, Joanna convinced me what several others had already tried to tell me: less is more! The result is this considerably reduced and much tighter version of the original draft.

I am grateful to Derek Murphy of www.creativindie.com for the cover design and to Linda Davy in Hong Kong for diligently carrying out the final proof-reading.

One of the fun things of writing a book such as *Rare Traits* is the research. I have mentioned one invaluable book already, but thanks are also due to my good friends Messrs Google, Google Earth and Wikipedia who make it possible to explore almost anywhere from the comfort of whatever desk I am sitting at. Like so many millions of people in the world who daily access their boundless information, I thank their creators for their inspiration.

I have borrowed the names of various friends and family members as the characters were created, in particular, the names of my five grandchildren: Lily, Phoebe, Frank, Digby and Mali. To them I say that I hope if one day you read this book, you will be amused, even though your namesakes in the book are in no way meant to be like you.

Finally, I should like to thank the characters in the book who all came to life for me as they appeared. Some were very strong and virtually took over creating their accounts, kicking me off my chair and taking over the keyboard. I am very attached to all of them and I hope I have done their lives justice.

David George Clarke

*Rare Traits* is the first part of the *Rare Traits Trilogy*. News on progress and availability of the second and third parts – *Delusional Traits* and *Murderous Traits* – can be found on the author's website at www.davidgeorgeclarke.com

Printed in Great Britain
by Amazon.co.uk, Ltd.,
Marston Gate.